THE QUEEN'S CURSE

SOULFIRE DUOLOGY
BOOK 1

TAYLOR UGRINOW

Copyright © 2026 by Taylor Ugrinow

Book Cover Designer: Rachel Bostwick

Developmental Editor: Sydney Moses

Line Editor: Taylor Kamnetz

ISBN 979-8-9950580-0-7

ISBN 979-8-9950580-1-4 (ebook)

*For the ones who stayed silent
when they had so much to say.*

N
W
E
S
SOLHAVEN
NOCT
LUMIN
EIDOL
THE RIFTLANDS
PARADISE
JUNIA

LUNARIA
HARN
ZALQUAR
THALASSARA
THE VOID

CONTENT WARNING

This book contains mature and explicit subject matters that might not be suitable for all readers, including themes of sexual violence, physical abuse, and alcoholism. Reader discretion is advised.

PROLOGUE
ARI

Silas claimed my arrival in this world cursed his land and his luck, and maybe he's right.

But it's what he deserves after everything he's put me through.

The day I stepped into the soulfire mines was the day I vowed to do whatever it took to save myself—no matter the cost.

I was only ten when my life changed forever.

The sun had just started to dip behind the trees, casting long shadows across the forest floor, and I used them to my advantage. I crouched low, my fingers curling around the rough edges of the wooden stake I carved—the marker that I needed to plant on Noah's side to win. I didn't bother hiding the grin that tugged at the corner of my lips when I stood and saw his stake still impaled in the earth on the other side of the clearing, the same clearing that serves as our battlefield in a game we call Circle of Crowns. The first person to plant their stake on the other person's land could claim it, and I was about to win *again*.

We play this game every day in the forest of our neighboring properties, but his side of the clearing was vastly different from mine.

Noah's parents never had any issues with greenery on their land. Tall grass and moss-covered stones flourish on their side, but where I stand, not a single green blade or wildflower grows; just cracked soil and brittle yellow weeds.

I raced through the brush, dodging trees, running along the perimeter of the clearing to get to Noah's stake, staying a few paces away from the portion of the woods deemed off-limits.

The Eidolon Forest was not marked, but you would know if you got too close—the quiet change that settled over everything was alarming enough. The forest always reeked of sour sap and rotting bark, and underneath it, the unpleasant scent of old rain lingered, as if the earth was constantly wet just past the tree line. This must have been the reason why the trees grew taller there, darker even. The light seemed to fade even in the daytime, and it was worse at night, like the moonlight was afraid to touch it. I swear, sometimes I saw someone running alongside me in the distance, just for a second, like a phantom between the trees, following me as we played.

I came to a halt on Noah's side. His stake was now just an arm's reach away, but he was still nowhere in sight. I paused, listening for a moment, giving him time to catch up. But I heard no crunching of leaves or heavy footsteps. I should have felt bad for beating him every time, and for a second, I did, but he never complained, and it was fun being one step ahead.

I glanced over my shoulder, searching for Noah one last

time before crouching down and yanking his stake from the ground. I entered the clearing and stood at its center, claiming my victory.

He had one last chance to battle me for it if he wished, and deep down, I hoped he did.

I enjoyed hand-to-hand combat more than I should. Although we agreed not to throw any physical punches, the idea of rendering someone powerless sent a thrill through me.

Wind rushed around me, like the forest itself was alive and mine for the taking as I triumphantly raised both stakes in the air.

"Noah!" I yelled, heart pounding with excitement. "Do you wish to challenge me to a duel to keep your kingdom under your reign?"

I allowed a beat of silence to pass before I slammed both stakes into the ground, marking my claim. "I am the great conqueror!"

Finally, Noah sprinted into the clearing from behind a big mossy rock, always arriving too late.

He skidded to a stop, panting.

I grinned. "Told you I'd win again."

He shook his head but laughed, still gasping for air. "Next time, I'll be faster." He dropped to one knee. "What is your first decree, my queen?"

"I do like the sound of that," I started to say when a blood-curdling scream pierced my eardrums.

I froze, rooted in place, alarmed by the agonizing, high-pitched tone that stopped as fast as it started. And for a moment, all I could hear was the blood rushing to my ears and the deadly silence that followed as fear coiled tight in my gut.

Noah came up beside me, like a shadow at my shoulder, fear clinging to him.

I spun in the direction of my house over the tiny hilltop, catching the slightest glimpse of dry land. Mama was inside preparing dinner. There was only one reason she'd scream like that, and it wouldn't have been from cutting her finger.

My legs moved before my brain could catch up, bolting toward my home. Branches slapped at my arms as the air rushed too fast into my lungs. I found myself flinching the closer I got, scared of what I was about to discover.

I hauled myself up the hill, hearing Noah's footsteps pounding behind me.

Another scream, full of raw and broken emotions, sent ice down my spine.

The trees gave way to the back fence in my yard. I threw my body over it without thinking, scraping my knee on the bent wood. I winced, stumbling to get to my feet, not caring if I injured myself.

"Ari, slow down!" Noah said, reaching for my arm, but I was already moving again. His fingers grazed the hem of my shirt, but I continued to push forward.

"Be quiet," I hissed over my shoulder as dry grass crunched beneath my shoes.

I sprinted toward the small one-story cottage I called home. Its white paint clung to the siding like dead skin. One of the kitchen windows was wide open—the old one above the sink that never fully shut, and from it, you could hear the faint sizzle of food frying.

I slid my body against the side of my house, Noah following close behind. Chipped and peeling paint caught on the backs of our shirts as we moved, trying not to make a sound.

Noah's hands trembled at his side as we crouched under

the kitchen window, and his voice quivered as he spoke. "Maybe we should go."

A strangled whimper had me standing on my tiptoes to peek through the window before I had time to answer him.

Inside, the stove was on, the food unattended and burning. I spotted Mama on the floor, crumpled into herself, while a prominent figure loomed over her, hand outstretched. Their arm came down, and her body jerked from the movement.

My body went numb at the sight as blood began to trickle from her mouth. Not because I didn't understand what was happening. *No.* I understood all too well what was happening the second it did. Silas was home early, and it was never a good omen when he was.

I inhaled deeply, in an attempt to steady my ragged breathing. I planted my feet flat on the ground once more, resting my forehead on the chipped paint, and snapped my eyes shut.

Breathe. Breathe. Breathe. I chanted over and over again in my head.

Silas was drunk, which only meant one thing.

He was going to hurt Mama.

Again.

"Noah," I whispered. "We need to help her."

Nothing but silence greeted me. I opened my eyes, peering at where Noah was, yet I was alone.

"Noah?" I whirled around, watching as the back door to his house swung shut.

I clasped my hand over my mouth, smothering a cry before it slipped past my lips. I was alone in this, and always when I needed someone most.

I crouched down and squeezed my legs in close, trying to control the tremors that raked up my spine.

Why does Noah always run away?

"Pick up extra shifts! I don't care what you do! I will sell you off if I have to!" Silas roared with anger inside. "We need more gilds, or we won't survive another week."

He always complained about how many gilds we had or didn't have. That's where the curse of land and luck came in; not only did his land die, but his wallet dried up, too.

I matched my breath to the sound of his boots trudging across the kitchen floor. But the air stalled in my lungs when they abruptly stopped at the same time the fridge door slammed against the wall.

I flinched at the sudden noise, a knot forming deep in my stomach.

I needed to do something—anything.

I needed to help Mama.

I let out a heavy breath, determination setting in.

My hands were shaking uncontrollably, but I pushed myself up anyway. My cheek brushed the wooden window frame as I stood.

Mama was facing me, her blonde hair clinging to the blood on her lip, staining the golden strands. The sight of her on the kitchen floor, trembling in fear, ignited something in me.

I hated Silas.

I hated *him*.

"I'm sorry." Mama's eyes locked on mine. "I'll do better."

Silas spun around faster than I thought possible in his state, following Mama's gaze. He looked me dead in the eye, lips curling into an evil grin.

"YOU!" he exclaimed, spewing spit from his mouth.

I ducked down, and not even a second later, large hands gripped my shirt, pulling me up through the window and into the kitchen. Silas dropped me on the ground like I was nothing. I stifled my cry as I hit the cold tile. I had only a moment to collect myself before a searing pain spread across my scalp. Silas was dragging me across the floor by my hair.

I'm dead. I'm dead. I'm dead.

I felt sure he was going to kill me this time.

He released me with a thud. My head hit the floor, cracking one of the azure tiles. Mama's lightless brown eyes came in and out of focus as I willed myself to stay conscious.

She stared at me emotionless, like a shell of the woman I knew. Silas stood over us, arm pulled back, ready to strike, his face twisted with rage. Mama trembled beside me, but neither of us tried to move. We just stared at each other, waiting for the inevitable. It wasn't the first time Silas had hit me, and it wouldn't be the last.

The first was two years ago. I asked for a second serving, not being filled by the first. Silas struck me instead and called me ungrateful. I never understood what I did wrong. I thought maybe he had a bad day. I didn't want to believe that he would intentionally hurt me.

But now, lying here, I knew better.

"Please stop," I cried.

Mama remained unblinking, frozen like a statue, as if the silence might make Silas forget she was there.

All the times she watched as Silas struck me.

All the times she'd smile like everything was okay while bruises formed over our skin.

She never helped. She never stepped in.

If Mama didn't do anything, I would.

I would save us both.

"Please!" I choked out, beholding Silas's enraged expression. "Let me help!" I was determined to fix this. "I'll do anything, please just stop hurting Mama."

Silas stared down at me, the gears rotating behind his gaze, like he was rearranging pieces on a board only he could see. I held my breath waiting for his answer. His jaw tightened, eyes scanning my body, and I knew deep down that he wasn't trying to figure out how to make this right; he was deciding how to do it in a way that would benefit him in the long run.

A ghost of a smile pulled across his haggard face at his resolve. "You know..." he said, running a hand through his grease-slicked hair. An agonizing silence filled the room as Silas paused for a moment before continuing.

"There are countless areas of the mines we haven't fully reached before because, well..." he nonchalantly looked down at himself, and then back at me. "We simply don't fit." His knees popped as he crouched down. He gripped my chin, fingers digging into my skin. "You, on the other hand, are the perfect size."

I felt Mama's hand graze mine as a lone tear slipped free, tracing a path down my cheek.

I would do it. *I had to.*

I would be strong for both of us. I would accept this fate if it meant Mama was protected.

If I didn't, then nothing would change.

And I was determined to be that change.

CHAPTER 1

SOULFIRE COLLECTION
ARI

16 years later

The crystal is buried deep in the obsidian rock.

I wield my chisel, slamming it into the unforgiving earth. My muscles strain from the impact, and still, there is no movement. I glide the back of my hand over my brow, wiping away the sweat that threatens to sting my eyes. Despite the cool air down here, perspiration somehow manages to cling to every inch of me.

I carefully wedge the side of my chisel into the dark surface, my hands straining. "C'mon, you stubborn little thing. Get. Out," I grunt.

Pop.

The crystal springs free, with a faint crack that echoes through the small cavern.

"Finally," I sigh, sitting back on my heels. My knees ache from being crouched down for hours with no reprieve.

I slide the pebble-sized piece of soulfire into my palm, eyeing the narrow groove it came from. The dark stone emits a small ray of light for a breath before dimming out.

The light appears whenever the crystal is removed from the rock, as if a piece of the land dies with its departure.

I roll the pale green crystal between my fingers. It's warm and thrumming with life, pulsing as if it has a beating heart. "You have the king wrapped around your finger, don't you?" I whisper.

I have been working on this corner of the mine for a month, and this is all I have to show for it. It amazes me how a seemingly insignificant thing could cause such a fuss.

I pull a cloth from my pocket, tucking the soulfire into its folds.

A torchlight flickers above me, marking the way out of the mine. I slip the crystal into a side pocket of my cargo pants and button it shut. I grab my chisel and secure it to my waist, beginning the slow climb up.

I will my tired body to keep moving, following the faint glow until I reach the top. I haul myself out of the tight tunnel and follow the path out of the mine. The scent of pine floods my senses the second I emerge, and I tilt my head back, taking a deep breath. I almost forgot what it felt like to have clean air fill my lungs.

The sky unfurls endlessly above me as my eyes follow the golden hues fading beyond the horizon. Seven days have passed since I've felt the warmth of the sun on my skin, and it doesn't look like that is changing tonight, either.

Suddenly, the king's royal insignia—a vulture perched atop a crown stitched in gold threads—blocks my vision. A valorguard extends his hand, waiting. I dig in my pocket and drop the crystal in his palm.

"Next!" the valorguard shouts. The guard's voice is firm, as if he's done this a thousand times this week, which he probably has.

I step to the left, allowing the other miners to enter the

clearing. Only fifteen of us are allowed in the mines at a time, and on a good day, all fifteen will make it out. But today is not a good day. The possibility of death climbs at a devastating rate during soulfire collection week. Besides death, which is morbid but inevitable among mortals, soulfire collection week means the king's privileged valorguards grace us with their presence. And valorguards are the worst kind of eldarim.

Eldarim are the chosen souls of Althara, so they say. I, on the other hand, think it's nonsense.

Thankfully, we don't encounter them often.

Most mortals live on the outskirts of the kingdom on the furthest borders of Noctharn, forced into a life full of servitude in the lower, less cared-for sections. At the same time, eldarim live in the higher sections closest to the capital, and only the most powerful immortals get to live in Lunaria.

We mortals never receive word from the king until it's time to collect his soulfire. Regardless of the news, the people here are always the last to hear it. Needless to say, growing up in the only mining town in the kingdom has been dreadful.

"Name!" another valorguard bellows in front of me.

Only three guards are working tonight. The bulk of the soulfire was collected hours ago by the other guards in preparation to transport the crystal to Lunaria in the morning.

"Ari."

"Last name?" he spits.

I look up at the guard. "Just Ari."

I don't claim Silas's last name, and that will not change tonight.

The guard's eyes narrow, and I arch an eyebrow, silently challenging him to question me further.

We continue to glare at each other, his presence making my skin boil.

The way valorguards demand authority, thinking they are untouchable by mortals, fills me with rage. It repulses me how they can walk into our town, protected by status, punishing innocent people.

I think they forget that, although they don't age, they can still die. It's probably the only useful information I gained in my few years of schooling—how to murder them. Everyone has a weakness, whether they are powerful or not.

My hand hovers at my waist, itching to snatch my chisel and stab the valorguard in the neck. I wonder what power courses through his veins. Would he unleash it before I had a chance to attack?

Fortunately for me, he's not a mind reader, or he would have already arrested me for the direction of my thoughts.

I huff through my nose in annoyance, tapping my boot on the cold, hard ground.

Three...

Two...

One...

The valorguard's eyes bulge, and he quickly averts his gaze to the miner to the right of me.

The corner of my mouth curls subtly at the sight.

Elitist pricks. Every last one of them.

And that right there makes the lack of power worth it. Eldarim tend to struggle to keep eye contact with me. I like to think it's because I intimidate them; it's a nice boost to my ego, but really, it's because my light green eyes have a unique effect. They tend to do that since they are a similar shade to the king's soulfire.

Some mortals think the king collects the soulfire to wear as jewelry, but I disagree. No one would go through the hassle of collecting so much crystal to use for vanity. Others believe the soulfire amplifies eldarim's powers. There is a theory that the king made every immortal swear an oath never to use it, which to me would make sense, since laying eyes on the king's soulfire for too long is punishable by death.

I can't say the same for us mortals, though. We never swore an oath, nor do we abide by these laws. It's not like we can use the crystal anyway.

I listen as the valorguard continues down the line, writing down names. I count twelve. Twelve names, including mine, which means more of us made it out today than yesterday. I can find some joy in that.

"You are all released!" the valorguard yells. "Now scatter, you vermin."

His words strike me like a whip, searing my skin.

"Rot in hell," I mumble under my breath.

The miner beside me chuckles, and I give them a flat, unamused look. I don't recognize them. To be honest, I never bothered to learn anyone's names. Every day in the mines could be our last, so it feels like useless information.

I stride out of the clearing without another word, grabbing my bag and sword that I stowed in the tree by the mine's entrance.

I sling it over my shoulder, hooking my sword to it, and head in the direction of town.

A miner sprints past me in a hurry. "Good luck tonight."

I grunt in acknowledgment, keeping my pace steady, passing crooked houses barely illuminated by the dim lights that line the streets.

Lumin is quiet tonight, eerily deserted, but it usually is on fight night.

The only movement is the few last-minute stragglers

that rush out of their homes in the direction of the tavern, getting ready to watch the biggest event of the month. Truthfully, it's the only thing we have to look forward to.

I don't hurry, though. There's no reason to, especially when I am the main event.

"Ari, wait up!"

A smile tugs at the corner of my lips at the sound of the familiar voice, knowing all too well whose rushed footsteps I hear behind me. I peek over my shoulder, spotting Noah's blonde hair glistening in the fading light. My gaze trails down to his mouth, and my heart skips a beat.

Noah has always been devilishly handsome, but when he wears that playful, boyish smile of his, I always find myself staring longer than I should.

"I was starting to think you got lost in those mines," Noah huffs out between strangled breaths.

I stop in my tracks and turn to face him. He steps forward, coming to a halt just inches away. His ocean-blue eyes roam over me with quiet intensity, taking in every detail without a word. His smooth, callus-free hands settle on my bare shoulders, tepid against my skin. I shudder under his touch, welcoming the feeling of his soft palms.

Noah's parents own the local bookstore, so he gets to work there, too. He rarely has a physically taxing day, and it shows.

I fold my arms over my chest. "You should know better than to think anything would happen to me."

Noah chuckles, trailing his pointer finger across my collarbone. "I forgot how big and strong you are," he says, circling his hand around my bicep.

"Hey!" I playfully smack his arm away. "Remember what happened last time you underestimated me?"

Noah catches my hand and pulls me in for a hug. The

smell of fresh rain hits my nose. You know, that smell right before a storm is about to roll through.

It's one of my favorite scents.

"I am shaking in my boots at the thought," he jeers.

I bury my face into his chest. "I know you are."

Noah hastily pulls away, putting me at arm's length. His button nose crinkles as he takes a deep breath. "Sweetheart, I hate to be the one to tell you this..." he recoils dramatically to make a point. "But you smell like rotten fish."

"I do not!" I fire back defensively, lifting my chin in offense.

I casually sniff my armpit as discreetly as I can and instantly jolt at the stench that wafts off me. Maybe Noah's right, but I won't tell him that.

I shrug, hiding my grimace. "Smells like daisies and sunshine to me."

Noah shakes his head, fighting a smile. "If you say so," he teases, voice low.

I roll my eyes, looping my arm through his, pulling him in the direction of the tavern. Our steps fall into an easy rhythm, comforting in a way as his skin brushes mine.

"Do you know who I'm fighting tonight?"

I fight once a month—not for myself, or even because I enjoy it, but because Silas demanded that I bring in more gilds for the family, most of which he spends on ale. But he always seems to forget that part.

Noah smirks at me mischievously. "It looks like it's Raven. I saw it hanging in the center of town earlier today. It should be an eventful night for the king's valorguard."

Of course. I should have known. With the valorguards in town, it means higher bets and bigger pools of gilds. The king pays his valorguards well, which means it was inevitable that I'd be fighting the best tonight. It also means I'll have to forgo my comfortable leathers.

"Oh, how I love prancing around in skimpy clothing for the valorguards to get a hard-on." I exhale heavily through my nose, irritation prickling beneath my skin. "It's one of my favorite pastimes."

Raven and I fight when special guests are in town. We have a deal with the tavern to put on a show to bring in extra gilds, which means more for us. Embarrassingly, I struggle to fill the scandalous outfits they make us fight in. Raven, on the other hand, has no problem with that.

I blame it on the scarcity of food in Lumin. Our rations usually go to Silas, who distributes them between himself and Mama. If I want to eat, I have to hunt for it myself or take what Noah can skim from his family's rations.

We round the corner to the tavern, following the roars of a cheering crowd toward The Broken Fang.

I note how a larger-than-usual crowd gathers by the front door as we make our way to the entrance.

Noah grips my hand and leads me inside. He nods toward the pit as we pass by. "Silas is almost up."

I refuse to follow his gaze. "Hopefully, the drunk bastard gets knocked out early."

The only thing I've ever been grateful to Silas for is forcing me to learn how to fight. His mentality has always been to swing first or bleed, so I decided to swing first.

Noah's hand slips from mine as we reach the dressing room at the far end of the tavern.

"I'll grab us some drinks while you get ready," he shouts over the crowd. His eyes sparkle slightly as he turns to make his way to the bar.

"Thanks," I murmur under my breath, eyeing the bartender.

Octavia is working tonight. Noah has always shown an interest in her. I gave up on the idea that Noah and I would be anything more than friends long ago, and that was solidified when Octavia started working here.

My heart aches for a moment—a brief, hollow feeling that consumes me temporarily before I steel myself and reach for the handle, pushing the dressing room door open.

I shut the door behind me, mentally preparing myself for the long night ahead of me.

CHAPTER 2

GET ON YOUR KNEES AND BEG
ARI

Steam curls lazily in the air as I slowly lower myself into the bathtub. The water rises around me, just hot enough to sting at first. I sigh in relief and sink in further, letting the liquid melt the tension out of my body.

Warm water is a luxury. Clean water is also a luxury, and frankly, I don't have either at home.

I rest my head on the cold porcelain edge of the tub, allowing my eyes to flutter shut. The dressing room isn't the nicest place to relax, but it's better than my current living situation. And that's beside the point, because right now this feels delightful after the long, grueling week I had.

I just need to get through tonight, then I'll have a few days' break before my next shift in the mines. Only recently has my body been betraying me. When I was younger, I could work back-to-back shifts without feeling a thing, but now I struggle to work a whole day without feeling like my body is going to give out.

If I could sleep more than a few hours a night and occasionally eat something that actually fills me up, it would help. The lack of food keeps me slim enough to climb into the regions that other miners can't fit into. I have gotten myself into some scary close calls, but I'd rather it be me getting stuck in the mines than a child, forced to work in them at a young age like I was.

I embrace my semi-quiet moment, allowing the weight of the day to dissolve into the rapidly cooling water.

A few minutes pass before goosebumps rise on my skin.

I release a tired breath. "It was nice while it lasted."

I scrub my skin until it's raw and red, never truly feeling clean.

The chanting behind the bathroom doors becomes louder and louder, buzzing with anticipation for the next fight. I swiftly stand, grabbing the towel I draped over the edge of the tub. I step out onto the cool stone floor and head to the changing room.

I pat my hair dry and toss the damp cloth to the ground. My onyx-colored strands skim my waist, sending a chill up my spine from the contact. Wringing out the excess water, I collect my brush and immediately start detangling it. I slick my hair back into a tight braid, fastening my snake barrette into it. I have had the barrette since I was a child. It's the only thing that's ever been just mine. I wear it every second I can for that exact reason.

I pull on tight leather shorts and a cropped black tank top. Although I have a more petite frame than Raven, the outfit accentuates the little curves I do have, which I am grateful for.

I drag a wand over my lashes, painting them an inky black before pinching my cheeks to bring some color to my face. Being trapped in the mines day in and day out doesn't help with the paleness of my skin.

"Just win the fight, then you can rest," I whisper to

myself, plastering on a smile. It feels stiff and unnatural, but convincing enough.

I swing open the door and head back into the tavern.

The Broken Fang is dark and dismal. The only source of light comes from the barely lit lanterns hung in the corners of the room. They flicker faintly, casting harsh shadows across the wood-paneled walls. Beams made of oak stretch high above, closing us into the confined space. At its heart is the pit, sunk below the ground's surface. Patrons lean against the sides of the railings, drunkenly betting on the next fight.

I search the crowd in a practiced motion, my gaze sweeping over every face before zeroing in on Noah's familiar shape.

I scowl at him, spotting him still at the bar with two ales in hand—condensation undoubtedly coating the outside of the cups already.

I chew on my lip. By the time I get my drink, it'll be flat, that's for sure, and I really could use a drink right now.

I turn, trying to hide my frustration as I search for an open table.

"Good luck tonight!" a cheerful voice says beside me.

"Jenny!" I spin to face her. "What are you doing here?"

Jenny's gaze drops to the floor, twisting her hands in front of her. "I wanted to see you in action," she admits sheepishly. "If I want to be the best, I need to see how it's done."

A sincere smile forms on my lips.

Jenny is young. Only sixteen. She'll be joining the pits when she's eligible at eighteen. Eligible fighters are usually sold to the tavern. People can enter the pits willingly, but I've never heard of anybody doing that besides Silas. I've been fighting monthly for the past eight years because of him.

I took it upon myself to help Jenny train in combat and weaponry in my spare time, as Raven did for me, hoping she'll survive once she enters the real fights. She's a bit awkward, not confident in her body yet, or quick on her feet. We don't fight to the death, but the untrained ones always tend to die first.

I grip Jenny's shoulder, giving it a slight squeeze, "Thanks, Jenny." I lean forward to whisper in her ear. "Can you do me a favor?"

She nods without a second thought.

"Can you tell Noah to hurry the hell up with my drink?"

She flushes and turns to find Noah, spotting him at the bar. "Of course!" She slides out of my grip and disappears into the crowd.

I weave through the sea of people, claiming the closest table to the pit.

Silas's fight is about to start. He stands near the edge, shoulders squared, jaw clenched in a too personal and unwelcoming way. It's the same look I see so often at home. His hair lies slicked back with sweat hiding the specks of gray that stain his strands; he jabs his hands in front of him, sparring with an invisible fighter. The slight shake of his left hand gives him away, though. He already started drinking.

There is nothing noble about Silas. He doesn't fight to win; he fights to punish.

I stretch my legs out in front of me, resting them on the railing as the bell rings to start the match. He's up against a man with at least fifty pounds on him. Silas is already getting his face pounded, but I can't seem to bring myself to look away. Blood gushes from his nose, flowing down his chin and onto his chest.

I can't help myself; a smile forms on my lips at the sight.

I should feel sorry for him, but I don't. I could never feel sorry for someone like him.

"Enjoying the show?"

I whirl around, my legs falling off the railing from the motion. My hatred for Silas consumed me entirely—I didn't sense someone approaching me.

The chair beside me creaks as a man sits down. I glance behind him, finding Noah still flirting with Octavia.

I cross my arms, staring back into the pit.

"Can I help you with something, officer?" I ask, noticing the vulture insignia etched on the man's uniform.

The valorguard leans in and touches the tip of my braid. "Yes, I was wondering what a beautiful girl like you was doing all alone."

I stiffen at his touch, feeling his fingers trail across the exposed skin on my back.

I scowl at him, catching sight of his sandy brown hair and the wretched smile he wears, revealing his yellow-stained teeth. He is vulgar, and I don't just say that because he is a valorguard. His presence reminds me of my father's.

I shift in my seat to put some distance between us and nod in the direction of where I know Noah stands. "I am accounted for."

The guard smirks. "By whom? The guy flirting with the bartender?"

I return to watching the fight, dismissing him. He's wasting his time and mine. I have zero patience for being polite to someone who doesn't deserve my attention. You'd think he'd get the hint to leave me alone.

The valorguard raises his hand, moving it toward me, and I stand abruptly, annoyed. "Sorry," I say, smiling down at him. "I meant to say I'm not interested."

I turn to leave, stepping away from the table, but he doesn't let me go far. His hand clamps around my wrist, yanking me back into my seat.

I jerk my arm in an attempt to free myself, and at the same time, he leans forward, invading my personal space *again*. His lips brush against my ear, and hot, rancid breath washes over my face, making me wince. "You know the consequence of disrespecting a valorguard. Just be a good girl tonight and entertain me."

Fury simmers over every inch of me, and with a shove, he releases me. I glare at the guard, analyzing his every movement, trying to get a read of what I am up against. His power is what scares me the most. The powers held by valorguards are unmatched, spanning from elemental manipulation to mind control. The most elite are assigned an animal during the binding ritual, and I know nothing about the man before me.

I observe the other valorguards behind him—all in their clean black uniforms, blending into the dim tavern light. I quickly count eight of them. And that scares me even more...eight guards with powers they haven't yet displayed.

I can't do anything foolish unless I want my head on the chopping block.

"So, what's it going to be?"

I return my attention to the vile man. "What is what going to be?"

"Are you going to entertain me?"

My fingers twitch, instinctively wanting to reach for something that I know is not there. I would have drawn my sword if it had been strapped to my back, but you can't exactly hide weapons on you when you are dressed the way I am.

"No, I am not, but I'm sure there are plenty of other

women here tonight who would love your company and the idea of bedding the king's valorguard, so why don't you go waste someone else's time and leave me the fuck alone." I spit each word with venom, hoping he'll get the warning that he is messing with the wrong person.

He seizes the nape of my neck at an unnatural speed, gripping tightly. Maybe he has the power of a blitz, and if that's the case, I'll never be able to get away fast enough.

"I love a woman who plays hard to get." He sniffs my hair. "It turns me on."

My stomach twists in disgust. "Get your hands off me," I sneer back at him. "You won't like what I do next."

"Oh, baby, I know I'll like anything you do."

I adjust myself to face him fully, my gaze burning with hatred. He lets go of my neck, succumbing to the inability to look into my soulfire-colored eyes. With the slight distraction, I lift my leg and my heel finds his groin.

The guard falls out of his seat and onto the ground, cowering in pain. Another guard races to his side.

"Finley, what happened?"

Finley glowers up at me as much as he can from a fetal position. "That fucking bitch hit me in the balls," he whines.

I crouch in a defensive stance, realizing there are still eight guards at the table.

Did I miss one? I squint in their direction as the ninth comes into view. The valorguard sits in the shadows, away from everyone else, barely visible. Goosebumps rise over my skin while I struggle to make out his shadowy figure in the inadequate lighting.

Someone grabs my elbow, pulling me from my trance.

"Ari, what did you do?" Noah asks, voice tight.

Why am I always to blame?

"I didn't do anything; the guard couldn't take a hint."

Finley struggles to his feet, using the back of his chair and the other valorguard for support.

Noah straightens, his hand still gripping my elbow, using me to steady his trembling fingers. "I'm sorry, officers, we don't want any trouble," he says, trying to sound confident, but I see right through it.

"Pussy," I mumble under my breath for only Noah to hear before raising my voice louder. "He's right, officer; I didn't realize your ego was so fragile that a woman denying you would make you act so brash." I place a hand over my heart. "My apologies."

Finley's features darken with rage. "You are dead, mortal." He uses the word like an insult, spitting disdainfully at our feet.

"That's enough, Finley. We will not be killing anyone tonight." The valorguard that came to Finley's aid flicks his gaze to mine for a second. I see the sympathy in his eyes, as if Finley isn't the company he wishes to keep. "Come now, let's leave the girl alone."

But part of me can't let this go. I never can. I open my mouth without a second thought. "Yeah, Finley, why don't you listen to your little friend?"

Noah scowls. "Ari...seriously?"

Finley squares his shoulders and begins pulling his shackles from his waist. "Disobeying a valorguard's word is a crime against the kingdom; you will come with me."

A wicked smile stretches across my face. "If you wanted to tie me up, all you had to do was ask."

"Was that really necessary?" Noah hisses. "Officer..." Noah starts to say, just as Finley interrupts the grand 'ole speech he is about to give. At least I don't have to suffer through that right now.

"Can I tie you up?" Finley asks.

This guard must be an idiot. That is the only rational explanation at this point.

I bat my eyelashes at him. "Only if you get on your knees and beg," I demand.

Finley drops to his knees in front of me, and I can't help but chuckle at the sight.

What the fuck is wrong with this guy?

The tavern crowd has grown quiet around us. I glance toward the pit just as Silas collapses to the ground. I wince internally, knowing that he's going to be pissed when he wakes up. I'll worry about that later.

I turn my attention back to the valorguards in front of me. The guard, whose name I still don't know, pulls Finley, who seems on the verge of fainting, back to his feet.

In a dim corner in the back of the tavern, a door swings open, casting a beam of bright light inside The Broken Fang. A short, stocky figure emerges from the doorway, moving at an unhurried pace. The man comes to a stop in front of me, his eyes fixed on the valorguards.

"Is there a reason you're interrupting my fights as guests in my tavern? I'd hate for the word to get back to the king that his valorguards were seen in the underground pits with his precious soulfire in hand," the man quips.

Olen, my generous employer, owns The Broken Fang and controls every fight.

The guards' postures harden instantly.

"Is that a threat?" Finley asks through clenched teeth.

"Just an observation," Olen says, reaching behind him and pulling me forward. "You see, Ari, here is my prized fighter. While I'd love to see her fight one of the king's valorguards, we already have a great event planned for everyone tonight, and I can't have anything happen to her before then."

I keep my face blank, staring at Finley. His gaze roams down the length of me, understanding lighting up his eyes.

"I see..." Finley mutters, a sinister look flickering in his gaze. "I approached this all wrong." He pulls out his pouch of gilds. "I didn't realize I needed to pay for your service."

I open my mouth to snap back at the barbaric pig, but Olen waves his hand in front of Finley, uninterested in his offer. "She's all booked tonight, maybe next month."

My cheeks burn with embarrassment. Olen has never sold me for sex work. Some freaks love to get beaten by beautiful women, and it pays well, but I don't think that's what Finley had in mind.

I force a smile to cover the sudden rush of color that bloomed across my skin and blow Finley a kiss. "Maybe next month," I coo. "I'm all booked tonight."

I turn my back to him without hesitation and confidently approach the pit.

Raven and I are up next, then I can fucking sleep.

CHAPTER 3

FLOPPY HOOD

ARI

I somehow managed to avoid the valorguards for the rest of the night.

Keeping my promise, I let Raven get in a few solid punches. There is a mutual understanding between us: put on a good show, agree on the winner beforehand, and split the gilds we collect afterwards. Neither of us wants to be here, so this way, we both win—at least a little bit. It's a miracle that Olen hasn't caught on yet. He always calls our fights the 'ultimate rematch.'

I escaped the pit with only a tiny cut on my lower lip. On the other hand, Raven is unconscious in the back room. Next time we fight, it'll be my turn to be knocked out, but that is a problem for another day. All I want right now is my bed and a good night's sleep.

The Broken Fang has quieted down since our fight ended. A few lucky patrons won big tonight and are celebrating in the early hours of the morning.

"Another beer?" Octavia's voice chimes from behind the bar.

She's beautiful—bouncy brown curls halo her cherub

face, accompanied by large chestnut eyes. I can see why Noah is interested in her. I spot him across the tavern, his back facing us. His blonde hair is slightly disheveled, probably from anxiously running his hands through it.

I can't help but wonder if someone might be the reason his hair looks that way.

We have been friends forever, but our love life has never been a topic of conversation. I should ask Noah about his relationship with Octavia, but I just can't bring myself to. So, I choose not to know; it's easier that way.

I tightly clutch the handle of my tankard, beads of condensation forming around my fingertips. I glance at the clock hanging above the pit.

It's already 2 a.m.

The smile I manage to give Octavia is slow and tired, barely there at all. "I should probably call it a night," I slur. I swiftly finish my fifth beer. Flat ale slides down my throat, leaving a bitter taste behind. I push my tankard toward Octavia, placing a few gilds on the counter.

I clumsily stand up, pulling my bag onto my shoulder, and strap my sword to it. I sway on unsteady feet out the door, exhaustion weighing down on me.

"Get home safe!" Octavia calls out.

I wave my hand over my shoulder as I walk out into the frigid early morning air. Lumin is deserted at this time, but in just a few hours, the streets will be bustling with morning commuters. I often wonder what it would be like to have a regular job.

When I was younger, I thought I'd end up working in a shop like Mama.

Oh, how naive I was.

Things would have been different for me if I had grown up in a stable household like Noah's.

But my life didn't pan out that way.

I can't picture myself working in the small boutique in the town center, anyway. Dresses and heels work for other women, but I would feel out of place in them. Boots and cargo pants are all I know.

I stop just outside the tavern doors and sigh, staring up at the sky. The moon hangs low, tucked behind clouds that lazily drift in the endless darkness. I rest my hand at the nape of my neck and sway my head side to side, tension slowly releasing from my shoulders.

"At least I'll sleep well tonight," I mumble.

It's been a long week, but the worst of it is over. By morning, all the valorguards will be heading back to Lunaria, and the mines should return to business as usual since collection is complete. There will be no more long days without breaks, at least for a little while.

"Nice fight back there."

I jump at the deep voice that cuts through my thoughts at my rear. I unsheathe the dagger that rests at my hip and whirl around awkwardly, barely able to keep my footing. I surge forward in a weak attempt to protect myself.

The world spins for a moment while I fight to steady my vision. Somehow, I manage to pin a man against the tavern wall, my blade resting on his throat.

It's unlike me to be caught off guard, but it has happened twice this evening, and it's not something I can blame on the one too many drinks I had. My vision finally sharpens, and I feel my face pale to a ghostly white.

My blade is not on this man's throat like I initially thought. Instead, it rests on his chest.

He's taller than any mortal I've ever seen in Lumin.

But that's because he's not mortal at all.

And not just any eldarim.

He's a valorguard.

Dressed in a crisp black uniform, the most undeniably handsome man I've ever seen stands before me.

Ink spills out of the collar of his uniform, creeping up his neck, and feather tattoos shift against his skin as if rustling in the wind. I can't help but wonder if they cover his entire body.

But the floppy hood that shadows the guard's face intrigues me most. Hoods are not a part of valorguard's uniforms. I'd recognize him anywhere—the valorguard hidden in the corner of the tavern. The one that I missed.

I take a step back, dagger still raised. "You shouldn't sneak up on people."

I don't sound as confident as I'd like.

The valorguard head cocks to the side, eyes drifting down my body.

Even fully clothed, his gaze makes me uncomfortable. I shift my weight to my other foot, heat rising to my cheeks.

He raises gloved hands cautiously to show me he means no harm. But I can't help but notice the way his lips curve in amusement.

"You walked in front of me," he says, like he's stating the most obvious thing in the world.

I scan my surroundings, finally registering how close I was to him when I first walked out of the tavern.

"You should be more careful, or someone will jump you," he adds, lowering his hands. "Wouldn't want that to happen."

I stiffen, tightening my grip. I glare at the guard, willing him to look away.

But he doesn't.

I grit my teeth. "Is that a threat?"

He doesn't answer, just drops his hand into a pocket at his hip.

I adjust my stance, ready to fight, my body clenching in anticipation.

Slowly, he pulls out a cigarette, lifting it for me to see before placing it between his perfect lips and lighting it. Gray smoke coils through the air around us, his eyes tracking my every movement. I study the dark chocolate brown hair that ruefully peeks out from under his hood.

"Just a friendly reminder," he murmurs between puffs.

I exhale jaggedly through my nose. "I—"

BANG!

Noah stumbles out of the tavern, opening the door with such force that it slams against the wall.

I stare at him, and the guard continues to stare at me.

"Ari, you aren't avoiding me still, are you?" He sways a little as he makes his way toward me. His smile falters when he sees my dagger, oblivious to the valorguard in the shadows.

Noah wraps his arm around my waist protectively. "Is everything okay?" His gaze follows the direction of my weapon. He pulls away when he finally notices the guard.

"Can we help you with something, officer? I'm sure Ari didn't mean any harm."

I shoot him a sharp look.

The valorguard pushes off the wall and flicks his cigarette, smothering it with his boot. He steps out of the shadows, quickly engulfed by the silvery light of the moon. He is striking, no doubt—broad-shouldered, straight nose, eyes like a pool of liquid gold. Noah is the tallest man I know in Lumin, but this valorguard makes him look like a child. His presence is alarming. Every inch of him screams not to cross him, but I can't bring myself to sheath my dagger once more.

"Sergeant." The valorguard corrects Noah before facing me again. "Your friend fought a good fight." His lips twitch as his gaze shifts to my split lower lip. "It was almost like each movement was preplanned by both parties."

His eyes snap back up to mine.

I swallow my nerves and narrow my eyes at him, still far too intoxicated. But like hell, was I going to let this privileged, elitist asshole ruin my life.

I politely smile, though every inch of me wants to snap. "Thank you. I have been training for years in preparation for them. It's an honor to be recognized for my talent by the king's best."

The valorguard's stupidly perfect mouth quirks into a smug little smirk.

Noah's head swivels between the sergeant and me, his grip on my waist tightening. He leans in and presses a kiss to my cheek.

A wave of heat rushes up my neck, and the valorguard's smirk widens into an evil grin at the sight. Mortified, I stare down at my boots.

"I've watched Ari train hard for her fights; she is right about that," Noah says with pride. "We were just heading home. It's been a long night."

My gaze finds the sergeant's from under my eyelashes, a few spidery strands of makeup remaining.

"We were," I mutter. "It has been a pleasure meeting you."

A dark chuckle slips from the valorguard. "Have a good night."

He strides away, melting into the shadows of the narrow street.

I grit my teeth until they throb, watching his silhouette fade into the darkness, the ghost of smoke lingering in the air.

I whirl and smack Noah. "What the hell was that all about?"

"Owww!" he howls. "You should be thanking me, sweetheart," he says, rubbing his arm. "Especially because I am always coming to your rescue."

I snort in disbelief. "Rescue? I think you are confused about the definition of rescue, Noah. Kissing every valorguard's ass isn't valiant." My hands curl into fists at my sides. "You seriously need to grow a pair."

Noah's usual boyish grin lights up his face, and I resist the urge to smack it off his lips. "You're welcome," he teases, poking me in the ribs. "Maybe we should act like a couple more often; it seems to do the trick."

I let out a clipped laugh as I storm away from him.

I just want this night to end.

CHAPTER 4

STUPID FUCKING PIECE OF PAPER
ARI

Noah and I make our way to the furthest point of town, cobblestone turning to dirt beneath our feet. I step over scattered bottles and spilled ale, passing houses where everyone is already fast asleep.

Nobody lives well in Lumin. We're too far from anywhere of importance, too low in the king's eyes to matter, and too smart to expect that would change anytime soon. We learned to survive without power because we had to, and having a warm hearth and a loaf of bread that doesn't taste like ash is a miracle.

Luxury is a foreign concept in our section. We exist simply to survive because wanting anything more would get you killed. But sometimes, when the ale is deep in my blood and the night feels too long, I wonder what it'd be like to have more.

Noah stumbles into a fence post beside me, cursing under his breath.

"You alright over there?" I ask, my voice cracking from lack of use. I decided silence was what I wanted between Noah and me after our encounter with the valorguard.

"I'm fine," he mumbles, which means he absolutely wasn't. "I think the post moved."

I laugh, stopping to lift my gaze to the stars that spin above.

Spin? I focus on them.

The stars were indeed spinning.

Okay, maybe I wasn't fine either.

"Mhmmmmm," I hum. "Sure it did."

Noah frowns as if I've insulted him, which makes me laugh even harder. Moisture forms around my eyes, and he grins, closing the space between us. He cups my face with his hand, wiping away a tear that fell without my permission. "I've always loved that sound."

I try not to react, but my smile comes anyway. "You only love it because it means I'm not scowling at you."

Noah takes a step back, shaking his head. "You know me so well."

We begin walking again, reaching a split in the road. Noah's cozy one-story cottage is to the left, and mine is to the right, run-down and messy. But home, nonetheless.

Noah pauses, eyes lingering a moment, roaming over my features. "See you tomorrow," he murmurs, his voice soft and sincere.

I grip his hand and give it a light squeeze. "Tomorrow."

He pulls away from me, dancing to his front door. It's stupid, what he's doing, the way he's acting, but I laugh anyway. Noah always tries to lighten every moment, even when he gets under my skin. At this point, I don't know what I would do without him. I've known him for so long that I don't know how I'd function if he weren't in my life, and I can never stay mad at him for long.

I turn to face my slanted, decrepit home. Gravel crunches under my boots as I make my way down the walkway. I come to a stop at the front door, letting out a shaky breath, hand hovering above the doorknob for a moment before quietly twisting it.

Stale air hits my nostrils, sending a jolt of sobriety through me. I tiptoe into the living room, which is actually my bedroom, closing the front door with a small click.

My parents didn't plan to have a child, so they made do with what they had. I slept in a crib in the corner of their room until I grew out of it, and since then, I've slept on a small cot under the stairs in the living room.

I have never known privacy my entire life.

I quickly scan the room and the outline of a man cast in the darkness vaguely reminds me of the valorguard as he disappeared into the night. Startled, I flick the lights on, staring at the person who occupies the couch.

Anger radiates from every inch of Silas.

"You're the reason I lost my fight tonight," he seethes.

I don't say a word.

I learned a long time ago that I won't win this argument.

Silas stands and crosses the room in three long strides. He raises his right hand, and I flinch a second before the pain from the blow settles in. The anticipation always hurts worse than the actual assault.

"Did you hear me, bitch?"

"Yes. I'm sorry."

"Sorry? That's all you have to say for yourself? You humiliated me," he snarls. He rips my bag from my shoulder and dumps its contents on the ground. He sifts through my belongings with his boot, searching with a purpose.

I stand still as a statue as Silas rummages through my possessions like they are nothing, carelessly tossing my things to the side. He suddenly bends down, and I eye the lump in my spare cargo pants.

No. No. No.

He picks up my pouch of gilds instead, opens it, but discards it just as fast. "You can't fool me, girl."

Silas reaches over and snatches my cargo pants, slowly pulling out a pouch from one of the pockets.

He stands, dangling it back and forth in front of me with a smile. "I'll be taking this," he says, claiming my gilds as his own.

A burning hatred claws through my veins.

I hate him.

I *hate* him.

I hate *him*.

I should kill him, I conclude.

Silas turns away, heading toward the kitchen, putting his back to me like I am nothing. Acting as if I'm not worth another second of his time, even though he continues to take and take and take from me. My hand trembles just above my dagger, eyes never leaving the spot between his shoulders.

He underestimates me.

He knows I won't do it.

And he's right.

I drop to my knees, sweeping my things back into my bag. It feels as though the walls around me are closing in. I bring myself upright, stumbling toward the front door. Adrenaline surges through me, and the moment I swing it open, I'm gone. Silas curses behind me, but I sprint, vanishing into the night.

∼

Trying to run for your life while drunk is a special type of torture. My head pounds from too much alcohol and too little water. Every one of my steps is a gamble on loose legs and blurred vision. My heart pumps wildly, lungs burning, and mouth dry as I push forward down the road that Noah and I walked down moments before. I smiled then, laughed even, but all I feel right now is the throbbing of my face where Silas struck me.

I can already tell I'll have a black eye.

But that's tomorrow's problem.

I run until my body threatens to give out. Ahead, the town's center comes into view, a cruel reminder that I have nowhere to go. I veer down the narrow alley that runs parallel to the boutique where Mama works, sliding in the shadows.

The world teeters as my vision swims from exhaustion, and the moment my back hits the wall of the building, I collapse. The cold stone meets my backside, and I sit there defeated, trying to catch my ragged breath.

I've had nowhere to sleep before, but I usually went to Noah's. He made the chaos back home bearable. Tonight, though, I don't want to be an inconvenience to him. Not this time. He always thinks he needs to rescue me, but I don't need him to save me this time.

I'm supposed to be strong.

I am strong.

Tonight, I need to be alone.

I lean back, my shoulders sagging against the wall. I tilt my head up, looking, searching for anything in the emptiness. Anything to hold on to. But there's nothing. Hot tears spill down my cheeks, and I don't bother to wipe them.

Maybe I'm still learning how to be strong on nights like this.

I cry from the loneliness that wraps around me like a cloak. I have nothing but the bag on my shoulder and the clothes on my back.

"I can't live like this anymore," I weep. "I don't want to."

As if Althara heard me herself, the air suddenly stirred, bringing with it a gust of wind. It lashes against my skin, pulling my focus, the exact moment a white orb smacks my face.

I snatch the material that's now glued to my tear-stained skin. For a moment, I just hold it tightly between my hands, staring at it. A laugh bubbles out of me, borderline hysterical.

A piece of paper. A stupid fucking piece of paper.

I crumble it between my hands, and dark ink transfers to my skin from the movement. Each stain on my fingers is a silent reminder of every scar that refuses to fade. I nearly destroyed the paper so easily, without a second thought, leaving it fragile and broken.

I gently straighten it back out to the best of my ability, trying to return it to its original form. But it will never fully be the same again.

I begin to read the bold text with blurred vision.

THE KING REQUESTS AN AUDIENCE

The greatest fighters, assassins, and hunters are summoned to Lunaria in three days' time to search for the lost heir of Noctharn before they reach the age of twenty-five.

I straighten instantly. The award for finding the king's missing heir is substantial—one hundred thousand gilds.

A flicker of warmth fills my chest, fragile but unmistakable.

Hope.

I could have a better life.

A life in a superior section of the kingdom. With that many gilds, I could do anything. Attend the lavish balls the king hosts for the most elite, drink their fancy wines until my head spins, and live in a beautiful three-story home for no other reason than that I could.

I've dreamt of a life like this since childhood, one completely different than the one I have in Lumin. A life where I have a home to myself, a large bedroom with privacy, with linens so soft I would never want to leave my bed. I may not have power, but I could pay my way through with one hundred thousand gilds.

And the heir of Noctharn. I haven't heard any chatter about them in years. Rumors about the king's lost heir have faded over time, and I figured they were long gone by now.

The Queen of Noctharn's betrayal is well-known. She was an oracle and foresaw that the king would kill his first-born. So, she fled. She turned her back on her kingdom and disappeared with the king's only child while she was pregnant. The queen was eventually found and killed for her treason, but the king never located his child. And now he must be trying to find them before their binding ritual, stopping their chance to claim their rightful power from Althara. But where could they be? Surely the heir would have been seen by now if someone was hiding them in Noctharn.

The hair on the back of my neck prickles, and I snap my head to the far end of the alley—the sudden feeling that I'm not alone washing over me.

I rise soundlessly, folding the paper and placing it in my

pocket. I make my way to the mouth of the alley, peering over my shoulder every few steps. I enter the town's center, keeping to the shadows until I stand in front of a familiar wooden door.

I attempt to pry it open, my fingernails screaming in protest, threatening to tear off with each tug. The backdoor of The Broken Fang finally gives way and flings open.

I step into the dressing room, the sound of my ragged breath the only noise as I take my damp towels from earlier in the night off the drying rack.

I swiftly assemble a make-shift bed by the door with them.

It's not the most comfortable, but it'll have to do.

I place my bag beside me, making sure it's within arm's reach, before lying down on the cold floor. The towels beneath me offer me no warmth, and I'm vulnerable if anyone walks in.

I try to remember that I've slept in much worse and that no one was going to hurt me here.

I lay there, gaze lingering on the ceiling above, my thoughts drifting in circles. This quest will be my way out. *It has to be.* I will find the king's heir and finally leave this godforsaken town.

I'll bring Mama with me.

Would she even want that?

I no longer want this life for myself.

I never did.

Maybe she feels the same.

The same questions and fears loop endlessly in my mind.

But I know one thing for sure.

I'd rather die trying than stay in this town another day.

Tomorrow, I'll leave for Lunaria.

CHAPTER 5

ABOMINATION
LINCOLN

My gloves are suffocating me.

I hate them, always have, but I hate what they resemble even more. They are like a special prison, crafted just for me. And no matter how thin or soft, they hold me hostage.

I will never be able to escape them.

Tonight is no different. I miss the days when I was young and didn't have to wear them.

A cigarette dangles from my lips, the smoke curling beneath my hood and stinging my eyes. I breathe in fire, dragging it deep into my lungs, letting it burn. *It hurts.* But it's the closest thing I have to feeling alive.

I keep my head low, scanning the streets, not expecting anything. Habit, mostly. No one can catch me off guard, even if they tried. With the flick of my thumb, the cigarette hits the ground. I bury its glow with my boot. It makes a faint hiss as it's crushed to ash. It dies in a single breath, just like everything else in my life.

I yank my hands free from my gloves, stretching my

clammy fingers in front of me. I greedily soak in the sensation my hands have been starved of.

I round the corner of the narrow street, just one more block to the quaint hotel where the valorguards are being housed. It's rundown and anonymous, the kind of place that guarantees an uncomfortable night's rest.

Fortunately, and unfortunately, I don't have any time to rest, even as my head pounds from lack of sleep. Staying at the tavern so late and leaving the flyers until the last minute were both mistakes on my part.

I slip through the hotel's grimy doors. Thick, musty air submerges my senses and swallows me whole. I bury my hands deep into my cloak, careful to blend into the shadows as I make my way to the end of the hall. I duck into my room, the frame rough against my shoulders.

It's small and cramped, almost claustrophobic. It's acceptable for mortals, but nowhere near big enough for eldarim. I'd expect nicer accommodations from the king, but I suppose that was too optimistic, especially in a low section like Lumin.

I mount my quiver onto my back, strapping my bow to it before gripping my duffel of spare uniforms. I give the room a quick once-over and step back into the hallway.

Soulfire collection week is my least favorite time of the year, but participating in it is the only way I can quickly climb the ranks. If there were any other way, I would have taken it.

I rush out of the hotel onto the uneven cobblestone streets, striding past rundown storefronts and sidewalks littered with the aftermath of the evening before. The mortal sections of the kingdom always intrigued me. They live so poorly. Always given the scraps of the kingdom, plagued with disease at every corner, yet the King of Noctharn relies on them so heavily to mine his precious crystal. It's terrifying that we've come to accept that this is just the way things are.

Mortals do bore me, though. They are bland creatures, with no powers, no drive to live—short existences filled with mundane labor and nothing to look forward to, or at least I thought so until I met that one woman. That woman is different. I haven't stopped thinking about her since I left the tavern.

Her soulfire-colored eyes and sharp tongue have haunted me since.

The first hints of morning brush the horizon, casting a yellow glow over the dreary town. I reach the outskirts of Lumin, heading directly toward the horses that stand in a tight circle around the steel carriage containing the king's soulfire. Valorguards mount their steeds one by one as I approach.

I nod at the man at the front of the line. "Finley," I greet him.

Finley grunts in my direction before turning to face his squad.

How did that mortal woman have a valorguard as powerful as Finley on his knees? It is something I have been pondering since she stepped into the pit. Her fight drew me in, as did the way she carried herself with such confidence. I'm not sure how the tavern owner hasn't caught onto her scheme. It's apparent from a mile away.

I swiftly approach the carriage and climb in, swinging the door shut behind me and latching it. You'd think guarding the soulfire inside the carriage would be a privilege.

It's not.

The air barely flows inside the steel container. Just breathing in here is exhausting.

Sighing, I run a hand through my thick hair, taming it after being constricted under my hood all week.

Don't get me wrong, though. I'm not complaining. I will admit, I do like it better that way, hidden beneath my clothing, walking in the shadows, away from everyone. I tell myself that if I stay out of sight, I can't harm anyone.

Because if they knew what I was, then they would run. They would scream for their lives and beg for mercy.

I'm unnatural—an abomination.

It's a truth I've learned to live with.

I hastily slip my gloves back on, ignoring the ache that pulses through my hands from the constant constraint.

The carriage lurches forward, marking the beginning of our trek back to the capital.

CHAPTER 6

DEATH IS BETTER THAN THIS
ARI

Sleeping on a thin layer of damp towels wasn't the wisest decision.

I groan, rolling onto my side, trying to ignore the splitting headache that shoots across my forehead.

Years ago, I could slam back ale and wake up like nothing happened the night before. Hell, I used to sleep in the woods with only dead leaves for comfort and would wake up ready to take on the day. Now? Working in the mines has aged me, and I'm pretty sure my spine is permanently tangled.

I prop myself up on one elbow and rub my eyes. Dusty morning light seeps through the cracks in the door, casting small beams across the back room of The Broken Fang. The floor is littered with bottles, splinted wood, and...

"Long night?"

Olen's voice startles me.

I spring to my feet and wince. Something in my shoulder pops from the sudden movement. My hand finds the strap of my bag, and I pick it up to survey its weight. All my belongings are still here, and my sword still lies where I left it. I trust that Olen wouldn't steal from me.

I bring my attention to my employer. He sits legs extended, perched on an empty barrel of ale, eyeing me with evident annoyance. I shift under his gaze, standing a little straighter, as much as my spine will allow.

Olen clicks his tongue, the sound sharp and full of disapproval. "This isn't a hotel," he drawls. "First, Raven. Now you?"

There's no use in pretending I hadn't been caught red-handed sleeping in The Broken Fang.

"And how is Raven?" I ask.

"Alive," he says flatly. "Now, why are you sleeping in my tavern?"

Olen is harsh, but I know he means well. He has taken better care of me than my father.

I grip the back of my neck, dropping my gaze to the floor in submission. "I'm sorry, I just..."

Olen raises a hand dismissively. "Save the sob story. I'll be charging you for your stay."

I groan, rubbing my temples—willing my headache to disappear. "Seriously?" Like sleeping on the floor wasn't punishment enough, I now have to pay for the terrible night of sleep I had? And better yet, I don't have a gild to my name at the moment.

Olen sits there, waiting.

"Take it out of next month's pay," I offer him. It's the only solution I have.

I sling my bag over my shoulder, securing my sword to it, and pull open the back door before he can protest.

"You know I will, girl!" Olen shouts just as I step out into the morning light, knowing full well that I will not be fighting in the pits next month. "And Ari." I peer at him over my shoulder. "You've looked better."

I pinch my eyebrows together in confusion at the same time he taps a finger at the corner of his eye.

His laughter is the last thing I hear as the door slams shut.

I forgot about that damned black eye I was going to wake up with. I hastily unfasten my barrette, strategically placing the strands of my hair in front of my face to mask it.

I inhale a deep breath; the frigid air instantly clears my head. It's a beautiful spring morning in Lumin, the kind that rejuvenates something deep inside you after a brutal winter.

I pause for a moment, savoring the soft caress from the sun brushing against my skin. I'd almost forgotten how pleasant its touch can be after so much time lost in the mines.

I allow myself a short moment of peace before pulling out the flyer for the king's quest from my pocket. I walk into the town's center as I do, following the hum of morning commuters. I keep my gaze down, trying to stay hidden in the rush of people. Flyers flutter on every surface—lamp posts, shop windows, even floating in the wind. The same flyer that I hold in my hand is plastered all over town. It was too dark to see them all last night, it seems.

I pick up my pace as the crowd thickens. Voices overlap each other in a mix of laughter, and mindless conversation. I don't slow down until I reach a building with faded blue paint. I stop just outside, staring at my reflection in the bookstore window. I grimace—not because Noah hasn't changed the display in years—he's proud of it and refuses to touch it. It's the woman staring back at me that takes me by surprise.

I almost don't recognize myself.

My face is pale, too hollow, with cheekbones too high. I look tired, from lack of sleep and something far worse. I gingerly touch the tender skin around my eye. A bruise has already begun to creep down my cheek.

I run my hands down my shirt, straightening out the wrinkles as best I can. My clothes are just as disheveled as my appearance.

"Did you see the flyers hanging around town?" someone murmurs behind me. I crook my head toward the sound of the voice, hiding my bruised eye with my hair. Two women sit on the nearby street bench, enjoying a cup of coffee. "Only a person with a death wish would join that quest," the other adds.

I peer down at the flyer still clutched in my hand.

Death is better than this, I remind myself.

A rush of patrons swarms the bookstore door, and I spot Noah through the window. He's chatting animatedly, casually leaning against the counter in a deep purple tunic. A customer laughs at what he says, nodding along, wholly caught up in whatever story he is spewing. And of course, it's Octavia. I observe them through the pane, and my hand flexes, crinkling the paper within it.

Noah has Octavia now. He'll be okay.

I slip into the bookstore, hiding behind the large group, and head down the first aisle.

I move a book on the shelf just enough to peer around it. Noah gives Octavia that boyish grin he always wears, running a hand through his tousled hair simultaneously. He looks so...carefree.

I whistle softly.

A distinct whistle we would use when we played hide and seek when we were young. Noah's head shoots up, eyes sharp, and scans the room.

I whistle once more, and his gaze finds mine, just long enough for him to see me before I slide the book back into place.

In a breath, he rounds the corner, stopping directly in front of me. He stands so close that I can feel the heat radiating off his skin.

Noah brushes the hair from my face, eyes widening as he does.

"God, Ari...you look like shit."

"Thanks," I murmur, my voice thick with sarcasm.

He cups my cheek with his hand, gently moving the pad of his thumb against my swelling eye. Silence falls between us as I melt into his touch. Every line on his face is filled with worry, and the way he's looking at me right now makes me want to crumble.

How do I tell him that I'm leaving?

My mouth feels dry as I search for the right words. My decision is final, regardless of how much I'll miss Noah. I have to go. I need to.

"Silas?" he asks.

"Yes," I whisper.

Fury washes over Noah's features. I don't need to explain Silas's behavior to him. He's seen it firsthand.

Noah's hand slides down my face, dropping to his side. "Why didn't you come over last night? Where did you go?"

I step back, putting some space between us.

"I didn't want to be told that I did something wrong. You berated me last night for the valorguards speaking to me, and I just...I just needed to be alone."

Noah grips my shoulders sternly in his hands, pulling me forward. The smell of fresh rain fills my nose as he leans in close. "You know that's not what I meant. You're always welcome in my room." His lips brush my ear. "Where did you go?"

I draw back, laughter bubbling up uncontrollably.

He covers my mouth with his hand. "Shhhhh!"

I smirk against his palm. "My my, Noah, do I detect a hint of jealousy?"

"I don't care what you do and who you do it with," he hisses.

I bat my eyelashes at him. "You wound me."

Noah's eyes narrow, clearly unamused. "Ari! I care about you. Is that what you want to hear me say?" he growls, raking a hand through his hair. "I don't want anything to happen to you."

I've never seen Noah act like this. Why does he have to do this right now?

I grab his hand, concealing it between mine. "I slept on the tavern floor in the dressing room. Olen kicked me out first thing in the morning, but I'm fine."

Noah exhales jaggedly, as if he were holding his breath, and I inhale, about to ruin his brief moment of peace.

I need to get this over with. I need to tell Noah what I intend to do.

"I only came here because there's something I have to tell you." I pull out the crumpled piece of paper from my pocket and hand it to him.

Noah's eyes dart back and forth across it. "Shit," he mutters. His knuckles turn white from gripping it so hard. "Why do you have this?"

"Why do you think?"

"You can't join the quest," he snarls. "You hate King Malvok. Why would you help him?"

Help him? I'm doing this to help myself.

"I can get out of Lumin and make a life for myself, for

Mama. It'll be a life worth living. Far, far away from here." And far away from Silas, but I don't add that part.

"There are other ways!" Noah shouts. He stops himself and returns to a whisper. "There are other ways. Please, think this through."

I rip the paper from his hands and shove it in my bag, wrath pounding through my veins. "You would say that. You and your perfect life and perfect family. You never had to fight in the pits or work in the mines. You get to work here." I wave my hand, motioning to the clean, orderly bookshelves. "You have a normal life, while I've never had a normal day. Don't you understand?"

Noah seizes my wrist between his hands, pleading with his eyes. "Why do you always have to go to the extreme? Going on a quest that will likely kill you isn't worth it."

My skin boils beneath his fingertips.

Noah will never understand. I realize that now.

I glare up at him. "Get your hands off me," I command. His hold on me disappears instantly, and I slowly retreat, growing the space between us. "I'm going. It's final. You can support me or not, but I need to do this for myself."

Noah shakes his head, defeated. "Just don't die."

I scoff, putting my back to him without a second thought. "Have a little faith in me for once."

I feel Noah's gaze boring into me, but I don't stop, even when my feet wobble beneath me like the ground itself is unsteady. Pressure builds in my chest, begging me to look back just once, but my mind is set.

I'll do whatever is necessary to achieve the life I deserve.

There's no going back now.

CHAPTER 7

SMALL PAWN
ARI

I stopped to see Mama at the boutique before I left.

She didn't protest when I told her I planned to join the king's quest. She didn't even try to stop me. Her tired eyes held a quiet understanding, as if she already knew.

She pulled me into the back room and, with gentle hands, wrapped a small bundle of bread and nuts from her lunch in a cloth. She pressed it into my palm. It was a small offering, not enough for my journey to the capital without starving, but it was an offering filled with care, nonetheless. The way her gaze lingered on my bruised eye said enough. She caressed my cheek, skimming the area with the faintest touch, grounding me in a way that I needed in that moment.

"I always knew this wouldn't last forever," was the only thing she said to me.

She was a woman of few words, and deep down, I knew she cared, but it wasn't a tearful farewell. There was no dramatic embrace, just an acceptance of what I had to do.

Now, I'm a day out, in clothing that's grown too warm during the day and too thin at night. I crossed the last ridge beyond Lumin hours ago, leaving the southern border of the kingdom behind. The bundle she gave me is running low, even though I have been trying to ration it the best I can. I will have to hunt for my next meal if I want to survive.

The journey to Lunaria is not an easy trek. There is one path from each mortal section to the capital and another path for the eldarim. The path I travel on is extremely overgrown, with ancient trees pressing too close, while I can only assume the path for the elite is well-groomed.

Weeds poke through stones, and tree roots protrude from the earth with each step. I spend most of my time staring at the ground to make sure I don't trip.

I haven't passed one living soul since I left Lumin. The only company I've had is the flash of a deer in the distance and the birds chirping nearby. Last night, I had no other choice but to sleep on the forest floor. I kept one hand on my sword the whole time, though nothing came. I don't think sleep actually found me.

A sudden shift in light ahead pulls my attention from my boots to the area where the trees part. It's thin at first, like a small thread that barely slipped past the branches, but with each step I take, the wider it gets. I hasten my pace at the scent of fresh water and moss, a rush of excitement blooming inside me.

I push through a curtain of vines, and a large clearing unfolds before me, bathed in sunlight. At its center lies a glittering, crystal-clear lake. Its surface is as smooth as glass, reflecting the fluffy clouds that float aloft.

The tension I held, coiled tight inside me, loosens.

I stride to the water's edge, and the soft earth sinks slightly beneath my boots. My bag slides from my shoulders, dropping to the ground with a thud. I rest the hilt of my sword on top of it, and relief shoots down my spine. I allow my knees to buckle, sinking to the ground.

I tentatively dip my hand into the luminescent water. It's colder than I expected, but the perfect temperature to cut through the burgeoning warmth of spring.

I rise once more, unclasping the button of my worn-down cargos. I strip down to my undergarments and unclip my barrette, tucking it into the side pocket of my bag. I speedily unbraid my hair, letting the strands fall loose down my back.

I scan my surroundings, remembering that I'm on a direct path to the capital, and anyone could be walking by.

After a few brief moments of silence, I slip my toes into the crisp water. It rises around my ankles, then my calves, pulling at the grime from my skin. Something brushes against my leg, and I jump from the sudden contact, searching for the culprit.

My lips curve upward as small fish dart between my legs. Their tiny fins brush against my skin, and it tickles in a way I wasn't expecting. I choke out a laugh. "You wicked little things," I squeal, trying to get away from them.

I have always been terribly ticklish. Noah has taken advantage of the fact on multiple occasions, especially in an argument—one good jab to my ribs and I was undone, entirely consumed by laughter.

I wade deeper into the lake until my shoulders are entirely submerged. The fish trail after me, their silver bodies gliding through the water. "Let me be," I protest with a laugh, but they seem undeterred by my jerky movements.

I kick up from the sand and float onto my back, staring up at the sun. I bask in its warmth, letting it soak into my skin. It's a welcome contrast compared to the frigid bite of the water clinging to my limbs.

I lay there in the stillness of the lake, and in its vastness, feeling minuscule in a kingdom I have yet to explore. Worthless, even. It's a humbling kind of loneliness, making my fears and worries seem insignificant in this moment. I'm just a small pawn on the board while bigger pieces play. But just like this lake, the slightest movement can change the surface, and that's precisely what I intend to do.

I have made my choice. I will find the lost heir. Nothing will stop me. And when this is all over, everyone will finally know my name.

I submerge my head, allowing the lake to carry my thoughts away.

I just hope I'm not making the biggest mistake of my life.

CHAPTER 8

HALF-BREEDS
ARI

By dawn, I'm on the road again.

The morning mist curls low over the path, laced with the earthy scent of damp leaves.

I adjust my belt around my waist while I walk, securing my fighting daggers to it. I'm not sure if what I carry will be enough, but two daggers and one sword will have to do.

Hours pass before the capital city reveals itself. The forest thins gradually, the trees growing sparse, opening into a broad field that stretches like a golden sea. The ground cracks beneath my boots, like life itself has been drained from it long ago. There is no moisture in the air, like all the humidity from the promise of spring has been stripped away.

Each step through the field sounds like bones breaking, and it makes the hairs on the back of my neck stand. I press on, passing through the field as fast as I can, eyes fixed on the city walls. They glimmer like a mirage carved from pearl.

The field ends, transforming into a well-kept road, just wide enough for a horse and carriage to fit.

The city gates unfold in front of me. They are iron-bound and flanked by stone towers that rise like sentinels from the ground. My gaze shifts to the emblem carved on them—a shadowy vulture with outstretched wings, its eyes gleaming like dark jewels. And just past them, in the distance, the castle looms. Its ridges pierce the gray sky like black spears, touching the clouds and extending beyond them, a complete contradiction to the vibrant white stone that makes up the city. Goosebumps rise along my arms like a quiet warning at the sight.

I have never seen Lunaria before, only heard stories from the lips of travelers—all stories too grand to believe and utterly impossible to be true.

I come to a halt, standing before a group of valorguards dressed in their pristine black uniforms. Their swords gleam in the hazy morning sun as they advance to meet me.

"State your name and purpose, mortal."

I clear my throat. "My name is Ari," I say, trying not to stammer. I pull out my frayed flyer and hold it up for them to see. "I came to join the king's quest."

The paper is faded now, with ink running in places where it touched my sweaty skin.

The valorguard at the front of the group studies me, eyes fixed on my face, then my weapons. The intensity in his stern demeanor unmistakably marks him as the leader.

I keep my attention downward, not wanting to cause a stir. I stand there, waiting to be questioned or scolded for thinking a mortal could take on the quest, bracing myself for laughter or worse. But it never comes.

I lift my gaze.

"Head straight to the castle. Someone will be waiting to collect you there," the valorguard finally says. "The king will be addressing his participants soon, and once the doors shut, you will not be let in." He moves to the side, and the guards behind him drag the gates open. "Welcome to Lunaria."

I fold the flyer and put it back in my pocket. I straighten my posture and, with my chin held high, I stroll past the guards and head into the capital.

I saunter through the city in awe, greedily taking in everything around me. Lunaria is even more beautiful than I imagined. The walls tower high, banners sway in the wind, and eldarim stand by carts of fresh fruit, bartering with patrons. It's all surreal.

I pass vendors who sell foreign silk, stones said to be blessed by Althara, and roasted nuts in colorful stalls. The scent of fresh-baked goods and herbs engulfs me as an unrelenting pain gnaws at my stomach. The leftover rabbit I ate this morning from yesterday's hunt only filled me so much.

The streets are packed with immortals dressed in elegant finery—jewels adorn their collars and cuffs of their robes. Their faces are serene and ageless; untouched by time itself. My Lumin style of dress stands out painfully, like a smear of grime amidst polished grace.

"First time in the capital?"

The voice startles me. I spin around to find a man standing near a glowing fountain filled with a silver liquid. His arms are full of scrolls, so ancient they look like they could disintegrate if a light breeze passed through.

He appears no older than I am, with smooth almond skin and cheekbones shaped like they were sculpted from marble. Something twitches over his shoulder, and I gasp.

"You have wings," I blurt out. I slap my hand over my mouth in horror.

I can't believe I just said that out loud.

He peers behind himself, his wings shifting from the movement. They are broad and strong, each feather coated in an oily sheen, and when the light hits them just right, hints of midnight blue and purple peek through. They are stunning and terrifying at the same time.

Eyes the color of a lush forest met mine, sparkling with amusement. "Unfortunately, I do," the man replies. "They make sleeping on my back a nightmare."

I blink. Can he never sleep on his back? Does he have a special bed? Or maybe... "Can you fly?"

The man chuckles. "That's always the next question."

I snap my mouth shut, realizing it is still hanging open. Heat pools beneath my skin, and I flush. "I'm sorry. I don't mean to be rude. I just never knew eldarim could have wings."

The man repositions himself, adjusting the scrolls in his hands. "They don't, at least not indefinitely. If an eldarim were assigned an animal with wings, then yes, they could transform and fly." He stalls for a moment. "But I can never transform. I'm stuck this way forever."

"And that's a bad thing?" I ask, thinking about the freedom he must feel soaring high above the capital.

The man frees one of his hands and points to the tiny punctures tracing the length of his wings, marks I hadn't noticed before. "I can't fly. I was never given the chance to." His voice hardens. "It seems the king has been successful in keeping us half-breeds hidden from the lower sections."

I gape at him in horror, imagining the pain he has been through. Slowly, I tilt my head. "I don't understand. You are an eldarim..." I stutter. "You're powerful."

He smiles, folding his wings tight against himself. "Yes," he says, choosing his following words wisely. "But I failed when it mattered most."

How could he have failed? He has an animal assignment. "You are a shifter, though."

"No. I am not. I failed to obtain all my power. I woke before I could claim its entirety. I was weak-minded in the sense that I couldn't take it any longer." The man's eyes darken before he continues, lowering his voice to a hushed whisper. "The king doesn't celebrate the weak."

An eldarim's binding ritual is one of the most sacred and pivotal moments in their lives. It determines the role they will have in society for eternity. From the moment they consume the belknot root, their fate is sealed. Althara releases her power, and it descends upon them like a flame. Many falter under the weight of it, but if you do survive, you are reborn. No longer aging and emerging anew. The most powerful wake with the ability to shape shift, taking on the form of the animal that resembles them most. The man before me was destined to be great.

Part of me can't fathom that our king would treat any immortal with cruelty. And yet, as I stand here before the winged eldarim, I see it clear as day in his eyes—the same hatred I carry in my heart for the king, like mirrored bitterness held so tight, deep within us. I can't help but wonder how many half-breeds are trapped in the capital.

A bell chimes, marking the arrival of the next hour, and my heart jolts.

"I am running late. It was nice meeting you..." I trail off, realizing I never got his name.

"Ian," he says, finishing my sentence.

"Ari," I reply with a soft smile.

Ian gives me a slight nod, his eyes holding mine for a

breath longer than expected. "I'm sure we'll meet again," he assures me. He turns away from me and heads in the opposite direction.

For a moment, I just stand there, caught off guard at how certain his words sounded. I carve the image of his dark wings into my memory as he disappears.

I pivot and hurry toward the castle, not wanting to be late.

The busy streets of Lunaria grow quiet behind me as cobblestone becomes polished marble under my feet. The castle stands just past a drawstring bridge, spanning the moat that guards the entrance. The water below is dark and still, radiating with an unnatural heat. At the far end, banners flutter from iron sconces, bearing the insignia of the king. Archers in plated armor observe me with watchful eyes, and I quickly count twenty arrows pointed at my chest.

I cross the bridge, keeping a steady pace, each step deliberate, not wanting my next one to be my last.

A woman appears in front of the castle just as I stroll off the bridge. I examine her, noting the soft gray linen that wraps around her body, her loosely braided blonde hair, and her tail. *Her tail...*I realize. A fox-like, vibrant orange tail sways behind her. She's a half-breed and a servant.

She gives me a wary look. "Are you here for the king's quest?"

I nod, pull out the flyer, and show it to her.

She bites her lower lip. "Very well," she mutters. "The king is about to begin. Come now, or you'll be late."

I follow the woman through the doors.

Obsidian walls rise high around us, swallowing the sound of our footsteps. Golden chandeliers float eerily above the grand hall, shimmering with crystals that twinkle like stars in the night sky. We pass chamber after chamber filled with the most lavish furniture I have ever seen in my life.

The servant abruptly stops, pointing just ahead of us. "Right through these doors."

"Thank you." I soften my expression, hoping she'll see that we're not so different—us mortals and half-breeds. "I never got your name."

I want to remember every half-breed I meet. I won't allow myself to forget the king's heartlessness after I find the lost heir. I will make him pay for what he's done.

"Erica," she whispers. She turns her back to me and glides down the castle halls, her tail bouncing behind her with each step.

She must not think I will survive this because she never asked for my name in return.

She'll learn it soon enough.

CHAPTER 9

ASHFIELD

ARI

The doors to the throne room loom before me, carved from a dark stone, delicately engraved with winding patterns that I can't quite name. Some twist like flames, others stretch long and thin, depicting what I can only imagine air would look like in a breeze, swirling and reshaping itself over and over again.

I stand frozen, hand hovering just above the cold iron handle, fingers trembling.

I shouldn't be this nervous, but I am.

My fate lies behind these doors, and I don't know what's waiting on the other side. I don't know if I am ready.

What if everyone sees it—the doubt, the fear, the truth that I am afraid I might fail.

I close my eyes, swallowing the rising wave of uncertainty building inside me.

My mind cries for me to go back, but my heart urges me to go on. What if I die? Pressure builds in my chest. But what if I don't?

I'm tired of being a coward.

I'm tired of dealing with daily abuse.

I'm tired of being the weak little girl my father thinks I am.

And I'm tired of protecting Mama from that vile man.

Part of me wants to run home and tell Noah he was right, but I listen to the part that would rather die trying to make a better life for myself than to have never tried at all.

I didn't come this far to quit.

I force stillness into my quaking limbs and shove the door open.

Voices begin to hum as I cross the threshold into the throne room.

Light spills through the floor-to-ceiling stained-glass windows, painting the polished floor with fractured colors of rich blues and greens. Columns stretch into a ceiling lost in shadow and cast in darkness, engraved with the same strange shapes as the doors. And at the far end of the room, raised high above the hall, is the throne.

Men and women alike crowd into groups, dressed in various arrays of armor and weapons. Most appear young, stuck in the ageless time loop that comes with immortality, while others appear worn down by age and undeniably mortal.

I slip into the room, only heeding a few curious glances.

There must be at least thirty participants.

Maybe I was stupid for thinking I would be the one to find the king's heir. The thought crashes into me suddenly. I don't belong here. I'm only mortal, and more than half of the participants are eldarim. These could be professional investigators, assassins, or bounty hunters for all I know.

But it's too late now. The doors have already closed, and I have nowhere else to go. Lumin is not my home anymore.

I lift my chin and march further into the room. My gaze catches on a mural near one of the columns, faded from age but still powerful. It's a vibrant arrangement of colors depicting a young prince clad in regal armor, lined in gold. A bloodied sword is raised high, its length drenched in crimson red. King Malvok stands above a man with tired eyes—his father, the former King of Noctharn—his face caught in a moment of triumph. The former king lies at the foot of the throne, crown fallen, eyes wide with disbelief. Above them, in the swirling gray clouds, an angelic face weeps silver tears.

King Malvok has ruled Noctharn for a hundred years, with no heir to his throne. His reign marked a turning point, and no throne before his has ever cast such a long shadow. Shortly after he came to power, the sections fell into place, separating the weakest beings from the most powerful. Eldarim prospered while mortals lost everything.

I slam into something hard, the unexpected force knocking me back a step.

Curious amber eyes meet mine, piercing but bright beneath a furrowed brow. The girl's tawny skin glows softly in the light from the crystal chandeliers.

I narrow my eyes at her with a flicker of caution, hand instinctively dropping to my waist. "Sorry," I say, voice calm, not an ounce of unease in my tone. I observe her, searching for any threat, but all I catch is a small, almost hesitant smile.

"It's okay," she murmurs. "I couldn't look away either."

It hits me then, how young she is, too young to be here in the king's throne room, caught up in something bigger than herself. A sense of dread coils inside me.

She shouldn't be here.

I reach out my hand in front of me. "I'm Ari."

She places her slender fingers in mine. "Ella," she says. Gold bangles jingle at her wrists as we shake hands.

"Next!" a valorguard yells.

Ella whirls around to face him, and I join in line behind her.

The guard writes down our information, and we sign our names on a piece of parchment before being ushered further into the room.

I fall in step beside Ella, weaving through the crowd of participants. The babble of hushed voices well around us; whispers, and idle chatter, all blending into a hum.

We stop amid a throng of other mortals, each one with their own reason for being here written in their wary eyes. I inspect the throne room, seeing faces full of hope and fear, some proud, others resigned to whatever fate awaits them.

I take my time memorizing the crowd, committing faces to memory, when one in particular stops me cold.

By the column on the far right of the room, a group of men stand in a huddle. Valorguards dressed out of uniform in regular clothing, though that isn't what halts me in my tracks. The valorguard in the center, with his sandy brown hair, does. It's him. *Finley*. The guard I kicked in the crotch a few days ago at The Broken Fang.

Shit. I clench my hands into fists, forcing my features to remain neutral. I shield myself behind the participants who surround me.

Ella nudges my arm. "Everything okay?"

"Yeah." I force a calm smile. "Sometimes I forget how tall eldarim are." I look around the room, making it seem like I'm perplexed at the fact. I mentally note how Finley's back is now angled away from me.

She chuckles, easing the tension just a little. "Oh, I know! We rarely saw any in Solhaven."

Ella is from a low section like me; a mortal town located northwest of Lunaria.

She nudges me again, nodding in a different direction. "Look at that one over there."

I follow her gaze to a towering figure near the far wall, noting his wide shoulders, leather gloves, and his mysterious hood. The blood drains from my face. *His hood.* This just went from bad to worse.

Ella's voice drops an octave. "He's massive. He has to be almost seven feet tall," she says under her breath.

The valorguard with the hood, the one I keep missing. His focus is on me, and he's even more intimidating than I remember. He's dressed in worn fighting leathers, battle scarred and hugging his form, revealing every taut muscle beneath. A bow is slung casually over his shoulder, its quiver full of arrows.

"Did you hear me?" Ella's voice slices through the fog in my head.

"Hmmm?" I clear my throat. "Oh yeah, he's definitely seven feet tall, give or take a few inches."

"Being that tall should be illegal," she huffs. "I will say he does have that whole 'don't mess with me' look down."

I shrug, unfazed. "He looks like an arrogant brute." The kind of guy who knows he scares people and wears it like a badge of honor.

The hooded valorguard tilts his head, just enough to make it clear that he is studying me. Unreadable eyes drag over every inch of me. I keep my chin held high.

Ella laughs softly. "Ari, you're staring."

The guard's face hardens, an icy wave of anger flooding his features. The calm, impassive expression he held moments ago vanishes in an instant. He lifts his hand and taps the corner of his eye with one gloved finger.

A small gesture. But I understand immediately. My black eye is probably a pretty green by now, courtesy of Silas.

Ella's head swivels between the valorguard and me. She grabs my arm. "You know him? Don't you?"

I jerk my head side to side. *I don't even know his name.*

"No, I—"

A bell clanks, loud and jarring, cutting me off. It echoes through the room, and the murmur of the crowd dies instantly. Every head turns toward the dais, and a valorguard next to the throne clears his throat.

"Your Royal Highness, King Malvok, savior of the Noctharn Kingdom," the guard announces.

Every participant in the room bows. I follow suit, lowering my head, the motion smooth and effortless. I practiced it on my journey here, over and over again, until I got it right. I've never been in the presence of royalty before. My eyes face the floor, but I can still feel the hooded valorguard's gaze on me, branding my skin.

The king enters the throne room, flanked by guards, his footsteps the only sound. I inhale jaggedly, counting the subtle squeak of his shoes. He reaches the dais on the twelfth step.

The participant in front of me falters slightly, legs quivering in anticipation.

"Rise," the king commands.

We all stand, backs straight, eyes fixed on him. I scowl at the king as he observes us. His features are as cruel as his heart.

"I trust you all traveled here safely." The king grins as if he told a joke. "The fate of my kingdom relies on each one of you."

His words sink into my gut, like a stone.

King Malvok surveys the room but stops abruptly before he can reach Ella and me—his attention stalls on the mysterious valorguard with the hood.

"Lincoln Ashfield," the king says, a thread of surprise in his tone. "Here to bring honor back to your family's name?"

All eyes in the room swing in the direction that Ella and I were staring a moment before, and my heart stops.

The Ashfield's were the longest-running family of assassins in Noctharn, notorious for being lethal and showing no mercy. They held that title until they failed to locate the heir.

I get it now—why the hooded valorguard lurks in the shadows, how he's able to move unseen. And now he knows who I am and my scheme in the fighting ring.

If I survive this, I'm as good as dead.

CHAPTER 10

THE MAP

ARI

I regard Lincoln through lowered lashes, letting the weight of the knowledge settle like a blade across my throat.

I ignored what little I knew about him from our encounter outside The Broken Fang, and worse, I ignored what I didn't.

How could I have been so stupid?

I should have known the moment I saw Lincoln's face who he was. Not because he hides it poorly. He doesn't. In fact, he hides it too well with his hood pulled tight, masking his features, and this is the third time I haven't noticed his presence until he made it known.

It's painfully obvious who he is now. There's only one bloodline with eyes like his—eyes as golden as sunlight. His father had them too, and every Ashfield before them.

Lincoln stands before the king, impossibly still—a spitting image of his father.

"Yes, Your Majesty. If it's the last thing I do," Lincoln finally declares.

His words land like a warning, calm but glacial.

A savage smile spreads across the king's lips. "Very well."

I know what Lincoln is capable of, having heard the stories of the Ashfields before him; their cold-blooded precision, killing without a second thought at the king's word.

Lincoln's father, Lieutenant Ashfield, was tasked with finding the Queen of Noctharn after she fled. He was successful in locating her alive and well, but without the heir. He nearly tore the kingdom apart searching for them, chasing any whisper of the king's child.

Lincoln's father dedicated twenty years of his life to searching for them before the king inevitably had enough. They killed him, leaving his body strung up in the city square like a dog, just like they did to the queen's. They didn't bother to cut him down until vultures came to pick at his innards.

The news hit Lumin a week later that a new family of assassins would be taking the Ashfield's place, ending their legacy as the king's best.

And now his son is here, joining the king's quest. A ghost wearing his father's skin, wanting to finish what he started.

This is exactly what Noah was trying to warn me about, and somehow, I convinced myself I had a chance before I knew what I was up against. Maybe that's why Erica didn't bother to learn my name; she probably already thought of me as dead.

My gaze shifts from Lincoln to the king.

He sits tall and unyielding on his throne—a towering structure lined with jagged bones. His broad shoulders and harsh demeanor demand attention in the eerily silent room, with skin so pale it almost appears sickly, gleaming with the same polished sheen as the bones. A halo of onyx hair surrounds his gaunt face, emphasizing the harsh lines around his pure black eyes. Rings glisten on every finger of his hand, a glimmering crystal sitting atop each.

Rage wells up inside me at the sight of the soulfire.

I was wrong. The same crystal that countless mortals bled and died trying to collect, the king wears as jewelry. What a spineless prick, hiding behind his hollow display of power over the mortals, sentencing us to death for his own vanity.

I hate everything King Malvok stands for. I hate him with an unrelenting fury. And right underneath the hatred, there's something colder, a sense of disappointment. I wanted to believe what we sacrificed was for something bigger, and that our efforts made a difference, good or bad. But now that belief leaves nothing but a bitter taste in my mouth.

I let my anger burn through me unchecked.

"My child will be twenty-five soon," the king says, pausing to look around the room, eyes lingering on each of our tense faces. "They are almost of age to present power, and without a proper binding ritual, they cannot claim their right to immortality and obtain their full ability. I need them found," he declares with a sense of false concern. "They may not even know that they are my child, but I would do anything to have them back."

The king snaps his fingers, and servants file in, their heads bowed low. Each one carries a tray of envelopes.

"His lie almost sounds convincing," Ella whispers.

My lips curl subtly. "I bet he prays to Althara every night that his child is dead."

A servant hands me a sealed envelope, quickly retreating. My fingers graze the wax seal holding the paper closed.

"The bounty will be well worth it." The king points in the general area where Ella and I stand. "It should last the entirety of your short mortal lives, and if you wish to use it to live in Lunaria, I will gladly allow it. And for the eldarim." He shifts his attention to the right of us. "You will have enough to purchase the most decadent home in the capital."

"How will we know if they are the lost heir?" A mortal asks from the left of me.

The king rises, lips twitching. His eyes narrow, taking in the lanky boy who dared to speak out of turn. "Never speak unless spoken to," he hisses, voice low. "Disobedience has no home here, nor will it ever."

The boy swallows hard, shrinking under the king's intense scrutiny. I find myself searching for Lincoln among the faces. His golden eyes are impossible to miss, but right now, his attention is on the boy.

The king flicks his wrist, and the room transcends into darkness.

Before anyone can react, it brightens again. The boy lies lifeless on the ground—a pool of blood forming around him.

Ella snatches my arm, her fingers digging in as a pair of servants scurry over to drag the boy's body from the room.

"The envelopes contain all the information you need to find my child." The king continues nonchalantly, as if nothing had happened. "Go on...open them."

My hands fumble with the seal, pulling out a folded paper tucked inside.

"Now, the thirty of you—" King Malvok grins, darkly. "Excuse me, I mean the twenty-nine of you, will search for my heir using this." He unfolds the paper within the envelope. "My child is believed to be in these lands, an intruder amongst their kind. They will have a distinct birthmark." The king shifts his robes to the side, revealing a star with seven points on his chest. "All Beldara's are born with it."

I etch the image into my memory, my mind reeling from all the new information. I don't have time to keep up. Participants unfold their papers hastily, and I follow, the blood draining from my face when I do. I find a map of a strange world. I don't recognize any of it. Its borders are unfamiliar. Its landmarks are foreign and full of territories I never knew existed.

Voices swell around me, whispers stacking on whispers until they grow.

The king raises a hand, silencing the room. "This map is classified information, and by signing your name to participate in my quest, you agreed to keep it that way. Unfortunately, that means only the person who returns with my heir in hand can live." The king plasters a smug look on his face. "We can't have you running around with important intel, of course."

The room erupts in chaos, voices clashing in protest.

I seize Ella's hand amid the growing turmoil, my eyes darting around the room. I search desperately for an exit, looking for a way out before we are forced to face this harsh truth.

There are two possible ways to escape, both heavily guarded.

King Malvok remains silent before his throne, enjoying our distress. He opens his palms to face us, and I freeze. Shadows pour from his hands, racing toward us at a rapid speed.

"Bring my child to Noctharn's border before the month ends, and if you fail, just know I will find great pleasure in hunting you all one by one." The king's lips twist into an arrogant half-smile. "That is...if the terrain doesn't do it for me."

Ella's hand tightens around mine as shadows climb

upward, wrapping around our ankles. Higher and higher the darkness coils around us, circling our torsos, then our throats.

The king's eyes gleam, his hands moving in a rhythmic motion. The shadows answer only to him, and with the flick of his wrist, the ground below us is gone.

Air whistles past my ears as we free-fall into the abyss.

I pull Ella against my chest, a second before my back hits something solid, knocking the air from my lungs. I lay there, Ella draped across my body, struggling to draw in a breath.

I blink rapidly, trying to straighten my blurred vision through ragged gasps as the sun shines down on us, burning my skin. A cloudless blue sky welcomes me with open arms, and I get lost in its rich hues.

We must be in The Unseen—where our souls go after we pass to the other side.

Ella repositions herself against me, and her frantic amber eyes cut into my line of sight. She grabs me by the collar of my shirt, screaming. "Get up! Ari, get up!"

I crook my head to the side, rolling it against the ground, taking in my surroundings. A large circular clearing sits in the middle of a lush forest, filled with vibrant green grass that swooshes in the wind. My eyes land on the participants, all rising to their feet.

Ella yanks me off the ground. "Snap out of it!"

I stumble to my feet. "Where are we?" I ask, voice rough.

Ella raises her weapon, and a rush of adrenaline fires through me at the sight. I unsheathe my dagger at the same time Ella presses her back against mine. "Not in Noctharn, that's for sure," she says.

Other participants raise their weapons, and my attention snaps to a mass of sandy brown hair. Finley stalks toward a mortal woman, and I see the glint of his sword a second too late. Blood gurgles from her lips, and her body falls limp, steel protruding from her stomach.

He killed her. *Why did he kill her?*

"Run!" I command, ordering Ella to follow, not wanting to stay to find out.

I sprint to the edge of the clearing, heart pounding wildly at the sound of clanking metal. Ella flanks my side, matching my desperate pace. I stop and peer over my shoulder at the bloodbath behind us—countless bodies, too many to count, already lost to the king's quest.

I keep my dagger unsheathed and run as fast as I can.

CHAPTER 11

SILLY MORTAL
LINCOLN

The space between the mortal woman and Finley dies within seconds. She doesn't sense the danger yet. But I do. I already know what comes next. His blade finds its mark the exact moment I nock an arrow.

I stare down the narrow base of it, fletching brushing my cheek, taking in the scene unfolding before me.

Finley always strikes first, impulsive by nature, reckless as ever. The woman's body slides off the end of his sword, collapsing to the ground.

Participants sprint in every direction, but I stand steady, confident in my position. I let my arrow fly, concentrating on the faint whistling noise it makes as it cuts through the air. It hits its target with perfect accuracy, right in the back of an unlucky mortal.

I never claimed I wasn't like Finley; I just plan better.

I've waited for this day—trained for it my whole life because I know what's at stake. Finding the heir is the only way to restore my family's legacy, and getting rid of dead weight is necessary. I have no sympathy for the weak because, for me, failure is not an option. But for them, it's inevitable.

I nock another arrow, aiming it at Finley's back. Eldarim disperse around him, hovering close, showing where their loyalty lies. Unfortunately for them, I have no moral compass when it comes to killing immortals or mortals.

I pivot fast, pulled by an invisible force I can't ignore. I face the edge of the clearing; my arrow now pointed at the pit fighter from Lumin as she peers over her shoulder.

I grunt in annoyance at her presence. I knew the second she stepped into the throne room. A pulse of energy rattled through me the moment she did. I never truly believed she'd show up.

I saw her while hanging flyers after the fights. Her face was swollen and covered with tears. She clutched the flyer so tight that it almost crumpled in her grip. Determination radiated off her in waves.

I followed her all the way to The Broken Fang. I even snuck in later and watched her sleep. She was tense even then.

I didn't realize until I saw the yellow-spotted skin around her eye that her face was swollen and bruised by someone else's hands, and not just her tears.

I pull the arrow taut, a breath away from releasing it.

It's a pity I let her live, only to kill her now—a short life, cut even shorter.

She whips her head, and in that single moment, my grip falters. She flees, and I release the arrow, missing her entirely due to my hesitation.

I never *fucking* hesitate.

One last mortal slips out of the clearing behind her, their halo of disheveled blonde hair fading with distance, leaving only eldarim left.

"Did you know about this?" Finley growls, holding the map in the air.

I take my time securing my bow back to my quiver before I respond. "I knew as much as you did."

Finley strides toward me, flanked by valorguards. I adjust my glove in response, making him pause. He clenches his teeth. "That's hard to believe, seeing your father found the queen."

I yawn, too bored by his accusations to entertain him further. "I have no plans to kill you or your group, so let's keep it that way."

I turn away from them, taking my time leaving the clearing, stepping over bodies as I do. A faint swoosh fills my eardrums, and I sidestep. A dagger embeds itself into the ground at my side, a lion emblem carved into its handle.

I crouch down, yanking it from the soft dirt. "I needed an extra weapon." I strap Finley's dagger to my side and stand. "Thanks."

Finley snarls with anger behind me, fury tearing from his throat, but I don't bother facing him again.

Instead, I wave a gloved hand over my shoulder and transform.

CHAPTER 12

ALLIES

ARI

Our feet slam the ground, muscles numb, legs moving on pure instinct. The screams from the fallen participants faded with time, but we never slowed down.

I don't know where we're heading or what awaits us out here, but we have no other option. There is no room for doubt, only forward.

We continue to race through the foreign landscape. It flashes by in a blur of green and gold hues. The sun beats down on us, brutal and heavy. It is suffocating in a way. Every breath I drag into my lungs is thick with heat as if the very air has turned against us. The sun was never like this in Noctharn. You could feel the rays against your skin, but not their warmth. Sweat stings my eyes and drenches my clothing. Every inch of me is slick from it. If it were possible to drown from your own perspiration, I surely would in this moment.

After some time, we finally begin to slow down. My footsteps falter, no longer driven by sheer panic but exhaustion pulling on each of my limbs like lead. I double over, hands on my knees, sweat dripping down my brow. Ella does the same. My chest heaves with every breath, lungs raw from the overexertion.

Around us, the land stretches for miles. There's no noise, except for the rasp of wind through dry grass.

I stagger to the ground, collapsing, and for the first time since we left the clearing, I allow myself to feel relieved that we were able to get away.

Ella kneels beside me, her breath just as ragged as mine.

I scan her face from under my lashes, analyzing the girl I just met a few hours ago. *She's nervous.* I can see the tension in her shoulders, the way her fingers tap against her thigh, and how her eyes dart in every direction.

I adjust myself, shifting to face her fully. My hand closes around the hilt of my sword, and I draw it in one smooth motion as I stand. The tip rises until it rests just beneath Ella's chin.

She freezes, eyes wide and full of terror. Her hand drops to her waist, right where I know her dagger rests. I press my sword a little firmer, pricking her skin just enough to make a drop of blood fall.

I shake my head, staring down at her. "I wouldn't if I were you."

Her hand falls to her side instantly.

"Let's make one thing clear." I bite out. "Either we work together, or we don't. There's no in between. You can walk away right now, and I won't put this blade in your back unless it's necessary, or you can stay, but there's no playing both sides, because if you betray me, you are dead. Do you understand?"

Ella's throat bobs, lips quivering violently, the confidence she once wore in the throne room no longer present.

I lower my sword a hair to let her speak.

"I didn't ask to be part of this." Her voice trembles with each word. "But I'm in it now. And I promise I am not your enemy."

I keep my attention fully on her, searching for any half-truths or lies, but find nothing. "Tell me something," I say. "Are you actually mortal or not of binding age?"

Ella blinks, caught off guard by my question. "Why does it matter?"

I thrust my sword closer, the steel pressing into her throat again. "It matters because I need to know what I'm dealing with."

"Mortal," she whispers. "I promise I won't do anything to you. I was sent here by my parents in the hope that I could bring them into a better section."

I lower my weapon, letting it slide away from her skin. She's more like me than I expected, and for a moment the walls between us feel thinner—two strangers bound by the same fragile thread of longing for a better life.

I sigh. "Get up."

Ella rises cautiously, like she's ready to bolt the moment I give her reason. I have a feeling that allies out here will be rare, and I'll take what I can get at the moment.

I drop my bag to the ground. "I'm mortal, too," I declare. I undo the worn leather flap of my bag with a quick snap, pulling out what I've managed to hold onto; dried wild berries, a half-full canteen of water, and one spare set of clothing. "This is all I'm carrying." I drop the items into the dirt between us. "What do you have?"

Ella pauses for a heartbeat, then reaches for her own pack. She pulls it open and lays out its contents; another handful of dried food, but this time it's meat, a crudely wrapped bundle of herbs for healing, a small sharp dagger, and a few more sets of spare clothing than I carry. "Not much more than you," she admits. "Enough to survive but not to win the quest."

"You will never succeed with a mindset like that." I retrieve the map the king gave us and lay it on the ground. "It's not what we carry that will make us win. It's what we do with the little we have that will." I say '*us*' loosely, knowing full well only one of '*us*' will survive this.

Ella nods in agreement, crouching down beside me.

I press my finger on the strange markings, pointing to an area on the outskirts of our kingdom's borders.

"This looks like the clearing where the king dropped us. It's the only plot of land that would make sense." I point to another clearing on the map. "This one feels too far for the king to transport everyone."

Ella leans in to get a better look, her shoulder accidentally brushing mine. She warily studies the map without a word.

I've never seen anything like this before. All the kingdoms, flatlands, and mountains. Lands of creatures I've never heard of, and a body of water that surrounds the land. It stretches so far off the map that I wonder how far it goes.

I drag a finger over a blurred-out portion of the map. I wonder what lies there that the king wants to keep hidden. "Still so many secrets," I murmur. Secrets that I will get answers to, but after the bloodbath we just witnessed, the safest bet would be to continue toward a far kingdom, and one that is marked.

"This cliff area might be a good place to start." I point to a kingdom southwest of Noctharn labeled *The Riftlands*. "We'll collect berries as we go. Hunt when we can, fill up water at every river we pass."

"It's maybe a two-day walk if we head out now," Ella says, pointing to a different clearing on the map. "I'd say we are here." She trails her finger east. "Since we don't seem to be surrounded by many trees."

I take in my surroundings—the stretch of dry earth and dust. *She's right.* There's nothing around, minus some dead grass and no signs of life, except for one falcon perched in a decaying tree. It tracks us with its beady eyes, watching us like we are prey. And maybe we are, since there is not much out here. We need to find a better hiding spot. That's our first priority.

I run my tongue over my chapped lips. "Let's get moving then."

I open my canteen and take a small sip, passing it to Ella to do the same. I fold up the map and shove it back into my bag and pick up the rest of my belongings.

Ella mimics my movements, and I mentally note how her hands aren't shaking anymore.

We stand in unison heading in the direction of The Riftlands as allies, which is weird to me. I don't have allies, nor do I ever trust someone I just met. Every instinct in me screams against this. But Ella is young. And damn it, part of me feels like I need to protect her, even though deep down I know we both won't survive this quest.

I'll kill her if I have to.

I prefer to do things on my own, anyway.

But I hope it doesn't come down to that.

CHAPTER 13

IT BURNS
ARI

My shirt is soaked through.

It clings to my body as sweat drips down my sides, dampening the waistband of my cargos. I breathe in the dry, heavy air. It's thick with the scent of blooming flowers. Purples, reds, yellows, and some colors I don't even have names for spill out of the underbrush, climb trees, and push through cracks in the stone at our feet.

This isn't the world I've come to know. It's not even one I've ever encountered in books before. And yet, here it is, right across the same border I grew up next to.

Everything in Noctharn is dull in comparison to the land outside the kingdom, like a gray smear on the edge of a painting. We've passed countless creatures frolicking between trees—deer grazing without flinching, birds chirping from low branches. Even a fox trots across the trail ahead and doesn't bother to run. Nothing here is afraid. Nothing here *expects* to be hunted. They live separate lives, untouched by mortals and eldarim.

I unfold the king's map, squinting at the strange regions of land as we walk.

"I don't get it," I mumble. "We barely inhabit a quarter of the land. How could King Malvok keep all this hidden for so long?"

Ella keeps pace at my side. "The king seems to be capable of a lot more than we think."

"Yeah," I say under my breath. "And that's what scares me most."

"Me too," Ella admits. "I once heard that the king's heir is said to be able to..."

I jerk my head to the side, no longer listening to the words that leave Ella's mouth, focusing solely on the faint murmur of running water in the distance. It's the first sign of water we've had in days.

My steps quicken, and Ella follows. She's still talking, but I barely register the words she's saying.

I shove the map back into my pocket and force my way through knotted vines, swatting loose greenery from my vision.

"Have you heard of a power like that before?" Ella asks.

I take my next step and gasp, freezing in place. I'm standing on the edge of a cliff, and far below, a creek winds through a stretch of trees.

I peer over the ledge, gauging how high we really are and determining the best route to the water.

"Whoa," Ella yelps as she breaks through the vines. "Maybe you should back up a little bit."

I do as she says, only because I already figured out how to get down. "Follow me."

Ella and I descend the cliffside toward the creek. It's narrow but deep, running over white stones, and it doesn't take us long to get to it. I drop my bag with a grunt, legs shaking by the time we reach the water's edge.

"Did you hear me?" Ella asks, annoyed.

Shit. I don't know what's wrong with me. I rub my eyes with the heels of my hands. "Sorry, just tired."

That's an understatement, though. I'm more exhausted than I'd like to admit, and my eyes burn from lack of sleep.

We took turns keeping watch last night, Ella and I, but truthfully, I barely slept during my half. I could say it's because I don't trust her. But really, it's the way she speaks—how easy it is for her to open up to someone. That's the part that haunted me most, how vulnerable she is out here, mindlessly putting her faith in someone she just met.

Ella was poking at the fire with a twig, her eyes reflecting the flames' glow. "My town's nothing but goldsmiths. Every house. Every family. My mom runs the workshop, and my dad does detailing. My brothers do casting. I was supposed to follow in line."

"You didn't?" I asked.

She shook her head. "I burn everything I touch. Melt the mold, crack the metal. Once I set the chimney on fire." She laughed. "Twice, if we're being honest."

I quirked an eyebrow. "I didn't know that was possible."

"Oh, it is if you're the least skilled goldsmith in all of Solhaven. When the king asked for participants, my parents practically shoved me out the door with a packed bag and a smile."

"I get it."

"You do?"

I shrugged. "I've worked in the soulfire mines for as long as I can remember. The only difference between me and you is that I chose this because it was time for me to leave."

"What are you running away from?" she asked.

"Everything."

And that's all I gave her.

Ella places her things on a large boulder, a few paces away from me. "I said that this might be a good place to stop for the night," she huffs. "We'll be in The Riftlands by tomorrow."

"That's fine," I murmur, peeling my sticky shirt off my shoulder. I kick off my boots, roll my pants as high as they'll go, and step into the creek, needing it to wake me up.

I lean forward and splash the cool water onto my face. A shiver runs through me at the contact before it fades into a welcome numbness. I bend lower, and my barrette slips loose from my hair.

I catch it midair before it can hit the water, aware of Ella tracking the movement with her eyes.

I look over my shoulder, meeting her gaze.

"Where did you get that?" Ella asks.

I all but roll my eyes. She's so predictable, and she doesn't even know it.

I turn to face her. "I found it. One day, when I was playing by the Eidolon Forest back in Lumin. It was just there."

And it was. I was nervous to take it home, but Noah said it belonged to me now. And the way it glistened on the edge of the woods, calling to me as the sun sparkled off the scales of the snake, made me believe him.

"Someone must have lost it, but no one came back to claim it," I add.

"It's gold, no?"

I examine Ella, the gold bangles that clank at her wrist and droplets that hang from her ears. She doesn't come from a low-income family, by the looks of it, but that doesn't mean she acquired it all in a respectful way. I know I wouldn't have.

I hold my barrette up between two fingers so she can see it fully. "Yes. The bastard of a man that I lived with found it in my possession a few days later. He tried to take it from me to sell for gilds. He claimed it burned his hand when he touched it and that Althara must have cursed me, but it never burns me."

"Burns...burns as in..."

"Yes, burns," I cut her off. "Your skin will burn like a fresh piece of meat on an open fire if you touch it."

Ella's face twists in horror. "Why would you keep such a thing if it's cursed?"

I smirk at her and toss the barrette her way. Ella lets out a squeal and dashes off in the opposite direction.

"It won't burn you if you wrap it up in a cloth to hold it."

Ella grabs her bag and digs in it, pulling out a spare piece of clothing. She hesitantly walks toward the barrette that now sits nestled in the soft mud beside the creek.

"Go on," I say, coaxing her. "Pick it up."

Ella timidly wraps the cloth around her hands three times, covering her exposed skin. She stares at the barrette, eyes locked on it as if it might bite. "You better not be tricking me."

"Only one way to find out."

Ella's amber eyes meet mine, determination shining bright. She picks it up without a second thought.

"WAIT!" I yell.

Ella jumps, eyes widening. The barrette tumbles out of her hand and back into the mud.

"Kidding," I drawl.

"Not funny," she snaps.

Ella picks up the barrette once more, and I step further into the creek.

"The snake is so fierce but peaceful," she says in wonder. "I've heard of trapping magic in jewelry, but nothing of this nature."

I pause mid-movement. "You have?"

"Yes," Ella whispers. "It takes a powerful being to do it, but it can be done."

"Like a witch or a warlock?" I joke.

Ella's eyes flare. "Precisely."

"Which only exist in fairy tales," I mutter.

Ella continues to study my barrette, making me uneasy. I've never had someone examine it so closely.

I'm overly protective of it, sometimes to a fault.

I dunk my head under the water to ease my sudden panic, running my fingers through my hair to rinse away the sweat and dirt.

It's peaceful under here.

Quiet.

Allowing me time to think. If we could capture magic in items, mortals could have a better chance of survival. We could fight back; magic against power, mortals against immortals.

I stay below the surface for a few seconds longer before emerging once more.

Ella's back is now facing me, my barrette no longer in her hands—a wilted photo in its place.

So, she's not a thief, but a busybody, nonetheless.

I clear my throat. "Nosy much?"

Ella whips her head around, almost dropping the photo on the ground. "I'm sorry, I just..." Flustered, she places it back into my bag. "Is he your boyfriend?"

"No," I say, clipped. "Just a friend."

That photo of me and Noah is one of my favorites, taken on a long weekend in his backyard. Noah was showing me the timecatcher that his parents were going to start selling in their bookstore. It was new, something we've never seen before. The king created them, replicating the power of eldarim with photographic memory. We were close, lying down in the grass, our shoulders touching. I was watching Noah fiddle with the device, laughing at his failed attempts, when suddenly, a beam of light shot out of it, and the photo was taken. We laughed even harder when we saw the finished product. Noah was stuck in a moment of confusion, looking devastatingly handsome, but I was more shocked by myself. My face was caught mid-smile, eyes bright, staring at him. A moment in time that holds all the secrets of our friendship—all the missed chances, a day captured when maybe, just maybe, we could have been something more.

But we aren't and never will be.

"You're happy here," she hesitates. "In the photo."

"I was," I reply, my voice filled with a mix of bitterness and honesty.

I miss Noah. I do.

I miss his overbearing desire to protect me, but our friendship has never been anything more than that.

Ella doesn't say anything right away. Instead, she sits on a flat rock, tugging off her boots and rolling up her pants to her knees. "Then why did you give up on him?"

I bite the inside of my cheek. "I didn't. It would've never worked." I don't owe her an explanation. "Are you getting in, or just going to sit there?"

Ella snorts, clearly not believing my words, but thankfully doesn't question me further.

She rises and steps into the creek, gritting her teeth. "It's colder than I thought it would be."

I splash a bit of water her way. "Don't be a baby," I tease.

"I'm convinced you're evil," Ella yelps, stumbling back.

I grin, but the word sticks.

Evil. Ella meant it in jest, I know that. Still, it lands a little too close to things I don't talk about, a part of me I try to keep locked far away. I've done some unpleasant things in my life, but I made my choices, and I can't take them back now.

"Do you have someone waiting back home for you?" I ask, steering the conversation in a different direction.

"Yes," she sighs, longing in her voice. "I thought he would propose before I left, but maybe he is waiting until I return."

If she survives.

I know it sounds cruel, but Ella is young and naive—too pure for the harsh truths I carry. I can't bring myself to shatter the fragile world she lives in.

So instead, I ask, "How did you meet?"

"Oh, Ari, it was love at first sight! His name is Myke. His family are goldsmiths too. We were in class, and he saw how horrible I was at making the simplest ring shape," she giggles. "He leaned over to help me with my mold, and when his hand bumped mine, I swear I could feel electricity flow between us."

"Sounds like you read too many fairy tales," I mutter under my breath.

It's the type of love you hear about and never get to experience yourself.

"Every day with him is a blessing from Althara. I've learned so much from him." She flushes as she speaks. "He even taught me how to fight."

My eyebrows shoot up. "Really? I'll be the judge of that."

Ella shoves the cool water toward me, forming a small wave. "I swear," she scowls.

I shake my head, lying back to float, the weight of my body disappearing on the surface of the water. "And what exactly were you training for?"

"We always need to be prepared."

"Prepared for what?" I huff. "You burning down your whole town?"

"Not funny." She lies back to float next to me. "Anything could happen."

I can't fault her for that one, especially with how much we don't know in this world.

"Well, I guess Myke doesn't sound that bad. Still, I'm pretty sure I could take both of you in a fight, with my eyes closed and half asleep."

Ella snorts. "Then we should get in a few rounds before going into The Riftlands tomorrow. I love proving people wrong."

"A few rounds? Althara, spare me. You're serious...you actually know how to fight?"

Ella gives me a stern look, and I all but laugh at her attempt to appear intimidating.

"You know..." I wink at her. "I usually don't fight for free."

"And why is that?"

"Did I forget to mention I used to fight in the pits back in Lumin?" I ask, unable to hide the amusement in my voice. "Must have slipped my mind."

CHAPTER 14

COLD-HEARTED
LINCOLN

My father told me that to be an assassin, you need to lose pieces of yourself. What he didn't tell me is how willingly I would give those pieces of myself away. Growing up in a family of assassins meant my childhood wasn't measured by birthdays but by fights won, and blood spilled. From the moment I could walk, I had a weapon in my hand—mastering the art of deceit and swordplay. Family dinners consisted of strategy sessions and the rehearsal of escape routes. And being the oldest child made things even worse.

I have a legacy to uphold.

A family line to continue.

A curse to break.

Even if it means killing friends and foes to achieve it.

I stand over Nikolai Runebrook's body, my blade slick with his blood. He's the king's new assassin, belonging to the family line that ended the Ashfield's reign. And if it weren't for my father, it would have never had to end.

The Runebrooks and Ashfields have always been rivals,

and competition has simmered between the two of us since childhood. Our families always pitted us against each other.

But Nikolai and I are different.

Nikolai relies on the sense of surprise. He is skilled, but not the best. The gift of invisibility will only get you so far if you can't wield a weapon. Someone like him does not deserve the honor of finding the king's heir.

I do. This is my reason for living. To correct my father's failures.

I kick his dagger from his grasp, crouching down beside him—blood pooling around his body. His eyes flutter open, unfocused. But eventually, they find mine.

One by one, I tug my fingers free from my gloves.

Nikolai's chapped lips begin to move, his lungs fighting for air as his body flickers in and out of focus—his power failing him in his weakened state.

"Why?" he rasps.

I lift my hand, hovering it over his exposed skin, inches above his heart. "This is how it has to be," I tell him.

Nikolai's face pales, drained by fear, and I thrust my hand downward. His skin instantly cools beneath my touch, his eyes drifting past mine toward the sky as one final beat stutters from his heart.

I pry the steel ring from his hand, the king's assassin's sigil, and slip it into my pocket. I feel the weight of it pressing against my skin, a fond reminder of what was taken and what is rightfully mine.

The Runebrook family never deserved the honor of wearing my father's ring.

They never earned it.

Not like I have.

~

I kneel, the white stones shifting against my knees. Dark, dried blood coats my fingers, like tree sap clinging to my skin. I plunge my hands into the water to loosen it, grinding my palms together.

It takes longer than I expected.

My hands are raw by the time it is all gone.

I examine the purple veins that wrap around my pale gray fingers.

Always worse after a killing.

I fasten my gloves back onto my hands, concealing them away as a wave of self-loathing washes over me. Not because of what I am, but how good it feels afterward. I can't deny the rush of euphoria I get, and it makes me sick.

I lean back, letting the midday sun settle on my skin, and give myself a moment to breathe. My father trained me for a quest like this my entire life—a weapon to be used by his side. But he, like my family, is no longer here. Our line will die with me if I don't fix his mistake and mine.

And that's all the motivation I need. I push myself to my feet and nearly miss the faint grunt nearby, muffled just enough by my movement. My head whips in the direction it came from. I stalk toward it immediately, moving like death incarnate, when the noise comes again; this time closer and higher pitched.

I creep forward, each footstep muted by the soft moss-covered earth. I reach over my shoulder, nocking an arrow as the underbrush thickens, and the sounds become louder.

I crouch down behind a tangle of thorny vines and peer through the opening.

There in a small clearing by the creek, arms raised and knees slightly bent, a woman bounces up and down on the balls of her feet, waiting for the assailant in front of her to attack. She pivots, but not fast enough, as a fist connects with her stomach. She groans, hunching over in pain.

At last, I see her opponent clearly, and my palms grow slick.

The soulfire-colored-eyed woman from Lumin beams with excitement, staring down at the woman before her. Blood seeps from the corner of her mouth as she smiles—lips parted, and teeth stained a deep, glistening red.

I lower my bow, observing her as she glides into her next move, her body like liquid, flowing through each motion.

I ignore the tightening in the left side of my chest and the way my breath hitches at the sight.

"Last chance to tap out," she grunts to her opponent.

"Never," the other woman replies.

I can't bring myself to look away as they savagely fight like their lives depend on it.

I should step in. Killing both of them would mean two fewer participants in the quest.

But I don't.

I'm rooted to the ground like a fool under an enchantment. I don't know who these women are or why they'd think they'd survive this quest, but I can't seem to raise a weapon against either of them right now. Something in me refuses to, and that terrifies me more than any enemy ever has.

I scowl at their fragile mortal forms, loathing their existence with every ounce of my being.

CHAPTER 15

DAMN BIRD
ARI

Ella stands before me, arrogantly rolling up her sleeves. "Try not to get mad when I knock you on your ass."

I roll my eyes. "Confident...I'll give you that."

She shrugs, and I circle her, testing her weight on the uneven ground. She mimics me as I learn how she moves. Her feet are light, shoulders loose, stance balanced. Maybe she wasn't bluffing like I thought.

Ella lunges, and her fist connects with my jaw before I have time to register what happened.

I stagger back, blinking rapidly, the taste of iron filling my mouth. "What the hell was that for?"

Wild strands cling to Ella's grinning face, her eyes burning with triumph as she rises onto the balls of her feet.

"Can't keep up?" she teases, right before she lunges at me again.

Jab, jab, low kick.

I blocked all three. I counter with a left cross, but she twists under it, landing a hook to my ribs that knocks the wind sideways in my lungs.

"Shit," I hiss, stepping back.

Ella's smile doesn't falter; no apology in sight. "Come on, show me what you got. I thought you were a prized fighter back in Lumin."

I've sparred with many different fighters in the past, but something about the way Ella moves her body before each strike startles me. She advances like smoke in the air, impossible to catch and even more impossible to hold. One moment, she is in front of me, and the next, she is gone.

She has no tell.

So, she thinks.

But I see it a second before she strikes. She taps her left foot ever so slightly. If I blinked a second too long, I'd miss it altogether.

I wipe away the blood that trickles down my chin with the back of my hand. "I was going easy on you."

Ella quirks her brow, meeting my gaze. "Doubtful," she replies.

I launch forward and sweep low at her legs. She jumps over it, barely, but I was already onto my next move. I shoulder-check her, knocking her off balance. Her feet scrape in the dirt, but she doesn't fall. She throws an elbow into my chest instead.

I grunt and catch her arm, twisting hard. "Yield!" I yell, slamming my heel into the back of her calf.

Ella's legs buckle, and she stumbles forward. She spins, trying to catch me off guard, but I'm already in front of her. My fists snap in a blur, both connecting with her face like an unexpected storm. Her eyes widen in dismay, too slow to react. My next punch lands on her side, and the next, on her shoulder.

Ella falters a step, shaking her head, and just when she

thinks she's regained her balance, my fist connects with her stomach. Her body hunches over from the impact.

A bloody smile spreads across my lips, fully aware of the fact that my teeth were most likely crimson red.

"Last chance to tap out," I tell her.

Ella's eyes lock with mine from under her lashes. "Never," she growls as she stands straight.

Ella studies me as my fingers curl around the dagger at my waist. She can fight, yes. But I wonder if she's ready to face a blade.

"Let's make things a little more interesting, then." I flip the weapon between my hands. "No more going easy on you."

Ella grabs hers in one swift movement. "I doubt you were," she murmurs. "I told you Myke taught me how to fight."

"Hmmmm, we'll see about that."

We circle each other, my boots grinding softly against the earth. Ella is well-trained, but hesitant. I can see it in the way her dagger rests in her palm. Doubt clouds her features, making it seem as though wielding a blade is the last thing she truly wants to do.

My dagger feels warm in my hand, familiar and how it's supposed to be, while Ella's fingers quiver just a fraction.

Birds trade sharp calls from the treetops, their voices ringing over the clearing like eager spectators.

I make my advance, and the steel of my dagger clanks against hers. I jab my free hand forward, my fist meeting her side.

"Owww," she howls.

A shadow of pain crosses her expression, and I take advantage of the distraction, bringing my free hand to her jaw in the next breath.

Ella drops to her knees. Stepping behind her, I connect my boot to the middle of her spine, and she tumbles onto the ground.

I stare down at her, kicking her dagger out of range. In one fluid movement, I flip her onto her back. Her body slams the solid earth, and I straddle her hips before she has a chance to register her loss.

Fear fills her eyes as I place my dagger at her throat.

"I win."

"You got," she says, shifting her body underneath me, "lucky."

Breathless and grinning, I lean back on my heels. "Call it what you want, but you're the one with their ass in the dirt."

A faint red gash marks the base of Ella's throat. She instinctively rubs it as I grip her hand to pull her back onto her feet.

Ella composes herself, wiping sweat from her brow. "Rematch later?"

I smirk. "You want to lose again already?"

She snorts, picking up a twig and throwing it at me. "I want you to teach me how to wield a weapon better," she murmurs. "I don't want to be defenseless, especially out here." There's something raw and vulnerable in the way she says it.

I look at the creek, avoiding her gaze. The sun has just started to dip low behind the trees, casting an ominous glow on the cliffs' faces.

Ella reminds me so much of my fighting mentee. Jenny was always determined, always eager to learn, and who am I to stand in the way of someone who's simply trying to survive?

I nod, swallowing the sudden tightness in my throat. "Let's eat first."

The Riftlands await us tomorrow, full of mysteries, and I have to make sure Ella's ready for the worst.

I wash up, pulling on my spare set of clothing, my other set hanging to dry. We set up camp on a flat patch of land, a short walk from the creek, circled by towering trees. Ella gathers dry brush and wood while I make my way back to the water to catch us dinner.

Soft moonlight weaves through the trees, casting a pale light on the creek, the sunset's soft hues now gone. Dark shapes move in the water, creating small ripples on the creek's surface, flashing silver like scattered coins. Fish swim tauntingly under the surface.

I lean in, blocking out the evening sounds—the steady chirp of crickets and the soft snap of flames from Ella kindling a fire nearby.

Lighting a fire now might not be the best call, with participants trying to kill us, but we are extremely low on food, and starving to death is not on my agenda.

I crouch low, arm extended, ready to strike.

"Any luck?" Ella's voice drifts over with curiosity.

I anchor myself. "Shhhhhh," I hiss.

I thrust my hand forward, breaking the surface and forcing chaotic ripples to spread across the peaceful water. I clutch a dark shadow, my fingertips sliding against slippery scales. Tightening my hold on it, I rip my hand free. A silver fish thrashes in my grip, its gills expanding rapidly.

I rise with it and walk toward Ella, pulling out my dagger. The fish tries to wiggle free from my grasp, but I stab it between the eyes and cut downward before it has the chance to. Red blood gushes from its body, spilling onto my hands.

Ella grimaces as I pass it to her. She grabs it by the opposite end that I am holding and heads back to the fire.

I stare at my stained hands, smearing the blood between my fingertips. It always disturbed me how easy it was to kill something. I've killed animals to make ends meet, but that's the furthest extent that my killing has gone *so far*.

I clean my hands in the creek while Ella cooks.

We eat in silence, and the hollow feeling that fills my stomach dulls to a manageable ache.

When we finish, Ella and I train until our limbs grow heavy with exhaustion.

"I'll take first watch," I say, positioning myself against the base of a tree.

Ella folds inward, slipping into a peaceful sleep within minutes. I lean back, focusing on the darkness stretching out before me, a strange protective feeling washing over me.

We're both chasing something bigger than ourselves, for a better life, for our kingdom, and maybe even for glory.

I understand her more the longer we are together.

We both want the same thing.

And maybe, she's starting to grow on me.

Just a little bit.

My eyes fling open.

I didn't mean to fall asleep.

I scramble to find my sword, rising on uneven footing. The fire is now just small embers, on the verge of sputtering out.

My head tilted back against the tree, and that was the last thing I remembered. I meant to only count the stars in the sky, something I so rarely do. I didn't realize the notion would pull me into a slumber.

I blink the tiredness from my eyes, adjusting to the dark.

Squawk.

I jump, searching for the source of the sudden noise, heart hammering in my chest.

A minuscule black silhouette illuminates against the star-filled sky. I squint at the creature, high up in the canopy of leaves—beady black orbs meeting mine.

I lower my sword and take a deep breath.

"Damn bird," I mutter around a yawn. "Almost gave me a heart attack." I couldn't have dozed off for too long with how tired I still feel.

I slide back down the base of the tree until I feel the ground beneath me, rubbing my eyes with the heels of my hands.

Squawk. Squawk. Squawk.

"Ughhhh!" I groan.

I glance at Ella, still fast asleep, unharmed and safe. I relax back into the tree, my sword resting at my side.

Snap. A branch breaks, echoing loudly, and I jerk my head in the direction of the sound.

Only silence follows.

I didn't realize how heavy and unnatural the stillness truly was until now. It's the kind that makes the hair on the back of your neck stand. I look around the campsite, a chill creeping down my spine. No crickets. No wind. Even the bird has gone mute above me.

I get to my feet once more, each beat of my heart louder than the last. I see nothing but darkness, yet my skin still tingles with unease.

But sight means nothing right now. *I feel it.* The instinct built into everyone that whispers to you when you are not alone.

A branch snaps again, and this time it feels purposeful.

My eyes follow the noise, landing on an opening between the trees—a narrow gap in the dense woods.

Something is out there. Something is watching us.

I raise my sword high, muscles tense, attention unwavering from the tree line.

That's when they appear. A set of massive glowing spheres.

They glint in the moonlight, confirming the sensation that tormented me in anticipation.

I stumble back, crashing against the base of a tree. The spheres blink, and I realize they are eyes bigger than I've ever seen before.

"Ella!" I cry out, but she doesn't stir. "Ella. Wake. Up!" I command her, borderline hysterical.

Ella lurches to her feet to my left, spinning her head in every direction until she spots me. She raises her dagger the second she sees my sword, coming to stand beside me.

"What's wrong?" she asks.

I don't break eye contact with the being before me. The creature appears large and unnatural looking, with yellow eyes and black slits like a cats.

I'm at a loss for words, and all I can do is point.

Ella's head snaps in the direction of my hand, breath hitching.

"What..." she stutters, "is that?"

Branches begin to shudder and fracture, bark splintering and flying in every direction. I duck, dodging a stray piece as a gigantic hand wraps around the trees' trunks. The tree groans under the pressure, and slowly the creature lifts itself to its full height.

It steps out from the tangled edge of trees, drawing the darkness with it. Moonlight spills over its form, and my breath catches in my throat.

I tighten my grip around my sword's hilt, feeling small and fragile compared to the towering creature before me.

It's a giant straight out of a fairy tale, with weathering gray skin and yellow eyes. I read a fable about them once. Noah always let me read the books in his parents' store without having to purchase them. It was only a story, though; one your parents would tell you before bed to scare you from traveling too far into the woods. But I can't shake the feeling that fairy tales are seeming more and more real lately.

The giant inhales deeply through its nose, letting out a hot, rancid breath—rotten brown teeth on full display. A mixture of cloth and leather straps crisscrosses its body, sewn together like a bandage across its skin.

Ella trembles beside me, her breath coming in quick, uneven bursts. I keep my sword stable, fingers wrapped tight around the hilt, ready for whatever comes next.

"Oh, Gus is going to love this," the giant rumbles, extending his colossal hand toward us.

"Don't. Fucking. Touch. Us." I order him, trying but failing to add power to each word.

The giant's hand stops briefly, and he crooks his head to the side. He lets out a deep, throaty laugh, giving me a once-over. "You aren't strong enough to stop me, young one."

Before I have time to react, the giant sweeps us up, grabbing Ella and me in one swift motion. His other hand grips our belongings.

I stab the giant with my sword, leaving a deep gash, but not enough to harm him. He huffs out at my weak attempt like he heard a funny joke.

He squeezes his hand, and my lungs constrict. Black dots fill my vision, swirling at the edges until everything blurs.

The last thing I see is Ella's limp body as I fall into an abyss of nothing.

CHAPTER 16

NO TOUCHING
ARI

"I haven't seen their kind in decades," voices whisper, growing louder with each passing second.

I stay perfectly still, fighting to keep my breath even. I match each intake to that of a deep sleep.

Ella and I were taken, snatched away by a giant in the middle of the night. I try to piece together the memories, but they're fragmented, slipping away like water through my fingers.

I discreetly peek through my eyelashes, using them as a shield. I survey the room through a thin slit, just enough to see without giving myself away.

Burly figures fill the chamber, sitting around tables as if we were at The Broken Fang, chatting idly—waiting.

All of them are male, I take note.

The room stretches endlessly; a space clearly not made for mortals. Its walls ascend impossibly high, their beginnings and endings swallowed by murkiness. A breeze stirs my hair against my face, but I don't brush it away.

My attention lands on the massive openings carved into the stone far above. I drift my eyes downward, following the flicker of torches set along the walls. Their eerie light casts long, twisting shadows around the giants.

Anxiety surges through me, tightening my chest until my heart threatens to burst.

Where are we? And where is Ella?

I search the room, my gaze sweeping in every direction. I spot Ella sprawled across the same wooden planks I lie upon, not far away. The floor beneath me is splintered and pokes at my skin. She lies on her side, motionless, besides the gradual rising and falling of her chest.

She's alive, but why is she in her undergarments?

A shiver runs through me.

And why am I in mine?

I desperately scour the room to find any trace of our belongings. Giants sit in circles around us, crowded around a massive table at the center. My gaze moves from one to the next. Gray skin folds and wrinkles like aged leather over each of their bald heads, time clinging to every face. Yet none commands attention like the giant seated in the middle.

On a throne shaped like a colossal boulder, a giant with a stone crown sits in silence, staring directly at me. His crown sits atop a thick mane of fiery hair that tumbles to his shoulders, with a frame slightly larger than the rest, clad in armor that appears to be carved from living rock.

"Quiet!" his thunderous voice rolls across the cliffside, shaking the very air. He raises a hand high over his head, and the room falls into a heavy, expectant silence. He leans forward as he speaks. "Our guests have awakened."

My eyes flick open, taking in the room in full. Ella bolts upright close by, rubbing her face groggily, a flash of confusion crossing her features.

I push myself up awkwardly, crossing my arms across my chest, trying to shield what little dignity I have left.

The tables arc in a wide, intentional shape, each giant facing in, their eyes never wavering. It's a formation meant for a performance. Vulnerability clings to me at the realization. We are exposed and outnumbered, nothing more than prey surrounded by predators.

"I am Gus, King of The Riftlands," the giant, adorned with the stone crown, declares.

I shift my weight to the other foot, unsure what to do next. Ella stumbles to my side, fear clouding her amber eyes.

"BOW!" Gus bellows.

I lean forward, using my hand to cover my chest. I search the ground, looking for anything we could use to protect ourselves. I spot our belongings, piled at the foot of the stage, not too far away.

I wrap an arm around Ella's trembling body, pulling her close in a protective embrace. She shivers against my side as we stand together in unison. I squeeze her gently, a wordless promise that she's not alone, before letting her go. She remains rattled to the core, but there's a flicker of trust in her eyes.

I roll my shoulders back, shaking off the lingering fear, refusing to let it claim me. It's on me to find a way out of this, no matter how impossible it feels. We can't afford to let fear grip us both right now. If I falter, Ella will fall apart. I need to stand firm, for both our sakes.

The king's eyes roam down the length of me, licking his lips as he does. His suggestive gaze churns bile in my throat.

Squawk.

A sharp screech echoes off the walls, shattering the silence. *Not that dreadful sound again.* Nothing good ever happens when I hear that sound.

I plaster a smile on my face. "It's an honor to meet you and be in your presence."

Gus taps his pointer finger on his table, producing a loud thunking sound. "The honor is all mine," he drones, flashing me a mischievous grin. "We used to love your kind before your vile king cut us off."

"You did?" I ask, surprised. "Was it because of our undeniable charm?" I nudge Ella in the ribs, cringing inwardly at my own words. "It must be! We are pretty charming, if I do say so myself." Ella winces but manages a smile, clearly masking discomfort.

The king's laughter rolls through the room, and the crowd quickly joins in, their voices rising into a chorus of mirth. Gus places his hands in his lap, eyes gleaming. "You have a smart mouth," he says, each word dripping with ill intent. "There once was a time when you were our favorite source of entertainment."

I gape at him, completely lost, until it suddenly clicks and the pieces fall into place. No wonder we're here on this stage, half-naked and exposed before a crowd of men. Mortals must have been stolen by giants long before King Malvok's reign, forced to perform for their twisted pleasure.

I bite the inside of my cheek, tasting iron. "Why would our king cut you off?"

Gus wags his finger back and forth. "The better question is how did we get so lucky to have not one but two of you wander outside of the wards?"

Wards. The word screams inside my head, an alarm I can't silence. That can't be right. How could Noctharn be sealed off with magic so strong and yet remain hidden from us all?

I freeze, memories crashing over me like a tidal wave. Noah and I spent most of our childhood playing near the edge of the kingdom, close to the Eidolon Forest. It was a place that everyone feared, and no one dared to go. They said if you stepped inside, you'd never come back.

I remember sometimes catching sight of a figure in the shadows, as if someone or something were playing alongside us. But they were always distant, always just out of reach. Now, the image haunts me because the more I think about it, the more I believe it looked like me. A shadowed twin in the forest's depths. A reflection. My reflection...could it have been because of the wards?

I try to get Ella's attention, but she isn't looking my way.

"What do you mean by entertainment?" Ella blurts out.

"Dance! Dance! Dance!" the giants holler in response.

Gus lifts his hand, commanding the room into silence once more. The chants fade away, quickly replaced by the weight of expectation pressing down on us.

The king wags his eyebrows up and down. "What do you say?"

Ella's eyes find mine, searching for a plan, anything we can hold onto.

"Follow my lead," I whisper.

I'm not entirely sure what they expect from us or what the giants are looking for, but I take the risk. I lower my lashes, giving the king that doe-like expression I've learned works on most men. I clasp my hands behind my back and push my breasts forward, licking my bottom lip suggestively. "A question for a dance seems fair enough to me."

The king's eyes darken with a slow, dangerous heat, lips curling into a suggestive smile. "Fair enough," he rumbles.

A tight, uneasy knot twists in my stomach, spreading like ice, warning me that whatever game he's playing is far from over. My mind keeps wandering to how many mortals the giants have captured and how many never made it out alive.

I take a deep breath: weapons first, safety second, clothing third.

With a playful sway of my hips, I move closer to our belongings, each step purposeful. "My, my Gus." I all but moan his name. "You really are handsome."

The giants around him cheer.

Gus shifts in his seat, tracking my every movement—his possessive, hungry gaze searing my body.

I cringe, hiding it subtly with a sway. I feel sick to my stomach, but I don't see another way out of this.

I trail my hands up my body, cupping my breasts. "Why doesn't the king let us entertain you anymore?"

A guttural purr vibrates from Gus's throat, full of lust, and a wave of revulsion twists in my gut at the sound.

I inch closer to the edge of the stage, never breaking eye contact with the king. I feel the weight of every giant's attention in the room pinned on me. My sword is just within reach, close enough to taste, but lunging for it now would lead to our death.

Movement flickers at the edge of my vision. A giant seated in the front row reaches forward, his colossal hand brushing Ella's cheek. She flinches, stumbling backward.

I wag my finger playfully in his direction. "No touching," I order him with a wink.

The giant's hand drops to his side instantly. The king's attention shifts toward him for a second, so fast that I almost didn't catch it before it returns to me.

Ella steadies herself and mouths a 'thank you,' beginning again.

Clearly satisfied with our show, Gus begins to speak. "Your king," he snarls, "wants our land for himself. The wards that hold you in also keep us out. The more soulfire he collects, the further the borders stretch."

My body turns to stone, every muscle rigid, as the loose pieces click into place like a puzzle. The wards expand with soulfire, yet I can't grasp how.

Why did we never question the borders? We accepted them without thought, like children obeying bedtime stories meant to scare us into silence. The edge of the kingdom was the edge of the world, and we never challenged that truth. Stories of shadows in the woods and monsters just out of sight, were enough to keep us in line. Enough to keep us afraid. Now, I wonder if that was the point all along. But what happens to the beings on the land after they expand? Does King Malvok kill them, or does the ward do it for him?

"Keep dancing," the king demands.

I compose myself, advancing leisurely, just one more careful step. Our weapons are so close now. Ella moves with me, her movements matching mine.

If I can get to my sword, we might stand a chance. They're massive. Slow, I tell myself. All that bulk makes them clumsy. We'll slip through before they have time to react and grab us. *I hope.*

I continue to move my body seductively, acting like I plan to end up on my knees right in front of our belongings, and I almost succeeded.

But the king's hand wraps around my waist, and I am airborne in the next breath. I dangle a few feet above his table, trapped in his grip.

"Don't stop!" he barks at Ella. The giants around me roar louder, the only indication that she had listened.

"You are a sneaky little thing, aren't you?" Gus whispers, his breath brushing my face.

I grit my teeth. "Put me down."

He hesitates, and I swear his yellow eyes twinkle.

"We did keep mortals for more than just entertainment,"

he growls, tightening his hold. "We also feasted on them, and right now, I'm starving."

I click my tongue. "Didn't anyone teach you that it's impolite to play with your food?"

Hatred blazes across his features as his lips part. I'm trapped with no escape. My arms are pinned, frozen in place, while my lungs tighten from the pressure. Behind me, Ella cries out, but the ringing in my ears swallows her words whole.

Brown teeth fill my vision, looming unbearably close. I never imagined my death to be like this, nor did I ever think that giants were actually real, let alone that I'd be eaten by one. I begin to count every stain and crack on his jagged teeth.

One.

Two.

Three.

Four.

He really needs to take better care of himself.

Five.

Six.

Seven.

An arrow pierces the center of Gus's glowing pupil, blood spilling down his cheek.

The king howls in rage, and suddenly I'm free-falling through the air. I crash onto the cold stone table, pain radiating up my spine. Giants on both sides of the room roar in confusion as arrow after arrow streaks through the air, turning the chamber into chaos.

I roll onto my side, spotting Ella running for our belongings. Our eyes meet, her features full of terror, and a rush of adrenaline floods my system. I spring to my feet and sprint across Gus's table, my long legs carrying me in powerful strides. Monstrous hands reach out, trying to seize me as I jump through the air, launching myself toward Ella. I twist at the last second and land hard on my side next to her. I leap up and snatch my sword from the ground, slashing at the giants behind us.

"Follow me!" I yell as Ella passes me my bag. I vault off the edge of the wooden-planked stage, my bare feet pounding the stone floor. My knees shake from the impact, but I press on, slicing at the giant's calves as I pass. Ella follows close behind. The giants react too slow, like I suspected, unable to keep pace with the attack from above and below. Their deep, ferocious yowls reverberate as they search for us, while we dart and weave beneath the tables.

"Kill them!" Gus shouts.

We reach the wide opening at the far end of the chamber, arrows still flying through the air above us.

Ella bolts outside, and I follow. We race along the narrow ledge, our feet hammering against the stone as we cling to the cliffside. The path tightens dangerously, and I let her go first.

My gaze snaps upward to the carved openings high above, frantically searching for any sign of the assailant who turned the tide in our favor. Even though deep down, part of me feels like I already know the answer.

A movement in the shadows catches my attention, like a ripple in the void. I see it then, the string of a bow pulled taut by a pair of gloved hands. My breath hitches at the sight, a strange heat rising inside me.

I pivot sharply and flee, eyes fixed straight ahead, too terrified to look back.

CHAPTER 17

NEVER AGAIN
LINCOLN

A warning can go unheard when it comes to a stubborn woman.

I told myself I would not save her.

That a warning was good enough.

But here I am, breaking my promise, and saving her, *again*.

The King of The Riftlands' roar booms beneath me, a thunderous challenge that shakes the very air. I have no desire to raze his kingdom to the ground. This isn't my fight. What I do intend, however, is to buy the two women enough time to escape, to slip away from this nightmare while they still can.

I hadn't planned to step in; staying hidden in the shadows is something I am used to. But everything shifted the moment I caught sight of the soulfire-colored-eyed woman dangling dangerously close to death. The image twisted something profound inside me, a fierce knot of anger and protectiveness that wouldn't let me turn away. The shadows I'd clung to shattered in that moment, replaced by a resolve I couldn't ignore.

Now, arrow after arrow fires from my bow, each one aimed to keep the giants distracted. The chaos below rages on, but I focus only on buying them precious seconds.

I release my last arrow and ease myself down the cliff-side, moving with practiced care to hug the rock face.

I survey the sprawling landscape ahead, spotting the women racing toward a faint, distant light. Behind them, a silhouette moves like a phantom stalking through the night.

I shake my head, the cold truth settling in.

I can't protect them anymore.

Not her, not anyone on this damned quest.

This ends tonight.

It has to.

CHAPTER 18

PARADISE

ARI

Running for our lives seems to be a common occurrence lately.

The cliffs fade behind us, swallowed by distance, but our feet never stop. Time is a foreign concept; minutes feel like hours, or vice versa. I can't tell anymore. Blisters bloom on my feet, each step bringing with it a fresh stab of pain. I was moving too fast to lace my boots properly as I made my way down the cliffside. I was scared to look back again, too afraid of what might be following us, so I shoved my feet into them without a second thought. Now, they flop at my ankles, threatening to fall off. It's a small miracle I even managed to slip them on, considering our bodies are still fully exposed.

Side by side, Ella and I run in sync, trembling with fatigue. I *need* to know if someone is following us. But fear roots me forward, a silent command I can't ignore. I've cheated death again and again, each time because of the same person.

The first time was when I raised my blade to Lincoln's throat outside of The Broken Fang; he should have killed me then. He probably would have if Noah hadn't walked out. The second time was when we were dropped in the clearing, when the bloodshed started, and I saw Lincoln's arrow trained on me. And the third was when I dangled above the King of The Riftlands' mouth, inches away from becoming his next meal. Yet here I am, running for my life, all because Lincoln decided to save me, *again*.

He must be taunting me, using me as a pawn in whatever twisted game he's playing. Perhaps he gets a thrill from it, but he'll surely grow tired of it soon enough. And when the time comes, I need to ensure I'm one step ahead of him, because whatever his reason for playing this game with me is, mercy isn't one of them.

Kindness doesn't show up in the form of an assassin, especially not one with a legacy to restore.

Breathless, we press on, my lungs aflame as we chase a faint golden glow flickering ahead, while branches snatch and scrape at our arms.

A spark of hope ignites in my chest as we draw closer, and a village emerges, cradled gently between two low hills. We slow down to a stop, and the adrenaline that kept my legs moving disappears entirely, leaving me shaking and soaked in sweat. I hunch over, catching my breath, my eyes sweeping over the landscape. Every lurking shadow feels like a threat, but nothing flickers within the tree line.

My shoulders begin to relax as the weight of my bag slides away. Everything feels safe for now, but my weapon doesn't stray far from my grasp. The word 'safe' is one I've never trusted.

We dress in silence, shoving our tired limbs back into our clothing.

After situating ourselves, I pull the map from my bag and lay it flat on the ground.

"I don't see this village on the map." I trail my finger close to The Riftlands. "But it's still dark. We couldn't have gone too far." I take note of where the moon hangs in the sky. "I'd say it's 1 or 2 a.m."

I give Ella a sideways glance, just catching the confirming dip of her head. "What do you think we should do?" she asks, her gaze fixed on the village in the distance.

I look at her truly and fully. She is thoroughly shaken, and I don't blame her. I am still trying to wrap my mind around the world that is beyond the border of Noctharn. My eyes roam over her, noting the scratch on her cheek from an unforgiving branch, the sag of her shoulders, and mud on her boots. I didn't notice at first, but slowly, I've become protective of Ella. She's kind in a way that feels rare in this harsh world, sweet in her intentions but sharp-tongued when the situation demands. She was thrown into this, all in the hope of a better life. She might know how to fight and has learned over time how to hold her own, but that doesn't mean she's built for the kind of challenge she faces now. I don't know why I feel this way. She's not helpless; far from it. She can hold a blade and stand her ground when it matters. But still, there's this pull in me. A stubborn urge to protect her. Maybe it's the way she talks about her family, or the way her eyes soften when she's talking about Myke. Perhaps it's just that she still believes in something good in this world, or whatever it is that keeps her walking forward through all this. She has people waiting for her. People who love her. And Althara, spare me, I will make sure she returns to them.

My eyes drift toward the soft orange lights flickering in the distance, their glow pulsing through the dark. A thread of music rides the breeze, subtle yet inviting, as if the night itself is humming some forgotten tune.

My attention returns to Ella.

There's a quiet determination in the way she holds herself, even now, after everything.

I fold up the map and tuck it into my pocket. "Nothing can be worse than where we just came from." I grab her hand and whisper, "Let's go."

~

We step into the village following the dirt path past decadent cottages. I inhale deeply, the smell of fresh flowers and something else I can't seem to put my finger on floods my senses.

We follow the flickering glow of lamp posts into the village. Each post is carefully crafted, twisting with simple designs. At their tops, glass lanterns cradle flames fed by thick, ebony oil, most likely rendered from some animal fat. They burn steadily behind soot-streaked panes, casting the streets into a pale light.

We enter the bustling central square, with taverns lining both sides of the street, each building well-maintained with wooden signs hanging out front. Light spills out of open doorways, bringing laughter and music with it. The sound of clinking mugs and lively conversation fills the air as people gather inside and out.

I freeze mid-step, clutching Ella's arm. In the glow of a tavern, a man who closely resembles the same features of a lion dances out of an open door and into the street. His shaggy yellow mane is what draws my attention, and I gasp. *A half-breed.*

"Is that a fox?" Ella asks in a hushed tone.

"No, a lion—" I begin to say, but stop myself, noticing Ella's gaze in the opposite direction.

She's staring at a woman on the other side of the street

with soft orange fur. It follows the curve of her jaw, brushing down her neck and melting effortlessly into her skin. Delicate, pointed ears stand tall atop her head, peeking through a tangle of hair. Her slender fingers end in sharp, claw-like tips. She talks casually with a man whose furry legs shift into hooves just above the ankles.

"Is he a goat?" I ask in shock.

And as if he heard us, the man turns and smiles.

From the waist up, he's unmistakably mortal, with broad shoulders and a muscular chest that speaks of strength. His thick beard frames a strong jawline, and small horns curve from the crown of his head, giving him a distinctive and rugged appearance. But it's his lower half that holds my attention most. Thick brown fur coats his legs, the muscles flexing beneath as they bend slightly at the knee. His hooves strike the ground with a rhythmic clank as he moves toward us, the sound oddly graceful. My eyes roam down the length of him and back up to the thick dark curls that spill around his forehead.

"Yeah, definitely a goat," I murmur, strangely drawn to him. He's beautiful in a way I can't explain.

His cool sapphire eyes flash with a playful glint.

"Ladies." He stops in front of us and bows. "I'm Elliot," he pauses for a second, the edges of his mouth lifting in a hint of coltish delight. "Looking for some fun?"

I glance at Ella, our eyes locking for a moment. Fun? Did he seriously just say *fun*? After everything we've been through, he's asking if we want to have some fun? I can't hold it in.

Ella bursts out laughing first, and soon I'm doubled over in a fit of uncontrollable laughter, the kind that takes over your whole body.

We must be hallucinating. There's no other explanation.

"Fun?" I gasp out. "After almost being killed by giants, that sounds like a nice change of pace."

Elliot laughs with us, shaking his head. "Then you came to the right place."

"*Are* you a goat?" Ella asks.

I jab an elbow into her ribs, and she lets out a playful, "Owwww," rubbing her side. I've learned that Ella is always this blunt, like her mind has no filter when it comes to the questions she wants to ask.

Elliot gives himself a once-over, then returns his gaze to Ella.

"Are you a mortal?" Elliot throws back at her.

Feisty. I like him already.

I flash Elliot a coy smile. "Don't mind, Ella, she's too curious for her own good." I loop my arm through hers. "I'm Ari, by the way."

"Well, Ari and Ella, technically, I am a goat. And we," he says, waving his hand around him, "are velka. Similar to the most powerful eldarim, we are assigned an animal. But not at the binding ritual, Althara blesses us at birth. So yes, I am a goat, but I am also mortal like you."

My thoughts spin out of control. We share the same God. Do the giants share the same God, as well? What did Althara bless them with? I should have asked. I should have tried to obtain information from them.

I furrow my brows. "You are not a half-breed?"

Elliot tilts his head to the side, compassion shining in his sapphire eyes. "Many half-breeds came here seeking refuge from Noctharn, and we welcomed them with open arms. But we are not the same."

"I've never heard of velka before," Ella murmurs, her voice tinged with genuine curiosity. "Or half-breeds," she adds, shooting me an irritated glance.

There's so much left unsaid between us. Did Ella not question why Erica had a tail while she guided the participants to the throne room? I don't mean to hide anything from her. We're on this quest together, after all, but there are some things I still haven't fully come to terms with myself.

I give her an apologetic look and silently mouth *'later.'*

"Most haven't," Elliot says, smiling warily. "Your king's made damn sure of that."

"Oh, I'm well aware," I mutter, thinking about the map in my bag filled with a plethora of unknown kingdoms and everything else the king has kept hidden. "Half-breeds show up often then?"

"Not anymore," Elliot replies. "Not since the wards became more powerful over the decades. They vaporize anyone who crosses them instantly."

All the blood drains from my face at once. Is that how King Malvok acquires new land? By obliterating it and everyone who lives on it?

"That is awful," Ella rasps.

"It is." Elliot straightens his posture. "That's why we velka try to enjoy our little sanctuary while we can."

I look around, taking in the bright faces that surround us. It's almost unbearable. So much life...and knowing what King Malvok does when he expands his wards makes me sick. He destroys everything and leaves nothing behind. How many great kingdoms have fallen because of him?

My stomach twists.

I have to stop him.

"But enough of that!" Elliot claps cheerfully. "We're acquainted now, you know me, and I know you. It seems like the perfect time to have a little bit of fun, don't you think?"

I can't help but smile. There's an effortless charm to the

man that's hard to ignore. Ella does the same, clearly okay with dropping the conversation for now.

Without another word, we fall in step and follow Elliot's lead.

Something tells me I can trust him. Maybe it's the easy confidence he carries, a calm presence that somehow softens the weight of everything we've been through. This quest might very well kill us, and the idea of fun actually sounds like a welcome change.

"Where are you taking us?" I ask as Elliot leads us up a set of wooden steps.

He pushes open a set of doors and peers at us over his shoulder. "To let loose," he says with a wink.

We trail behind him into what I thought was a tavern. But it's not just any tavern...

There's music and dancing, and no fighting pit like The Broken Fang.

Melodies ring out from every corner, making the floorboards hum beneath my feet. Under the dim lights, a dance floor stretches wide, bodies swaying in time with the relentless beat.

Elliot directs us toward a table in the corner before gliding over to the bartender, whose cat-like whispers curl into a flirtatious grin. Ella and I slide into the booth, tucking our bags under the seats and concealing our weapons with them.

"Three ales!" I hear Elliot yell over the pulsing music.

He strides over a few minutes later, placing a drink in front of us with a casual flick of his wrist.

"So, what is this place?" I shout. "I didn't see it on the map."

"Paradise," Elliot states, clanking his glass against mine

and Ella's. He brings it to his mouth, tipping the ale down his throat.

I observe him, watching him gulp it down. I pause for a brief moment but decide to give in anyway. I guess I can spare one drink. After that, we'll get back on with the quest.

I follow his lead, letting the liquid touch my tongue. I'm hesitant at first, but it tastes normal enough. I take a full sip, allowing the golden ale to flood my mouth. A wave of euphoria spreads across my taste buds, igniting my throat as the enchanting beverage settles in my stomach.

Almost immediately, I feel myself giving in to the pull of the music, everything else fading—the quest, the heir, the king, even our inevitable doom.

I chug my drink, and Ella does the same, relishing in the feeling of it, while Elliot grabs us more.

CHAPTER 19

PROTECTOR
LINCOLN

I keep my distance just far enough that I go unnoticed, but close enough to follow every movement.

I step when they step, pause when they pause, breathe when they breathe.

My boots never make a sound.

I move in silence from the years of training drilled into me—each step against the ground masked by each of theirs. Mist curls low around our legs, carrying the mossy smell of damp earth with it. I stick to the shadows of the thick underbrush, using them to my advantage as I stalk my prey.

The cloaked figure pauses momentarily, glancing behind them. I slide behind a thick oak tree, blending myself into the darkness, my shoulder brushing against a tangle of vines. I angle myself to view them fully while they scan the area.

After a breath, they move again, left then right, weaving between the trees.

I follow them, my gloved hands casually resting at my waist.

I don't grab a weapon. There's no need to. No one truly stands a chance against me, especially not them.

The figure stops again, their dark silhouette unable to mask their tense shoulders. They must sense it, something behind them, stalking their every move. Their neck cranes beneath their cloak, angled in my direction.

I come to a halt behind them a few paces back, waiting in anticipation.

They spin around sharply; their eyes locked on mine.

I speak first. "Couldn't let your lover out of sight?"

They smile.

"I am her protector, and I need her to make it home to me safe," they say, voice steady.

I eye their weaponless body.

Poor excuse for a protector, if you ask me.

Love is a dangerous thing. It blinds you. Clouds your judgment. Consumes your being. Turns you soft in a world that is cruel. But love eventually sours. It leaves a scar on your heart that no one can ever repair. It'll kill any person before I do, and that is why it is dangerous. Because the ones you love most always leave first.

I clench my teeth in an attempt to keep any unwanted memories from flooding back.

"I pity a man in love," I snarl.

Their grin widens at my words, which only makes me angrier.

I unlatch my bow from my quiver, nocking an arrow simultaneously.

"I'll give you a head start." I smile back at them. "Now run."

A brief flash of fear spreads across their face as they retreat, heading in the opposite direction of their love.

And it's a shame that I know exactly where she is.

CHAPTER 20

FALCON

ARI

The tavern air clings to me, thick with incense and desire. It coils around my throat and sinks into my skin like a narcotic brew that I can't get enough of. All around me, waves of velka move in a riot of different colors; silk and fur shimmering in the tavern lights. The dance floor feels alive, like a beast feeding off each movement.

He found me. The man I first spotted when we walked into the village. The half-lion velka that made me stop in my tracks. There's something undeniably alluring about him, an effortless magnetism in the way he moves. I don't remember deciding to dance with him, only the moment I realized I already was.

We move together, my back against his chest, swaying to the rhythm of the music like it's the only language we speak. His hands glide up my sides until they find the base of my neck. With a gentle tug, he presses me closer, wholly lost in the heat of the moment. I push my hips back against him and let my head tilt to the side, coming to a rest against his chest. He purrs softly, the sound vibrating against my skin as his lips trace a slow path down the base of my throat.

I move my face toward him; eyes locked on his lips. I watch as they part, and my pulse quickens with each breath passed between us.

I reach up and loop my fingers into his hair, pulling him closer without thinking. His lips crash against mine, claiming my mouth with an urgency that steals the air from my lungs.

"Althara, spare me," a familiar voice rings out, dripping with amusement. "I hope I'm not interrupting anything important."

I pull back, staring at Ella through hooded lids.

She stands there with a sly grin, shaking her head—one hand clutching a drink, the other perched on her hip.

I laugh at the impish sparkle in her eyes. Reaching out, I snatch the drink from her hand and chug it.

She arches a single brow. "I left you alone for five minutes."

"C'mon," I pout. "I have to live a little."

She has Myke at home. She doesn't get how hard it is to find someone decent enough to entertain, especially when the love is always one-sided.

Ella's gaze flicks to the man behind me. "Well, are you going to introduce me or what?"

I laugh again, the sound growing warmer, less strange; something that's become easier to do the more ale I consume.

"This is—" I trail off, realizing I don't even know his name. "Ermmmm, what is your name?"

The velka chuckles, extending a hand in Ella's direction. "Selvan," he purrs. Turning back to me, his hand still outstretched, he waits. "Ari," I reply, taking his hand and shaking it.

Ella lets out an exaggerated huff, rolling her eyes. She reaches out and plucks the now-empty glass from my hands, fingers curling around the cool handle.

"I'm off to get a refill," she says. "Try not to get into too much trouble while I'm gone."

With that, she turns and weaves her way through the crowd. I playfully tilt my head toward Selvan.

"Friend of yours?" he asks.

I glance back at Ella, now nestled in the sea of velka. "Yes," I admit quietly.

I take hold of Selvan's hands, guiding them back to my hips. He chuckles at my boldness and leans in, his lips brushing against mine once more.

We fall into a rhythm again, and I don't know how long we've been dancing. The constant beat of music makes me lose track of time. I'll have to thank Elliot for inviting us, especially with all the shit we have dealt with on this quest. It feels good to slow down and enjoy something for once.

Selvan's hands remain firm on my waist while my eyes sweep across the tavern, drinking in the swirling bodies that move around us. For once, I am not thinking of anything but the current moment; the blur of the dance floor, the heat that makes my skin pebble with sweat, and the flush that is apparent on my cheeks. I peer down the hallway toward the bathroom, noticing couples coming and going. My gaze lingers, half closed and filled with yearning.

It's been so long since I've been laid.

Something shifts in my peripheral vision. A flicker, really, so fast that if I blinked, I would have missed it.

I narrow my eyes down the hall, searching for whatever hides in the shadows.

The bathroom door swings open, illuminating the area, and my body goes still.

My heart hammers in my chest as I fix my gaze on the silhouette lurking in the darkness. The shape. The size. All too familiar as of late.

I blink, trying to refocus. Maybe I am seeing things. Maybe I...

No. I am not seeing things. They are standing there; eyes latched on me with an intensity that sends a chill down my spine.

I move before I think, pulling away from Selvan. "I have to use the restroom."

I pick up speed, weaving through swaying bodies on the dance floor. The roar of the tavern fades, swallowed by the pounding in my ears. I sprint down the bathroom hall to the back door and kick it open.

I stumble into a dark alleyway, chest heaving.

"HEY!" I shout at the man at the end of the alley. "STOP!" I holler as they slip around the corner.

I race after them, approaching the end when a gloved hand wraps around my waist and another clamps over my mouth. I'm yanked sideways into a hidden alcove veiled in darkness, barely wide enough for two people.

I struggle against the forceful hands that hold me in place, instincts telling me to escape.

"If you scream, it will be the last thing you do," a deep voice rumbles in my ear.

I stiffen, my body coming to a sudden halt.

"Do you understand?"

I nod.

"Good girl."

I shiver at the sheer violence in his tone.

His hand drops from my mouth as the other spins me

around. My vision blurs from the unnaturally quick movement.

My eyes roam up the muscular chest of the man in front of me before landing on a set of eyes like molten sunlight.

Lincoln Ashfield is mere inches away from me. My gaze drops to his lips fleetingly, still feeling aroused from my time in the tavern. It doesn't help that he looks better than I remember.

"Stalker much?" I grumble angrily.

"I've been accused of being a stalker once or twice in my life."

This admission should scare me, but I think the mixture of arousal and ale is altering my brain chemistry.

I tilt my head back. "So, you are following us?" I ask, still very aware of his tight grip that holds me in place.

"As I recall, you are the one who came barreling down that alleyway following me," he mutters, annoyed.

"Semantics," I huff.

Lincoln's eyes shimmer with a brief spark of humor, mocking me, no doubt. He probably sees me as a weak, pathetic mortal who needs saving.

I scowl at him. "I saw you at The Riftlands. So, I'll ask again. Why are you following us?"

Lincoln's body tenses, pressing rigidly against mine.

I hold my breath, waiting for his reply.

But he stays quiet.

He stands there, half hidden under his hood, watching me.

Silence stretches between us, humming with tension. I don't know who he thinks he is, or what twisted game he's playing, but I'm done humoring him.

I lift my hand, his eyes tracking every movement I make. "Unless you are trying to kill me or my friend," I say, trailing my finger across his throat, noting how fast his pulse pounds against my skin, "then I suggest you stay the fuck away from us."

Lincoln's eyes flare with anger, but the emotion disappears just as fast as it appears. "Fine."

I scrunch my eyebrows together. "Just fine?"

He inches closer until there's no space left between us. His mouth brushes against my ear, sharpening every one of my senses as the intoxicating scent of cinnamon and leather fills my nose. "I don't need to kill you," he states, his fingers tightening around my waist before releasing me. "Someone else will do it for me, sunshine."

I smile at him, all teeth and no warmth. "My name is Ari," I sneer, tapping my foot impatiently. "And you never told me why you are following us?"

Lincoln steps back, smirking down at me. "Coincidence, I guess. We are searching for the same thing, are we not—," he gives me a menacing look before adding, "sunshine?"

I cross my arms over my chest, frustration burning through every one of my veins. I am more annoyed with myself than anything for chasing after him without a weapon because I have an undeniable urge to stab him right now.

"I said my name is Ari, asshole," I snap back, each word dripping with venom. My eyes flick to the daggers at his waist, easily accessible if need be.

Lincoln's hands clench into tight fists at his sides, leather straining with the force of his grip. The air around him seems to crackle with raw fury, every muscle in his body coiled tight.

"You're not worth my time," he growls.

I'm not sure if he's talking to himself or me, but the words still hit hard, sharper than I expected, and I flinch.

Lincoln fixes me with a cold, unblinking glare. But I'm used to the challenge, I play this game all the time with valorguards. He'll undoubtedly look away first because he has to.

A sudden gust of wind rips through the space, violently tearing my hair loose. Strands whip across my eyes, blocking my vision, and my ears pop from a strange pressure.

I frantically brush my hair away, but Lincoln is already gone. A bird now flaps its wings in his place.

"No," I gasp.

It's the falcon that has been following us since Ella and I ran from the clearing.

Squawk. Lincoln chirps, his beady eyes set on me.

I stare at him, dumbfounded by my own stupidity. I push out of the alcove and sprint back down the alley, hearing nothing but his wings beating behind me.

I need to find Ella immediately.

CHAPTER 21

LEGACY

LINCOLN

The wind lifts me higher and higher.

Wings outstretched, I ride the breeze, feeling it carry me farther away from the bustling rows of taverns that crowd the streets of Paradise. Below, merchants' carts groan against cobblestone, and velka laugh, the sound entirely influenced by the ale they divulge in.

I push myself further, soaring past rooftops with every powerful beat. The houses and streets grow smaller, melting into a soft blur on the horizon. If I fly fast enough, I'll be able to outrun my thoughts of *her*.

She's infuriating in a way that I can't explain. I find myself saving her over and over, yet she has the nerve to insist that she doesn't need it. Every word out of her mouth feels like a challenge, one that I find myself continuously failing to surpass. She moves through this world like she is untouchable, making her impossible to ignore, especially for a mortal. And yet, somehow, I let her live, even though I could end her life with a single touch. All I would have to do is remove my gloves, and she'd be dead. Yet, she lives. She lives because of me; both she and her friend do. I keep telling myself that having two fewer participants would make things easier, but I struggle to act on my own words when it comes to her.

She makes me question my abilities, and I want to strangle her for it. I want to grip my hands around her delicate little throat and squeeze until the light leaves her piercing green eyes. Maybe it's for the best that she's stuck in Paradise forever. She's probably back inside the tavern she walked out of, drowned in ale, with me already wiped from her mind.

I bank left, steering toward the tree line. I shift into my eldarim form, the wind whispering my failures around me. I sit perched high in the canopy of leaves, my legs dangling in the open air as I lean back against the base of a giant oak.

I rub my hands down my face, dragging them from my forehead down to my jaw, leather catching on the prickle of hair that has begun to grow.

I am tired.

I am tired of this godforsaken quest, tired of searching for the lost heir that plagues my thoughts, and tired of the curse that haunts me in the darkest hours. And the worst part is, I am no better off than I was before. I've completely lost sight of why I'm here and what I'm supposed to do. Playing savior isn't going to wash the blood off my hands. I've slain too many to ever change that.

I pull the ring I stole from Nikolai's corpse out of my pocket, twirling it between my fingers. It feels heavier than it should. I turn it over once more before slipping off my glove. The metal feels cool against my bare skin. It's a sensation I'm not accustomed to after decades of being constantly wrapped in leather.

I cast one final glance at Paradise, my mind firmly set on

where I need to go next—a place I am sure to find answers about the heir.

I slide the ring on my finger and clasp my glove back into place. I push off the branch, plummeting to the earth. The ground inches closer with each passing second. I wonder if this is what death feels like, facing the inevitable, accepting your demise while your body is dragged toward its doom. I relish the feeling, allowing it to consume me while I free-fall through the air. No one would mourn me if I died. I sure as hell wouldn't. Whatever I was, whatever I could've been, that version of me is long gone. If death came for me now, it would be more of a release than a tragedy.

I transform quickly, the feeling of loneliness heavy in my chest as my wings catch the next gust of wind.

Unfortunately, it is not my time to die *yet*.

My legacy will not end like my father's. I won't allow it.

I will bring glory back to the Ashfield name, if it's the last thing I do. And then maybe, just maybe, I'd allow myself to fall and splatter onto this very earth.

CHAPTER 22

DREAMING
ARI

The back door of the tavern slams shut behind me, its frame slightly warped from when I barreled through it earlier. Eyes flick toward me, a few curious, others full of yearning as I make my way down the hall.

Blood thrums wildly in my veins, my heart still racing from the encounter with Lincoln. He looked at me like I wasn't worth his time, like my death was surely coming. And the way his hand gripped my waist with unrelenting strength sent a jolt through me. Fear prickled at my skin from the contact, but beneath it, a heat I couldn't ignore bloomed. His touch was like fire and ice coiled together, and it left me trembling long after he let me go.

I shake my head, forcing the tangled thoughts to unravel. What unsettles me most is knowing he's been following us for so long, ever since the clearing. That quiet presence lurking just beyond sight. He's saved me, stalked me, confirmed his watch over every step I've taken, and yet he still lets me live this fragile, pointless mortal life. The weight of the knowledge presses down on me, but I can't afford to dwell on it. I have to focus. How would I have known that he was a falcon? I've only seen a handful of valorguards transform into their animal forms in my lifetime.

I force the panic that threatens to consume me away, reminding myself that my days are limited, and wasting them dancing and drinking is no way to face what's coming. I have been sloppy, chasing after an assassin without a weapon. If any quest participant walked through the tavern's door, we would have been defenseless. The fog from the ale clouds my mind and clearing it won't be easy. I need to find Ella so we can both sleep this off.

I step back onto the dance floor, slipping between sweaty bodies. They press against mine while I scan the masses of velka for Ella, struggling to resist the pull of the festivities around me.

I push forward before I can second-guess myself, and my eyes lock onto a figure in the crowd.

I arch an eyebrow, spotting Selvan already intertwined with someone new.

"Typical man," I mumble.

I spin around, ducking under a raised tankard of ale. Hands brush against my skin as I make my way through the crowd. I examine every face I pass and every table that lines the back of the room. There's no sign of Ella. I searched the back hall, the bathroom, and the center of the dance floor. Fear claws at my ribs. *Did she leave?* Did someone take her? Where did she go?

At last, I spot her, leaning casually against the railing at the corner of the bar. Her dark hair cascades over one shoulder, laughter spilling from her lips like a balm to my frayed nerves.

Relief settles over me as I stumble in her direction.

"Ella!" I shout.

Her eyes flick to mine, her grin stretching wider when she sees me.

I smile back at her, my chest warming at the vibrancy of her, unharmed and untouched. *Safe.*

"What has you looking so happy?" Ella places a hand over her heart. "Surely, it's not me. Did you...you know..." She wags her eyebrows up and down in a teasing manner.

I cross my arms over my chest. "Oh, come on..."

"I saw you come out of the bathroom hall," she says, suggestively.

"I thought I saw someone I knew!"

Ella chuckles. "An ex-lover? All the way out here?"

"None of my ex-lovers would dare travel outside of Noctharn," I mutter, taking the glass of ale from her hand.

"Hey!" Ella protests, glaring at me. "Stop stealing my drinks."

I set her glass down far away from us, motioning for the bartender to take it.

"We have to leave." My voice sharpens. "Now." I don't wait for her to argue. "It's not safe here, and we can't risk any of the participants in the quest finding us in this state." Because one already has, but I leave that part out.

Ella's eyes widen with a sudden understanding.

I grab her hand. "C'mon, let's get out of here."

She doesn't ask any questions as we weave through the packed room, heading toward the booth where we stashed our belongings.

We don't waste a second, quickly grabbing our bags and strapping our weapons back onto our bodies. I curse under my breath at how utterly screwed we would have been if a participant had actually walked in here.

A mistake I won't allow to happen again.

"Leaving so soon?" a voice calls out.

I face Elliot, eyeing the glasses of ale in his hands. "Unfortunately, yes." I raise my voice just enough to be heard over the music. "We have something we need to take care of."

"One more?" he asks, the liquid sloshing over the rim of the glasses.

I shake my head. "Thank you so much for showing us around. We really appreciate it, but we need to get going." My eyes meet his with sincere gratitude, willing him to understand.

Elliot nods. "Hopefully, I'll see you ladies again soon." With that, he turns away, taking a sip of one of the drinks as his body disappears on the dance floor.

We slip through the tavern's door and step out onto the crowded streets. Ella follows close behind me as I lead us out of Paradise, eager to put space between us and the village.

We don't slow our pace until the lights fade into a soft glimmer in the distance, the noise and bustle gradually giving way to quiet.

We reach the edge of the forest and step beneath the thickening canopy, shadows wrapping around us as the leaves blot out the sky. Moving carefully, we find neighboring trees sturdy enough to hold us high above the forest floor. Climbing up, we settle into the safety of the high branches, hidden within the dense canopy where no eyes could find us.

I lean back, letting the weight of the long night settle into my bones.

I hear Ella murmur from a tree over. "I'm really happy I met you." Her voice is soft in the stillness, the first words we've exchanged since leaving Paradise. "I don't think I would have survived this long if I hadn't."

A lump rises in my throat as I look in her direction. I can't see her face through the darkness, only the faint outline of her form. Still, I can hear the honesty in her voice, and that alone is enough to make my chest ache.

"I'm glad I met you, too," I admit.

And I mean that. Ella is more like me than not, but she still has happiness in her soul, and I will make sure it stays that way. She deserves a good life, and this quest is the only way she can get one. The king might not see reason and may only want one victor, but I can be persuasive. I always have been. I can talk anyone into giving me what I want.

"We'll leave tomorrow," I say softly.

"Tomorrow," Ella repeats as my eyes flutter shut.

My eyes snap open, though I'm not sure what woke me. A sharp throb pulses across my forehead, and I wince, pressing the heel of my palm to it in a weak attempt to ease the pain.

I think I slept, but it doesn't feel like it. I know my eyes closed, but it couldn't have been for long.

I shift against the rough bark, my limbs stiff as I reposition myself atop the tree branch. Leaves rustle above me, swaying in a breeze I hadn't noticed until now.

"Ella?" I whisper, voice rough from disuse and lost in the wind.

There's no response, minus the muffled sounds below me. The noises are distant, almost like they're underwater. There's a low grunt, followed by the sound of something heavy moving on the forest floor. I blink, disoriented, my thoughts still in an alcoholic fog. I twist carefully, trying to get a better look at what lurks below.

My hand moves instinctively to my waist, gripping the dagger at my side. The cool metal is a small comfort against the rising heat in my chest.

Moonlight filters weakly through narrow gaps in the branches, not enough to fully light the forest floor. I squint into the darkness at the same time the clouds decide to shift just enough for a sliver of light to slip through, casting broken strands across the ground. My breath hitches, barely above a whisper.

A group of three men huddle around something below. Low snickers pass between them, punctuated by a wet, tearing sound that makes my stomach twist. It's hard to tell exactly what they're doing from this height, but the ripping sound—like cloth stretched too far or flesh torn—sends a chill through me.

I slowly edge my foot against a branch for balance, eyes flicking toward Ella's tree. There's still no movement from her.

One of the men mutters something low and indistinct, his words lost in the rustle of leaves as the other shifts aside, revealing a glimpse of a face that makes my blood run cold.

Finley. He's someone I hoped I'd never see again. I grip my dagger tighter.

I keep my eyes fixed on the scene unfolding below as I rise to a crouch, balancing myself on the branch that holds me high above them.

But my composure shatters completely the second I see what they're doing. The world begins to tilt, my breath catching in my throat as a wave of nausea and shock crashes over me.

The shape on the ground is too still. Too lifeless.

I slam my hand over my mouth, desperate to muffle the cry that threatens to claw its way out. My eyes stay locked on the lifeless form, disbelief rooting me in place as the men's cruel murmurs crawl into my ears.

Ella's amber eyes stare directly at me, stuck in a permanent plea for help.

I'm dreaming.

I'm dreaming.

I'm dreaming.

I chant over and over again in my head. But this isn't a dream, and my friend is dead.

I tighten my grip on the slick handle of my dagger, blood roaring in my ears. Her murderers stand there cloaked in the shadows, hovering over their victim. And I am going to kill every single one of them.

They will pay for what they've done.

Finley and his group don't deserve to live.

Ella did.

Ella *deserved* to live.

My body violently shakes, every tremor fueled by a raw, burning rage. I line up my dagger to throw, quickly formulating a plan. I'll lodge my first dagger into Finley's back. And while he tries to remove it, I'll throw the other at his companion. With them both distracted, I'll climb down with my sword and slaughter the third. I'll murder all of them for what they have done, without an ounce of remorse.

I jerk my head to the side, a sudden whooshing noise passing by my ear. An object flashes in my peripheral vision. For a second, I thought I threw my dagger in a fit of rage, but I realized too late what had happened. I desperately grasp the air with my free hand, trying to keep my balance. My fingers graze the metal, but it's too late. My barrette slipped from my hair, and now glistens through the open air, before hitting the ground with a soft thud.

Finley pauses and raises a hand, signaling the others to stop.

I stay perfectly still, barely daring to breathe.

"What was that?" one of the men asks.

Finley walks toward my barrette, bending down to analyze it. He picks it up and twirls it between his fingers.

It's not burning him. *Why isn't it burning him?*

I aim my dagger at Finley's back.

"We're not alone," he says, excitement apparent in his tone.

I release my dagger, time seeming to slow as it flings from my hand. Finley sidesteps behind the base of the tree I'm perched in, my dagger missing him by a hair.

I fumble at my waist for the next one, losing my balance. My hand reaches for the branch that held me high above them, but it slips away. The air howls around me, mocking my failed plan as I plummet toward the earth. My back crashes hard against the ground, the breath knocked straight from my lungs.

I gasp, attempting to get to my feet but failing. I reach for Ella's body that lies lifeless a few yards away.

"Restrain her!" Finley shouts.

I tense as a valorguard seizes my ankles. Another presses my wrists down above my head, holding me in place before tightening a rough rope around them.

Finley clicks his tongue sharply, standing above me. "What a lovely surprise, I was wondering when I'd see you again." I eye the dagger I threw at his back now resting in his palm as he crouches down. "I've been praying that we'd cross paths," he continues, using my dagger to push my hair from my face. "Maybe I'll take what should have been mine since you denied it to me the first time."

I clear my throat and spit phlegm in his face. It splatters on his cheek, and I smirk.

Finley's eyes narrow, and he places my dagger beside him to whip it off his face. He stares at his fingers, rubbing my phlegm between them with a grin.

The sight repulses me, and I open my mouth to speak, but he beats me to it.

"Cover her mouth," Finley sneers.

Before I can object, a hand clamps over my mouth, stifling any noise.

Finley rolls up his sleeves, unhurried, savoring every second of the motion. My body trembles beneath the hands pinning me in place, helpless to do anything but accept what's coming next. I see him so clearly, and Althara, spare me, I wish I hadn't. There is no humanity in his eyes, only cruelty. The kind of person who kills because they want to, not because they have to.

Finley leans in, nodding toward Ella. "She didn't scream. Will you?"

I want to scream until my throat is raw, cry until there's nothing left. The weight of Ella's death crushes my chest, pressing down like a boulder I can't move.

Hot tears roll down my face as I try to break free of the hands holding me down. But I can't move. I can't do anything.

Finley clutches the top of my shirt and rips it open. "People like you deserve to be put in their place. And I'll gladly be the one to do it." He stands suddenly, pulling something from his pocket.

Fire ignites from his fingers as he tosses an object in the air. I catch the glint of my barrette through the flames, and I realize too late why it's not burning him.

Finley is a fire wielder, and he is going to burn me alive.

He smiles down at me as the realization sprouts across my features. "This is going to hurt," he states.

It's the only warning he gives me before stamping my heated barrette on my stomach.

I swallow my cry as the smell of burning flesh fills my nose, willing myself not to react, not to give him the satisfaction, but the pain is nauseating.

Is this what it feels like for others when they touch it?

My barrette stays pressed to my skin, the heat burrowing deeper until the pain becomes blinding. It's too much. I can't take it. I want to beg, to scream for it to stop, and I was about to when suddenly it did.

The searing heat lifts away, and so do the hands that were holding me down. Fire erupts around me, but sputters out just as fast, replaced with a violent roar.

I bolt upright, gasping for air.

Both valorguards that held me in place now lay dead at my feet in a pool of blood. Confusion washes over me as I scan the area searching for Finley, just catching the tail of an animal disappearing into the shadows of the forest.

"Ari," a deep voice growls.

My gaze snaps to a cloaked figure standing before me, the world tilting from the movement.

I don't have time to register what has happened before darkness swallows me whole.

CHAPTER 23

THE PULL
LINCOLN

A muffled cry echoes through the trees, barely audible, yet heavy with fear. It was faint, so faint no mortal or immortal would hear. But I am not normal; my abilities never allowed me to ever be normal, and a terror-filled cry is one that I know well.

I stand slowly, dropping the rabbit I was skinning. Its carcass lands with a thud. I move without thinking, my body already in motion, drawn to the sound. The cry didn't belong to any creature of the wild. That cry...it was mortal—a woman. And something fierce stirs deep within me, not just a simple instinct to protect, but a raging fire I can't control. It's as if every fiber of my being is screaming to shield her from whatever dark fate awaits her. Maybe it's urgency, an unrelenting drive to stop the cruelty before it's dealt, a force that pushes me forward without hesitation. Or perhaps it's the cry itself, so raw, and achingly familiar. The same cry I heard my mother let out in her final moments; the cry that still haunts the edges of my memory and drives me forward now.

My body shifts, morphing into its animal form, wings

propelling me through the forest. Everything is silent except for the ringing in my ears. It's the kind of silence that descends when death is closing in, when the predator has already ensnared its prey.

Branches reach out like jagged fingers, tearing at my wings as I close the distance between me and the flickering movement ahead.

I glide low, my talons transforming into boots, damp moss absorbing the impact as my feet hit the ground without a sound. I stalk through the underbrush, my eyes locking onto the three men I recognize immediately. The valorguards that I should have finished off back in the clearing.

I crouch, melting into the shadows that cloak my body like a second skin. My eyes catch on the lifeless form of a woman first, lying still in the pale pre-dawn light. Her amber eyes are vacant, searching for help that never came.

But it's not the lifeless woman who makes my blood run cold. It's the other, the one beside her. The woman whose name I have yet to say out loud, the one I've carried with me in every restless thought since I met her. Her hands are bound, her skin flushed from tears carving paths down her face. She is laid bare, her body vulnerable to every unwelcome gaze as it burns.

Something in me snaps at the sight.

I grip my bow, nock an arrow, and let it fly before I have time to think. Another arrow follows, both striking true.

The valorguards didn't see what was happening to them until it was too late. Both men die on the spot, arrows protruding from their chests. All my weapons are coated with the oil of belknot root. It's a poison derived from the very plant that grants us immortality. When boiled, it becomes deadly. Every blade, every arrow I carry is laced with it now, guaranteeing I can kill any being, mortal or immortal.

I nock my next arrow, aiming it at Finley's chest. A wall of fire erupts in the sky, igniting it the second it leaves my hand. His clothes suddenly disappear as fur bursts across his skin. I lock eyes with the beast standing at the edge of the tree line. It snarls a warning, and I pull my bowstring taut, readying to strike again.

Ari jolts upright, gasping for air, eyes wide with shock. My gaze flicks toward her as she takes in the bloodied bodies at her feet, then shifts to where Finley stands.

My focus snaps back to him, but I am too late. One blink, he was there, and the next, gone.

I lower my bow and step in front of her, my cloaked body standing above hers.

"Ari," I growl, tasting her name on my lips for the first time.

Her gaze travels up my body, lips parting to speak, but no sound follows. Her head tilts to the side, and her body goes limp.

I catch her before she hits the ground.

"Shit," I groan.

She fainted. Of course, she fainted.

I lift her, carrying her to rest beneath a sprawling oak tree, far from the lifeless bodies scattered across the clearing. I open my canteen, pull a small cloth from my pocket, and dampen it with water. I gently swipe it across the blood on her face and let it settle on her forehead. I take the time to examine her delicate features, the thick lashes that brush her pale cheeks, and the strands of hair falling messily across her face.

My eyes travel down the length of her, stopping at the snake imprint on her stomach. They branded her, leaving her with a mark that will never fade. I'll find Finley for what he's done, I'll make sure he *wishes* he'd never touched her.

I unfasten my cloak, draping it over her exposed body.

I begin to clean up the bloodshed, pulling my arrows from the valorguard's chest, and return them to my quiver. I drag their bodies away, leaving them deep in the forest and far away from Ari.

Morning breaks as I head back, the chill in the air easing with every beam of sunlight that slips between the branches. I leave Ari's lifeless friend where she is—a gift to her in a way, allowing her a chance to say goodbye.

I gather their belongings from high in the trees, catching the faint shimmer of gold on the ground as I make my descent back down. I kneel beside it, picking up the snake barrette that now imprints Ari's skin. I brush a gloved finger over its scale before tucking it into her bag.

I pile everything beside her before settling in to keep watch.

I can't leave her exposed like this. But I do plan to leave the second she wakes.

CHAPTER 24

MAY SHE STRIKE US DEAD

ARI

A heavy warmth settles over me, sinking deep beneath my skin. It seeps into my bones and wraps tight around my chest, making my breath come in shallow waves.

It feels like sunlight, but also like something else entirely.

It almost feels like *that* heat.

The kind that burns and leaves scars.

My stomach lurches and my skin prickles, caught somewhere between past and present, and the reminder of a reality far worse.

The memory doesn't return gently. It crashes over me.

She's gone. Ella's gone.

My eyes fling open, adjusting to the brightness of the midday sun. A thick fabric is draped over me, sun-warmed and suffocating. It sags against my torso, stinking of leather and...*cinnamon.* I rip it off and discard it.

I lie still, heart pounding, throat dry. The ground beneath me is hard with tiny stones that dig into my back. I'm bare from the waist up, save for my undergarments, and my body aches like it's been dropped from a great height. But it's my heart that's shredded, bleeding in a way no bruise could touch.

I shouldn't be alive.

But I am.

And Ella isn't.

I sit upright, my fingers finding the cloak again. I lift a corner, pinching the edge between my thumb and forefinger. I used to love the smell of cinnamon, but now, the scent of it can only mean one thing.

I inspect my surroundings, searching for Lincoln. My gaze settles on my belongings perfectly piled on the other side of me, Ella's included.

A crushing feeling constricts my lungs, squeezing tight until my breath shatters into quick, ragged gasps.

I can't get enough air. I can't breathe.

Where is Ella?

I scramble to my feet, hands trembling uncontrollably. The edge of my vision pulses as I scour the area on legs that feel too light, as if I might collapse if I don't find her.

"Look who's finally up."

I spin around faster than I intend, stumbling forward a few steps. My hand shoots to my chest, attempting to steady the wild pounding beneath my palm. If my heart doesn't slow down soon, I swear it might burst.

Half-hidden in the dappled shadows, Lincoln leans against the trunk of a tree with his arms crossed loosely.

Althara, spare me. I don't know how I managed to miss him. His face is blank, like a mask carved from stone, betraying nothing as his eyes sweep over me.

I don't care why he's here.

And I don't care that he saved me.

All that matters is Ella.

"Where is she?"

He tilts his head, analyzing me while I struggle to breathe.

I know he sees everything written on my face, the panic, the loss, and I swear I even see a small amount of sympathy in his gaze. Without a word, he lifts a hand and points toward a dark shape nestled between two trees.

My stomach twists and drops, but the ache is distant, as if it belongs to someone else. Tears prick at the edges of my eyes, but they don't fall, like my body forgot how to feel. The world narrows into a dull, cold numbness that percolates through my bones and settles heavy in my chest. I had prayed this was just a nightmare, a vivid, terrible dream I could wake from. But it isn't.

Ella is dead.

And I'm left here empty, and all alone.

So utterly and terribly alone.

I move on shaky legs toward her. "I..." my voice cracks, "I was supposed to protect her." I sink to my knees beside her lifeless body. "I told her I would."

I wanted to save her from the madness she got herself into. She had a whole life ahead of her. She was going to be engaged soon.

"Myke," I sob. "Oh no."

I have to tell him. I have to. But what would I say?

That I failed?

That I failed her?

That the future he dreamt of with Ella was now gone?

A gust of wind whistles through the trees, carrying the fading sound of wings retreating—a haunting reminder that Lincoln's still out there.

I don't have time to question why he won't leave me alone. All I do know is that he won't kill me.

And part of me is glad, especially in this moment.

I scrape my hands against the soft earth, dirt caking under my fingernails as I dig and dig and dig.

Ella deserved better than this.

I will make Finley pay for what he's done, no matter what it costs me, even if it's the last thing I do.

I pile the last handful of earth onto Ella's grave; a final goodbye etched in dirt and fading light.

I slump against the rough bark of a tree, sliding down it until the mossy earth cradles my weary weight. A layer of dirt covers my hands and up my arms, fingernails cracked and angry. A feeling of emptiness filled my chest hours ago that I haven't been able to shake.

I tug my barrette free from my hair, gathering the loose strands that have fallen out, and clip it back into place. When I found it tucked away in my bag, I didn't question it. I knew there was only one person who would help me and make sure I had all my belongings.

I look down, tracing the angry-snake imprint that now marks my skin. I'll have to clean it before it gets infected.

I grab my bag, pulling out the crumbled-up map that dictates my life. I trail my finger around The Riftlands in the general direction of where I think Ella and I ran off after being brutally attacked.

If my calculations are anywhere close, which they probably aren't, considering Ella was way better at reading this wretched thing than I was, a river shouldn't be too far from here.

Of course, that's assuming I even know where 'here' is. It would be easier if Paradise were on the goddamn map.

All I know is I need to get this burn cleaned, fresh water, and this grime scrubbed off my skin.

Squawk.

I sigh. "Of course, he's back."

I hear his boots hit the ground close by.

I scowl in annoyance but continue to study the map in front of me, examining the various terrains of the continent.

After a long pause, I look up, and my heart leaps into my throat.

Lincoln's dark hair is tousled, like he's been dragging his fingers through it for days, each pass more anxious than the last. And the purplish bruises under his golden eyes give him a haunted look, like sleep hasn't touched him in a while. He doesn't speak, just watches me with that same unreadable expression. The one I've come to hate like he's dissecting every inch of me.

I still haven't put on a shirt. The realization hits me suddenly as the wind brushes over my bare skin, sending a shiver through me. I fold my arms across my chest, glaring at Lincoln.

"No, 'thank you for saving my life' speech?" he asks.

I rise slowly, keeping my eyes locked on him the entire time. "I didn't ask you to save my life. You should have saved hers."

My eyes sting, but no tears come. They stay stubbornly dry.

"You're welcome," he deadpans. "If I hadn't, you would have been stuck in Paradise for the rest of your life or, better yet, dead, like your friend."

I flinch. "I wasn't stuck in Paradise."

I bend over, shoving my things into my bag, ignoring him. My fingers brush over the soft fabric of Ella's spare shirt, and I pull it over my head. The smell of her lingers, but it still doesn't bring tears; it only amplifies the hollow ache deep inside me.

Lincoln clears his throat, his eyes looking everywhere but at me.

"The ale does that." He grumbles the words as if he'd rather be anywhere in the world except here.

Which is funny, because he could be anywhere else. No one's forcing him to stand here. Yet every time something goes wrong, there he is. A savior that no one asked for.

I snatch the strap of my bag and sling it over my shoulder, flicking dirt from my sleeve. "The ale does what?" I snap, refusing to let him off easy.

Lincoln jerks his head in my direction, gloved hands clenching and unclenching at his side. He strides toward me, annoyed. For someone who acts like he hates being here, he has a bad habit of not knowing when to walk away.

I hold my ground as he stops directly in front of me, hovering close, lips pressed into a thin line. "Why do you think Paradise isn't on the map?" he growls. "Either you leave and never remember where it is, or you never leave at all."

I stare at him blankly, and he leans in closer.

"Now, tell me. Since I saved your life multiple times now, I think it's only fair that you share with me what you learned while you were in Paradise for five days."

Five days?

It's only been a day, maybe two, but not five.

I straighten and match his stance, tilting my head back to stare up at him, the silence between us thick with unspoken challenge. "First off, I wasn't gone for five days, and second off, why would I tell you anything? I don't even know you."

"Don't beat yourself up too much," he says, the remark

tinged with insult. "From the looks of it, you were having fun. I hear velka make excellent lovers."

I exhale angrily through my nose. Lincoln has no right to judge me, not for anything.

"I'll ask again, since you seem to like to avoid answering questions, why would I tell you, of all people, any information I have? I don't trust men like you."

Lincoln's expression doesn't change, but something in the way his jaw tics like he's gritting his teeth tells me exactly how much I've irritated him.

"What kind of man do you think I am?"

I smirk. "A man who thinks he's untouchable, one that believes fear gives him power."

"Fear is what keeps people alive in this world. You'll learn that soon enough."

"I'm not afraid of you."

A low chuckle rumbles from Lincoln's throat. "That's the kind of foolishness that'll be your downfall."

My nostrils flare, but I stay firm despite the growing tension. "Why won't you just leave me alone?"

He shakes his head. "You ask the wrong questions."

"And weirdly enough, you never seem to know how to answer them."

Lincoln glowers at me, the darkness in his eyes promising pain. "Let's just say you piqued my interest."

I take a small step back without meaning to. Something about Lincoln unnerves me. He is quiet but threatening in a way that makes my skin crawl.

I roll my shoulders back, straightening myself. I realize how much power I handed over the moment I retreated. Like hell I'm going to let him see how intimidating he really is.

"I need to win this quest more than you do. You've had

the chance to make something of yourself; I was never given the opportunity," I explain. "And don't give me that, bringing glory back to my family name bullshit, at least you live in Lunaria. Why would I share with you, of all people, any information I've learned?"

Lincoln leans forward, his breath brushing against my skin. "Need I remind you, you'd be dead if it weren't for me."

"And as I told you before, I never asked for your help."

His tongue clicks against his teeth in cold disapproval. "Stubborn woman."

My hands twitch with anger at my sides. "Arrogant brute."

We stand face to face, two strangers in the middle of nowhere, two people with different experiences of this world. He's made it clear he thinks I need saving, and I don't need to know why. If Lincoln's so set on helping me, then I will use that to my advantage. I formulate a plan quickly, every detail sharpening in my mind like a weapon. I have to stay one step ahead, because trusting him isn't an option, not after what happened to Ella.

I loosen my hands, placing them on my hips. "I need to win this quest," I say simply. "I want a better life. Something you will never understand." My thoughts churn rapidly in my mind. "If you are so willing to help me...which, it's obvious that you are..."

Lincoln's gaze drops to where the burn on my stomach throbs beneath my shirt.

I square my shoulders, trying to appear in control. "We should work together," I insist.

"I'll help you," Lincoln says instantly, "but you need to do something for me in return."

I swallow hard, forcing my voice to stay incessant.

Lincoln agreed immediately. I don't know if I should be scared or relieved.

"And what is that?"

"Let me kill the king's heir. In return, you can get all the glory, and I'll disappear. He said to find them, but not in what condition, and we all know that they aren't returning to Noctharn to live a happy life."

I blink, surprised at how much easier this was than I expected.

The king didn't say how he wanted his heir returned, but in the end, we all know it's a power play. He doesn't care for his child's well-being, only about saving his reign. And the odds of me finding them are much higher with a valorguard at my side, especially one that comes from a family of trained assassins.

"How do I know that you won't betray me when the time comes?"

Lincoln extends his hand. "You don't, but I can assure you that I want to kill the heir more than I want you dead."

I hesitate for a moment before extending my hand to meet his. "No blood oath?"

"No," he replies. "Althara has heard us; if either of us breaks our word, may she strike us dead."

"She can try," I mumble, wrapping my fingers around Lincoln's massive hand. His touch hums with a low vibration under the rough leather of his glove. The sensation unnerves me, a reminder of the power he holds, one I have yet to uncover.

I pull back, rubbing my hands together, wishing the uneasy feeling away.

"Well, I'm glad we were able to come to an agreement." I turn away from him, pick up my sword, and latch it to my bag. "Now, I'm in desperate need of a bath, so let's get moving."

I march away from Lincoln and head in the direction of the river I had spotted on the map. It shouldn't be too far from here.

I step into the underbrush at the same time Lincoln clears his throat, the sound distant.

"The river is this way," he calls out from behind me.

I whirl on my heels; gaze fixed on Lincoln's retreating form.

"What if you're wrong?" I shout. "What if it's this way?"

Lincoln waves a gloved hand over his shoulder, cloak whipping in the wind behind him. "Suit yourself, sunshine."

I pull the map from my pocket and study it, tracing where I think we're standing. A moment later, I realize I was wrong. I exhale roughly through my nose, annoyed, and fold the map before shoving it back into my pocket.

I shoot Lincoln a hard look as he slips between the trees, but I follow after him despite myself.

CHAPTER 25

ACCURACY

ARI

Lincoln stalks just ahead, his tall frame brushing the lower branches of the neighboring trees. His broad shoulders shove through the tangled vines like they're flimsy curtains in his way. A quiver is slung over his back, pressing against a skin-tight black shirt that leaves little to the imagination. Feathered tattoos spiral from his neck down to his arms, mirroring the hues of his falcon form—an unmistakable sign of what he is, and a stark reminder of how oblivious I'd been.

His cloak hangs off one shoulder, tossed aside in the heat, exposing ragged cargo pants stained from whatever mess he's been through. He could snap me like a dry twig, hell, even like those brittle branches crushed beneath his boots.

Lincoln reaches into his small pack, pulling out a cigarette and lighting it. The smoke coils around him like a dark ribbon. I hate that smell. It's the same bitter stench from last night when we set up camp.

Unfortunately, I was mistaken in more ways than I realized. I not only thought the river ran in a different direction, but I also underestimated how far away it actually was. And I couldn't sleep last night knowing the man who's been following me was so close. And better yet, I'm still filthy from digging Ella's grave. Now, with that smoke curling around me, I roll my eyes, unable to keep my mouth shut.

"You know that stuff's bad for you."

Lincoln doesn't even bother to look over his shoulder to acknowledge me.

"Like you care," he mumbles.

Of course I don't. But the way he drags on his cigarette grates on my nerves.

Would he even hear me if I unsheathed a dagger and sent it spiraling into the center of his back? The thought flickers in my mind. It would be simple, too simple. But part of me knows he'd sense it. He's too alert, too damn sure of himself to be caught off guard like that.

Still, I weigh the options silently, considering the cost of what I want against what I'm willing to risk. There's a part of me craving the finality of it, a cold satisfaction in ending this problem once and for all. But the other part, the smarter part of me, reminds me that he's useful. He probably knows this land better than anyone, thanks to his father's past missions to find the lost heir. And if I am going to be stuck with Lincoln, I might as well make the best of it.

So, my dagger stays sheathed...for now.

"What do you know about the wards?" I ask.

Lincoln continues trudging forward. "My father never shared much about his missions."

"Liar."

Lincoln stops dead in his tracks and turns, flicking ash to the ground. I don't bother stopping, quickly closing the distance between us.

I push past him, slamming my shoulder into his.

"You are awfully rude for someone who can barely keep themselves alive," he growls.

I storm ahead of him, shoulders tight, boots hitting the ground harder than they need to. "You just lied to me when you said we were working together. Wouldn't that make you the rude one?"

Lincolns at my back in a second, and before I have a chance to get away, he grabs my wrist, the leather from his glove melting into my skin. He holds me in place, forcing me to come to a halt.

I yank my arm, trying to pry it free, but his hand doesn't budge.

"I know as much as you do. The king collects his soulfire, he expands his border a little further each year, and no one in Noctharn questions it because of an enchantment."

He repeats to me verbatim what Gus said in The Riftlands, everything the same, minus that one word. *Enchantment.*

My eyebrows pinch together. "So, you do know something."

"I just told you..."

"You said enchantment," I interrupt. "The giants never said anything about an enchantment."

Lincoln glares down at me. "Educated guess," he says, taking a drag from his cigarette. "How else would we have stayed oblivious for so long?"

Irritation buzzes beneath my skin. He's stalling, I can see it in the lazy way he exhales smoke like we have all the time in the world. He clearly doesn't want to share his knowledge.

And yet, there it is again, just like with Ella and her fairy tales.

"Magic, fables, warlocks, and witches," I say flatly. "That's what you're circling around, isn't it?"

Lincoln doesn't answer, but I didn't think he would. He just stands there, smoke curling around his head like a veil with an unreadable expression that makes me want to hit something.

Fine. Lincoln can keep his secrets. I've made it this far without his half-truths and smug silences.

"Let go of me," I command.

Lincoln's grip on me loosens in an instant, his hand falling to his side.

If he wants to play games, so can I.

"What's your power, anyway? I know every eldarim has one, so what's yours? Besides your cute little bird form, what else do you have to offer?"

"You think I'm cute? That's sweet."

I huff in annoyance. "That's not what I—"

"Peregrine falcon," he cuts me off, flicking his cigarette on the ground and smothering it. "Known for their precision and accuracy when killing their prey."

I shrug. "Sounds lame."

An annoyed chuckle escapes Lincoln's lips, cold and dry, like he's laughing out of irritation more than anything.

Lincoln reaches behind himself and grabs his bow at an unnatural speed. He pivots on his heels, nocking an arrow in the same movement.

I step back instinctively. My hand lands on the hilt of my sword, fingers wrapping tight around its worn leather grip.

The muscles in Lincoln's arm ripple as he flexes, giving the illusion that the feathers on his skin are moving. "When Peregrine Falcons hunt, it is all calculated. It requires a lot of focus, almost like an archer taking a shot with perfect accuracy." His chest rises slowly, and when he exhales, the arrow whistles through the air, traveling so far that I can barely see it as it hits something close to the river and falls to the ground.

Lincoln slings his bow back over his shoulder and starts toward the river once more.

I jog behind him, trying to match his long strides but failing.

I approach him moments later, his bent frame hovering over a small animal.

"Hungry?" he asks, pulling a squirrel off the end of his arrow.

"So, your power is accuracy?"

"No, sunshine," he chides condescendingly. "Farsight and extreme strength. We can't all be elemental wielders. The best power is one that you don't have to rely on to win a fight."

Lincoln starts gathering twigs and dry leaves, piling them beside the squirrel.

"Well..." I unsheathe my dagger and spin, releasing it in the same movement. It flies through the air with a whistle before skewering a bird to a tree. "Maybe I have power too."

Lincoln falls silent, staring at the lifeless animal now pinned to the bark. If only I could have been this precise when it actually mattered—when Ella needed me most. She wouldn't be gone if it weren't for me, or at least Finley would be dead alongside her. She should be here with me right now and not this brutish valorguard with a superiority complex. The thought gnaws at me incessantly, a constant reminder of my failure. Every misstep, every mistake, loops in my mind like a broken record, and I hate myself for it.

I shift my gaze to the gently flowing river, letting its soft gurgle dominate my senses. It's a simple, unremarkable sound, but today it's like a lullaby. I never realized how intoxicating the sensation of water could be. Immersed, I feel untethered to the world around me, and that's exactly what I need right now.

I peel off my clothes down to my undergarments, paying Lincoln no mind. It's not as if he hasn't seen me like this before, twice now if we are keeping count. I sweep my hand through my hair, freeing my barrette, feeling the weight of his stare pressing against my skin.

I inhale deeply, drawing in a lungful of crisp air. Turning just enough to catch Lincoln's eye, I let my gaze carry a warning as I wade into the water. "You know," I murmur, "I'd be careful if I were you." I jerk my head toward the tree where my dagger remains lodged, gleaming faintly in the light. "That could be you next."

And I mean it.

Without giving him time to react, I slip into the water, submerging my head. The river swallows me whole, and for a moment, the world—my regrets, my guilt—dissolves beneath the surface.

CHAPTER 26

KILLED FOR LESS
LINCOLN

She sleeps with her back toward me, curled near the dying embers of our campfire. The night wind pulls at the spare clothes that she draped over herself, but she doesn't flinch. I offered her my cloak, but she declined. Now she lies there, stiff-spined and tense, pretending to sleep—her shoulders rigid from the effort. Ironically, she still thinks she can fool me with it. I can see every detail of her clearly, every exaggerated breath she takes, stirring the braid that falls to the middle of her back. A few strands have slipped free, swaying in the breeze. The braid is loose, not out of carelessness, I can tell, but because she doesn't waste energy on vanity. Everything she does is intentional, even when it looks like it isn't. She's always too sure of herself, like she's playing a game that she'd already won.

Truthfully, everything about her bothers me. And the way she holds herself bothers me even more. Every word that leaves her mouth is preplanned, and every sentence of hers is soaked in defiance. She's rude and unapologetic about it and laughs at danger like she's untouchable. Her very presence crawls beneath my skin like a splinter I can't dig out. She's mortal, breakable, and yet she acts like she's invincible.

And what unsettles me most is that she isn't afraid of me.

There wasn't even a flicker of fear in her eyes when we first met, no trembling or wide-eyed awe. Just that damned unimpressed expression she always wears, as if I'm nothing more than another man with a weapon. Her only tell is the subtle way she inches backward, as if some part of her senses that something isn't right.

I could kill her with a single touch. I could drain the life from her before she even opened her mouth to scream. And yet she mocks me, talks back, and challenges me like she's testing how far she can push before I snap.

And the truth that haunts me in the night, beneath the stars and shifting shadows?

I haven't snapped.

I have killed for less, but I haven't killed her.

I surge to my feet so fast the world seems to tilt with me. Dead leaves scatter where I'd been sitting from the movement. Agitation burns through me viciously, like something wild clawing at the inside of my ribs.

I drag a rough glove down my face, leather catching on stubble, trying to force the storm in my head to quiet.

What the hell is wrong with me?

I glare at her, and my jaw tightens. A scowl pulls at my mouth before I can stop it. She is unbearable. Mortal. Weak.

I pound my fist into my head, trying to clear my mind.

I can't think straight.

I *need* to think straight.

My body transforms on its own accord, bones and muscles bending into a lighter form as wings unfurl from my back. The night wind catches me in the next gust.

I soar into the open sky, leaving the campsite and her sleeping form below, desperately wanting to put space between us. Up here, there's no stubborn disobedience; just stars and silence.

I circle overhead once, twice, long enough to calm the restless energy burning in my blood. I settle into the high branches of a nearby tree, talons curling around the bark.

I still can't wrap my mind around how it's come to this, me, up in a tree, protecting *her*. I should never have agreed to this arrangement. I should've walked away the moment she voiced her proposal.

I should have said no.

But I didn't. And I don't know why.

I willingly signed up to protect a mortal destined for death, driven by something I can't fully name. Maybe it's the part of me that craves companionship, or it's something softer—a flicker of pity for her. The truth is, I can't tell where one ends and the other begins.

There's a lot about this world that we still don't understand, and working with someone is a welcome change for once.

I knew King Malvok was up to something, but I didn't exactly know what. How could I have known? My father's conversations were always so clipped, every word distant after a failed mission. And beneath the surface, I could feel the weight of his hatred aimed squarely at what I had done. He didn't shout or throw it in my face; it was in the coldness of his tone and the way he avoided my presence that made it known. That silent resentment settled between us like a shadow I couldn't escape, no matter how much I tried to make things right.

So, my father never told me anything, but as I grew older, I started to suspect some things. Our borders never made sense to me. Although learning that the soulfire expanded them was something entirely new, I had never thought to investigate further. I am intrigued by the soulfire. I'm not sure of one eldarim that isn't, but we are bound by oath to never stare at it too long, an oath we all took after our binding rituals.

I click my beak, eyes fixed on the horizon, counting each passing second. I pray to Althara to end this night, urging daytime to come faster so we can move once more.

This alliance, if it can even be called that, exists for one reason and one reason only. I keep telling myself this over and over, because if I forget, I risk falling into Ari's trap. A trap designed to lure me in to save her life, even though I have no apparent reason to do so.

With a mighty sweep, my wings catch the breeze, propelling me through the night sky.

I will not save her again.

I swear.

I swear.

I swear.

I swear I will not.

CHAPTER 27

SHARP REFLEXES

ARI

Lincoln chose our next destination because, according to him, my judgment is severely lacking. To be fair, how was I supposed to know The Riftlands were home to giants and that Paradise had magical ale that'd hold us captive?

We head to a region named Zalquar next, a place made entirely of sand. I asked Lincoln how he could tell, but he just shrugged and said it was obvious. The map was empty, with not a single patch of green in sight. He confidently called it a desert, insisting it was something he'd learned about back in his schooling in Lunaria. He made it sound like common knowledge, as if anyone would have known it. I wasn't totally buying it, though.

I flip a photo of Ella and Myke between my fingers as we walk. I found it tucked deep in her bag, like the photos I have stashed away in mine. It makes sense now why she thought Noah and I were together, with a similar image of her and Myke in her possession. They look so happy, full of life. It makes me sick. How am I supposed to tell him that she's dead? What if he asks how she died, and I have to admit to failing her when she needed me most?

I slam into something hard, the sudden jolt snapping me out of my thoughts. I stumble forward, my hand shooting out in front of me to catch my balance. My fingers graze warm, sweat-slicked skin. It's a fleeting, accidental touch that sends a jolt up my arm. The heat of it lingers longer than it should, even when I pull away.

The broad planes of Lincoln's back fill my vision but are quickly covered as he pulls a shirt back over his head.

He shifts his body, nodding toward an opening ahead. "Let's stop here for the night."

It was the first time I'd heard his voice in what felt like ages, filling the silence that had been eating me alive. I follow him without a second thought between two large boulders that form a natural nook just big enough to fit us both comfortably.

I step carefully between the jagged masses of rock while Lincoln moves around the perimeter, inspecting the area. The weight of my bag slips off my shoulders, and I sigh out in relief. Slowly, I stretch my arms above my head, feeling the tension loosen with every inch I reach. My eyes flutter shut for a moment, savoring the brief but welcome reprieve. A cool breeze brushes against my skin, carrying the faint scent of cinnamon with it.

Even with my eyes closed, I know Lincoln is near.

"Do you need something?" I ask.

Dirt shuffles behind me, as if Lincoln's restlessly shifting his weight from one foot to the other.

"Nope," he replies, voice tense. "I'll take first watch."

I peer intently over my shoulder, taking in his stiff frame retreating just outside the protection of the boulders. I don't understand him. I never wished for a valorguard to look me directly in the eyes for longer than a moment, until right now. Part of me wants to uncover his secrets, to tear down the walls he's built and reveal what's really going on inside. I shake my head, feeling foolish. I hate valorguards, I hate eldarim, and I hate King Malvok even more; that will never change, especially not for him.

I peel off my filthy clothing and fold them carefully on the ground, using them as a rough pillow. Reaching into my bag, I pull out my spares. I slide my cargo pants up my legs and tug a shirt over my head, the fabric clinging to my skin as I prepare to settle in for the night.

I collapse on my makeshift bed. It's not the comfiest sleeping situation, but the ground is soft for once. I longingly remember the bed I made at The Broken Fang, which feels distant now. My life will never be the same after this. There's a clear line now between who I was and who I'm becoming. Everything has an ending, even when we think it will never arrive. I just didn't realize how quickly this one would transpire, even though I've dreamt of this moment since I was young.

Stars splatter across the dark sky, each one shining with purpose between the two towering boulders. My focus involuntarily returns to Lincoln, drawn to him without thinking. He's just a silhouette against the dark, hardly visible, observing the same night sky that I do. I wonder if he ever searches it and sees something more, or if that's just me, trying to make sense of the stars above.

Part of me likes to think that I can see straight through the facade he wears, that he's more caring than he lets on. He holds himself as if the weight of the world might finally crush him if he lets his guard slip for even a second. It's in the tension of his shoulders, and in the way his jaw sets like he's bracing for something that is inevitably coming. And maybe that's what I can relate to the most. I recognize parts of myself within him, like he's carrying a burden he never asked for. It makes me feel seen in a way that's both terrifying and comforting.

I cough into my fist obnoxiously loud.

The silence between us is suffocating. I can't take it any longer. It's driving me insane, and if we are going to work together, we might as well get to know each other.

"How old are you?"

Silence.

Crickets actually.

Crickets chirp in unison, taunting me, no doubt.

I reach over and grab a small stone, chucking it at the back of Lincoln's head.

"Fuck." He cranes his neck, rubbing the spot where I hit him. "What was that for?"

I chuckle under my breath. "Sharp reflexes weren't a part of your power package, it seems."

Lincoln throws me an irritated look, angling himself against the boulder to face me. He doesn't say a word, but the tension in his expression says enough.

"I asked you a question," I grumble, not bothering to hide my annoyance.

"I heard you, and I chose not to answer," he fires back.

This man is unbelievably infuriating. Just when I dared to believe we could be civil, he proves me wrong.

I prop myself up on my elbow. "How are we supposed to work together if you won't even talk to me?"

Lincoln regards me silently, hands balled into fists at his side, as if telling me anything about himself pained him.

He exhales unevenly through his nose, a flare of anger escaping with his breath. "Twenty-eight," he finally says.

I tilt my head. "You are a new immortal then."

Lincoln averts his gaze suddenly. "Good job, you really know how to state the obvious."

I clench my jaw. "Are you going to ask me how old I am?"

"No."

I huff out in frustration, snatching another small stone and throwing it at him. He catches this one effortlessly, without even looking.

Lincoln presses his lips into a thin line, discarding the stone beside him. "You're going to have to try harder than that, sunshine."

I lower my voice, trying to imitate his tone as best I can. "How old are you?" I ask myself, mimicking him.

The corner of Lincoln's mouth twitches, as if he actually found me amusing.

"Oh! I'm twenty-six, thanks for asking," I chirp, voice dripping with sarcasm.

"I didn't," he mumbles.

"You really suck at this whole communicating thing. No wonder you're only a sergeant. There's no way the king would ever let you lead a team." I lay back down, folding my hands behind my head.

I study the night sky once more, trying to calm the pounding in my veins, when a sudden whooshing sound and a clank ring clear as day next to me.

I follow the noise to find a metal handle sticking out of the ground. The face staring back at me in the blade's sheen is one of pure shock.

He did not just throw a dagger at me.

My patience has worn razor-thin, and a surge of anger roars up from deep inside me. I refuse to hold back any longer. I snatch the weapon by the hilt and hurl it back in his general direction, sitting up in the same motion. The blade whistles through the air, missing him by a hair.

Lincoln stares at me, unfazed by my attack, which only angers me further.

Fuck. Him.

I push to my feet, grab my sword, and launch into a sprint.

One step, he rises and grabs his bow.

Two steps, an arrow is nocked.

Three steps, it's pointed directly at me.

Four steps, his lips curl mockingly, and he releases.

I lunge to the right, my foot slamming against the rough surface of the boulder. Harnessing the force of the impact, I launch myself into the air. I twist with intent, my blade slicing through Lincoln's arrow with a crisp, satisfying snap.

I land a few feet in front of him, the amused smirk he wore now gone. I'm too close for him to use his bow, and I take advantage of the fact.

I unsheathe my dagger with my free hand and throw it at his chest before he has a chance to retaliate.

He catches the dagger by the tip and flips it in his palm. I leap forward, thrusting my sword.

One second, I'm standing, the next, my feet are swept out from underneath me.

Lincoln stands over me, his boot digging into my wrist, forcing me to let go of my weapon.

"Not bad, but your attacks are obvious. Unfortunately for you, it looks like dancing around in the pit didn't help you in the real world," Lincoln says, taunting me, clearly trying to get under my skin.

I purse my lips. "My dagger was inches away from landing in your chest."

Lincoln chuckles, meeting my gaze. "I saw your next move before you even decided on it. Nothing was going to happen."

I take note of his stance above me. He's tall, but I have long legs. If I reach just far enough…I swing my leg up, aiming right for his groin. My hips lift off the ground to reach.

Lincoln falls to his knees, bracing my hips. He groans in pain, discarding my dagger beside us.

I push up, flipping him on his back, catching him off guard. I snatch my dagger and rest it against his throat.

I lean in close, my lips brushing against his ear. "Let's make one thing clear," I growl, feeling the rough stubble on his jaw scrape against my skin. "If we're going to work together, you need to start talking. I've had enough of your silent treatment."

I pull back just enough to see his face, adding pressure to my dagger as I do.

A spark of humor flicks in his pain-filled gaze. "Whatever you say…" he croaks, "sunshine."

I sit up straight and point the tip of my dagger at his crotch. "I'd stop calling me that if I were you."

Lincoln pins me with a cold, menacing glare. "I answered your question about my age, did I not?"

He has to be the most frustrating man I have ever met.

I apply pressure to my dagger in warning. "Answer one more question. Prove to me that you want to work together."

Lincoln eyes me skeptically, then sighs, the fight leaving his features. "Fine," he says, grudgingly giving in.

"Why did you join the quest?"

He blinks once, slower than usual. "Isn't it obvious? I'm finishing what my father started. If you asked more interesting questions, maybe I would feel more inclined to answer them."

My throat rumbles in anger, but I sheath my dagger back

onto my hip, nonetheless. "Asshole," I mutter under my breath.

Lincoln lets out a quick, dry laugh that makes his body shake, the movement pressing his hips flush against mine. I sit back, closing the gap in the same motion.

Heat rises to my cheeks before I even have time to realize what I had just done. Lincoln's pupils dilate as he rakes his golden eyes down my body, stopping at the exact spot that our bodies connect.

I clear my throat, rising to my feet, holding my hand out for Lincoln to grab onto. "Wipe that look off your face."

His hand circles around mine, gripping tight, using his whole strength to pull himself up.

"What look?" he asks.

I pick at my fingernails, focusing on anything but him. "I thought we weren't asking stupid questions?"

Lincoln takes a step around me, heading back to the entrance of the boulder.

"Goodnight, sunshine. Maybe you can dream of some better questions to ask me while you sleep."

I suppress a groan as I make my way back to my makeshift bed.

Damn me.

This did not play out how I wanted.

CHAPTER 28

BURIED

ARI

I can't move my arms or legs.

Something holds them down, pulling them taut. It feels like my limbs are being yanked from their sockets. I try to scream, but no sound leaves my throat.

I take in my surroundings, noting the small light that trails between the trees, barely illuminating the area.

Dirt and rock dig into my shoulders as I angle my head, shifting against freshly turned soil.

A sudden recognition washes over me.

I know this place.

I know this place because I lie atop of Ella's grave—the one I dug for her.

She lies deep in the ground beneath me, layers of earth separating us, but I swear the faintest heartbeat pounds at my back.

Did I bury her alive?

The pounding continues, gaining momentum and growing louder with each beat.

Ella is alive.

I dig my fingers into the soil, clawing at the ground with the limited movement that I have.

She's alive. I must have buried her alive.

I blink back tears that threaten to blur my vision as my fingernails fill with dirt. My hands are bound, and I'm not going to be able to save Ella.

The truth hits me like a blow to the chest.

I might have saved her if I hadn't been so drunk. Maybe then I wouldn't have slept through it all and seen the moment she needed my help.

A branch snaps in the distance, but I don't stop digging, even when I spot something moving in the shadows. I can feel their presence like a heavy weight settling in my chest, squeezing tighter with every breath.

I close my eyes, a reluctant acceptance washing over me. The weight of inevitability presses down, and I brace myself for what's coming. I know I should fight back, but fear pins me in place, turning my attention inward while the presence draws closer.

I am a coward in more ways than one.

I feel them hovering over me, the smell of burning flesh filling my nostrils.

"You could have saved her," a deep voice says, "but you chose to sleep while she fought for her life."

My eyes shoot open, tears spilling down my cheeks. Finley stands above me. I thrash against the bonds holding me in place. I feel him glide a point object down my body in a warning of what's to come.

"Why didn't you save me?" It's her voice. *Ella's.* "I thought you said we were friends."

I steal a glance over Finley's shoulder and catch sight of a gaunt face emerging from the shadows. Ella's face is stuck in a permanent expression of horror, amber eyes wide and pleading, as if she's still silently praying for the help that never came. Desperation clings to her like a second skin, haunting the air around her.

"Ella," I sob. "I'm sorry."

Finley's lips curl into a dark, twisted grin as flames erupt in every direction, instantly engulfing the space.

My throat clears suddenly, allowing me to scream as my skin begins to burn. It's a sound that tears from my heart and rips through the forest.

I wake up gasping, clutching the burn that aches on my stomach. My fingers graze the tender skin beneath my shirt. I count my breaths, trying to soothe my frayed nerves. It was just a nightmare, I tell myself.

Ella is *still* gone.

I failed her once—not again.

I bolt upright, suddenly remembering that I'm not traveling alone. Lincoln sits in the same spot as before, back facing me, oblivious to the nightmare that nearly swallowed me whole.

I let out a rough sigh and straighten my clothing. I can still feel the sting of dried tears on my cheek, a reminder of everything I lost.

I'm not sure if it's time for Lincoln and me to switch, but either way, sleep won't find me again tonight, not after that.

I rise to my feet and approach Lincoln's side. His tired eyes blink out in the distance, avoiding mine. If he heard me, he isn't letting on.

"Go rest," I whisper.

Lincoln stands stiffly, brushing past me. He slips through the gap between the boulders, leaving me to my thoughts without a word.

I press my back against the rough surface of the boulder, letting it take the weight of my tired body as I lower myself to the ground. Settling into the dirt, I pull my knees up to my chest and wrap my arms tightly around them, seeking some small comfort in the tight embrace.

The moon hangs low above the treetops, casting a trail of silver toward me like it's reaching out to comfort me in the darkness.

"I'm sorry, Ella." I breathe out, defeated. "I truly am." I release a long, weary breath, gathering myself before speaking again. "I failed you, and I'll carry the weight of that for eternity, so I never forget, even if it breaks me in doing so."

I rest my cheek on my knee, avoiding the moon's gaze, knowing that I am not deserving of it.

CHAPTER 29

CINNAMON-SMELLING SWEAT
ARI

Waist-high grass claws at my arms, golden and dry, brushing against my exposed skin and making me itch. It sways in the light breeze that pushes through the brutal heat, allowing only the slightest reprieve. Every breath is heavy, as if inhaling the flames of a forge. I had never heard of lands like this, not in any book, not during my short and scattered years of schooling, and not even in the old fireside tales whispered to keep restless children close to home. No one had warned me that such a place could exist.

This region wasn't just dry land or some sun-scorched wilderness I couldn't name. This stretch of earth is so stripped of life that it feels like even Althara herself has given up on it and moved on.

I can only assume Lincoln's father must have spoken to him about his travels through this region, perhaps in hushed tones, late at night, long after the candles had been blown out.

It's the only explanation that makes sense. Our schooling may have differed—Lincoln's family comes from a line of power. Even so, no one ever knew there were other kingdoms besides Noctharn.

The sun beats down mercilessly from its throne high above, a relentless predator scorching my pale skin. Its fiery gaze leaves behind angry red blotches that sting and ache, a brutal reminder that clemency is a stranger here. Occasionally, a tiny wisp of cloud drifts across the sky in an attempt to challenge the sun's dominance. But it never lingers long enough to cast a true shadow or offer even the smallest truce from its burning glare. Instead, it passes like a hesitant visitor, utterly powerless against the furnace blazing all around us.

In Noctharn, the sun always felt like it was stuck behind a haze, masked by a slow-moving fog. I wonder if the wards weren't in place, if Noctharn would be less dreary. Warm summer days in the kingdom are nothing compared to this. This kind of oppressive heat seeps into your bones, leaving your mouth unbearably parched as if the very air is draining every ounce of moisture from you.

In the distance, the grass begins to disappear entirely, promising something far worse than what we are experiencing right now. The sunbaked sand glistens like glass, its grains shimmering and stretching out toward a series of dunes that rise into the bone-dry air. They tower above the horizon, each slope bringing a new challenge. I squint, searching for any signs of Zalquar, but see nothing that resembles a kingdom.

My gaze follows the ripples in the sand before landing on Lincoln. I can tell the heat is getting to him. He travels slower than he has in the past couple of days, a few steps ahead. Light sinks into his tan skin, giving him an iridescent glow as beads of sweat trail down his neck, darkening his shirt.

His hands hang loose at his sides in their leather gloves. It's an odd ensemble, wearing gloves while your body screams for salvation. My eyes follow the drops of sweat that cling to every curve of his muscled arms, like jewels against his body.

I wonder what his sweat would taste like on my tongue.

Would he taste like cinnamon?

My tongue sticks to the roof of my mouth, and each swallow is more painful than the last. I attempt to lick my chapped lips, imagining the salty taste of Lincoln's sweat filling my mouth.

I shake my head at the disturbing direction of my thoughts. The sun must be altering my brain chemistry. I pull out my canteen, allowing the smallest drop of water to slide down my throat.

I screw the cap back on, noting how light it has become. My water supply is dwindling fast. I don't bother to ask how much water Lincoln has left in his canteen, partly because I already suspect he'd rather stay silent than say anything at all, and partly because getting him to answer a question was tiring in itself.

Perspiration might be my only option to survive if my canteen runs dry. Is that possible? Can you survive on drinking sweat? Maybe cinnamon-smelling sweat is different.

I bite my lip, staring at the enticing beads that roll down Lincoln's arms.

Just one lick. There's no harm in one lick.

"What are you thinking about?"

I jump.

Lincoln's voice cuts through the heat like a blade. My eyes snap to his, which were already on me.

I clear my dry throat, scrambling to contain my embarrassment.

Think. Think. Think.

I swiftly crouch down; my eyes locked onto an object partially hidden beneath the brittle strands of dead grass. My hand curls around a large leaf, its surface rough but sturdy between my fingers. I rise back up, holding it in front of myself for Lincoln to see, forcing a smile.

"I was thinking that this leaf is the perfect size to shield me from the sun." I blurt the words out awkwardly, wiping the back of my free hand across my slick forehead. My smile stretches wider than it should, lips cracking at the edges from the strain as my cheeks flush.

Lincoln arches a brow, skepticism written plainly across his expression.

I shift uncomfortably, clutching the leaf a little tighter. "My skin. It's burning," I add without thinking.

What is wrong with me?

I glance down at the leaf in my hand and can't help but think how ridiculous I must look.

I silently curse myself for being so foolish, but lift the leaf over my head, nonetheless, pretending it's the fanciest sunshade ever invented.

CHAPTER 30

BLONDE BOY

LINCOLN

I feel her eyes on me before I see them.

It's not her usual alert and assessing gaze, like she is waiting for me to give her a reason not to trust our alliance. This expression is different, hesitant—as if she were about to do something irrational.

I don't turn around right away. I keep walking, letting Ari's eyes bore into me, tempting me to read her intentions. Each step I take stirs up a cloud of dust that sticks to my boots and settles on my skin. I can feel sweat running down my back in steady, hot trails, soaking into my shirt as it slips lower down my spine. I listen closely to the sound of her feet dragging behind me, each one weighed down with exhaustion.

I cast a fleeting look over my shoulder, barely moving my head, acting like I'm checking something beside me. Her gaze lingers on my forearms, studying them without a word as she pulls her lower lip between her teeth and bites down softly. There's a subtle intimacy in the way she does it that holds me captive, drawing me in.

"What are you thinking about?" I ask, catching her off guard.

She jumps, her eyes widening just enough to betray the swirl of thoughts behind them. She quickly drops her focus to the ground, as if the earth beneath our feet has suddenly become utterly fascinating.

I stop walking and face her fully, an amused smile playing on my lips. She avoids my gaze, and after a brief pause, she clears her throat and crouches down to pick up a large, dried-up leaf.

She stands upright, her smile stretching so wide that her lips start to crack. "I was thinking that this leaf is the perfect size to shield me from the sun," she mumbles, searching for the right words. Her cheeks flush with a soft pink, so entirely different from the red splotches scattered across her skin.

I raise a single eyebrow, studying her as she brings her other hand up to her forehead, wiping the sweat away. Seriously, for someone with such a clever mouth, this is the best she can come up with? She stands there, clutching that absurdly oversized, brittle leaf like it's some forgotten relic from another world.

"My skin...It's burning." She adds out of nowhere, as if it's not the most obvious thing she could say, before lifting the leaf over her head.

She smiles at me innocently, holding her stupid leaf high. I put my back to her and start walking again. She quickens her pace to match mine, falling effortlessly into step beside me, as if daring me to say something about the ridiculous thing in her hand.

"Are you alright?" I ask.

She hesitates for a moment, then forces a breathless

laugh. "Of course—" Her voice cracks, betraying her tough front. "It's just obscenely hot. Like, really hot."

Her cheeks stay flushed with a pink hue, the color lingering on her damp skin.

"Is that so?" I drone.

"Yes," she says, nodding her head. "I didn't know a desert would feel like this. It's like walking into an oven. Not a nice oven though. Well, I mean, ovens aren't nice because they can burn you, but anyway, I'm totally fine. Just hot is all."

She rambles on, probably the heat getting to her, making her restless and spilling words without much thought.

"You really didn't know any of this was out here?" she asks, waving her hand dramatically around her, quickly changing the subject.

"I did to an extent. I knew my father wasn't searching in Noctharn." I lie only a little. "I just didn't know how big the land actually was."

I've seen photos from my father's missions, but nothing more. He showed me images of dunes that stretched for miles, small cottages in a lush forest, and creatures of both land and sea, before our relationship took a turn for the worse.

"I'm sorry about what happened to him," she says quietly. "He shouldn't have been executed the way he was."

I stiffen at her words, a wave of old anger rising like bile in my throat. "My father got what he deserved in the end." I clench my jaw so hard it hurts. "He failed."

The words taste bitter, and I know they're not entirely true. My father wasn't loving like a parent should be. He was cruel in ways that didn't always leave bruises but always left marks. Every day, I curse him, and I'll continue doing so for the entirety of my long, immortal life.

"What about you? Do you have a father?" I ask, grasping for anything else to talk about besides him.

Ari's head jerks toward me, like she didn't expect me to ask her anything about herself.

"Yes." She clears her throat. "He isn't a good man."

A small chuckle slips from my mouth at her words.

"I'm not a good man either, but here you are."

Ari clenches her hands into fists, and the leaf crunches from the strain. "I doubt you beat helpless people, force them to fight for your survival, and make your own child work in the mines just to grow wealthier."

I stop without warning, and she mirrors me.

"I don't need your sympathy," she growls before I can respond.

I grit my teeth at her dismissal. "Is that why you joined the quest? To get away from him?"

Her eyebrows scrunch in the middle, making a crease. "I want to start living the life I deserve." She lets out a slow breath. "Everything I have done has been for my mother. Fighting back is the only way I can repay her now."

I search her piercing green eyes for as long as the oath will allow me, seeing all the pain and hurt hidden within them. "And what do you deserve?"

She squares her shoulders. "I don't deserve anything if I don't win this quest."

Ari pushes past me without another word, determination filling each of her steps. She shifts her giant leaf back and forth, creating a slight breeze that catches the edge of her shirt.

I can't help but shake my head at the sheer absurdity of this woman.

I catch up to her in three long strides.

"You wouldn't move your lover with you?"

She laughs, confusion sprouting across her features. "Lover? I don't have a lover."

I rub my gloved hand on the back of my neck, trying to think of a way to save myself right now. "What about that blonde boy from the tavern back in Lumin? I thought he said you and he were together."

She tilts her head, recalling our first encounter.

I remember it vividly, the way her blade rested on my chest, unaware of who she was threatening. The way her breath hitched as her eyes roamed up the length of my body and met mine. But I also remember her deep in an embrace with a velka in Paradise, moments after seeing him.

"Noah?" She laughs again, harder this time. "Oh, Althara, no. We grew up together. He's my neighbor and my best friend."

That explains some things.

"Well, that's good, you need someone stronger than that." She gives me a sideways glance, but I keep my attention fixed ahead. "You protected him more than he protected you."

"It's a good thing I don't need protecting," she mumbles.

"You keep saying that, but I don't believe you."

She purses her lips, and I can practically feel her eyes rolling.

"This," she says, pointing to the desert. "I don't know what I'm up against out here. Back in Lumin, I knew what I had to do to survive. It's different."

"I'll believe it when I see it," I mutter, "though I'm not betting on it anytime soon."

She lets out an irritated huff, the final sound before silence settles thickly between us. The dry grass becomes sparse with each step we take, and patches of yellow brush creep into the lush sand. My boots sink in the loose, shifting grains. If she believed the stifling heat trapped in the tall grass was already messing with her mind, she's in for a rude awakening.

It's about to get worse.

"Do you have a lover?" Ari asks, startling me.

I flex my gloved hands at my side. "I don't do relationships."

She breathes her next question more than she says it. "What do you do then?"

I regard her—eyes shimmering with that tempting hue of hers, lips slightly parted, silently awaiting my response.

"Nothing."

She scowls. "Liar."

I can't help but laugh at her response; if only she knew. "Think what you want, sunshine."

Ari shakes her head, staring off in the distance, avoiding my gaze. It's not that I don't want to be loved by someone else; I do, more than I'm willing to admit. There's a continual ache beneath the surface, a longing that won't fade. But I won't risk hurting anyone to fill my own emptiness, not with this curse hanging over me, not after everything that's happened. I've already lost everyone important to me. It's not something I want to gain, only to risk losing all over again.

"You seem like the type that couldn't hold a relationship anyway," she grumbles.

"What is that supposed to mean?"

Ari shrugs nonchalantly, quickening her pace. "Just an observation. That's all."

CHAPTER 31

ZALQUAR

ARI

It's hard to say how much time has passed since the tall grass faded, swallowed by the soft, shifting sands beneath our feet. Hours, at least. Maybe more. The change was gradual at first: yellow blades thinned out, giving way to dry earth and fine grains of sand that stretched farther than the eye could see. Since then, we've seen nothing but a never-ending expanse of golden emptiness. No paths to guide us, no ruins, no distant towers on the horizon, just an endless stretch of land as if the kingdom of Zalquar didn't exist at all.

Sand spills into my boots no matter how tightly I lace them, gathering at my heels and grinding against my skin until it's raw. I don't even try to shake it out anymore. There's no use.

We trudge up a large dune, barely making progress. Every two steps we take, we slide back one.

Gusts of wind hurl dust against my skin, offering no relief, doing nothing to ease the heat. I squint into the haze, biting back a curse as needle-like grains sting my eyes and force them shut. Even with a spare shirt wrapped tightly over my nose and mouth, the sand slips through every gap, turning every breath into a mouthful of grit.

I want to scream, but my mouth is too dry.

I want to cry, but no tears fall.

I want to lie down and rest, but I fear I won't get back up if I do.

Lincoln walks ahead of me, his movements sluggish and weighed down by fatigue.

"Say something," I plead, my voice rough. "Anything. Please. I beg you."

He doesn't answer, just keeps walking with his head down, focused on the sand at his feet, as if it might change if he concentrates on it hard enough.

The silence is worse than the heat, worse than the burning in my legs or the sand grinding in my boots.

"Lincoln!" I shout his name this time, voice cracking. "Please talk to me. I don't care what you say, but if you don't say something, I swear I'm going to lose my mind."

He doesn't reply.

My legs finally give out, and I collapse to the ground. It takes Lincoln only a second to realize that I'm no longer following behind him. His shadow is upon me in an instant.

He hooks his hands under my arms and lifts me with surprising ease, holding me close against his chest. I lean into him instinctively, seeking comfort I didn't know I needed. His arms tighten around me in response.

"Please," I whimper. "Talk to me."

Lincoln sucks his bottom lip into his mouth, biting it. "I don't know what to say."

"Then lie," I snap. "Make it up, tell me anything to help me take my mind off the fact that we're most likely going to die out here."

Lincoln exhales slowly. "Alright," he says after a pause.

"Sometimes I wish I had a more interesting power. It is kinda lame, like you said."

A frail laugh escapes me, barely more than a breath. "I was only kidding."

"I know. But you're right, I am strong and weak at the same time."

Lincoln is many things, but 'weak' was one word that never came to mind when I look at him. "What was it like?" I ask. "The binding ritual. What was it like?"

He ponders my question for a moment. "It was brutal...It felt like my body was being ripped to shreds and put back together again. And that wasn't even the worst part. The animal assignment was. I almost gave up then. I understand why some eldarim can't make it to the end. It's a pain I never want to endure again."

I settle in closer to Lincoln without thinking, wrapping my hands around his neck as he carries me. "And the ones who fail," I choke out. "The half-breeds. What really happens to them?"

"If the king had his way, they'd be dead the moment they didn't succeed. But we keep them around, they're still useful for the grunt work in the capital."

"I get it."

Lincoln nods, understanding precisely what I meant. Our eyes meet and hold, a silent exchange passing between us, more honest than anything we've shared before. I examine him. His strength, his resilience, everything—in complete awe of how gentle someone like him could be.

Lincoln inevitably looks away but frees one of his hands in the next breath and points. "There's some shade up there."

I cling to him, afraid to fall while he seems completely

unfazed. He holds me now with one arm, cradling my entire body, and doesn't falter an inch.

I follow the direction of his finger toward a narrowly curved dune and the sliver of shade it has to offer.

Lincoln hikes across the sand, the distance to the dune feeling longer than it should, but bit by bit, the shade grows closer.

We finally reach it and Lincoln stops, crouching briefly before sitting down. I loosen my arms from around his neck as he gently slides me off his lap, setting me down beside him. The sand beneath my hands is noticeably cooler, but a welcome contrast to the burning sun. I press my palms into the grainy surface, letting the chill seep into my bones.

Lincoln lingers on the edge of my vision, his closeness impossible to ignore. The space between our bodies feels almost nonexistent, and every slight movement he makes brushes against me. His hand moves to his waist, unfastening his canteen. He passes it to me, and I grasp it eagerly, unscrewing the cap. I remove the fabric from my mouth and take a dire sip of the lukewarm water. It floods my mouth, allowing me a small reprieve amid the endless desert.

I hand it back to him. "Thank you."

He takes the canteen, sipping from it before securing it back to his waist.

I lean back, watching him.

"Why do you wear gloves?" I ask. "Aren't your hands sweaty?"

Lincoln stares ahead, hands clenched into fists. "It's better you don't know."

"Why?"

He lurches to his feet suddenly, breaking the fragile contact we'd held just moments before. Something unseen seems to have caused him concern. He hovers above me like a shield, bow drawn tight, the arrow aimed at a distant dune.

I scramble upright. "Lincoln?" I blurt out, concern creeping into my voice.

My hand moves instinctively to the hilt of my sword, gripping it tightly. I draw the blade free with a crisp, ringing sound that cuts through the stillness. The steel feels heavy in my palm, my body still fighting exhaustion.

"Lincoln," I repeat. "What's going on?"

The sand begins to shift beneath my feet. It's a slow, ominous ripple at first, but transforms into a violent wave just as fast. It drags the dunes back like curtains, unveiling distorted figures.

"Welcome to Zalquar." I hear a scratchy voice say, just as the dunes collapse around us.

One moment, the vast expanse of blue sky stretched for miles, and the next, everything vanished, swallowed by a suffocating darkness. It's as if the sun itself had been snuffed out, and the world plunged into a shadow.

The ground groans, a low, mournful sound as the desert unleashes its fury. Sand tears at my skin like tiny blades, each cut a sting that sets my nerves aflame as the wind roars in wild laughter around us. The grains pierce my eyes, burning so fiercely that I'm forced to squeeze them shut. I cough through the haze, the dust choking me as I try to breathe. I barely have time to register the chaos before Lincoln's body collides with mine, shielding me. I cling to the fleeting hope that this torment would pass, that Althara herself would save us.

Lincoln and I crouch low, bodies pressed tight against one another, trying to become as small and unnoticeable as possible.

I discard my sword beside us and bury my face against

his chest. My fingers curl around his shirt, and I pull it over my mouth and nose. He mirrors the movement, pressing his mouth to the base of my neck, using the fabric around it as a barrier against the storm.

Lincoln's grip tightens, and he squeezes so hard my ribs ache. My lungs rebel against the pressure, craving air that the storm refuses to give. Yet despite the pain, I never want to let go.

I never imagined I would die wrapped in the arms of a valorguard. I loathed valorguards and eldarim my entire life, and now I feel like if I were to die, maybe death from something I hated with every ounce of my being would make sense.

The world likes to play twisted games like that.

I've wasted so much time hating what I thought I couldn't change. No one forced me to live under Silas's roof for as long as I did. I should have tried harder. I should have made something of myself sooner. I never fooled myself into thinking I'd grow old. I always felt there was a harsher fate lying in wait, ready to claim me first.

Noah is going to be so disappointed in me. He warned me not to go on this quest, but I didn't listen. He's always been the one standing between me and danger, protective to a fault; sometimes smothering, but always because he cared. Even when I pushed back, even when his caution felt like chains, I never doubted that it came from love. And somehow, that makes this all hurt even more—the thought that I might have let him down, that I went against everything he tried to protect me from. But I had to do this. I wanted to do this for myself, even if it meant leaving him behind for a bit of freedom. I just hope that if death awaits me, that Ella is at the gate with open arms. I pray she can forgive me, but I'd understand if she didn't.

Lincoln's grip slackens, his gloved hands gliding over the bare skin of my lower back, sending a sudden chill running straight up my spine.

I grip him tighter.

He can't let go. He can't.

"Ari—" His voice vibrates in my ear.

"Don't leave me," I rasp, each word dragged out.

"You can let go now."

My eyes shoot open.

The roar of the sand around us has faded, and the last of the dust has already settled, revealing sand-colored stone structures that pierce the clear blue sky.

I release Lincoln, easing the death grip I had on him, and brush the dust off my clothing as I rise. "You could have told me sooner."

Lincoln's gaze sears into my skin, but I don't dare meet it. He stands tall, handing me my sword. I tighten my grip around it, struggling to steady myself as I turn toward the beings I saw hidden within the dune.

Three figures stand before us, resembling mortals but never fully solid. Their bodies shift and flow like grains in the wind, never deciding on a fixed shape. They wear the same white cloth, draped loosely and covering only a small part of their skin. I scan the various weapons hanging at their hips.

"You're made of sand," I say in awe.

The middle figure's eyes glow in response.

"Yes." The single word scrapes the air as if he hadn't spoken in a century. "We're sandlurkers and this," the creature waves his hand behind him, "is Zalquar."

I look beyond them, finally taking in the kingdom we've been searching for. Sand trickles down the edges of the stone structures, mirroring the way it flows around the sandlurkers before us.

"Who are you?" Lincoln growls, standing protectively close at my side, weapon drawn.

The sandlurker in the middle lifts his hand to his chest. "My apologies, I am Rami, the king's messenger." He bows his head in a gesture of respect before straightening.

Rami examines us from head to toe, his eyes narrowing for a moment before brightening with sudden recognition.

"And you are from the kingdom of Noctharn," he says with a burst of excitement, clapping his hands together. "What a pleasure."

I offer a slight bow in return. "I'm Ari, soulfire miner from Lumin."

A crease appears on Rami's face as he brings his attention to Lincoln. "And what do they call you?"

"Lincoln."

Rami clears his throat, a subtle smile playing at his lips. "Very well. What brings you to Zalquar?"

"We'd like to request an audience with your king," I reply, meeting his gaze. After what Ella and I learned during our short time in The Riftlands, I decided that the fastest way to get the information we need is to go straight to the royalty of each kingdom.

Lincoln offers no objection to my request, which tells me he agrees.

Rami nods. "Of course. The King of Zalquar foresaw your arrival."

"He did?" I ask, unable to hide the suspicion in my tone.

Rami's smile widens just a bit, but his eyes remain unreadable. "Word travels fast outside of Noctharn. All the kingdoms are aware of your king's quest."

"Let's waste no more time then," Lincoln says firmly.

Rami steps aside, motioning toward a sand path that leads into the kingdom. "Very well. Follow me."

I hesitate for a moment, analyzing the sandlurkers' retreating forms as uncertainty wells up inside me. Lincoln follows behind them, not saying a word. He even lowered his weapon, his face frozen in an icy and detached expression. I keep my grip tight around my sword, staying a few steps behind.

He doesn't seem phased by anything, which unnerves me. Either he knew their people already existed, or he trusts others too easily. But I fear it is the latter, given how easily he agreed to work with me.

I don't put my faith in others so blindly, and neither should he.

~

We enter Zalquar, passing beneath towering pillars that frame a pair of gleaming golden gates. They feel symbolic in a way since the actual city of Zalquar remains hidden to anyone arriving at the desert's edge, no matter how long they've traveled.

The buildings beyond the gates are crafted from pale stone, weathered and worn by centuries of persistent sand and scorching sun. Each block is carefully stacked in intricate patterns, shaping homes, storefronts, and the road beneath our feet.

Vendor carts line the central plaza, half-shielded by loose, tattered cloths that flutter gently in the breeze, guarding fresh food and exotic goods from the dust. One by one, people begin to emerge from shadowed doorways and narrow alleys, their glowing eyes fixed intently on us.

"Do you have visitors often?" I ask.

Rami regards me over his shoulder, calm as ever, yet I can't stop my skin from tingling under his stare.

"Not many," he replies.

Lincoln walks behind Rami, his shoulders stiff and his eyes peeled, constantly scanning the surroundings. Every subtle movement of the sandlurkers pulls his focus.

We approach the exterior of the castle. It's a breathtaking fortress, shifting and reshaping itself as grains of sand swirl in the wind. With each gust, parts of the castle appear to crumble, only to rebuild moments later, as if the structure is stuck in an endless cycle of decay and renewal. I am mesmerized by the silent, graceful act of it.

Rami claps his hands three times, the sound slicing through the silence. Slowly, a grand entryway rises from the ground, its towering frame carved from smooth stone made from fine grains of sand. Rami steps inside, the two other sandlurkers close behind him, their forms changing with each movement.

"The king has extended an invitation to you both for dinner," Rami announces, his voice firm as he gestures for us to follow him down a narrow corridor that winds deeper into the castle's heart.

We stop before two sculpted doors, each flanked by a female who waits patiently, their calm eyes observing us.

I glance at Lincoln, searching his face for a hint of what to do next, but he avoids my gaze. Frustration bubbles deep within me, and my hand trembles beneath the weight of my sword. I thought we were finally opening up to each other, but clearly, I was mistaken.

The two women step forward, bowing low in unison.

I sheath my sword, sensing no apparent threat.

"Hello," I say kindly to the one in front of me. "That's not necessary."

Timid eyes find mine, and I give her a soft smile. "What's your name?"

The woman straightens, eyes wide, almost startled, as if the question caught her off guard. Her lips part, but no answer comes. Instead, her gaze moves to Rami, lingering there, searching his face for some kind of direction or approval, as if she needs him to speak first, or simply to allow her to speak at all.

Confused, I stare at Rami, waiting in expectation. There's a weight in the moment I don't fully understand.

"They are mute," he says. "All women are."

Bile rises in the back of my throat as I struggle to process his words.

"Mute," I repeat. "Why?" The question slips past my lips before I can stop it.

"Silence," Rami says softly, almost reverently, "is the first step to obedience for a servant."

My blood runs cold. "You silence them...on purpose?"

"It relieves them of the burden of questions and the need to make choices. The world runs more smoothly when no one expects to be heard. Don't you think?"

Lincoln tenses, muscles coiled like a predator ready to strike. "No," he growls.

Rami arches a brow. "I don't expect you to understand our traditions."

Lincoln takes a step toward Rami, and I grip his arm firmly in a silent plea for restraint.

Rami's gaze roams over us, taking in the hold I have on Lincoln. He chuckles under his breath, low and cold. "You'll find that Zalquar runs much better this way." He pivots and strides back the way we came, the sandlurkers following. "See you at dinner."

I return my attention to the servants who both stand patiently, arms outstretched in offering.

Lincoln shrugs out of my grip and takes the servant's hand in front of him, allowing her to lead him through a set of sculpted doors into a room.

"Yell if my help is needed," he says, tone clipped.

Anger courses through me. After everything that it took to get here, that is all he has to say? "Like I told you before —" His door closes, swallowing my words with a click. My voice falters, a sting of hurt hidden beneath my anger. I swallow hard, fighting the queasy knot tightening in my stomach.

"I don't need your help," I whisper, knowing he can't hear me.

CHAPTER 32

DIVINE

ARI

Steam rolls in lazy plumes around the stone bath, the water's surface glistening with aromatic oils. The servant moves with grace around me, her hands solidifying like the stone buildings before plunging into the water. A sponge glides across my skin, banishing the dust from the desert and the weight of the quest with each pass.

I wince when it grazes the burn on my stomach, the pain unpleasant enough to remind me it still lingers. The woman hastily sets the sponge aside and reaches for an ewer. She tilts it, and warm water flows over my head, coaxing my hair to tumble down my back like a waterfall. Her fingers work gently, lathering soap into my scalp. A sense of calm settles deep in my bones, unraveling the tension I've been holding onto. My mind wanders to Lincoln, the way his body felt pressed against mine, how safe I felt in his arms—a rare feeling I'm not accustomed to and one I won't experience again. Not with him. I do wonder if he is getting the same treatment, if they are touching him the same way they are touching me.

It's not that I really care, but curiosity gnaws at me, especially given how indifferent he acts toward me. He treats me like I'm nothing more than a burden that slows him down rather than someone worth his attention.

The water in the tub drains, carrying away the grime and sweat that have clung to me for days. As I rise, a soft, perfumed towel is wrapped around my shoulders. Beads of soapy bathwater trace down my skin, slipping back into the tub like a final farewell to the exhaustion and filth I've been carrying.

Despite the pressure to find the king's heir, I can't help but feel a small flicker of relief. For the first time in what feels like forever, I'm clean. It's a fleeting moment of tranquility, a brief refuge before the hunt begins again.

I'm helped out of the tub, my feet meeting the cool stone floor. It's a distinct contrast to the soothing water I just emerged from. A tender hand guides me into a short-backed chair situated in front of a gold floor-length mirror. The servant's fingers run through my damp hair, detangling the long strands that fall down my back.

I watch her intently, wondering how long she's been mute—how long silence has been forced upon her. At what age do they take their voices from them? Is it a punishment handed down in childhood, or some immoral tradition based on status? The thought unsettles me more than I want to admit, weaving through my mind as her fingers untangle the knots in my hair.

A soft tap on my shoulder pulls me back to reality, my eyes snapping open. I don't remember falling asleep, yet somehow, I must have because the person in the mirror looks like a stranger.

My hair has been dried and shaped into luscious curls that tumble gracefully over my shoulders. They frame my face with an effortless elegance I've never seen before. A delicate line of black traces the edges of my eyelids, making the striking green hue shine even brighter, in a way that feels almost foreign. My cheeks carry a rosy glow, and my lips are painted a rich, inviting shade of red.

I blink, half-expecting the image to fade away, to reveal the tired, worn woman I've grown accustomed to, but the reflection remains.

The servant holds up my barrette, waiting for my approval.

I nod, still at a loss for words.

She gathers a few curls and fastens my barrette behind my ear.

I look beautiful, almost regal. It's a thought that surprises me, something I never imagined I could be.

The servant strides across the room and comes to a halt in front of shimmering fabric. I twist in my chair to find a scandalous gold dress hanging there, accompanied by equally scandalous heels.

I shake my head. I've never worn anything besides my linens and cargo pants.

The servant grabs a piece of paper from a side table and scribbles on it with a chunk of charcoal before handing it to me.

How did I not think of this sooner?

I grab it eagerly. '*I'm Lilia*,' it reads.

"It's nice to meet you, Lilia." I extend the paper back to her. "I'm Ari."

Lilia smiles, snatching it back.

'*You were made for a dress like this. Just try it on, if you hate it, I will find you different one*,' she writes.

I bite the inside of my cheek...It is a beautiful dress.

I study my reflection in the mirror once more. If I were to wear a dress, putting one on when I look like this would make the most sense. It wouldn't feel like I was pretending to be something I'm not in this state.

I briefly make eye contact with Lilia in the mirror. "I guess I wouldn't be opposed to trying it on."

Lilia's face beams with excitement. She grabs the dress and begins to help me into it with attentive hands, lifting the gold fabric over my body and fastening the clasps that trail down my lower back.

The dress fits like a glove, every curve of it accentuating mine as if it were indeed made for me. I run my hands down the soft fabric that hugs my body like a tender embrace. A smile naturally blooms on my lips.

I collect one of my daggers and strap it to my leg, feeling more comfortable with it there. Lilia holds the scandalous heels in front of me to take.

A crease forms between my brows. "I've never worn heels before," I say, almost ashamed. "And there's no way in hell I'd be able to walk in those."

Lilia places the shoes on the ground and raises her hand to indicate one moment before hurrying out of the room.

Moments later, she returns with a different pair in hand. She points at the height of the heel. They are barely two inches high, more manageable compared to the ones she first showed me.

I twist my hands nervously, losing my confidence. "I guess I could give it a try."

I sit down and stretch my legs out in front of me. Lilia slides the heels on my feet and hooks the straps around my ankles with a featherlike touch.

I rise slowly, feeling off-balance as I take a tentative step forward.

Lilia is by my side in an instant, holding my elbow while I practice walking back and forth across the room. I stumble, my legs tangled in the gown, but her grip never wavers. After a while, her hand eventually fades, and my ankles finally support the weight of my body.

I saunter before the mirror, each step a silent declaration of the new skill I just learned. Lilia's smile brightens the room, encouragement shimmering in her eyes. Laughter rises from me, light and free, as the weight of the past few days begins to lift from my shoulders.

A pang of longing stirs in my chest. I wish Ella were here to share this moment with me. She would've adored every bit of it. Maybe, in some small corner of the world beyond, she's watching me right now.

I cast Lilia a mischievous wink before spinning in a circle, my golden gown catching the light and scattering it like liquid sunlight.

A throat clears behind me, too deep to be a woman's. I freeze. My fingers slip to the dagger I strapped to my thigh, unsheathing it, ready to face whoever just entered without my permission.

My heart leaps into my throat the moment I spot the intruder.

Lincoln stands in the entryway of my room, poised with the confidence of a proper nobleman. A simple but elegant white tunic hugs his frame, accompanied by a dark sash that wraps around his waist like a snake. So effortlessly powerful without trying and so striking that the sight of him robs me of my breath.

I lower my dagger. "Well, don't you clean up nice."

"Is that a compliment, sunshine?"

I bite my lower lip, forcing down the flicker of nerves. I roll my eyes like I'm unbothered to mask it. "Don't let it go to your head. I'd hate for your ego to get even bigger."

Lincoln taps the doorframe, each thump of his gloved

finger matching the pounding of my pulse. "Wouldn't want that, would we?"

I move in his direction, sliding my hand between the slip of my dress to sheath my dagger once more. His finger stalls midair, eyes darkening to a deep caramel. He studies me closely, devouring me with a single look as if carving me into his memory. I stop just in front of him, tilting my chin up to meet his gaze, unflinching under the heat of his intense presence. "Of course not. You're insufferable enough as it is."

Lincoln's mouth quirks to the side. We stand so close now that I can feel the brush of his breath against my skin.

"You look—"

"Out of place?" I interrupt.

"Divine," he declares.

Lincoln's compliment is simple, almost cold in delivery, but it stirs something deep inside me that I can't name. My lips twitch into a smile, but I quickly suppress it before it can fully bloom. A flush creeps up my neck, nonetheless, betraying the illusion of indifference I meant to portray. I look just past him, hoping he wouldn't notice, wanting to pretend it meant nothing, but the truth is stubborn. The tiniest emotion still lingers, a reminder that even with perfectly constructed walls, there were cracks.

"Thank you," I manage to say, masking my true feelings with those two simple words.

CHAPTER 33

A DELICACY
ARI

We follow Lilia through the castle halls, her pale linens matching the dull stone that lines the walls. Each turn carries us into yet another corridor, indistinguishable from the last, mirroring the barren repetition of the desert outside. It feels like we're moving in circles, lost in a maze built to confuse.

Lincoln's hand lingers just above the small of my back, barely grazing my skin. It's a whisper of a touch that leaves me longing for more.

We've slept on forest floors, in dingy caves, and crossed endless scorching dunes, and yet I never thoroughly saw him for what he is. He's a protector. He said so himself, but something about the way he looked at me in my room made me newly aware of how kind a man he might be, even given the circumstances. Or maybe I'm just merely aware of the space between us and the way my body reacts when he's close.

"You're quiet," he murmurs. "For once."

"I'm just thinking—" I veer my attention upward, noticing how the banners sway in the breeze overhead. "I'm a little concerned that the king welcomed us so easily into his kingdom."

Lincoln's expression tightens, lips pressed thin. "Don't worry, sunshine. I won't let anything happen to you." There's no teasing in his voice, even when he says that awful nickname he knows I hate, just an unapologetic admittance for what and who he is.

A valorguard, an eldarim, an assassin, a killer.

No one has gone to great lengths to protect me. Not my father. Not my mother. Not even Noah at the times I needed him most. And yet Lincoln continues to, as if I'm someone worth saving.

I study him, taking my time memorizing the way his jaw clenches, the subtle furrow of his brow, and the intensity that burns deep within his golden eyes.

"I know," I admit. I wholeheartedly believe that Lincoln will never let anything happen to me.

He moves closer to me, resting his gloved hand on my lower back, unable to keep it hovering any longer.

A jolt of euphoria shoots through my veins at his touch, leaving a lingering ache in its wake. The feeling settles deep in my bones, building into an unrelenting desire for him to touch me, to feel his skin against mine. Not hidden behind those wretched gloves that leave me drowning in my own sense of loneliness and detachment.

I've spent my whole life craving connection, yet even though Lincoln may look at me and touch me, he'll never truly see me or feel me.

I wish my eyes were a different shade of green, any color other than the soulfire.

I wish the leather that wraps around his hands didn't steal the warmth of his touch from me.

It's nice being feared by the most powerful, but it also gets lonely.

So painfully lonely.

I've seen everyone's happiness unfold around me while mine was pushed to the side, stuck in the same story with my barbaric father. Part of me even feels like maybe Noah wouldn't have stuck around as long as he did if we didn't live next door.

But right now, for the first time in my life, I feel like I matter, that I'm someone worth knowing. It's a fragile feeling, but it fills me with hope. If only Lincoln could hold my gaze a little longer, really see me—not just with his eyes, but with everything he is. If only he could reach past the distance between us and touch my skin, breaking down the barriers that keep us apart. I long for the connection in a way I hadn't realized I needed.

The hallway narrows and opens again, leading toward a wide arch. Lilia stops in front of ceiling-high doors, with two sandlurkers standing on either side. With a nod, they pull them open, revealing the dining chamber.

A gasp tears from my throat before I can stop it.

Crystal chandeliers sparkle overhead, illuminating the circular room, each one mounted firmly to the hardened ceiling above. The floor is a mosaic of colored stones, the first and only color I have seen in the entire castle. Light spills through open windows, casting elaborate lines that swirl across the walls, depicting graphic scenes delicately etched by a firm hand.

My eyes scan the detailed drawing. I recognize the giants from The Riftlands, the velka from Paradise—surrounded by a vast number of kingdoms and lands we have yet to explore. And Noctharn. Freshly engraved lines mark the border, suggesting that the sketch had been recently updated. The land appears flattened, as if what was once there no longer exists.

My heart thuds in my chest as the realization of what it means hits me. *Soulfire collection week.* It was, what, a few weeks ago now? I've been unintentionally helping the king destroy people's homes, and I never realized.

At this point, I am no better than he is.

"Welcome, Lincoln and Ari," a deep, boisterous voice rumbles.

I direct my focus toward the long table that stretches beneath brightly dyed linen in the center of the room. An array of fruits covers its surface, while liquid-filled clay pitchers sweat from the heat. At the head of the table, in a chair made of bleached stone, the king sits.

A golden crown floats above his head, suspended in midair as it morphs and transforms, endlessly changing its shape. Unlike the other sandlurkers in Zalquar, the king's skin is a rich brown, paired with piercing red eyes.

Lincoln bows at my side, and I move with him. I dip at the hips to mirror his gesture, his hand still warm on my lower back.

I observe the king, hiding myself under my lashes, barely catching the flash of an impish smile before it disappears.

I straighten to my full height once more. "Thank you for inviting us so graciously into your exquisite home."

The king's eyes narrow, his face full of hard lines and pointed features. There is nothing soft about his appearance apart from the fine silk robes that drape his body. Six guards flank him, three on each side—all wearing armor lined with curved blades at their hips.

He gestures for us to sit. "I'm delighted that you both

accepted my invitation. I cherish the opportunity to host anyone from the Noctharn Kingdom."

Lincoln and I part ways, his hand sliding away from me, and I immediately yearn for the sensation of his touch to return. I cross the room and take my seat opposite him at the table.

The doors to the dining chamber swing open, and Rami rushes in, making his way toward the king. "Sorry, I'm late." He nods at us as he passes, taking a seat to the left of the king. "I had some last-minute business to attend to."

A servant steps forward and unfolds the king's napkin, placing it neatly across his lap. I reach for my own, noticing that no one moves to assist Lincoln or me.

My fingers skim the material of my dress as I settle the napkin into place. "You have a ravishing taste in clothing, Your Majesty." I allow a soft smile to present itself across my lips, in an attempt to warm the king up to my questions. "This is the most stunning piece of clothing that has ever touched my skin."

His eyes sweep over me unhurriedly, lingering on every inch of my figure. I straighten my posture, a wave of discomfort creeping over me under his lingering gaze.

"You wear the color of my people." His voice is as dry as stone. "It suits you deliciously so."

Lincoln's body stiffens, the leather of his gloves straining from the tightness of his fist.

The words may have sounded complimentary, even flattering, from anyone else's tongue, but his.

"Deliciously so indeed," Lincoln repeats.

"Well." I bite the inside of my cheek to mask my annoyance. "Being told I look delicious is new."

The king tilts his head back, a mocking grin curling his lips. His laugh rings off the walls alongside Rami's, only to fade just as fast as it began. He claps his hands together suddenly. "Let us eat," he says.

Figures emerge from shadowed alcoves, gliding into the room with trays of food in hand.

Lincoln fixes the king with a cold glare, his face tight with unspoken violence. He starts to speak, the rigidity in his shoulders making it clear that whatever he is about to say will only bring us trouble.

I extend my leg under the table and kick his shin. His eyes snap to mine, blazing with anger. He clamps his hand around my ankle just as I go to pull it away. A rush of fire surges through me from the contact, flushing my skin pink and betraying me. He holds me captive a moment longer before letting go, just as bowls of leafy greens topped with vibrant, colorful vegetables are set down in front of us.

An arm extends from behind me, holding a large pitcher filled with a ruby red liquid. Wine pours into my crystal glass; its scent fruity, and full of spice, like berries crushed with cinnamon. It's the same alluring cinnamon scent that coats Lincoln's skin.

I eye it suspiciously, noting how the King of Zalquar's and Rami's glasses sit untouched. I lift my own glass to my lips, pretending to sip it and place it back down.

The king takes a bite of his food. "I am aware that Malvok launched a quest in search of his lost heir." He clicks his tongue between chews. "Sorry bastard is still searching for them, it seems. I figured we'd have some stragglers show up at our gates sooner or later."

I push my fork around my plate. "And are we your first stragglers?" I ask.

"Of course not," the king says. "But I wish you were."

Lincoln grits his teeth, jaw ticking. "Has the heir ever set foot in your kingdom?"

The king crunches down on a leaf. "Just once."

I lean forward. "When?"

"Very recently. There were rumors. People reported seeing someone with a seven-pointed star on their chest. It was hard to miss, but they didn't linger. Here one moment, gone the next."

"Man or woman?" I inquire urgently.

The king shrugs. "No one specified."

My eyes narrow. "You didn't think to investigate?"

The king lifts an eyebrow, unbothered. "Rumors are cheap. I don't chase ghosts, nor do I help the Noctharn Kingdom."

Lincoln opens his mouth, but the king lifts a hand, silencing him with a dismissive wave. "Let's save the back and forth. I'll tell you exactly what I told everyone else. No citizen of your kingdom has survived in Zalquar longer than a day, so the heir is either long gone or dead."

"Because of the heat?" I question him, pressing for more information.

"Because of the heat," the king repeats with a smile.

I have a nagging feeling he isn't being completely honest, but the lie is believable enough that I decide not to press further.

Lincoln lets out a harsh, impatient cough. "What can you tell us about the wards?"

A rumble of disapproval leaves Rami's throat. "Eat first, and then we can discuss. You both look famished," he says. "We shouldn't be discussing such sensitive matters on an empty stomach. Isn't that right, King Tharion?"

I study the king, at last discovering his name.

He grunts, flicking his gaze to our untouched food as if to remind us that it's there. "The main dish will be ready shortly, and you both haven't taken one bite."

I lower my fork, my stomach rumbling in anticipation of the meal ahead. The king's stare lingers on us, his expression unreadable, while Lincoln mimics my movements from across the table.

I stab the leafy greens and place them on my tongue. I pick apart every flavor as I chew, but it tastes normal—delectable, actually.

I finish my plate and push it to the side.

The servants hurry in, clearing them to make space for the next course. They quickly remove the decorations from the table, laying down placemats in its wake.

Clearly satisfied, the king begins to speak. "The wards around Noctharn are impossible to break. Each year, they expand and take more and more from the continent." He clasps his hands in front of him. "Many great kingdoms have collapsed under Malvok's reign."

I tap my foot lightly under the table. "And there's no way to stop him?"

King Tharion chuckles. "If there were, I would have already. There's word of another soulfire mine, but no one has been able to find it. Without the soulfire, we are defenseless." He sips his water. "That's why I find it humorous that your king thinks that his heir would be anywhere in these lands. Althara blessed my kingdom with the ability to survive in this terrain. Even if the king wanted it, he and his people would never survive. His child has probably been living right under his nose for the past twenty-five years, and he doesn't even know it."

Lincoln and I sit up straighter in our seats.

Would they live in the kingdom knowing that the one person who wanted them dead was in reach? It's a possibility.

"And surely if Noctharn's heir were here, King Tharion

would have killed them by now for their crimes against the land," Rami adds.

"Did the Queen of Noctharn pass through Zalquar?" Lincoln asks, his tone full of challenge.

Tharion regards Lincoln impassively. "No, but your father has. How is he?"

A cold grin forms on Lincoln's lips. "Dead."

The king sets down his glass. "What a shame," he mutters.

I sense the tension thickening in the room, catching a hint of malice in Lincoln's expression. "I must say, Your Majesty." Lincoln's attention snaps toward me the second I open my mouth. "The food tastes incredible."

The king features lighten at my compliment. "That's not even the best part," he chimes. "We have a special treat for you tonight. A delicacy."

On cue, the servants begin rolling in a large tray, sliding it down the length of the dining table.

Steam rises, curling from beneath the platter, releasing a warm, earthy spice that makes my mouth water. The servants lift the lid and clear it from the table, disappearing from the room. I squint through the haze, focusing on the food laid in front of us.

My hands fly to my mouth before I can stop it. Not out of hunger or intrigue, but out of shock and pure disgust. Beneath the pleasant spices and honey glaze, a mortal body lies on the tray, cooked and lifeless, a sight so grotesque I have to look away.

I recognize them immediately. A boy from the clearing. A boy participating in the king's quest.

Lincoln's hand moves to his waist, sliding beneath his sash.

"You—" I trail off, the sight overwhelming me. "Eat us?" I ask, voice thick with revulsion.

"Of course not," the king replies with disdain. "We eat mortals." His eyes lock on mine. "I thought your kind had the same appetite."

I drop my hand below the table to the dagger strapped to my thigh. He thinks I'm eldarim.

"We don't eat mortals," Lincoln barks.

A wicked grin contorts the king's face—gone was the indifferent man who spoke to us. "Why would your king lock them all up behind your wards then?"

Lincoln scowls in disgust at his words, while mine reels in shock. Mortals never truly existed to the extent they do now, not with the binding ritual stripped away from them. Eldarim's power is passed down through bloodlines, and beings without high blood cannot obtain it. You are either born into a powerful family or a weak one, but every being in Noctharn has the right to gain immortality from Althara, even if they are not eldarim born. It's just a name the king invented to divide us further. Under Malvok's rule, he declared it pointless, arguing that life had no meaning without power. Still, stories speak of those who never desired immortality or power, taking pride instead in living a brief but meaningful life. However, no mortals were ever eaten in Noctharn.

I swallow the bitter taste on my tongue. "We don't eat mortals."

"A misunderstanding," Rami says calmly.

The king's gaze flicks between the meal at the center of the table, then to me, and finally to Lincoln, his eyes shining with an emotion I can't quite place.

And then he laughs. The king laughs. I don't understand what he finds so funny.

Lincoln stands abruptly in response, his chair tipping over behind him. "Thank you for the hospitality, but I think we will be leaving now. Ari, get up."

I glare at him, trembling with rage at the display before us, but also at Lincoln's demanding words. No one commands me. I allowed Silas to command me long enough, but never again. "You do not tell me what to do," I declare, coming to my feet.

King Tharion rises, using the table to come to his full height. "You're on a fool's quest, valorguard, one you will never win until you accept who you are."

Lincoln's nostrils flare with each breath he inhales. "And what am I?" he snarls.

The king's red eyes glow as he speaks. "A monster."

Lincoln freezes, but it's his expression that gives him away, haunted and filled with an acceptance I've never seen in him before. "If that's what I am," he sneers. "Then so be it."

I reach for my dagger at the same time Lincoln pulls one from beneath his sash, throwing it directly at the king.

CHAPTER 34

CAGED ANIMAL
ARI

Rami lunges in front of the king, taking the dagger in his shoulder. A gasp of pain tears from his throat as he hunches over, hand clutching the wound, fingers now slick with a strange liquid. Somehow, he manages to stay on his feet, holding himself between the king and danger.

The sandlurkers stationed behind the king quickly close ranks as the doors to the dining chamber explode inward with a thunderous crash, sending clouds of dust and sand swirling through the air. The edges of the room blur momentarily, then settle like a ghostly veil over overturned chairs and scattered plates.

A rush of guards pour in, curved blades raised high, faces expressionless.

Lincoln had made his move, heedless of the consequences. He had attacked the king—another kingdom's king, in his own castle—while we sat at his table, and surely, we would pay for this.

I struggle to find my bearings as the chaos unfolds; every passing second filled with panic. Yet through the haze, my eyes catch Rami and King Tharion slipping into the shadows. Behind them, the guards descend in waves, a tide of steel and shouts, closing in on us as the two disappear from the room entirely.

Lincoln raises his hand, and the air shifts. A fierce rush of wind whips through the room, knocking guards off balance as his bow materializes out of nowhere.

How did he...

How did he do that?

"ARI! MOVE!" he bellows.

A sandlurker lunges at me, and my senses ignite all at once. I dip under the guard's clumsy assault, raising my dagger. His eyes lock with mine, revealing a mix of shock and pain, the moment my blade slits his throat.

A radiant yellow liquid spills from his wound, shimmering with an almost otherworldly beauty. The sight is mesmerizing and tragic all at once. My fingers tremble as the luminous fluid drips between them, and the guard collapses to the floor.

I freeze in place, disbelief coursing through me as the weight of what I've done sinks in.

I've never killed someone before.

I peer downward at the body crumpled at my feet, and I feel absolutely nothing.

I always thought the first time I took a life, it would destroy something in me, that I'd scream for what I've done until my voice was gone. I imagined blood on my hands would come with the crushing weight of becoming something I never wanted to be.

But now that it's done, I feel none of that.

I don't feel sorrow.

I don't feel regret.

I don't even feel the tiniest hint of remorse.

What I do feel is clarity.

But this is no grand awakening or heroic rise with destiny burning in my blood.

This feeling is something else entirely.

It isn't noble.

It isn't power.

It isn't a strength that shapes kingdoms or commands attention. But it does feel like control. And for someone like me—someone who's has nothing and been nothing—that illusion is dangerous.

A beastly emotion decided to break loose the moment my blade slid across the sandlurker's throat, something that had been caged inside me for far too long.

I curl my fingers tight around my dagger, eliminating any hint of weakness in my grip. I grasp the hem of my dress and slide the blade into the fabric. It parts smoothly beneath the sharp edge, slipping through like silk as I shorten it to a more manageable length.

I spin around, taking in my surroundings. Among the throng of guards, I catch sight of Lincoln. His skin is smeared with a vivid, terrifying red.

I gasp at the sheer amount of blood that covers him.

I don't understand. Lincoln is powerful...immortal, yet the sandlurkers have taken him down so easily. It's almost ironic how King Malvok reveres the powerful, as if they aren't just as capable of falling as the rest of us. A sandlurker raises his weapon, and I catch a glimpse of it. A green sheen glints along its edge just before it slides into Lincoln's thigh.

Poison. It has to be.

But there are multiple wounds. I examine Lincoln's body from afar, my gaze bouncing quickly from one injury to the next, noting the torn fabric, and the way he falters when he transfers his weight. His first hit must have been what slowed him down.

How long has the poison been working through him before I noticed it?

The question strikes me like a lightning bolt, igniting a fierce, inexplicable fury deep within me.

I will not allow anyone to take Lincoln from me. Not now. Not ever.

I've already lost too much in my life. I refuse to lose anything more.

My anger grows and rips through me, flooding every fiber of my being until it consumes me entirely.

"Each of you will pay with your lives!" I roar.

A dozen guards' attention snaps in my direction, their faces vacant, weapons raised.

Lincoln collapses, his knees hitting the floor with a crisp crack. One guard returns his focus to him, and my legs move on their own accord.

I leap into the air, using the table to launch myself forward. I land behind the sandlurker, my weapon lodging into his back.

Warm liquid splatters my face, and I grin, entirely lost in the feeling, knowing this is the exact moment everything falls apart.

CHAPTER 35

HER VOICE
LINCOLN

Darkness.

It's not peaceful like I always thought it would be when it was my time. I always assumed if I were to die—truly die and be taken from my misery—that it would be serene and silent.

But it wasn't.

The room rumbles around me, pulling me in and out of consciousness. Even as I drift further and further away to the edge of nothingness, I still hear everything, especially Ari and the commanding tone of her voice. It alone could revive me, like the sheer weight of it could bring me back to life. If I could move, I'd obey without question. I'd kill every sandlurker in the room for her if she asked.

I'm terrified of how far I'd go.

I feel Ari's hands on me. "You're fine" she whimpers. "Everything is fine."

Her voice reverberates with rage and grief, almost primal like a ravenous animal.

I don't know how much time has passed. Seconds.

Minutes. Hours. I'm not sure. The only thing tethering me to my body is the pain that laces through it and her voice.

I exhale heavily, eyes still shut. "Leave me," I rasp, barely getting the words out.

"I can't." Ari growls, resolve clear in her tone.

I cling desperately to the sound of her voice, though she only said two words. I don't understand why it draws me in. She should mean nothing to me, but it hooks me like a knife inching between my ribs.

I've thought about death more times than I can count; I always knew it would come, and I've accepted that it would.

I need to warn her.

I want to warn her.

I want to call out to her.

I need to tell her that I am not worth saving and that she should run, not from the sandlurkers or the king, but from me and my curse.

But darkness fully claims me before I have the chance to speak.

CHAPTER 36

INDEBTED

ARI

A dozen guards lie dead around me.

The once-grand dining chamber is deathly quiet now, save for Lincoln's ragged breathing. Gold platters and shattered glass litter the floor. A single goblet rolls in a slow circle near me—its wine spilled and mixed with blood in sluggish pools that spread across the mosaic stones under my feet. The long dining table has been split down the middle, and every chair has been over-turned. I stand in the center of the wreckage, gripping the edge of the splintered wood.

Blood streaks down my arms, staining me from wrist to forearms. It soaks into my dress, the scent of it overwhelm-ing, and yet I can't get away from it. It is everywhere, on the floor, on the walls, and most of all, on Lincoln.

I breathe in jaggedly, nearly gagging on the coppery air. My thoughts won't line up. Everything blurs at the edges. I try to make sense of it, try to *understand*, but all I remember is mayhem. Panic presses against the edge of my mind, threatening to break free.

I don't remember how it happened, how I did it. But every sandlurker is dead now because of me.

I glance at the far door, half-expecting more guards to come storming in, but the silence stretches. I stand among the dead, alive and untouched.

There's no time to dwell on what happened or piece everything together. Lincoln needs me. If he dies, then I killed them all for nothing.

I sprint toward his crippled body, the edges of the room blurring and fading with each step. The world narrows until it's just him and the fragile rise and fall of his chest.

I drop to my knees beside him, assessing his injuries.

Curved blades protrude from his shoulder and thigh, each rapidly gushing blood. I press my hand against one of his wounds, repeating over and over again that he is going to be okay.

That everything will be okay.

He groans under the pressure of my hand, but his eyes remain shut.

"You're fine." The words leave my mouth in a strangled whimper, caught somewhere between fear and hopelessness. "Everything is fine."

I'm stuck between wanting to help and not knowing how to. I survey the dining chamber, eyes darting from shattered furniture to blood-streaked walls, desperate to find anything that could offer a way out.

But there's nothing.

I've never felt so helpless in my life.

He's going to die from the poison before I have a chance to save him.

I whip my head suddenly to face the sound of footsteps closing in, every muscle snapping taut. I press harder into Lincoln's thigh and edge my body between him and whatever's coming. With my free hand, I snatch the last dagger strapped beneath Lincoln's sash.

Lilia steps into view from behind a pillar, her hands raised high in a gesture of peace. She moves cautiously, each step uncertain, keeping her figure partly shrouded in shadow. Her eyes flit over every surface in the chamber, taking in the fallen guards, the disarray, and me. She lifts her hand, and gestures for me to follow her.

My eyes narrow, lips curling into a snarl as suspicion rises like a flame inside me. Lilia's people eat mortals. Her people tried to kill us. And following her could result in both our deaths.

"Give me one good reason why I should trust you," I demand.

Lilia presses her hand to her chest, fingers trembling against her heart. Her lips part, struggling to form words. She slaps a hand over her mouth, more distressed by her inability to speak than anything else—the plea for me to understand etched plainly across her face.

She gestures for me to follow her again, more urgently this time.

I stall for a moment, every instinct shouting at me to stay on edge, but with Lincoln's body beneath me, his increasingly shallow breaths, and the blood that pools around him; I have no time to second-guess myself. I lock eyes with Lilia, searching for the betrayal she is bound to inflict on us, but find nothing. She appears torn herself, gaze filled with doubt. We're both risking more than we can afford to lose, and if there is a chance that Lincoln lives, I need to take it.

"Help me get him up!" I order her.

Lilia hurries to my side.

I rise just long enough to mount Lincoln's quiver to my

back, then drop back down beside him. He exhales heavily from the movement, eyes still shut.

"Leave me," Lincoln rasps, his voice no more than a whisper. A cold knot forms in my stomach at how fragile he sounds; the strength I knew in him now hanging by a thread.

"I can't," I growl.

I don't bother hiding the urgency in my tone or the direness of the situation.

I clutch Lincoln's arm, nodding to Lilia to do the same on the other side. After tremendous effort and a few close calls, we manage to hook them around our necks, and together, we haul his body toward what I can only pray is safety.

We leave the dining chamber and travel down a narrow corridor, each step feeling like a mile.

Lincoln is deadweight between us. I hate that I even have to use that word to describe him. His breath stutters often, each one weaker than the last. I flinch when a muted whimper slips past his lips.

We hastily move through the passage, turning right, then left, then right again. The darkness thickens around us, swallowing the walls and floor as we push deeper into the unfamiliar space.

A shape takes form ahead, outlined by a dull, pale light. It's distant at first, but it pulls my attention, nonetheless. I tighten my hold on Lincoln. His body hangs limp between us, and I use the glow to guide us forward through the choking dark.

I see it then, an entrance I would recognize anywhere.

A mining shaft.

It's old, but functional. A wooden cart rests on its rails, teetering at the edge of endless shadow.

We hurry toward it as fast as we can manage.

"Where does this lead?" I ask when we reach the mouth of the tunnel.

Lilia peers at me, the trust she's asking for written clearly across her face. Little does she know, trust has never come easily to me, and if only she knew how little I have left. Every time I place my faith in someone, it crumbles. However, right now, it's the only choice I have.

I meet her gaze with a guarded expression. "Help me lift him."

We carefully lift Lincoln into the cart first, doing our best to maneuver him without jostling the blades embedded in his body.

After he's settled, I face Lilia, seizing her wrist firmly. "I don't think you're trying to trick me." I like to think I have a good sense for it, after all the pretending I've done my whole life. "Thank you for showing me kindness. I'll be forever in your debt."

A sad smile flashes across her face, fleeting and tinged with pain.

I drop her hand and pull my body over the cracked wooden frame of the cart. I sit down between Lincoln's legs, tucking my body in close. Lilia throws our belongings from our rooms onto us. She must have grabbed them the moment everything started to fall apart. But how did she know?

I jerk my head to face her. "Why?" I demand. "Why are you helping us?"

Lilia stays silent for a long moment, her face shifting through caution, and a softer, unspoken emotion. She opens her mouth to speak, and this time, words fully form. "For a better future," she croaks, voice frayed at the edges.

It's the first time I've ever heard her speak, and the

sound shatters me. I barely have time to register it before she pushes us into the tunnel.

"I'll come back for you!" I shout, but my voice is overpowered by wheels clattering harshly against rusted metal rails. Each jolt of the old wooden cart shakes us as we descend into darkness.

I lean back, resting my head against Lincoln's chest, seeking a small measure of comfort. My fingers move intentionally over the veins in his arm, tracing the faint pulse beneath my touch, eager to know if the blood still flows.

The cart sways with the curve of the track for what feels like hours before the howling wind finally dies down. We burst out of the tunnel and skid to a stop. I squint, blinking rapidly to adjust to the sudden change.

Tall trees sway overhead, their branches weaving together to form a natural canopy above the patch of overgrown grass where our cart now rests in the moonlight. Lincoln's throat makes a wet, unsettling gurgle behind me, reminding me that we are running out of time.

I haul myself out of the cart, clutching it for support. "Please help me! Anyone, please! I need help!" I plead repeatedly. I don't even know why I'm yelling or who I'm yelling at, only that the hopelessness inside me won't let me stop. I reach over and grip Lincoln's face between my hands, tears swelling in my eyes. He's slipping away right in front of me, and I am running out of time to save him.

"I need you, goddammit." I rest my forehead against his, my body convulsing from sobs. "You cannot die."

My tears fall freely now, tracing lines down his cheeks, and I wish I could pour all my fear and rage into the space between us, hoping it could somehow make him wake. I press my face closer, inhaling his cinnamon scent. "Please, wake up."

A musical hum drifts toward me, barely louder than a whisper.

I blink tears away, angling my body in the direction of the sound, exhausted to the point that I don't even lift a weapon.

An orb of light floats between trees, like a firefly in the night, inching closer to me. The circular shape soon takes the form of a small woman—her cheeks flushed with a pink glow. Wings flutter behind her in swift bursts, catching the moonlight like shards of shimmering glass. She drifts gracefully in the breeze, her tiny form no larger than the length of my arm.

"I can help you," she coos in a clear, melodic voice.

I stare at her in awe as an overwhelming feeling washes over me, settling deep in my gut.

I can't explain it, but I believe with everything in me that she will save Lincoln—her voice carries a truth I can't ignore.

I wonder if this is what it feels like for others.

CHAPTER 37

JUNIA

ARI

Lincoln has been unconscious for three days.

His pulse is the only thing holding me together, a fragile anchor preventing me from sinking completely. Still, worry tightens its grip on me with every passing second that Lincoln remains unresponsive, consuming my thoughts and twisting them into fear. I find myself thinking that maybe he won't wake at all.

Twice today, I've opened the windows, hoping the breeze might coax Lincoln back to life. Yet, he still lies unmoving.

His motionless body haunts me in my sleep, depriving me of the rest that I so desperately need.

I sit by his bedside, just as I did yesterday, and the day before that. My mind doesn't allow me to focus on anything but him, silent, on the narrow bed that's too small to fit his massive frame.

I haven't seen him stir an inch. Not since the fairies drew the poison from his blood that coated the tips of the sand-lurker's weapons. They called it ebonkiss; a clever name for something so savage. It's a common poison sandlurkers are known to use. It first shuts down the nervous system, then enters the bloodstream until the person's soul separates from their body. It's fatal for anyone who lacks immortality.

I want to reach out, to hold Lincoln's hand and whisper that everything's going to be okay, even if I don't know if that's true.

I cautiously reach forward and trace the edge of Lincoln's glove with my finger. When we first arrived, the fairies warned me never to remove them. I still don't understand what could be so dangerous that his gloves must stay on, even with him on the brink of death.

The only possible explanation is that Lincoln is keeping something from me. And the real question is just how deeply is his secret buried?

I want to trust him, I fear a part of me already does, but trust doesn't erase the fact that he isn't telling me the whole truth, and I'm starting to wonder why.

I peek out the window, taking in the sight of the fairy kingdom of Junia sparkling like a dream I'm struggling to believe is real.

The skies are different here, painted with a soft lavender hue, as if stuck in a permanent dusk.

Once we crossed the border of the kingdom, everything changed. The air itself seemed charged with magic, as if the land was woven in an enchantment—not like a ward that keeps the Noctharn Kingdom locked away, but almost like a spell that allows Junia to stay in a constant state of peace.

The fairies welcomed us with open arms, lending a helping hand in our time of need. They are said to be able to heal anyone. But if Lincoln doesn't pull through, it will all be for nothing.

I lean forward, resting my elbows on the corner of his bed. I've had more than enough time to study every crevice and dip of Lincoln's face over the past few days.

A small scar rests atop his lip, invisible unless you lean in close. His chin is slightly squared, framed by stubble that dusts his jaw, and between his brows, faint lines crease into a permanent scowl, softened only by the long black lashes that fan around his eyes.

I skim my fingers lightly across his forehead, drawing in an uneven breath. "You left me here all alone," I murmur. "I don't want to be alone."

Because being alone is more than I can handle right now, it's too much. I can't afford to lose another person on this quest. Especially not him, and especially not after losing Ella. We have uncovered too many secrets for it to end like this. Countless times, he's saved me, yet I've barely returned the favor.

I lift myself upright and move away from Lincoln. I leave him frozen in place and step into the hall.

The cottage was made for small bodies, yet it never feels cramped. The rounded corners and arched doorways curve so naturally that walking through them feels like moving inside a living tree. I run my fingers down the smooth bark of the walls, following the threads of green that spiral through the wood like veins, flowing beneath my fingertips. I let them guide me until the hallway expands into a kitchen.

Shelves hover in midair, never quite touching the walls. The jars on them are filled with things I've never seen before. Dried blossoms, twigs of gold, and liquids that shift color depending on the angle you are looking at them.

I linger in the archway, watching Evie flutter around the kitchen. She saved us that night, the night the sandlurkers almost killed us both. I will forever owe her and Lilia a debt, one I still don't know how to repay.

Evie removes a steaming kettle from the stove. "I'm

working on tea for him. He should be waking up any day now."

I smile, letting my gratitude show. "Thank you."

Evie sets the kettle down and floats toward me, her long brown hair swaying with the movement.

The slight curve of my lips falters as she approaches.

She places a small hand on my cheek. "It has been my honor to help you."

Her words land heavily in my chest, leaving a lump in my throat. "I am not honorable nor valiant. I need to do more."

Evie's eyes soften. "You will."

I let out a long breath, my shoulder sagging with the exhale.

Evie saved Lincoln with her healing abilities—a righteous gift from Althara. I, on the other hand, am a simple mortal who isn't worthy of being blessed with anything. Everyone I care about either disappears or dies. Then there's Noah, to whom I am more of a burden than anything. And I still can't wrap my head around the fact that I murdered so many.

My heart aches and hardens at the thought.

I run my hand through my hair, fidgeting with my barrette, eager to change the subject.

"What do you know about my king?"

Evie's hand drops from my face, terror flickering in her hazel eyes. She drifts back to the tea she was making. "Malvok is ruthless, with ambitions to conquer the continent," she says, straining the concoction into a cup. "He spreads his wards further around this time each year."

I nod. "Soulfire collection week."

"Yes, and one day, we'll all be completely pushed off the land."

Anger laces through me. "No one has tried to stop him? The King of Zalquar said that there could be another soulfire mine. Have you heard anything about it? Can't Althara help?"

Evie shakes her head. "Althara can't help. She doesn't know what's going on."

"How is that possible? She is our God. She is supposed to protect us."

"The wards block everything, not just us. No one can look in and see what Noctharn is up to, not even Althara."

"But the binding ritual," I mutter.

Evie's lips press into a thin line. "The binding ritual draws on Althara's power stored within the earth's center. Her supply is endless, and there is no need for her to worry with the rituals still taking place. Noctharn's heir is our only hope."

I furrow my brows. "How will they stop him?"

"They will know what to do when the time comes."

I rock back on the balls of my feet, suddenly feeling overwhelmed. Evie has a lot of faith in someone who doesn't want to be found.

I walk to the center table in the room and pick up the pitcher resting on it. I pour myself a glass of water. "And you're sure the king's heir has never traveled through here?"

"No, there isn't much safety for them in Junia. Our territory is too small, and therefore, our housing is limited. It's not the best place to hide, especially one on the run, which is why I hope Lincoln wakes soon so you can get on with your quest." Evie picks up Lincoln's cup of finished tea as I bring my glass of water to my lips. "Not that I don't enjoy your company," she smiles. "But you are not safe here."

My eyes roam across the room, and I nod my head in agreement. No eldarim or mortal would go unseen here.

Evie floats by me, holding the tea in her hand, heading down the hall toward Lincoln's room.

I follow close behind, praying that he wakes soon.

Sunlight filters through the window, casting delicate strands across the wooden floor, while Lincoln lies in the bed, still wounded but healing.

I've waited and waited, counted each shallow breath, but I can't sit idle any longer. The days are ticking by, and we are no closer to locating the heir than we were before. I need to figure out what information other fairies might have.

I lean forward and press a hand to Lincoln's forehead. It's a part of my routine now, and each day his skin feels warmer against it.

I quickly dress, strapping on my boots and slinging my bag over my shoulder. I cross the room and pick up Lincoln's bow and quiver resting by the door.

"I'll be back later," I say, unsure if he can even hear me. "Maybe I'll have some good news to share."

I step into the hall, marching down it, and slip out the front door without another word.

After being cooped up for the past few days, it takes my eyes a couple of minutes to adjust to the light.

I head into Junia, following the narrow dirt path that winds from the cottage. I inhale the fresh air. It's the first real breath I've had in what feels like forever. Wild grass borders the path, littered with glowing mushrooms and morning mist.

The trees part, revealing glimpses of the village rooftops, each blanketed in soft moss. Magic clings to Junia, a constant reminder that the impossible exists. I can't help but smile at the thought. I sweep my hands through a row of vibrant flowers, brushing the silky petals with my fingertips. A subtle bounce lifts my steps, each one lighter than before, and for a fleeting moment, I nearly break into a skip like a fool.

I shake my head and keep walking toward the village, slower than before, savoring the euphoria the forest brings.

"Quit acting like a damn idiot," a man hisses. "We have to go."

The sound of the voice stops me in my tracks.

"We don't know what's there!" someone counters.

I scan my surroundings, alert to everything. The path I follow continues toward the village that's just within reach, but the voices come from the left, where the forest is denser, and vines grow thick and tangled.

"I don't plan to die because of your stupidity," the first man yells.

I tiptoe to the path's edge, quietly stepping into the forest. I fight through the ferns, their pointed fronds tugging at me. There's no trail to follow, just earth covered by roots and spongy dirt.

"You'll die anyway if I find the heir and you don't!" the other man shouts.

My breath hitches, a tightness gripping my throat. I found participants of the king's quest, so close to where Lincoln and I have been safely residing.

I crouch low behind dense brush, using it for cover. Silently, I inch toward the voices.

Just a few paces ahead, two eldarim stand face to face, each unnaturally tall with bodies built like a fortress. Broad shoulders and muscular arms flex under tight compression shirts, their very presence commanding power.

I recognize them from the king's throne room. I memorized every participant's face just in case.

"We are going to the void, and that's final," one of the eldarim says, shoving the other in the chest.

The man stumbles back, eyes flaring from the assault.

I reach over my shoulder, fingers curling around Lincoln's bow.

The eldarim lunges forward, attacking again, snarling something muffled under his breath. At the last second, the other one sidesteps, his movement sending a rush of air crashing into his assailant's chest.

I press my hand over my mouth to hide my gasp.

An elemental bender. An air one at that.

The other man howls in rage, stumbling backwards. In the blink of an eye, his fist connects with the air wielder's face, drawing him into a chokehold.

A blitz. I've never seen a blitz move in real life. A speed so unnatural, you are already dead before you can realize what or who attacked you.

I nock Lincoln's bow with ease, eyeing them down the length of an arrow. I will forever be grateful for the various weapon training I received from Raven. I will have to thank her next time I see her. If I shoot now, I could hit them both in the heart with one shot—a perilous attack, especially when I have no power to help me succeed if I fail.

The blitz squeezes his arm tighter around the air wielder's neck. "The witch kingdom is our only option. Why would the heir go anywhere else? Why do you think the area is voided out on the map?"

The air wielder flails in a fit of fury, flinging his fists behind him, but misses the blitz entirely. "Let me go," he growls.

"No," the blitz snarls in rage. "Use your worthless brain a

little bit; the king and his men haven't ventured to that land yet. The answer is there, and we will find it."

The voided area on the map...I recall how easy it was to overlook it when trying to figure out where to go next. It could be a trick of the mind, or the answer was right in front of us all along. But if witches live there, how does the king not know? And how do they know?

Snap. My gaze drops to my feet when a twig lies crunched beneath one of them.

I tilt my chin back up, and both men's eyes meet mine. I have seconds before I am dead. One second before the blitz is on top of me, and one second before the air is pulled from my lungs.

I have no time to think, only act. "Stop!" I command them.

They freeze, caught off guard, giving me the split second I need to aim Lincoln's arrow and release it. It whistles through the branches and lands in the air wielder's chest. The blitz tries to move but can't, as if stuck in a trance. I nock another arrow and send it flying. It hits its mark, lodging in his throat.

I retreat behind the base of the tree, the bow trembling in my grip. It drops to the ground, and I claw my hands through my hair, pulling hard at the strands. My scalp screams in agony under the strain. I clench the strands tighter, welcoming the pain.

It's proof I'm alive, though remorse is nowhere to be found.

My heart doesn't grieve for the lives I just took. If anything, it grows colder.

CHAPTER 38

NO TEARS LEFT

ARI

The whole day has slipped away; the once-lavender sky is now a deep, shadowy purple.

I had only meant to sit down for a moment, but I ended up lingering far longer than planned, perched on a weathered boulder tucked deep within the forest. The stillness around me made it easy to lose track of time.

Hours have passed since I covered the eldarim's bodies with branches and large leaves, not even bothering to bury them beneath the earth. My fingers bear the stains of dried blood from pulling the arrows free from them, a reminder that I haven't washed away. I find myself staring at my hands, searching for the moment when the reality of what I've done will finally settle in. Yet, it never comes; even when I replay the moment over and over again in my head, praying for any emotion to break through, to grab hold of me and shake me awake.

But, instead of relief, there's only a growing emptiness inside me. A coldness I can't escape, and the realization that perhaps this is who I've always been. And that haunts me more than anything else.

I pull a worn-down photo out of a hidden fold in my bag and rub my fingers over the faces. Blonde hair softly frames Mama's warm, radiant skin—her smile full of happiness, like all of ours in that moment. I stand between my caretakers, Silas's hand resting on my shoulder. He stands tall, a wide smile lighting up his features, his dark hair, like mine, perfectly combed.

Then there's me, so young and completely unaware of the challenges life would bring.

My chest constricts, the only emotion I've truly felt all day.

If I had had an easier childhood, I would have turned out differently. I would be a kinder person, one who cries when others are hurt. I would have become someone who hesitated before releasing an arrow, not someone who releases it without a second thought. Unfortunately, that person will never exist.

I tuck the photo back in my bag and pull out another.

My eyes roam over Ella's face, memorizing her features for fear I might forget them one day. The ache of missing her lingers within me, and I can't help but pity Myke, who waits patiently for her to return home.

I slide the photo back into my bag and pull out the map.

I study the blurred-out portion, a fierce instinct telling me that the answer I seek is hiding within it. The king's heir must be in the witch kingdom, and I am determined to find them, no matter the cost.

Hunger twists in my gut, reminding me that I haven't eaten since dawn. I push myself up from the boulder, my legs stiff from sitting in a tight ball for so long. I meticulously fold the map back up and slide it into my pocket.

I follow the path I took into the forest to head back out, using my old bootprints to guide me. Each step I take feels like lead as I walk down the dirt path toward Evie's cottage.

I pull the wooden door open, crouching slightly to fit through the frame.

"Ari! Just in time! Dinner is almost done!" Evie practically sings, her voice bright with excitement.

I place my belongings by the front door and kick off my boots. The warm, inviting smell of a home-cooked meal fills the air, causing my stomach to rumble despite everything else on my mind.

Evie flutters across the room, placing steaming rolls on the table, eyeing me.

I tuck my hands behind my back to hide the blood that covers them.

"Are you okay?" She frowns. "You look like you've seen a ghost."

I examine the table, and my breath catches in my throat. "Why are there three place settings?" I ask, ignoring her prior questions altogether. "Are we expecting a guest?"

"Lincoln! He's up!" Evie squeals.

I spin on my heels, my legs moving at their own free will. "You could have led with that!" I shout, running down the hall.

I reach the bedroom door and slam it open.

Golden eyes find mine, still heavy with sleep but clear enough to have anticipated the moment I would step into the room.

"You're up," I say, trying to keep my voice from cracking. I sink into the chair at Lincoln's bedside, tears spilling over and streaming down my face uncontrollably. "I thought I lost you."

Lincoln lifts his hand, brushing a tear from my cheek. The coolness of his leather glove against my skin sends a shiver down my spine. He inspects me, eyes roaming over every line and curve of me. I return the gesture, studying him just as carefully. His attention shifts downward, brows creasing, lingering on my soiled clothes. I tuck my fingers into the folds of my shirt, trying to hide the bloodstains that mar them. If he notices, he doesn't mention it.

Lincoln adjusts himself into a sitting position, his large body leaning back against the bed frame. "What happened? Evie filled me in on where we are, but I don't remember how we got here."

I sink back in my chair. "You nearly died. The sand-lurkers had poison on their weapons. It consumed your whole body at one point. You," I exhale jaggedly. "You almost didn't make it. I thought maybe I lost you, too. But Lilia saved us, helped us escape through an old mining shaft. And Evie was able to remove all the poison from your blood." And I did nothing, powerless amongst the powerful, but I leave that part out.

"You stayed," he rasps. "I heard you. While everything was dark, your voice was like a tether. It was the only thing I could hear."

I swallow hard, forcing myself to meet his gaze. His eyes are calm but weighted, filled with a fierce protectiveness that leaves me feeling exposed and vulnerable.

"I don't want to be alone anymore," I admit, my voice shaking from the truth in my words. If only he understood the burden I carry—the weight of what I've done and what I'm about to do.

Lincoln's eyes never waver from mine with a tenderness that makes me blush, and I realize then that he is staring at me longer than he should, longer than he ever has.

"Thank you for saving my life," he says, extinguishing

any flicker of warmth that had remained untouched within me.

I force a smile, but it never fully reaches my tear-filled eyes.

It wasn't me who saved Lincoln's life; it was everyone else. He'll realize his mistake soon enough.

There's so much I want to say to him, so many things tangled in my mind, waiting for the right moment to come out. So much I need him to understand. But that moment isn't now. There will be time for all of that later. There's still a few more things I need to do first.

"Dinner's done!" Evie's voice rings, echoing down the hall.

I reach for Lincoln's hand and give it a small squeeze. "Let's eat," I whisper.

CHAPTER 39

CURSED

ARI

It's not about his torso.

Let's just start there, so we're clear. Because yes, Lincoln is shirtless *again*. And yes, it's hot out. And *yes*, his torso looks like it was carved by someone with emotional issues and a chisel obsession. But that's not the point. I'm not going to dwell on the way his shoulders look in the sunlight, or how the sweat glides down the center of his back like it has somewhere important to be.

That would be stupid.

Besides, it's not about *that*. It's about how calculated Lincoln is. The shirtlessness? It's a tactic. A distraction. But I'm taking notes, I'm watching the way his hands twist in his gloves, and the way he constantly fiddles with the straps on them.

Lincoln has a secret, and I am determined to figure it out. And sure, sometimes I notice how perfect he is in the process. I'll let it slide for now, but only because we're traveling along the border of the desert, and it is, in fact, excessively hot.

Our new enemies are just in arm's reach. Not out of

ignorance, unfortunately, it is the fastest route. Evie helped us map out the best path to the kingdom by the water, home to the selkith—people of both land and sea. She knows the continent better than we do; every territory and its people. So now, we walk a delicate dance along the border of Zalquar. One wrong turn could alert the sandlurkers that we are here, and Lincoln's bronzed skin isn't helping.

Fortunately for me, convincing Lincoln to go to Thalassara wasn't difficult. Ever since he woke up, he's been extremely cooperative and maybe even a tad bit overprotective.

I trust Lincoln to an extent, but not enough to divulge my whole plan to him about the witch kingdom, so I let him believe we're on the same page. But my real plan lies deeper.

I need to win this quest, which he knows, and when the time comes, I'll act alone. Althara's wrath will never come. If she hasn't been able to figure out what is happening in Noctharn, then she surely isn't paying attention, especially keeping tabs on a deal between a valorguard and a mortal.

So until then, Lincoln will play his part, and I'll keep my cards close because, as much as I never want to be alone again, deep down, I know I always will be. It is a depressing thought. One, I keep to myself, even when I vocalize the opposite. Not because I want my life this way, but because it's the inevitable truth.

The sun begins to set in the distance, slipping leisurely behind the dunes. "We should stop for the night," I decide, noting the instant shift in the air. The heat we've hiked through all day is fading fast, causing my sweat-soaked shirt to dry rapidly.

Lincoln comes to a halt in front of me. "Probably for the best." He looks around, running his hand through his damp hair. "I'll start hunting for something to eat."

With a whoosh, his body transforms. He launches into the sky, wings beating powerfully as he soars overhead.

I push my way through dense underbrush. Gnarled roots twist beneath my boots, threatening to trip me at every step as the last light of day slices through the leafy canopy in fractured beams. I drop my bag beside a large tree trunk, far enough from the path we followed to stay hidden.

I peel my shirt off and drape it over a low branch to dry. Fumbling in my bag, I pull out a cloth Evie gave me and dampen it with a little bit of water from my canteen. I guide the fabric up my arm, savoring the relief it brings.

"May I?"

I jump, taken by surprise. Muttering a vulgar curse, I glance over my shoulder. "May you what?"

Lincoln's gaze fixes on a point between my shoulder blades, eyes blazing with a hunger that makes my skin prickle. He points to the cloth in my hand. "Help you," he whispers.

I spin to face him fully. "I've got it," I reply unsteadily, the tremor in my voice betraying me.

Lincoln takes a step forward, closing the distance between us. "I know," he croaks. He clears his throat before speaking again. "But it's okay to let others take care of you for once."

His words hit me like a punch to the gut.

Lincoln doesn't understand. He will never understand. No one ever does. Help never comes for me when I need it most, and when it does—when it stares me right in the face, the damage is already done.

"If I don't do it—" My voice fails me. I inhale deeply, feeling flustered. "I've learned a long time ago that no one is going to catch me if I fall."

Because no one ever did. I've caught myself for as long as

I can remember. Noah tried, and I applaud him for doing so, but he never truly understood my pain. He never tried to. He always turned a blind eye, masked under a handsome smile, but laughing through the pain doesn't make it go away.

I drop my gaze to the ground.

But Lincoln tilts my chin back up just as fast. "I want to be the one to catch you," he confesses. "Let me catch you."

I see the longing and care in his stare, like a plea buried deep within him, as if Lincoln has been waiting for this moment his whole life. But I also see the terror in his eyes, the closeness in this moment.

I extend the cloth toward him. "Okay."

Lincoln pulls off one glove, keeping his exposed hand far away from me, and grabs the cloth with his other.

I hesitate, but put my back to him, my body tensing as I brace for contact. Lincoln's hand, free from constraint and fiery beneath the fabric, slides over my shoulders. He wipes the sweat pooling there, tracing a slow path down my spine. The thin cloth catches on his calloused hand, scraping my skin with each pass.

I have a feeling that whatever game we are playing is a deadly one, but I lean into his touch anyway, savoring the rare feeling of someone taking care of me.

A firm gloved hand grips my waist, whirling me around with effortless grace, on his part, not mine. I stumble forward, using his chest to balance myself.

We're inches from each other, his parted lips drawing my attention, every shared breath lingering between us.

I wonder what it would feel like to press my lips to his—would they be as soft as they look?

Lincoln's hand moves unhurriedly over the plane of my stomach, hovering over the snake scar that now mars my skin, his free hand digging into my waist a little harder. After a breath, the cloth resumes its path upward between my breasts and over the wrapping that holds them, leaving goosebumps in its wake before landing at the base of my neck.

I look up at him, a sudden flush coloring my cheeks. He's so close that his sweet cinnamon scent maddeningly wraps around me. The urge to trail my hands down his body rises in me, and I find myself acting on it unintentionally. I trail my fingertips across his chest in lazy circles.

A feral expression washes over him at the contact, like a beast holding back with all their restraint.

Lincoln takes a step back, leaving the air between us thick with tension. I drop my hand to my side, trying to hide the embarrassment that wells up inside me unexpectedly. His eyes flicker with a confusing mix of longing and uncertainty, the two emotions fighting beneath the surface before he finally drops his gaze to the ground.

"Have your eyes always been that green?" Lincoln asks.

"Yes," I murmur. "They have been the same color since I was born."

I reach for him, my hand landing on his forearm. He shivers at the touch. "Lincoln," I say softly. "Please look at me."

He shakes his head, pulling his glove back on and securing it. "I don't want to."

Lincoln's words shatter me. Since Junia, he has been peering into my eyes at me longer than he used to. I don't understand how or why, but he has, and now he is choosing not to.

I clear my throat to speak, but he beats me to it.

"Rabbit for dinner," Lincoln murmurs, turning away from me. "I'll get the fire started."

My mind fractures, crushed by pain and rejection as he walks away, more confused than I've ever been in my life.

The fire roars, filling the night with orange flames and the scent of burning wood. I gnaw on the tough, stringy rabbit meat—an animal I've eaten more of on this quest than I'd like to admit.

"Where did you get that?" Lincoln asks.

"Huh?" I answer in a daze.

"The barrette in your hair that you have been nervously fidgeting with, sunshine."

I drop my hand instantly. I didn't realize I was twisting it between my fingers. "I'm shocked you know what a barrette is."

"I do have a sister," he divulges nonchalantly.

"Really?" I arch an eyebrow, surprised that he's willingly sharing something about himself for once. "How old is she?"

Lincoln shakes his head, wagging a rabbit bone in front of my face. "Answer my question first."

I cross my arms, pressing my lips into a thin line. "Is that an order?"

"No." A sly grin spreads across his face. "But I'm happy to go back to not talking. Then I won't be able to give you an order, and we'll both be happy."

I glare at him. "Fuck you."

Lincoln chuckles, clearly enjoying himself.

I roll my eyes, weighing my pride against the pull of curiosity. The hurt from before still prickles at the edges, but I give in, nonetheless.

"I found it," I say, answering him. "One day, when I was

playing by the Eidolon Forest. It was just there, sitting in a pile of grass." I unclip it from my hair and flip it over in my hand. "I suspect I was only allowed to keep it because it is cursed."

Lincoln's brows furrow. "What do you mean by cursed?"

"No one can touch it but me." I offer it to him, palm up. "Here, try to hold it, without your gloves."

"Place it on the ground."

I eye him suspiciously but oblige. I still have so many unanswered questions.

Lincoln unclasps a glove, slender fingers springing free. "So, you do know how to follow orders," he chides.

I grin at him, delighted by the torment he's about to endure. "Go on, touch it."

Lincoln extends a finger and skims it across the snake's scales. "Shit!" he hisses, pulling his hand back. "What the hell is that thing?"

I burst out laughing. That's what he gets for being an asshole. Lincoln scowls at me, cradling his hand, causing me to laugh even harder.

I grab a chunk of my hair and secure the barrette back in place. "I don't know what it is, but it's pretty and the one thing that's never been taken from me."

"But Finley was able to touch—"

I stop him, all amusement gone at the mention of Ella's killer. "I've thought long and hard about that. The only explanation I could come up with is that since Finley is a fire wielder, he can't feel the barrette burning him."

"Hmmm," Lincoln drones, dragging out the sound. He examines his finger for a moment, then brings it to his mouth.

I turn my attention elsewhere, forcing myself to focus on anything besides his mouth and the finger between his lips.

"I still don't understand the gloves. Your hands look normal to me, if that is what you're concerned about."

Lincoln freezes mid-movement. "I am cursed, too."

I stare at him in disbelief, expecting a joke that never comes. "You are...cursed?"

"Yes," he quips. "And that is all you need to know."

All I need to know? If my traveling partner is cursed, I surely should know. I open my mouth to fire questions off, but he shakes his head.

"Your sister?" I ask instead. "You never said how old she is."

"Twenty-two."

"Is she joining the valorguard as well?"

Lincoln lets out a chilling bark of laughter. "She couldn't even if she wanted to. Women aren't allowed in the valorguard."

"They aren't?" I ask.

Lincoln regards me with an expression full of skepticism. "The king banned all women from joining decades ago. Eldarim women have taken a more traditional position within society."

"Even if they have power?"

Lincoln bites into a piece of rabbit. "Even with power."

The king's inhumanity runs deeper than I ever imagined.

I push my food aside, losing my appetite. "Will your sister inherit similar powers as you?"

"No. My sister is dead, just like the rest of my family."

My face pales. Lincoln's whole family? *Dead?* I stare at him, suddenly seeing him anew. My heart breaks for the man before me. He's alone. Truly alone—more than I am, more than I ever thought possible.

I have so many questions, but words fail me as I struggle

to find something to say. I'm no stranger to pain, but I've never been good at soothing it in others. Still, I breathe out, "I'm sorry," barely more than a whisper, knowing it's all I can offer.

Lincoln rises abruptly. "The Queen of Noctharn and the heir are to blame. I will get my revenge soon enough."

I look up at him, confused. "I'm not sure I understand."

"You don't have to," he grumbles. He kicks dirt onto the fire, sending sparks scattering into the dark. "It's late."

Lincoln cuts the conversation short before I can even process anything and respond. He moves a few feet away, putting space between us, making his bed as if nothing had happened. His moods shift so fast I can barely follow, and part of me longs to understand him, even as another part knows it's best to retreat.

I lie down where I am, keeping my eyes locked on him. I wrap my spare shirt around my shoulders, using it as a blanket. My fingers fumble with the fabric as I try to piece together my racing thoughts, wishing that I could predict him even a little.

I know how Lincoln's father died, everyone does, but I never learned about his mother or his sister. So much about him remains a mystery, and it unsettles me. One way or another, though, the truth always comes out, and if he doesn't wish to tell me, I will uncover it myself.

A shiver runs down my spine, my shirt doing nothing to protect me from the cool air.

"Lincoln?"

I see the outline of him shift, turning toward my voice.

"Yes?"

"I'm cold," I admit, unsure if it was wise to say.

Lincoln lifts himself, picking up whatever he was using to keep himself warm. His feet shuffle across the dirt, coming to a stop in front of me. After a brief pause—a silent struggle he clearly lost—he lies down next to me and pulls me against his chest.

His limbs wrap around me like a cocoon, and I nestle into his body. "Thank you," I breathe.

My eyelids grow heavy and close, sleep pulling me under in an instant.

CHAPTER 40

PUT IT BACK

ARI

A familiar confined space surrounds me. The air is stale and damp, filled with the scent of earth and decay. It wraps around me like an unwelcome memory I can't outrun, catching in my throat and refusing to let go.

I know this place, far too well.

I've spent countless birthdays down here. I could walk these tunnels with a blindfold if I wanted, every narrow crevice barely wide enough to pass through, every warped beam overhead threatening to collapse and entomb me. I know it all by heart. But what I don't know is how I got here or when I returned to Lumin.

I run my hand along the jagged wall as I wander deeper into the mine. The low ceilings press down, their weight almost physical. After so long away, I nearly forgot how claustrophobic this place can feel.

The mine has always been a haunted place, not by ghosts, but by the shadows of your darkest memories. The ones you bury deep, the moments you never speak of, and the cruelty endured at the hands of fellow miners.

Once you've been down here, it becomes a part of you, no matter how far you go.

I halt in my tracks, ears straining for any sign of life. Others are down here—I can hear the distant clatter of chisels, and the soft shuffle of boots on dirt. A footstep sounds nearby, closer than the rest. I spin on my heel, heart pounding, eyes scanning the shadows.

I exhale. *Nothing is there.* Nothing that I can see, and the noise I thought I heard is now gone.

I move deeper into the tunnels, pressing forward. The path turns in an unfamiliar way, catching me off guard. That should have been a right turn, not a left.

I stop in front of an old shaft, long forgotten. It collapsed years ago, trapping a dozen miners inside. I'll never forget that day. It was supposed to be me in there, but I never showed up for my shift. I felt unwell the night before from a meal Noah had prepared for me. The mushrooms he used from the Eidolon Forest never settled right in my stomach. I vomited the night away well into the morning. He took care of me the entire time.

His lousy cooking saved my life.

Now the rubble that once fell is cleared, and the shaft is wide open, breathing cold air.

I step in cautiously, all the light in the tunnel suddenly disappearing. A dark cloak of shadows shifts on my right side, twisting unnaturally up the walls like they have a life of their own. They rush at me and curl around my ankles, threatening to hold me in place.

My pulse quickens, pounding in my ears. I kick my legs free and back away, moving down the path I came, stumbling over my feet.

But no matter how fast I go, the shadows close in on me at a tantalizing pace.

They fall upon me, transforming into the shape of a man. He closes the space between us, and I recognize him immediately.

"No!" I scream. "NO! NO! NO!" A sob rakes through my body as the cold tendrils grip my throat.

"Finally," his deep voice rumbles.

My eyes fling open, my body paralyzed by the ice that has settled into my bones.

I am alive. It was only a dream. An awful, awful dream.

I stare up at the night sky, counting the stars, relieved that I'm not in the soulfire mine. I never want to go back. I've grown quite fond of my freedom.

A soft scrape of material captures my focus.

My eyes snap toward the sound.

Lincoln's body crouches low, his back angled away from me.

I realize now how cold I feel, not from the aftermath of the icy shadows that wrapped around me in my dream, but from the lack of heat without Lincoln's body close to mine.

I open my mouth to ask him to come back to sleep but snap it shut just as fast.

His hand brushes over the fabric of my bag as if he's debating whether or not he should go through it.

I'm frozen, my eyes fixed on him, following every movement he makes.

Lincoln tactically unzips my bag without a sound, pulling out a worn photo creased from years of handling. His fingers hover over the image of my family, analyzing it. His eyes, usually guarded, turn soft for the briefest moment in the moonlight, but it's gone as quickly as it appeared.

His gaze shifts to where I lie.

Shit. I slam my eyelids shut.

"He doesn't know I'm awake," I whisper, steadying my breath to mimic sleep.

Moments pass before I open my eyes again, peeking through my eyelashes, at the faint sound of Lincoln digging in my bag once more.

He goes through my belongings but comes up with nothing of interest—spare clothing, a photo of Ella, one of Noah, and some weapons. Nothing worth sneaking around in the middle of the night for. He closes my bag shut, and at the same time, his fingers swoop low, stabilizing it from shifting against the dirt.

I swallow roughly, and he stops mid-movement, confusion washing over his features. He glides his fingers over the lower planes of my bag.

Lincoln stops his descent, applying pressure to the fabric with his fingertips. He unsheathes a dagger and makes a microscopic cut, ripping the small seams I had sewn.

Adrenaline surges through me, and I feel like I'm about to be sick. Lincoln will never trust me after this.

He pulls out an object and places it in his palm. Its green hue catches in the moonlight, and I flutter my eyelashes nervously.

I stare at the soulfire resting in his hand, every fiber in my body screaming at me to say something, to ask Lincoln what he's doing, but my voice catches in my throat.

Put it back. Put it back. Put it back. I inwardly scream, willing Lincoln to return my soulfire.

I have meticulously stolen the smallest quantity of the crystal over the years I spent in the mines, just enough that no one has noticed. I chose to steal from the king right under his nose, in retaliation for all the pain and suffering he has put us through.

It is why I never leave my bag behind. I was scared that

Silas would find it and report me. I always told myself that I carried it everywhere because I didn't want Silas to steal my gilds. That never stopped him, though. Deep down, I never left it behind because I didn't want anyone to figure out what I've done. No one in Noctharn is allowed to own soulfire unless they are the king. I would be executed on the spot, like the last person who did.

I think of that day often. I stole soulfire the same shift he did, but the miner didn't hide it well. He stole a significant amount in one day. I stole a minuscule amount over the years, taking specs and dust particles to form my crystal. Valorguards killed the man and left his body to rot in front of the mines until the vultures picked his body clean. The smell was horrendous for weeks.

I would face the same fate if I were ever caught.

"Put the soulfire back, and come here," I whisper the words, barely louder than the wind itself, commanding Lincoln to listen.

As if pulled from a trance, he rolls the crystal in his palm one last time before tucking it back into its place.

I let out a shaky breath in relief, closing my eyes shut at the same time that he stands. I will have to find a better hiding spot for it tomorrow.

I count Lincoln's muted footsteps until they come to a stop behind me. My heart races under his gaze, feeling it sear my skin. After what feels like an eternity, he eventually lies down, pulling me close once more. I suppress my flinch and pray to Althara that he can't feel my rapid pulse.

Will he kill me? Will he turn me in?

It's a valorguard's duty to the kingdom to report me, and he has every right to do so.

Sleep doesn't find me for the rest of the night.

CHAPTER 41

THIEF

LINCOLN

Ari sleeps with her body pressed against mine, her face turned away, and for a long time, I watch her closely, noting the subtle rise and fall of her chest. It's different now, more controlled than when she was truly asleep. The natural rhythm is gone, replaced by something intentional. She's not sleeping. She's awake, and she wants me to believe she isn't.

Still, in the early morning hours, under the orange light that peeks through the trees, her features look soft. It's as if whatever's keeping her from finding the sleep she needs is buried deep inside her, hidden in a place no one can reach. And lying next to her now—our bodies pressed close on the hard forest floor—I've never felt farther away.

I've finally stopped lying to myself that the pull I felt for her wasn't real. The idea that I was attracted to her, in my mind, was a byproduct of traveling side by side. It was a convenient excuse, a story I told myself to avoid facing the truth. I saw her clearly for the first time in Zalquar, no longer through the haze of attraction or denial, but as she truly was, with all her contradictions and truths laid bare. A shift happened inside me, breaking the barrier that had kept my eyes from fully meeting hers. I could hold her gaze without the urge to look away, without the need to shield myself from breaking the king's oath. That's when I stared into her piercing green eyes and realized how screwed I was because the pull I felt for her was real.

But it's never that simple, is it?

There's still so much I don't know about her. I realized it the moment I found the soulfire hidden in her bag. It was a quiet revelation, one that spoke volumes about the secrets she keeps. I almost missed it. I would have if it weren't the faintest thud it produced against my fingertips, like a heartbeat.

But I should have known the moment I saw how protective she was of her bag. At first, I thought she was being careful, didn't want to misplace the only things she had on her, but she'd always have a hand on the strap and her bag in sight at any opportunity she could.

Ari has stolen from the king.

I've seen firsthand what happens when you try to wield the smallest amount of the king's soulfire without permission.

There was a jeweler in Lunaria. King Malvok trusted them to create and set all the soulfire jewelry he wears. Talara wasn't bound by oath like the rest of us, which meant she could carry out her duties without hesitation or restriction. That freedom gave her power, but it came at a cost. I was there to collect what remained after she wielded it, and the aftermath was undeniable. The crystal tore through her body as if she'd been struck by lightning. I remember the stench of her charred flesh.

The king ensured it was a lesson to all to uphold the oath we all swore to.

Ari is mortal, though, and not bound by the same rules —power doesn't flow through her blood. She can't do anything with it, which means she'll be publicly executed like my father if anyone found out what she has done. I just don't understand how the king didn't feel its presence in the throne room. He's always been able to sense when soulfire is near. He claims it whispers to him, sings to him in his sleep, for the Beldara bloodline is the only one that can wield it.

When I touched the small amount Ari carried, I felt it immediately, the hum of magic thrumming at its core. The energy pulsed in my palm, alive yet elusive, a restless force just beyond my control. No matter how hard I wanted to wield it, I let the magic remain still. I could barely bring myself to look at it straight on. I even narrowed my eyes. I thought maybe I could behold it the way I could now stare into Ari's eyes. This, however, felt completely different because Ari's eyes aren't truly soulfire, only a similar shade.

My attention falls to the halo of hair framing her face as she pretends to rest. She's painfully bad at it, unaware of how horrible her acting skills are.

I take the moment to memorize every detail of her while her eyes are closed, the slight parting of her lips, the small freckle by the corner of her eye, the softness of her skin. I wish I could trace the curve of her cheek and feel the warmth beneath my fingertips just once.

My chest tightens with a feeling I never meant to have. Beneath my calm exterior, restless tension simmers, and I can't shake the certainty that it's only a matter of time before it erupts.

She's trouble, but she's also sunshine.

She's the light after a long stretch of darkness—a light I didn't know was missing until it appeared.

I couldn't walk away from her now, even if I wanted to. I feel it deep in my bones that it's not a possibility anymore.

Her presence alone threatens to unravel me completely.

All I want is to protect her from the shattered part of myself she doesn't know exists.

A secret I've kept buried deep for so long.

A curse I am hoping I can undo when I kill the heir.

CHAPTER 42

LINK

ARI

Lincoln's laugh catches me off guard, more boyish and carefree than I ever expected from someone so serious. I've heard small chuckles, low and rough, but nothing of this nature. It's relaxed and utterly sincere. The corners of my lips lift in a subtle smile, drawn helplessly to the sound.

Lincoln is talkative today. Words pour out of him; stories, shitty jokes, and observations, like a dam cracked open.

It makes me uneasy.

Distracted.

So distracted that I trip over my damn feet a few paces ahead of him.

"Owww," I groan, barely catching myself.

Lincoln lets out a long whistle. "It looks like you are fighting invisible enemies up there, sunshine."

"Asshole," I grumble at the same time I raise my hand high above my head and flip him off.

Does he really think all this rambling is fooling anyone? Especially after what he found last night, I can't help but feel like I've been walking on eggshells since we left camp, like saying the wrong thing might set everything off.

I clutch my bag tighter against my side, more guarded than I've ever been with it. A creeping doubt settles in my chest, threading through my thoughts no matter how hard I try to shake it off.

Will he leave me?

Will he turn me in after we find the king's heir?

He hasn't mentioned a word about the soulfire. Not a single accusation or threat. And for someone of his nature, that kind of silence is worse than any confession. He is planning, waiting for the right moment to make his move, and I don't know if I'm safe or already doomed.

I swear to Althara that I have no intention of doing anything with it. I just wanted it. Holding it, knowing it's mine, makes me feel something I rarely do—powerful. Like, for once, I'm in control. Not just surviving but shaping my own fate. It's a feeling I can't quite explain, but I crave it all the same.

Maybe he'll try to steal it from me.

Is that why he's trying to distract me?

I banish the thought from my head.

He wouldn't do that. *Would he?*

Selling the soulfire now is out of the question; no one would dare buy it from me. But I didn't steal the crystal to sell it. I stole it simply because I could.

The king has taken so much from everyone that I just wanted to take something from him. And the soulfire's ability to expand wards was a hidden perk I wasn't aware of. It actually could be useful to us out here.

Some of the kingdoms we have stopped in haven't been the friendliest. Their traditions and ways of life made it clear we didn't belong. Still, that doesn't mean they deserve to lose their homes. In my opinion, everyone here, regardless of their differences, has found a way to coexist peacefully on this land. There are no talks about war between any of the kingdoms, only the mutual hatred for Noctharn. Don't get me wrong, I'm glad the wards are up to protect us from the mortal-eating sandlurkers and the giants' peculiar choice of entertainment, but that doesn't mean they deserve to lose their land.

Lincoln falls into stride beside me. His annoyingly confident grin doesn't fade, but now I notice something new—a dimple, faint yet unmistakable.

Great. Just when I thought this couldn't get any worse.

My attention falls to his arms, and the way the sun's rays dance across his bronze skin, giving him a subtle otherworldly look. And just like that, whatever anger I had starts to slip away. I can't stay mad at him when he looks so light.

I scowl at him anyway.

"Is Ari short for anything?"

"Now look who has all the questions," I mumble.

Lincoln tilts his head, grinning wider. His dimple deepens, and I moan internally at the sight.

"Nope, always been Ari for as long as I can remember."

Lincoln arches an eyebrow. "And no *last name*?"

I dissect his question over in my head. He's prying. I see right through his scheming; he's pretending to be casual, laughing beside me, and smiling as if I deserve his undivided attention. There's no doubt he's after information, and I'm not giving him a damn thing.

"I don't claim my parents' last name. Never have, never will." I keep my tone light, careful not to show that I'm aware of the game he's playing. "What do people call you besides Lincoln?" I ask, entertaining his question. "Link?"

A breathy chuckle slips past his lips. I've made a mental

note of every sound he makes, and this one might be my new favorite.

"I don't have many friends," he admits. "I am...hard to get to know."

It's my turn to laugh. "Yeah, clearly," I jest. "To be fair, I don't have many friends either."

"Clearly," Lincoln repeats, his tone dripping with sarcasm.

"Well," I start, slightly defensive. "I do have some."

He looks at me out of the corner of his eye. "I'm sure you do, sunshine."

I roll my eyes at the nickname he knows I hate. Sunshine sounds belittling, implying that I'm joyful and soft, both qualities I do not have.

"I do!" I fidget with the strap of my bag. "I have Noah. He's been there for me through everything, even though he doesn't really understand me. I guess Jenny, too. She is my fighting mentee. Her family sold her to the pits like mine did, so I have been training her in hopes that she will survive," my voice trails off. "Maybe she is more of an acquaintance. And Ella. Ella was my friend. But she's dead."

Lincoln stays quiet at my side for a breath. "We are friends too. Are we not?"

"I guess we are—" I peer at him, trying to gauge his reaction. "Does that mean I get to call you Link now?"

I swear his eyes sparkle at the sound of his nickname rolling off my tongue.

"Do I have a choice?"

"Hmmmm..." I lift a hand to my cheek and tap a finger against it, pretending to mull his question over. "Would you prefer I keep calling you an asshole instead? Or what about an arrogant brute? I like that one."

"You can call me whatever you'd like, as long as you don't turn your back on me."

His words frighten me, implying so much but also nothing at all.

"I don't plan to," I murmur against the ringing in my ears. "And since we are friends now, I guess we should get to know each other more?"

Lincoln inaudibly mutters something under his breath.

"Say that again?" I ask, challenging him.

He clears his throat. "Nothing sunshine, just that this conversation is absolutely liberating."

"Oh, please, you want to know everything about me. Don't lie to yourself."

Lincoln's gaze meets mine, pinning me in place—all humor suddenly gone. "I do," he confesses. "I want to know everything."

I flash him a quick, crooked grin. "Well, good thing we are still a long way from Thalassara."

The day has flown by, and I've learned more than I expected. We traded stories freely, sometimes sharing more than necessary, but somehow, we never crossed the line into anything truly personal. It was a methodical balance, opening up just enough to connect.

Lincoln hates oranges; he says the smell tingles his nose in a not-so-good way. He dislikes the feel of velvet fabric against his skin, the texture of bananas, squeaky shoes on marble floors, and, my favorite, being told to relax, which I had to ask him to do after he ranted about how he hates forced small talk, even though that was precisely what we had been doing on this entire quest.

But he also loves the smell of fresh bread, the way sunlight on his skin makes him feel, and how his favorite color is the glow in the sky right as the sun peeks over the horizon each morning. And don't get him started on lemon tarts. *Oh*, did he rant for a long time about his love for lemon tarts, to the point that it made us both aggressively hungry.

I draw in a deep breath, letting the salty breeze fill my lungs. Lincoln flies overhead, scoping out the large, crystal-like structures that stretch upward toward the sky in the distance. Thalassara's castle is breathtaking, framed by a vast body of water that shimmers like glass.

Lincoln swoops low, shifting with a flap of his wings. His form changes effortlessly, boots landing on the earth with a crunch.

We approach the gates that mark the entrance to the kingdom.

Lincoln reaches behind him without a word, drawing his bow from over his shoulder in one swift motion. It hangs loosely in his grasp, but there's a readiness in the way his fingers rest near the string. I follow his lead, letting my hands hover near my waist, close to my weapons.

A guard steps forward, raising a hand above his head to signal us to stop. "State your business."

I track his breath, analyzing the gills on his neck that flutter open and closed. At first glance, he looks mortal, but the scales splattered across his skin say otherwise.

Lincoln stands perfectly still beside me. "We would like to request an audience with your king. We are on a quest searching for Noctharn's lost heir."

"The heir is not here," the guard replies coolly.

I meet the guard's stern glare. "That may be. But we want to speak with your king about the treachery Noctharn continues to commit against the kingdoms of this land." I gesture to Lincoln. "King Malvok's own valorguard seeks retribution. We are not leaving until we speak to him." I both threaten and command him at the same time.

The guard's face pales, his gills losing their sheen. "I guess..." he stumbles over his words. "There is no harm in asking King Nerion a few questions."

Lincoln's golden eyes flick between the guard and me before settling back on my face as the gates groan open.

"Of course, there isn't. We mean no harm," I say with a soft smile, passing through the gates.

Lincoln catches up to me, grabbing my elbow. He leans in close, whispering in my ear. "What was that about?"

I shrug. "I know a weak man when I see one."

I remove his grip on me and rest my hand in the nook of his elbow in return. I feel his attention linger on the place where we connect.

We fall in step down the peaceful streets of Thalassara. Quaint homes line the streets, their walls sun-bleached and weathered by salt, fading a little more with each passing day. Small shops and cozy restaurants spill onto the sidewalks, their doors wide open. The loudest thing we hear is the sound of the waves crashing against rocks, and not one selkith turns to look at us as we pass, as if we don't exist at all.

We reach the massive stone stairs leading up to the grand castle and begin ascending them. Our heads snap up in unison at the sound of the castle doors rattling open.

A man dressed in regal attire emerges, flanked by a line of guards. Atop his head rests a crystal crown, intricately woven with white stones I can't name. Greenery cascades gracefully over his flowing white robes, adding an almost ethereal touch. Beside him, a breathtaking woman steps forward and takes her place, her presence commanding as much attention as his.

"Welcome to Thalassara," her angelic voice coos.

Lincoln and I bow before them, and I speak before he can. "Thank you for welcoming us into your kingdom. We appreciate your candor."

The King of Thalassara smiles stiffly. "My guards told me we didn't really have a choice."

I offer him a polite smile back. "It was urgent. We traveled a great distance to see you."

The king studies us, taking his time. "Tell me your names."

I meet his silent scrutiny. "I'm Ari." My attention shifts briefly to the queen, who stares off into the distance. "And this is Link," I add, gesturing to Lincoln by my side.

Lincoln casts me a dirty look at the use of his new nickname. "We have questions about Noctharn and the king's lost heir that we'd like to ask you," he says, annoyance apparent in his gaze.

"That's what I've been told," the king replies, eyes roaming over the dirt that smudges our clothes. "But questions can wait. First, let's get you cleaned up. Sera and I have arranged a room for you two overlooking the sea. It's quite romantic. Couples love it."

My cheeks burn with a sudden heat. "Oh," I stammer. "We aren't—"

Lincoln clears his throat. "Thank you. We appreciate your hospitality."

"Nerion and I want nothing but the very best for our guest," Sera adds, practically singing each word.

The king nods, draping his arm around the queen. "Precisely," he purrs, stepping through the castle doors. "This way."

I glare at Lincoln, and I swear he smirks as we step over the threshold

I keep close to his side as we follow the king and queen. "One room? Romantic? For couples?" I repeat the king's words to him.

"Easier to keep you safe that way," he whispers, tilting his head toward me.

I roll my eyes. "Overprotective much, don't you think?"

"Only for you," he replies.

CHAPTER 43

THALASSARA

ARI

I've never seen anything like this.

Walls and columns rise in seamless transparency, catching and bending light like frozen waves. An endless body of water surrounds the castle on nearly all sides—its restless surface mirrored in the gleaming floors beneath my feet, giving the illusion that the entire structure floats atop it. Sunlight pours through every surface, refracting into shimmering rainbows that dance across the walls, while shadows of passing clouds ripple like ghosts through the translucent corridors.

Lincoln and I follow close behind a selkith woman whose scales glow with a beautiful shade of pink. She wears simple clothes, plain but impeccably clean and well-fitted. Despite the simplicity of her dress, there's an undeniable elegance in the way she moves, like someone who's valued and treated with respect without the trappings of rank or wealth.

We come to a halt before a hanging veil of lush green foliage, a drastic contrast to the crystal structure we walk in. With a snap of the selkith woman's fingers, the curtain of vines parts, revealing a breathtaking room suspended over a cliffside. The view is so majestic that it's impossible to tell where the blue of the sky ends and the water begins.

A sudden surge of panic stirs deep within me, fluttering against my ribs like a trapped bird. The king was right,. This room is undeniably romantic. Why would Lincoln want to spend the night here with me?

I steal a glance at him, and as if he senses the pull of my thoughts, his eyes meet mine for a brief, charged moment. A flicker of raw desire lights in his gaze, but disappears just as quickly, leaving a veil of tension hanging between us.

I clear my throat, refocusing on the servant standing before us. "Will we need to snap our fingers to leave?"

"Oh, of course not! You simply walk toward the vines, and the curtains will draw. While entering, there will always be a guard at the post to let you back in," she says, guiding us through the greenery.

I step into the room, my face flushing as I fully take in the space and the imposing four-poster bed that dominates the center.

There is no couch, no spare bedding—nothing.

"The bathroom is through those doors," the woman's voice peals, gesturing toward a loosely veiled entryway to our right. "My name is Gloria. If you need anything, please just say my name." Her lips curve into a brilliant smile. "Welcome to Thalassara."

Lincoln nods in thanks at Gloria's retreating form. The curtains part for her and close, leaving the room wrapped in silence.

I turn away from him, hiding my face. I let my bag slide off my shoulders and drop to the floor with a thud. Every muscle in my body aches after weeks of relentless travel, and no matter all our efforts, we seem no closer to answers than when we first began. I cling to the optimism that here, somewhere within this place, we'll finally find some answers, or at least some information about the void.

I lift my arms high and stretch, letting go of the stress as it unwinds from my body. A soft moan slips past my lips, and my eyes close briefly. I count each wave that crashes against the rocks below, finding it incredibly soothing.

"Ari—"

My eyes flutter open. "Yes?"

I turn slowly, every nerve alert.

I meet Lincoln's gaze, and my stomach lurches under the weight of his stare. His stone-cold expression makes him look every bit the assassin I know he is—an assassin who's ended hundreds of lives without hesitation.

I retreat a step in response, not just from him, but from everything that the fire in his eyes threatens to awake within me.

"Don't look at me like that."

He doesn't listen and closes the space between us, suddenly towering over me. My breath becomes shallow, heart pounding like it's trying to break free. He doesn't touch me, but it feels like he could, and the thought alone sends a rush of desire through my body, making it hard to breathe.

"Tell me," he murmurs. "How am I looking at you?"

A flush spreads across my cheeks at his question. Maybe I'm overthinking it. He would never want someone like me. Lincoln is a valorguard, an eldarim. He's an immortal with a long life ahead of him. My life is fleeting in comparison to his.

I pause, steadying myself before I speak, unsure if I'm about to embarrass myself. "Like maybe you and I—"

Lincoln's lips flatten into a thin line, and I don't dare finish my sentence.

"You're mistaken," he says, clenching his hands into fists. "There will never be an us, not like that."

My pride stings, and I knew I should have stayed silent. I grit my teeth and somehow manage a controlled smile. "Thank Althara," I scoff. "I could never be with someone like you."

Lincoln flinches, leather straining from his grip. He takes a step back. "You can wash up first."

I clutch the strap to my bag and move toward the bathroom. I peek over my shoulder as I do and see Lincoln standing rigid, exactly where I left him. My eyes follow the length of his body, resting on the curve of his back.

I ache for him, even though I know I shouldn't. It would only complicate things. I have a quest to win and information to find and having feelings for Lincoln will only make me weak.

I step into the bathroom and draw the curtains closed, giving him time to himself.

CHAPTER 44

SECRETS

ARI

A simple white dress falls gracefully over my body, its smooth fabric melting into each one of my curves. The material clings to me in all the right places, flowing like the water outside with each step I take. I gather the silky hem between my fingers, lifting it to keep it from twisting around my ankles.

We follow Gloria through the castle halls, and I make sure to keep my distance from Lincoln.

I hang back a step, feigning interest in the crystal walls and the water that surrounds us. But really, I'm hiding from him, from my emotions, and, most importantly, from my wandering thoughts of our sleeping situation.

Lincoln is dressed in the same white, flowing silk as I, radiating lethal elegance and completely unbothered by the tension thrumming between us. Each breath and each glance crackles through me, but he moves like it means nothing. He's distant and composed, perfect in a way that disgusts me. I want him with a hunger I can't silence.

But it's wrong.

It all is.

I didn't join this quest to get distracted by feeling that I never intended to develop. I keep reminding myself that Lincoln is eldarim and I am mortal. A relationship between the two never ends well; history tells us so. Every eldarim who had ever loved a mortal after King Malvok came to power either chose to die at their mortal love's side or moved on, as if they had never existed. Neither of those outcomes is what I wish for Lincoln or myself, which is why we would never work.

We are simply not meant to be.

I scowl, furious that I let things come to this. If he would just stop showing up and let me die like I should have countless times now, maybe it wouldn't feel so impossible to keep my distance. It would certainly make things a lot easier.

Truthfully, I can't make sense of why Lincoln saved me in the first place. Somehow, he always seems to show up right when I need him most. He keeps choosing me, again and again, and I'm left questioning why.

I shake my head, forcing the unwanted thoughts away. There's time to sort through it later, when I'm calmer and not caught in the middle of all of this. Right now, I need to stay composed, keep my distance, and focus on anything but the storm brewing inside me.

"Just a little further," Gloria says.

Lincoln grunts in acknowledgement, the sound unintentionally quickening my pulse. I hate that he has this effect on me.

If anything, it's another reminder of why I do everything alone. He's a deadly temptation. One I can't afford to continue to grow feelings for, at least that's what I keep telling myself.

We slow our pace approaching the king's war chamber.

Doors adorned with intricate gold details stand before us, flanked by guards who remain motionless at the entrance.

Gloria pushes the doors open, bowing as she enters. We step into the chamber, and I sweep my eyes across the room. Light spills through the floor-to-ceiling windows, reflecting the ripples of the sea on the polished floor. I lift my gaze, and my eyes lock with the king's icy blue stare.

King Nerion sits at a pristine white desk, his posture stiff, tracking our every movement.

"Ari and Link, Your Majesty," Gloria announces. She bows one last time before leaving the room and closing the doors behind her.

Lincoln and I bow in unison, just as a splash disrupts the stillness. I straighten and turn to see a large creature floating in a tank of murky water. I gasp and take a step back. Lincoln finds my arm and pulls me close to his side as if to protect me from whatever is swimming in the depths of the tank.

The creature is massive, sliding through the water in a smooth, oily motion. Its size and presence are impossible to miss, yet I didn't see it until now. The murky water distorts its shape, but there's no mistaking the power behind the creature.

"A sea serpent," the king declares, pushing away from his desk. His shoes create a strange sloshing noise that I overlooked before.

I pull away from Lincoln, his touch lingering longer than I'd like. Even with his gloves on, I can still feel the ghost of his hand.

Dark green scales flecked with gold glisten on the serpent's long body as it moves through the tank, and my hand involuntarily touches the snake barrette in my hair. The similarities are striking.

I stand beside King Nerion, watching the serpent as it slithers through the water.

"They are very similar to a snake, but sea serpents can't survive on land." The king smiles. "And this one seems to like you."

The serpent stops, fixing its beady eyes on me. A ringing noise fills my ears, and the corners of the beast's mouth lift into a mocking grin. Not fully. Not humanly at all. But in a deliberate way that makes my skin crawl like it knows something I don't.

"Ari," Lincoln says, demanding my attention.

I stay rooted in place, unable to tear my gaze from the serpents in front of me. I feel as though it sees straight through me, everything I despise about myself, every dark secret laid bare before the creature. And I see everything about it, too—its struggles, its pain, its loneliness. We are more alike than different, both of us having spent most of our lives hidden away.

Lincoln steps into my direct line of sight and places his gloved hand beneath my chin, tilting it upward.

"Ari," he growls. "Are you okay?"

I retreat beyond Lincoln's touch, well aware of the fact that we are not alone. "Yes. The creature just reminds me of someone, that's all."

The king waits patiently before his chair. Somehow, he retreated from my side, and I hadn't even noticed. "Come sit," he insists.

Lincoln's eyes stay fixed on mine, filled with confusion. I look away from him and take a seat across from the king.

Lincoln eventually follows, sitting next to me.

I clasp my hands together in my lap. "Your Majesty," I say, voice calm. "We need information on the lost heir of Noctharn. We are running out of time."

"You aren't the first to stop by, nor will you be the last." The king drums a finger on his desk, impatiently. "Why should I give you information willingly without anything in return? Is that how you operate in Noctharn?"

"No," Lincoln replies sharply. "But as Ari said, we are running out of time. We have less than a week before the Noctharn heir can claim their power."

"And why would that concern me?"

"If you want to keep your land under your control, it should be a concern of yours," Lincoln snaps.

I clear my throat, sensing the growing agitation in the room. "Don't mind my friend. He can be quite blunt with his words to no fault of his own." I pat Lincoln's thigh sympathetically. "We understand what you are saying and are willing to work on your terms for the information we seek."

The king runs a finger over his bottom lip, tapping it. "I like you," he says, eyes flaring. "How about this? I'll give you information for your deepest, darkest secret in return."

The serpent splashes in the water next to us, and I jump.

I readjust myself in my seat. "Who's?"

The king points at Lincoln. "His."

Lincoln clenches his gloved hands into tight fists. "No," he says blankly.

"No? And what if I already know your secret, Ashfield?"

A chill runs down my spine. "You know the Ashfield family?"

"A long time ago, Darian Ashfield set foot in my kingdom, looking for help," the king deadpans. "He was torn over the loss of his wife and daughter. He bartered for information to save his cursed son. So, I ask Lincoln for a simple thing. Do you not trust your companion enough to know your secrets?"

My mind reels, struggling to grasp the meaning behind

the king's words. I have a feeling he holds the answers we've been searching for, but Lincoln is ready to walk away without them, all because he doesn't trust me with his secret.

"Come on, Lincoln, it can't be that bad," I whisper.

"No," he sneers. "If you know my secret, then why do I have to say it?" he asks the king.

"Because I fear you don't understand your curse, it's more a gift than it is not."

I look at Lincoln's gloves, knowing deep down that his secret is wrapped in leather.

"Lincoln," I demand. "Just say it. It'll be alright. We need the information, and maybe this is the closure you've been searching for."

Turmoil laces across Lincoln's features, already set on his answer. "You don't know what I'm searching for. I'll do anything but this."

The king shrugs indifferently, almost bored. "Very well then. A fight to the death against a fighter of my choice. Win, and the information I have is yours. I'll even allow you access to my library," he grins as if he's doing us a favor.

"No," I hiss, at the same time Lincoln mutters, "Deal."

I whip my head toward him, my thoughts spiraling out of control.

What secret does Lincoln have that he'd rather die than reveal?

CHAPTER 45

GLOVES

ARI

The pit lies sunken below, a hollow scar at the middle of the crumbling coliseum. It's wide and uneven, its edges jagged with time, and its center filled with blood from the weight of a hundred battles. Stone terraces rise in rings around it, stacked high into the sky, each level crammed with bodies. Flags snap in the wind, bearing the emblem of Thalassara and its people.

The crowd is a living beast. It moves and writhes and roars, feeding on its own excitement. Selkith children perch on shoulders, men beat their chests, women wave scraps of cloth, and vendors slither between them all like rats, shouting over the chaos to sell flasks of sour wine and roasted nuts. Not one of them averts their eyes from the pit or dares to blink; their hunger for blood evident in every piercing stare.

I sit motionless, observing them. Memories of my time at The Broken Fang rush back to me. They feel so distant and pointless now, brutal for no reason. Nothing is worth fighting to the death for.

My tongue feels dry in my mouth, at a complete loss for

words at what Lincoln has done. After he agreed to the fight, he was ushered out of the room. He didn't say anything, not even a goodbye, nor did he glance over his shoulder as he left. An uneasy feeling filled my chest in that moment, and it's been growing ever since.

I lean forward, elbows digging into my knees as I fight to steady my ragged breath. Around me, noblemen rise to their feet in unison, bowing.

The king enters the viewing box where I sit, accompanied by the queen.

I do not rise.

I do not speak.

I do not look at them.

My body pulses with an anger I can barely contain.

The king passes by me, and the queen follows close behind, her citrus perfume a complete contrast to the scent of iron rising from the pit. She sits beside me, her silk gown rustling as she adjusts herself.

A servant appears wordlessly, filling goblets with wine. I don't reach for it. I would surely wretch up anything I put in my body with the anxious nerves that course so heavily through my veins.

The king adjusts a small device attached to the collar of his clothing, tapping it before speaking. "Silence!" he orders, his voice echoing off the open-air arena in a way I didn't think was possible. "We have been blessed with the presence of eldarim from the Noctharn Kingdom."

The crowd of selkith boo in distaste. Every last one of them hates us. That would explain why they were so indifferent when we first arrived; they didn't want to waste any time acknowledging our presence.

The king's lips curve into a knowing smile. "My people, prepare yourselves. I've arranged the entertainment of the century. These fighters aren't just eldarim but Noctharn's finest." The crowd erupts into a chant, anticipation crackling through the arena. "King Malvok's valorguards themselves."

A low thrum pulses through the ground, rising to the soles of my feet. A gate groans open far below, and Lincoln stumbles through the archway at the far end of the pit.

He blinks the sun out of his eyes, using his hand to shield himself. He scans the arena, searching, before his gaze finally lands on mine. My eyes roam down the length of his exposed body and over the loose shorts that hang at his hips, hunting for any new injuries that mar his skin, but find nothing.

I watch intently as he strides into the center, each step avoiding the splattered blood at his feet.

Another gate groans open from the opposite side of the pit. A figure stands in the shadows, visible only as a silhouette at first. Large-framed, and tall—extremely tall, like Lincoln. The shadowy figure emerges from the archway, and my face pales.

"Let them bleed! Let them bleed!" the crowd bellows.

Finley stalks toward Lincoln with an unhurried pace, lips pursed with vengeance burning in his gaze.

This is not a duel. It's not even a test of power.

This is the execution of one person, and I will accept only one outcome. Ella's killer will not be leaving Thalassara alive today. I will not allow it. Finley will die, by Lincoln's hands or mine.

I spring to my feet, eager to go anywhere. I'll throw myself into the pit and end Finley's life with my own two hands if I have to. King Nerion seizes my elbow, holding me fast.

Rage races through me at his touch, painting the world scarlet.

I give him a murderous look, meeting the frozen weight of his ice-blue stare. He leans in, his breath brushing my ear. Fury spikes hot beneath my skin. "Watch closely, my dear. Betrayal comes in many forms," he whispers. He releases me with a thrust, sending me crashing back into my seat.

It's a shame the guards took all our weapons the second Lincoln agreed to the fight. If I had my dagger right now, I would slit the king's throat in front of all his people and let his blood drip down the terraces, splattering onto the selkith below.

"What aren't you telling us?" I snarl.

King Nerion raises his goblet to his lips, peering just above it as he takes a sip. "A war is coming."

I narrow my eyes. "You say that like it's certain."

The king tilts his head. "Do you doubt me already?"

"Yes," I reply. "War is the language of kings who fear losing power."

The king chuckles darkly, sliding into the empty seat beside the queen, not entertaining me further.

No one has spoken of a war in all of our travels. Whispers, yes. Maybe even some unspoken truths, but war? A war between whom? Noctharn and the other kingdoms? When do they plan to attack? Mama is there, too close to the border. She won't be safe. She would be the first to die.

If a war truly looms, I'll find the answers.

"Hello, old friend," Finley's voice cuts through my thoughts like a shard of glass. It booms off the arena's wall amplified like the kings.

My stomach flips at the sound.

"How is he doing that?" I demand.

The king points to his collar, confirming my suspicion. "They wear it in their ear. Hearing them makes the fights more entertaining for the audience."

A horn sounds before I can respond, letting out one long note, while a single word hangs in the air. "Fight!"

Finley surges forward, a blur of motion I almost miss with my mortal eyes. The light catches something thrusting toward Lincoln, an object glinting in the rays of the setting sun. My eyes lock onto it, and I hopelessly spin to face the king. He must have seen the dagger in Finley's hand.

"He's cheating!" I yell. "The fight has just begun, and he's already cheating!"

The king shrugs and lets out a thoughtful hum before answering. "I must have missed it."

I curse under my breath, using every bitter word I can think of. I pin my eyes on Lincoln. He is speaking. His lips move urgently, but I can't make out a single word.

"Why can't I hear him?"

"He must have turned his device off," the king says casually. "Now, stop asking questions and watch."

Lincoln's shifts, and I gasp. Blood trails down his stomach and onto the grass. How did Finley best him already? Lincoln succumbing to poison in Zalquar was one thing, but a dagger to the stomach? That doesn't make sense. Why would he ever allow Finley to get that close with a weapon? He would have seen the attack coming the moment Finley decided to do it. He's acting like he's never fought in his life.

"Lincoln!" I shriek. "To your left."

Lincoln moves just in time to avoid a stab to the kidney. He stumbles backward, trying to regain his balance, but fails, collapsing to the ground.

I rise, gripping the railing tight, my eyes fixed on Lincoln's trembling lips as he mouths the words, *'I'm sorry.'*

"No!" He isn't trying. Why isn't he trying?

A violent kick lands in Lincoln's ribs, forcing him to curl

inward. Finley kneels, pushing Lincoln onto his back and planting a heavy knee on his chest. Stealing the breath from Lincoln's lungs, he presses a dagger to his throat for everyone to see.

The howl of the crowd pounds in my skull, but it doesn't matter. I will not allow another person I care for to die.

"Get up!" I order Lincoln, screaming over the noise. "Stand up and fight!"

One second, it looked like Lincoln was going to accept his fate, but now a cold, murderous gleam sparkles in his eyes.

Lincoln's hands twitch at his sides as he slides off his gloves, only now noticing the ring he wears on one of them. He presses his pale fingers down against the earth—Finley realizing too late.

Purple veins lance up Lincoln's arms, moving like shadows beneath his skin as the ground beneath him turns to a dry yellow patch.

Death spreads from his touch, and the grass is the first to fall.

CHAPTER 46

MY WEAKNESS
LINCOLN

A door groans shut behind me, sealing my fate with it. I stand alone in a narrow passage, waiting for the guards to open the gates that lead into the arena. The stone walls press in on me like a coffin, while just above me, through the small cracks in the masonry, selkith stand—their cheers, eager and hungry.

My ear buzzes, pulsing lightly. The device the guards forced me to wear is quite interesting, and unlike anything I've seen before. They said it was an amplifier for my voice, so my words can echo clear as day during the fight.

How kind of them to want to hear my opponent's dying breath.

I press my back against the wall, waiting. I don't dare look through the gate into the grassy arena, in fear that I might spot Ari. Instead, I keep my eyes locked on the stone wall in front of me, well aware of the royal box that sits higher than the rest, filled with the king and queen. She would be up there with them, either sitting or standing, clutching the railing in search of me. One look at her and I'd fall apart, which is the exact reason I didn't allow myself to look her way when I left the king's chamber. I would never go through with this if I had, but my secrets are the only thing I have left, and I don't plan to give them up willingly. Even though deep down, something tells me that my secret is already lost, and it will no longer be just mine.

I run a hand through my hair. Sweat beads at my temples and trickles down my back and into the thin shorts that hang low on my hips. They stripped me of the fine silk they gifted me, leaving me with no armor or protection. Just bare skin, my own two hands, and the gloves that I wouldn't allow the guards to take.

The king's voice cuts through the arena, and the crowd falls into a sudden silence.

I peel myself off the wall and walk toward the arch. The gates ease open with a creaking protest, and the guard beside me gives me a hard shove.

I stumble forward onto the grass, glaring daggers at him.

I will kill him next.

Final strays of sunlight spill from the cloudless sky overhead, blinding me. I lift my arm to shield my eyes and blink out the black orbs that float in my vision.

I inspect the arena as I make my way to its center. I spot Ari exactly where I thought she'd be. She sits perfectly still. Her hands balled into fists, knuckles white, eyes running down the length of my body searching for injuries. I knew I shouldn't have looked. I told myself I wouldn't, but I couldn't stop myself.

A second gate groans open on the far side of the arena, and I don't need my opponent to step into the light to know who it is.

Even tucked in the shadows, I'd recognize them anywhere.

Finley strides out of the darkness; a wicked grin plastered across his face. He appears rougher than the last time I saw him. How long has he been in Thalassara? By the look of his hollow face, he appears to be a prisoner of his own making.

My expression doesn't shift while the man who threatened Ari's life more than once stops a few paces away.

"Hello, old friend," Finley snarls. His voice reverberates through the arena.

I swiftly tap the device in my ear. I watched the guards activate it by tapping it before placing it on me, and I quickly learned how to deactivate it.

It's the only action I have time to do before a horn blares and a single word is shouted. "Fight!"

Finley surges forward, and I drop into a defensive crouch. The movement is automatic, muscle memory overriding the spike of adrenaline. I catch the glint of metal a split second before he drives it toward me.

Of course, he managed to sneak in a weapon.

From the rough handle and uneven edge, it's something he cobbled together from whatever he could find in here. Crude. Improvised. Which means it's not coated in anything lethal. Nothing that will kill me instantly, at least.

So, I let my eyes widen. Let my balance falter half a step. I let Finley believe he's caught me off guard as it slides into my stomach, making a small incision. I feel its effects instantly, pain blooming across my abdomen.

I spit phlegm onto the grass and begin to circle Finley as he does the same to me, never taking my eyes off the smug curl of his lips.

He always fought dirty, known for taking cheap shots.

I plant my feet, making sure my back faces the royal box, before I speak. "We both know how this is going to end," I growl. "I'd expect you to know better." I glance down at the blood that trickles from my stomach onto the grass. "Now tap your ear."

Finley does as I say, muting his voice from being projected. "It is only fair," he barks back at me before tapping his ear once more.

So be it. I look over my shoulder, my eyes locking with Ari's. I see everything in her gaze, how much she cares for me, even though she hasn't told me, and even though I haven't told her. Will she still care for me after what she's about to see? I feel Finley approaching me before Ari has the chance to shout.

"Lincoln! To your left!" she shrieks, barely loud enough to reach my ears.

I move in time to deflect a stab to the kidney, pretending to stumble like my life is hanging by a thread.

I fall to the ground, the grass catching me in a soft embrace. '*I'm sorry*,' I mouth, praying to Althara that Ari will understand why I kept this secret from her.

Ari's cry is the only thing I hear as Finley kicks me in the ribs. He pushes me onto my back and places a knee on my chest, forcing the air out of my lungs. A small, knife-like dagger rests against my throat.

"Get up!" Ari screams. "Stand up and fight!"

Her voice cuts through me, stirring a profound emotion, but I already knew it'd come down to this. I unclasped my gloves before I came out here, and now I slide my hands free from their tight restraint while Finley is distracted.

I press my palms flat against the earth. Life pulses beneath my fingertips as I take it all away. The once lush grass feels dry against my bare skin, scratching me.

My eyes glaze over, relishing in the new life now coursing through my veins. It feels so good, like euphoria. A feeling I have grown to love and hate.

I flash Finley a sinister grin, and the blood drains from his face, realizing too late what I have done. His hand trembles, forcing the blade to come crashing down, landing in the grass with a crunch.

I twist beneath him, using the movement to drive my head into his face. A sickening crack follows, and Finley groans, falling to the side. He hits the ground with a thud.

Wasting no time, I push myself up, dirt clinging to my hands and knees. I lunge for Finley's weapon. My fingers close around it, and I swing it through the air with a hissing whoosh. The sound slices through the crowd's cheers, and the dagger meets its mark, landing directly in front of the king's chair.

Flames erupt across the arena, scorching the now dry, brittle grass beneath our feet. In seconds, fire snakes up the walls, forming a blazing ring that surrounds us in a flickering halo of heat and light.

I smirk, taking my time to face Finley. "You always attack too fast. I thought I trained you better."

Finley bellows in anger, throwing fireball after fireball at me.

I dodge each one, grinning at his growing rage. "My point exactly."

Finley surges forward again and I transform. I shoot high into the sky, feeling the wind in my wings before spiraling back down toward the earth. My feet hit the ground behind him, and I snap my heel into the back of Finley's knee. He buckles and collapses.

I circle him, like a predator would its prey. "I always knew it'd come down to this, you and me."

Finley chuckles, the sound bitter. "Unfair advantage," he growls. "If I had your curse, I wouldn't waste it like you."

I loom over him, my shadow falling across his face—clenching and unclenching my fists.

"Just do it!" Finley yells, his bravado cracking.

"Finish him!" the king demands.

I don't dare look in King Nerion's direction, too worried that Ari already hates me for the secret I kept from her.

I kick Finley in the chest, and he topples onto his back. He stares up at the sky as I lean down, hand hovering over his chest. "Any last words?"

Finley bursts out into a hysterical fit of laughter. "My life may be short, but yours will be long and full of anguish."

"You'd better hope I don't see you in the Unseen when my time comes." I press my bare hand over his pounding heart, feeling the rapid beat beneath my palm as the color fades from his face.

The fierce flames that once danced around us sputter out, leaving only smoke and ash in their wake. Finley's body grows limp under my touch, his haunting laugh now mute.

A roar of jubilation rises from the crowd. I'm unsure if they understand the extent of what happened.

I stand, staring at the lifeless body of the valorguard I once bled beside, his energy now pulsing through me.

Slowly, I lift my gaze toward the royal box, searching for Ari, but she's already moving.

She's a flash of motion, tearing through lines of stunned selkith. Nobles recoil as she shoves past, guards too slow to stop her. She breaks through line after line of bodies, rushing toward the edge of the pit. She brushes past a familiar face—someone who reaches for her, recognition dawning too late.

I furrow my brows.

But Ari doesn't look back, and I don't have time to question why he's here. She's at the railing in seconds, gripping it with both hands, and without hesitation, she pulls herself up and over it.

Time seems to hold its breath as her legs dangle above the bloodstained earth below.

I break into a run, shouting her name. "Ari! Wait!"

She lets go, and my heart falters. She hits the ground with a sickening thud.

My legs keep moving, closing the distance between us as Ari rises to her feet. I stop directly behind her at the same time she spins toward me, her balance fragile. She wobbles but catches herself. Her eyes are wide, fixed on me with an intensity that sends a shiver down my spine. I'd gladly get lost in her piercing green gaze if she'd let me, and for a moment, I allow myself to.

The chants around us fade, and it's just the two of us, breathing hard, caught in a heavy silence filled with unspoken feelings. I find something raw burning in her eyes, fierce and vulnerable all at once, but I can't place exactly what it is. The care is still there, as far as I can see, but so is fear.

For the first time, I register fear in Ari's eyes. Fear of me. Even when she found out I was an Ashfield, she still never feared me until now. I deserve it, though. She should fear me. She now knows I can end a life with a single touch, and yet she still ran toward me, wanting to be near.

We stand within arm's reach of each other, but not close enough for our skin to touch.

I tuck my exposed hands tight behind my back.

"Are you okay?" she asks me, taking in the blood that smears my bare body.

"Yes—" My voice fails me, stuck somewhere in my throat.

Ari steps toward me, closing the small space left

between us. She lifts her hand and presses it against my chest, right over my heart. Her fingers tremble, shivering from the chill that always settles over me whenever I take a life. I feel her thumb moving against my skin, sending jolts of electricity through me.

The sweet, intoxicating scent of her overwhelms my senses as I inhale deeply. I stare down at her, suddenly aware of just how fragile she is. In this close proximity, the delicate edges of her frame and the fleeting nature of her existence hit me with a clarity I hadn't expected.

"I thought I was going to lose you," she says, her voice barely above a whisper, quiet in an intimate way, like it is only us in the arena.

"It's going to take a lot more than that to get rid of me."

Ari tries to stand taller, rising onto her tiptoes. Her eyes drift in the same movement, settling softly on my lips. "Good," she murmurs.

Her warm breath brushes against my skin, making my pulse quicken.

I clench my fists behind my back, aching to reach out and touch her as she slides her hand up my chest, fingers curling around the back of my neck. She pulls me close, shrinking the space between us until the air itself feels charged.

Our mouths hover inches apart, a long, aching pause hanging between us.

I shouldn't.

We shouldn't.

I moan inwardly, trying to resist but failing miserably.

Fuck it.

I press my lips to hers, and the world vanishes, leaving nothing but her and me.

A flood of new emotions rushes through me, like a thread finally snapping into place.

I part her lips with my tongue, greedily claiming her.

She brings meaning to my life, giving me a purpose I didn't even know I was searching for.

And for the first time in a long time, I have a reason to live.

CHAPTER 47

WITCH KINGDOM
ARI

King Nerion has agreed to meet with us tomorrow. Until then, Lincoln and I will remain in the kingdom for the night.

We need answers, but just as urgently, we need rest. The day has drained us both in more ways than one.

I wander the halls of the castle in the direction of the kitchen. Lincoln is having his wounds tended to, and I told myself I would find food for us—that it was the least I could do after everything we've been through. But deep down, I know that isn't the real reason why I left.

I couldn't be near him any longer. Being in the same room as him for even a second makes it hard to think clearly. It feels like a storm is gathering inside me, one I don't know how to stop.

My feelings for Lincoln have grown, no longer subtle or easy to ignore. We are friends and allies, that is what we agreed upon. Just two people with the same goal to find the lost heir, both benefiting from it in different ways.

How can we begin to understand what we are when I don't even know what he is? Lincoln can kill someone with a single touch, and I still can't wrap my head around how it's possible.

And that's not even the worst part.

The worst part is that we crossed a line we should not have.

Althara, spare me. I can still feel it, the pressure of his lips against mine. I've kissed others before, but never like that, never with feeling.

There was a sense of urgency in it, and it scared me, not because it was wrong, but because it felt right in a way that I didn't expect.

I hadn't realized how numb I'd become until our lips touched. That kiss stripped away the distance I'd been clinging to and left me exposed, craving more. More of *him*.

I want his touch, even through the barrier of his leather gloves.

I want to hear his voice, especially when it softens only for me.

I want the weight of his gaze when it lingers just a second too long.

I want whatever he's willing to give me.

But before I want too much, I need answers. I plan to ask Lincoln all the questions that have been brewing inside me when I return to the room.

I follow the scent of spices and savory aromas as they drift toward me, guiding me through the unfamiliar halls. Selkith rush by me in a hurry, some with linens in hand, others with food, and I know I am getting close. My stomach rumbles in protest, urging me to move faster. I can't remember the last time I had a full meal or a full glass of water. The weeks and days have blurred faster than I thought possible.

"Miss, can I help you with something?"

I jump, unsheathing my dagger.

I spin on my heels and grab the collar of a person's shirt, slamming them against the glass wall. I bring my blade to their throat without a second thought.

A young servant shakes violently between my fingertips, and I realize my mistake the moment I see the fear in the boy's eyes. He can't be any older than fifteen, and I almost just killed him.

Guilt washes over me, and I step back, putting space between us.

"Sorry about that," I murmur, managing a polite smile. "You took me by surprise."

The servant straightens his shirt, standing on wobbly legs. His dark blue scales reflect the moonlight, mirroring the stars' vibrancy.

He keeps his eyes down; attention locked on the polished floor. "No worries, miss. Er—" he stammers, lips quivering. "Can I help you with something?"

"Yes, actually," I say, overly cheerful, trying to mask the fact that I almost just slit his throat. "We leave tomorrow, and I was wondering if we could have some food prepared for it." He peers at me from under his lashes, his eyes searching my mine with caution. My smile widens, hoping to appear open and welcoming. "And some food for now as well," I add.

A moment passes before he finally relaxes, shoulders softening. He gives me a slight nod. "I'd be happy to help you, miss." His voice is steadier than before. "I'll have the kitchen bring food to your room. How long of a journey should we prepare for?"

A surge of relief sweeps through me, grateful that my brutality didn't drive the poor boy away. I lower my voice to a whisper. "I'm not sure of the distance, however far the witch kingdom is from here. Do you know how long that will take?"

The boy's complexion turns ghostly gray. "The witch kingdom? You wish to go to the witch kingdom?"

I hadn't meant to frighten him. I just wanted to gather as much information as possible. And clearly, he knows things that will benefit me.

"Don't be nervous," I purr, though my presence betrays those words entirely. Still, a part of me savors the fear the boy carries—a dark satisfaction in knowing I can evoke it. "I think we got off to a bad start once again." I extend my hand, eagerly awaiting his. "I'm Ari."

The servant's throat bobs, his clammy fingers touching mine. "Alfred," he mumbles, pulling away his hand just as fast as he had placed it.

I tilt my head. "It's nice to meet you, Alfred. I heard other servants in the castle talking about how they just returned from the witch kingdom, so I figured you would know."

Alfred runs a hand through his golden-brown hair, nervously looking around. "I don't know anything about the witch kingdom."

I lean in, our bodies so close I can feel the heat pulsing from his skin. I press my lips close to his ear, lowering my voice. "Tell me what you know about the witch kingdom," I demand.

"You don't just show up." Alfred gasps the words out like he's in pain. "You need to bring them something to enter. A life, a part of you, something, anything that they deem worthy."

"A sacrifice?"

"Yes."

"And how will I know if they will deem it worthy?"

"You'll know," he replies.

"Thank you, Alfred. You have been a joy to talk to. I appreciate all your help." I step back, allowing him the space to leave if he wishes.

"If..." he stutters. "If you still need food from the kitchen, I can bring you there."

"That would be amazing, Alfred."

He scurries down the hall, and I follow close behind.

I need to find a suitable sacrifice based on the information he provided.

But what exactly will it be?

The details he shared were vague, as if speaking them alone would lead to his death. I'll have to find something worth sacrificing before we leave Thalassara tomorrow, and right now, my options are limited.

I open the bedroom door and place the pile of food I acquired on the dining table. I snag a bundle of grapes from the plate, popping one in my mouth. Sweet juice slides down my throat, warming me to the core. My stomach moans in approval.

The bathroom curtains slide open, and my eyes dart in their direction. I stop mid-chew at the sight of Lincoln. He steps out in nothing, but a simple towel wrapped around his waist. His wet hair is tousled in every direction as if he just ran his fingers through it. There's a rough charm to him, magnetic in a way he doesn't seem to notice.

I lick my lips without meaning to, eyes locked on the beads of water rolling down his stomach, slipping along the grooves of muscle before disappearing into the towel. Lincoln freezes mid-movement, feeling my attention aimed directly at him. His head turns slightly, spotting me at the dining table.

I look away for a moment, then back at him, stuck between the temptation to keep watching and the fear of being caught staring.

I bite the inside of my cheek, trying to conceal the shy smile that tugs at the corner of my mouth. "Hi," I breathe, barely audible.

Lincoln walks to the bed and grabs the lounge shorts that the selkith laid out for him. He swiftly drops his towel, and I avert my eyes to the ceiling, popping another grape in my mouth. I hear leather stretching across wet skin, and feet padding toward me.

"Hi," he murmurs softly, taking a seat across from me.

I lower my gaze to meet his. "Are you hungry?"

Damn me...I'm totally losing it.

Of course, he's hungry.

What a stupid thing for me to ask.

Lincoln piles food onto the plate in front of him without a word. We eat quietly, everything that's gone unspoken pressing down on us. Time stretches, but only moments pass, and my throat tightens. I need to say something, to break this silence.

How long can I keep putting this off?

I clear my throat, the sound loud in the stillness, ready to confront the secrets between us.

"Your gloves," I say. "I think I deserve an explanation about them, don't you think?"

Lincoln's body tenses, his jaw clenching tight. "I was cursed long ago by the Queen of Noctharn in retribution for my father trying to kill her only child. The day my father found her was the day my curse took effect. I was four when it happened. She spoke in an evil tongue, in a language my father couldn't understand, like she was possessed. When the queen finally stopped and returned to normal, the damage was already done. An eye for an eye, she said, for hunting her child so relentlessly. She cursed me in hopes that he would stop, but my father tried to undo it by searching even harder for the lost heir. I suspect that's why he came to Thalassara."

I feel the color instantly drain from my face.

The Queen of Noctharn cursed Lincoln, the queen who was supposed to be good. She cursed the gentle man sitting before me, unleashing the darkness within him and transforming him into a monster. But I can't blame her for the aftermath of what would transpire when she didn't know the consequences, only possible outcomes.

"And your curse, what exactly is it?" I need to hear him admit it, I need him to put my suspicions to rest.

Lincoln clenches his hands into tight fists. "Death," he growls. "A single touch from me will stop your heart. I will never feel the warmth of skin beneath my fingers, only lifelessness." His eyes flash with a longing for something forever out of reach. "And I will never be able to fully commit to someone for fear that I will kill them."

I let out a shaky breath, reaching my hand toward him. "That doesn't make you unlovable."

Lincoln pulls away, leaving the space between us cold and empty. "It does. My hands have stolen the lives of all the people I cherish most. I will die alone before I allow it to happen again."

"Who? Who did you kill?"

"My sister and my mother. I ended their lives before my father had a chance to understand my curse."

I stare at Lincoln, my heart aching for the pain he has

endured. For the young boy he once was, who lost everything.

Our eyes meet and hold.

"You should be afraid of me," Lincoln says, defeated, convincing himself more than me.

"I'll never be afraid of you."

It's the undeniable truth; no part of me wants to run. Not once has an inkling of fear pushed me to flee; my only fear has ever been for Lincoln's life, never for who he is. I can't walk away now, not after everything we've been through, not when leaving would mean losing a piece of myself.

There's a part of me that's inexplicably drawn to him, pulled in despite the wrongness of the whole situation. It's dangerous, barely contained, one wrong move and everything will explode, because I already know full well how this will end.

Lincoln's eyes bore into mine, the intensity of them making me shift in my seat. "How do we reverse the curse?" I ask. "And how are you able to hold my gaze now?"

Lincoln lifts his fork, taking his time as he chews. "The heir is my only hope; with them dead, I would no longer have a tether to the origin of the curse. And to answer your second question, I don't have an explanation for that besides the fact that your pull on me is stronger than my fear of the soulfire, even when I am defying the king's word by staring at you longer than I should."

My skin heats, longing only for him. "Breaking the oath you made to King Malvok is punishable by death. You realize that, right?"

Lincoln's golden eyes darken, clouded with desire.

"Yes." The word leaves his mouth without a trace of hesitation.

A restless energy thrums beneath my ribs, impossible to

hold still. I abruptly come to my feet, the chair scraping against the floor as I push away from the table.

I don't know how to do this. All I've ever been good at is hiding, and the only thing that helps me think is putting distance between myself and everything else.

"I need a bath," I mutter.

I don't wait for a response as I turn and disappear into the bathroom.

The moment the door clicks shut behind me, I exhale jaggedly, as if I've been holding my breath this entire time. Steam soon fills the room, wrapping around me like a cozy embrace. I wash up, using the water to ground me, to strip away the intensity in Lincoln's gaze and the feelings that claw at the edges of my mind.

Clean and wrapped in fresh clothes, I pause in front of the mirror. I hardly recognize myself. My skin has regained its color, no longer lifeless from days spent in the mines.

There's something new in my face, too. I look lighter. Not quite free but no longer buried. Older, maybe, like someone who's just begun to live after being numb for so long.

I draw the curtains aside and step back into the bedroom.

I tiptoe to the bed, trying not to make a sound, though the silence already feels too loud. My eyes drift to the floor, where Lincoln has pieced together a makeshift bed. He's using his small pack as a pillow and a thin sheet to keep him warm. The sight evokes an emotion I've only recently begun to feel.

I slide beneath the sheets, the fabric cool against my still-warm skin. The contrast makes me shiver, though not from the cold.

The room is quiet, save for the steady rhythm of Lincoln's breathing, but my mind refuses to settle.

I close my eyes, willing the thoughts to go away, but Lincoln's voice echoes in my head anyway. My body may be still, but my mind is anything but. I try to block it all out; his curse, his loss, the emotion we both won't name, and our kiss.

I groan inwardly, thinking about his lips against mine.

I flip onto my side, turning away from him, as if the small distance might remove the thought from my head.

Just sleep, I tell myself, knowing it won't come easily.

I sink deeper into the bed, counting the sound of the waves on the shore below.

I make it to twenty before I cave in.

"Lincoln," I whisper. "Are you awake?"

"Yes," he answers immediately.

I nervously pick at the frill on my blanket, struggling to find the right words. "You don't have to sleep on the floor. The bed's big enough for both of us. I can put a pillow between us. We don't even have to be close." My voice cracks, my mouth suddenly dry as I stumble over the words. "You can sleep in the bed with me."

I wait for his reply, and the silence feels louder with each second without him breaking it. I swear I can hear the gears turning in his head—the war he's fighting between what he wants and his biggest fears.

I hear Lincoln stand, and relief rushes through me. He moves to the other side of the bed, and the mattress shifts beneath his weight the moment he settles in.

We lie facing each other, pale moonlight filtering through the window and painting soft shadows across his skin.

Tentatively, I reach out. My fingertips graze Lincoln's

cheek, moving to the curve of his lower lip. It parts subtly beneath my touch, a quiet invitation. I feel his hand slide around my waist beneath the blankets, pulling me closer.

I nestle into his side, breathing in the fresh scent of cinnamon that coats his skin.

My pulse pounds in my ears, matching the beating of his heart. I sink further into the safety of his embrace, feeling at peace in his arms, content with living in this moment forever.

CHAPTER 48

LETTING GO
ARI

I wake with a start, the air heavy in my lungs. Sheets stick to my skin, damp from a throbbing heat that radiates through me.

Where am I?

I blink the darkness out of my eyes, taking in the ceiling above, the canopy of cloth that drapes over the bedposts, the crystal transparent walls, and the distant sound of waves hitting the shore below.

Thalassara. *Right.* I am in Thalassara.

I reach for the blanket draped over my body, pulling it away, only to freeze mid-motion. My fingers brush against a strong, muscular arm stretched across my stomach.

Lincoln's body molds perfectly to mine, his chest pressed firmly against my back. The feeling is grounding, like he's holding me not just for comfort, but because he never wants to let me go. One of his legs is placed between mine, hooked tight, anchoring me in place.

Damn me. I should have left him on the floor.

I lie still as a statue, trying and failing to calm my racing heart.

My eyes drift down the length of his body, pressed so close. His hand rests on my stomach, fingers spread wide, the leather glove still clinging to him like a second skin. The contrast between the glove's roughness and the softness beneath makes me crave his touch even more.

I try to pull away, sliding my body meticulously from his grasp, desperate to carve out some space between us. But even the slightest movement makes him shift, his hold tightening. He presses closer. Closer than I thought possible, as if trying to merge our bodies into one.

Every inch of him touches me, overwhelming my senses. I want to push away the flood of thoughts crashing through my mind, the pull of his presence, the ache I try to deny. But they refuse to be silenced.

I'm stuck somewhere between the instinct to escape and the undeniable truth that I don't want to.

I listen to his measured breaths, each one causing the stubble on his jaw to scrape my neck. I hate the feeling it provokes in me.

I need to get away from him.

Far, far away.

I peer at him over my shoulder and catch myself staring at his parted lips. In sleep, he looks unburdened, his features bathed in peace. It's a side of him I'm not used to seeing, not often enough anyway.

I observe him, studying the lines of his face, curious about the world he slips into when reality fades.

Does he dream about...

Wait a minute.

I scrunch my eyes, analyzing the way his chest rises and falls. His hand twitches against my stomach like the stillness was unbearable to fake any longer.

I turn away from him. "I know you are awake, asshole."

The silence that follows makes me second-guess myself as I wait for his reply and get nothing in return.

I hesitantly look over my shoulder again, and our eyes lock.

Lincoln is frozen beneath my gaze, the tension between us tightening with every heartbeat. His eyes search mine like he's seeing straight through me—every thought, every unspoken desire, every feeling sparked by the closeness of our bodies.

And I feel it too, like a warning bell ringing in my head that won't stop.

Heat pools low in my belly. It's been there for a while now, growing stronger every time we're near each other. And every second that passes only feeds it more.

I should pull away. I know I should. But I don't move, because despite everything, I don't want to.

Lincoln repositions himself, resting his weight on his elbow, and at the same time, I hook one leg beneath his, moving him until he's hovering directly above me.

"You're awake," I whisper, softer than the words I threw at him minutes ago.

"I was trying to sleep," he rasps, his voice thick and gravelly. "But I knew you were watching me, and then I felt your heart beating like that."

"Like what?"

"Like you want me as much as I want you."

My throat tightens, and I swallow hard, fighting the dryness.

Deny. Deny. Deny.

"I don't," I lie. "You misunderstood."

Lincoln shakes his head, shifting his body weight. The hand that he had rested on my stomach now slides lower, tracing a slow path down. His lips brush the edge of my jaw, and against my better judgment, I find myself wrapping my legs around his waist and pulling him closer. He presses his lips firmly against my throat, and I moan.

"We shouldn't," I whimper.

"You're right," he hums against my flushed skin, pulling back just enough to meet my gaze. "Should I stop?"

Our eyes lock, burning with all the things we shouldn't want but so intensely crave.

I manage a shaky breath, my heart drumming a frantic rhythm beneath my ribs. "No," I admit, ignoring every warning in my head.

Lincoln trails a finger along my jaw. "Good," he breathes. "Because I don't plan to let you go anytime soon."

I yank him toward me without thinking, and our lips collide, quickly becoming ravenous.

Lincoln's tongue slides into my mouth, and I cling to him, drawn to the heat between us.

I need more. I want more. Nothing else exists—no worries, no doubts, no weight of the quest, the heir, or the soulfire. They all vanish.

"Ari," he moans, saying my name like it's both salvation and sin.

I move my lips down the base of his throat. "Yes?' I breathe.

"You don't want this." Lincoln forces out between strangled breaths.

I pull back, threading my fingers into the thick, dark strands of his hair.

"You can't tell me what I want and what I don't," I demand. "I want you, Lincoln, why can't I want you?"

"I'm not good for you. I am bad, broken. I, I..." Lincoln stumbles over his words in anguish, like he genuinely believes he doesn't deserve anything.

I look at him, really look at him, seeing only the good and none of the bad.

It hits me then, clear and undeniable. Everything I've done has been for everyone else's benefit; this is the first thing I'm truly choosing for myself. And I will keep choosing Lincoln. If everything had to fall just to keep him safe, I wouldn't hesitate. I will find a sacrifice. Something better.

"You're no more broken than I am," I tell him. "Maybe," I inhale, steadying myself before continuing, "we can piece each other back together."

Resolve burns through Lincoln at my words, every emotion written in the expression on his face. His hands tighten around my waist, guiding me with him as he lies on his back. I straddle him, my thin nightgown bunching around my hips.

Lincoln runs his hands up my thighs. "I will never be able to touch you the way that you deserve," he mourns. "You will never know my touch for as long as you live."

I hover over him, my lips just inches from his. "That doesn't change how I feel about you."

I barely have time to get the words out before Lincoln's mouth slams against mine. His hands roam eagerly across my body, tugging my nightgown over my head while I yank his shorts off, leaving no more barriers between us, just him and me.

We explore each other's bodies under the stars, and with him, I don't feel like I am missing out on anything. There's no pain for what he can't give me, because it is more than enough.

More than I ever dared to hope for.

CHAPTER 49

THREE WORDS
LINCOLN

I've never been good at sleeping next to someone. It's an intimacy I never allowed myself to have.

I like having my own space. It has always been necessary, but I wasn't thinking about that now. Not as Ari sleeps beside me, her bare body tangled with mine beneath the sheets.

I didn't expect tonight to unfold the way it did, not just because of what transpired between us, but because of the feelings it provoked.

I told myself I would guard her, protect her from any harm, because she is mortal and needed it. That's how it started and should have stayed. But somewhere between hiking through the desert and arguing over a map that she always read wrong, she became something more to me.

Althara, spare me. I can't believe I let my guard down and allowed myself to get this close to her, imagining a life between us that could never be.

I blame it on the agreement we made to help each other. It gave Ari power over me that I cannot break free from. She slithered into my life like the snake on her barrette, circling around me and holding me hostage. And the stubborn truth is that I never want her to let me go.

Ari shifts against my side, rolling toward me, wrapping her delicate arm around my waist. Her hold on me is featherlight, barely there, yet I feel like I can't move. The touch of her hand on my skin holds me captive, but I don't think I mind.

"Never leave me." The words slip through her parted lips, rough with sleep.

My muscles clench.

She's dreaming, but those three whispered words linger.

I don't answer right away, counting her breaths, each one dragging me deeper into thought. I stare at the woman who, without even knowing it, has unraveled everything I thought I knew. She tore down the walls I built so carefully to protect myself. Now, those defenses lie in ruins, and I'm left exposed, unsure of what comes next.

Her presence is a storm I never saw coming, powerful enough to uproot my entire life and change its course forever.

My throat tightens as I answer her. "I couldn't leave you even if I tried."

Ari doesn't respond, but her hold on my waist tightens.

My heart beats fiercely against my ribs, and I repeat her words over and over again in my head.

I will never be able to leave her.

I don't care that she stole soulfire from the king.

I don't care that she might have secrets.

I vow to give her whatever I can—whatever I am capable of.

I will protect her at all costs, no matter what.

Because, for once, being with her feels better than disappearing.

CHAPTER 50

ALTHARA

ARI

What was I thinking?

The question echoes hollow in my head, but I already know no answer could ever justify it. I can feel my choices pressing down on me, a suffocating guilt settling deep in my gut.

What happened last night can never happen again.

I rub the haze from my eyes, adjusting to the predawn light spilling through the glass walls. I try to ignore the arm wrapped around my waist, the pressure of Lincoln's body against my back, and the way he fits so effortlessly around me.

No version of us can last.

The hard truth slams into me, snapping me back to reality.

Only one person gets to survive this quest, and even if Lincoln succeeds in killing the heir, he still has no intention of returning to Noctharn after doing so. He doesn't want a life in Lunaria anymore, but that's all I ever wanted. I want to build something real for all my mother and Noah have sacrificed. It's all I've ever dreamt about. And that's the only reminder I need.

Feelings are a liability, and failure isn't an option.

Slowly, I lift Lincoln's arm off me, trying not to wake him. I slip out from beneath the sheets, letting the frigid air bite at my skin as I rise. I glance at Lincoln one last time. He lies there, face half-buried in a pillow, features soft with sleep. Peaceful. Vulnerable. Mortal-looking.

And somehow, that makes everything worse.

Because for a split second, I forget the plan.

I forget the quest.

I forget what this is supposed to be.

And I almost believe we could be something.

I move across the room, slipping into the bathroom without a sound—the morning light filters in just enough to catch my reflection in the mirror. The face staring back at me looks lost, gaze shadowed with doubt, lips still swollen, hair a tangled mess, cheeks flushed with the aftermath of something that never should have happened. My eyes are a battlefield, torn between what I want and what I know I can't have.

I shake my head hard as if it could rid the thought of him from my mind. Cold water hits my face a second later. I cling to the shock of it, willing it to wash away the feel of him.

I can't afford to be distracted.

I sigh, pulling a brush through my tangled hair, quickly braiding it. Grabbing my snake barrette from the bathroom counter, I clip it into place, smoothing down the loose strands.

Back in the bedroom, I slip into my familiar clothing. Without wasting another moment, I begin gathering my things, methodically packing them into my bag as my mind drifts back to the quest.

We have a meeting with the King of Thalassara this afternoon, and I'd like to use every spare second I can in the library, seeing what information I can find about the witch kingdom and Noctharn.

"Morning."

I stiffen at the sound of Lincoln's voice and what it does to me.

No feelings, I remind myself.

"Morning," I say coolly, not sparing him a glance.

I continue to pack my things, even as Lincoln's footsteps grow louder.

He stops my hand mid-movement. "Are you okay?"

I yank my hand free and close my bag shut.

I pivot to face him, trying to mask the storm inside me with a guarded glare.

"Why wouldn't I be?"

Lincoln analyzes me like he can't get a read on me, searching my eyes, trying to understand what's wrong.

I keep my face blank, choosing my following words strategically. "I had fun last night." I cross my arms tightly over my chest. "Thanks for helping me take the edge off. I guess valorguards are useful for something after all."

Lincoln's face hardens, jaw clenching so tight it might snap. "Is that so?" he drawls.

I shrug, like everything that happened between us doesn't matter. Like, *he* doesn't matter to me the slightest bit because if Lincoln hates me, he won't follow me, and I won't have to pretend that his presence doesn't affect me.

I'm running out of time, and dwelling on his feelings will only hold me back.

"I needed release," I say flatly. "And you were there."

Lincoln's expression doesn't soften, yet I glimpse a flicker of hurt in his gaze.

I step past him, slinging my bag over my shoulder and slipping on my boots, feeling the stiff leather tighten around my ankles.

I approach the dense vines, not looking back. "I'll be in the library if you need me."

Lincoln stays silent, and I don't wait for his reply. I keep walking, the knot in my chest tightening with each step. The vines close behind me, and I tuck my feelings away, burying them deep. Because if I let myself feel any of them, even for a second, I won't be able to keep going.

The castle halls buzz with life as servants hurry past me, their arms filled with various items.

I step in front of a woman who carries a golden tray piled high with food. "Good morning, could you point me in the direction of the library?"

Her eyes widen in surprise. "South wing, miss. Just past the king's gallery, second archway on your right."

I offer her a small smile. "Thank you."

She dips her head and continues on with her day.

It's easy to find; the massive crystal doors flanked by gold sconces stand as a clear marker.

I push the heavy doors open and step inside. The scent of ink and old parchment floods my senses, bringing me back to Noah and his parents' bookstore back home. Towering shelves stretch high above, packed tight with books of every size and color, each one holding stories like the ones I used to get lost in when I was young.

Just beyond the entrance, a man sits quietly at a desk,

adjusting a stack of worn tomes. He's an older gentleman; his face lined with wrinkles carved by years of laughter with streaks of gray that weave through his dark hair. He looks up, peering at me over the rims of his silver spectacles. The exquisite frames catch the light, mirroring the faint glint of silver scales that trail down the side of his neck.

He looks down at the watch on his wrist. "It's early, miss. Did you have a meal before coming here? There is a strict no food policy in my library."

"Yes," I lie.

"Very well," he nods. "I was informed to expect two guests today. While I'm unprepared to see you so early, I'm happy to accommodate. Is it just you?"

"My—" What exactly is Lincoln to me? "Partner," I decide. "Won't be joining us. He is still resting after his fight yesterday."

The man stands and walks around his desk. He pauses before me, extending a hand. I meet his grasp.

"I'm Rufus," he says. "The Kingdom of Thalassara's High Archivist and trusted protector of this lovely place."

Rufus's eyes gleam with pride, and I give him a polite smile in return.

"I'm Ari. It's a pleasure to meet you."

"The pleasure is all mine."

Rufus motions toward a table in the center of the room, and I make my way to it, sitting down in one of the empty chairs.

"So, what are you looking for today? Anything particular?" he asks, taking a seat across from me.

"As much history as I can obtain in a few hours, Althara's origin, Noctharn's family line, any information you have on soulfire..." I let my voice fade as I glance around the room, ensuring no one is nearby, before continuing. "And the witch kingdom."

That gets his attention.

He quirks an eyebrow. "I fear we have no documentation of the witch kingdom. The king will have to answer those questions for you, but I can help with everything else."

Everyone appears strangely tight-lipped when it comes to the voided-out area on the map, and I don't understand why.

Rufus pushes back from the table, his robe whispering as it brushes the floor. He weaves through the narrow aisles, disappearing among the countless tomes that fill them. A distinct whistle rings nearby, but I pay it no attention, patiently waiting for Rufus to return.

He eventually does, carrying a large stack. Each one is thick and worn with cracked spines and yellowed pages from age. He sets the pile down gently in front of me.

"Thank you," I murmur.

Rufus smiles. "Please don't hesitate to ask for anything else. I'll be at my desk if you need me."

I choose one of the heavier tomes from the pile. The spine groans as I open it, releasing the scent of aged paper. The pages crackle beneath my fingers, each one filled with elegant script and intricate illustrations, their meanings just out of reach. I flip through them, the motion of turning pages pulling me deeper.

I read in silence, chasing fragments of meaning, hoping a thread will reveal itself. The text is compact, layered with centuries of commentary and contradictions—sigils unfamiliar to me, references to volumes I've never seen, entire passages locked behind lost dialects.

Most of it feels like noise. Pages and pages of old power and older opinions, none of it pointing anywhere. The deeper I go, the more certain I am that I've misread the signs. That this hunch, that there is more to King Malvok's rule, was never more than a theory.

I flip the page, about to give up, when my fingers pause. I read it once. Then I read it again:

> *In the years where peace held strong, shrouded in mist and ruled by the divine, the kingdom of Noctharn flourished. Their fields were rich with harvest, no soul went hungry, and each being, powerful or not, was welcome. Yet, basking in an abundance of resources, the King of Noctharn was not content. He did not wish to be the only kingdom on the continent blessed with good fortune.*

> *He looked beyond his borders and saw kingdoms struggling with drought and poverty. So, he declared, not with pride but with purpose: 'What joy is it to drown in plenty, when our neighbors suffer so close?' The king shared Noctharn's wealth, offering up his resources to every kingdom, big and small. Creatures and beings of every kind thrived under Eryndor Beldara's rule. The realm as a whole no longer knew struggle. The king asked for nothing in return. As he, the son of Althara, was born on Earth, the first of her kin to walk the land.*

I turn the fragile page back and forth, my fingers trembling. There's nothing more. That's it.

Noctharn once being good, wasn't a surprise. Learning that the Beldara bloodline was divine was.

King Malvok carries a fragment of Althara's essence, which means so does his lost heir.

A knot of unease coils deep in my gut.

I close the tome, setting it aside, its pages still whispering to me as I reach for the next. This one is thinner, bound in deep green leather, softened and worn at the edges. It opens more easily than the other tomes, as if it's been waiting to be read. I scan the first page.

Where the last few tomes had been evasive, this one speaks clearly, as if the writer knew who would find it.

I flip the pages faster now, hardly blinking:

> *No one knows the true beginning of Althara. No scrolls bear the tale in full; the stars themselves don't mutter a word. She came before memory, before any being walked the land. Some say she was born before the world was created, willing it into existence: What is known is this: Althara gave freely and wholeheartedly, offering her gifts with quiet abundance that went unnoticed by many but was deeply felt by those who believed in her.*

> *Her blessings flowed through the land itself, an unbreakable bond that ties the people to the earth beneath their feet. Only her bloodline possesses the power to share what she created —a sacred gift rooted in the soulfire that rests at the very core of her work. Althara's sweet melodies awaken the land's power, channeling it into those she chooses. Through her*

> *gift, she provides her people with the strength and resilience they need to survive. Althara believes in what is good, for such belief is no weakness but the very flame that keeps darkness at bay.*

I lift my gaze from the tome, everything finally piecing together in my mind.

King Malvok can control the soulfire because the blood of Althara courses through his veins, a power no one else can claim but his heir. And if he's been collecting the soulfire piece by piece, it can only mean one thing.

He wants to become a God himself, destroying all the good Althara has created. That's why he raised the wards, why he hoards the crystal, and why he expands his territory. He is the only other person on this earth who can succeed in doing so besides his child.

Which means that there is only one being who can stop King Malvok, and only one way to save everyone. The Noctharn heir must live.

I have to tell Lincoln.

I rise, noticing with alarm that the sun is already higher in the sky than I expected and our meeting with the king is fast approaching.

I close the tome, the sound louder than I intended, and hurry past Rufus. "I need to see the king. Thank you again for your help."

Rufus dips his chin. "Good luck."

I leave without another word, already moving through the halls, driven by the need for answers.

CHAPTER 51

THE HEIR
ARI

I linger outside the throne room, trying to catch my breath from the sprint here, hoping to reach Lincoln before the meeting starts. He needs to know the new plan—what I found in the library changes everything.

I whirl around, fidgeting with the strap of my bag at the sound of his footsteps.

Lincoln strides toward me with the same callous look he wears so often.

Heat creeps up my neck, blotching my cheeks.

He's beautiful in a way that hurts.

I hate that he has this effect on me.

Before I can fully compose myself, he's in front of me, hand already on my waist. He pulls me behind a towering white pillar, shielding us from prying eyes.

"Lincoln—"

Both of his gloved hands come down on either side of me, effectively trapping me in place. The sudden closeness and the way his strength surrounds me sends a rush of desire through me. My breath catches, and I become acutely aware of every detail of him.

Lincoln's broad frame looms over me, so close that I can feel his body brush against mine with each breath.

I lift my chin, scowling, trying to mask the fluttering in my stomach. His golden eyes hold me captive instantly.

Lincoln lifts his hand, fingers brushing softly along my jaw before coming to rest beneath my chin, holding me in place. "Let me make one thing clear," he states. "I'm not one you can simply fuck to get the edge off."

I blink up at him, about to speak, ready to challenge him, but he shakes his head before a word can leave me. I swallow hard and snap my mouth shut.

Lincoln leans in further, his voice falling to a low murmur. "I can't keep pretending." He pauses. "I don't want to keep pretending," he declares, changing one word in his statement that makes everything else seem insignificant. "Every time I think about you, I forget everything. I tried to fight it. Tried to bury it deep down." His voice fails him, the words slipping away unfinished. He pulls his hand away from my chin and runs it down his face. "Do you not know what you do to me?"

I force down the lump in my throat, narrowing my eyes. "You're only working with me because you want something. Don't mistake that. We're on this quest together for one reason and nothing more."

"You are the most maddeningly stubborn woman I've ever met."

I fold my arms over my chest. "I am not."

A slow smile tugs at the corner of his mouth. "You are," he says, pressing me tighter against the pillar. "Tell me, sunshine, why does your breath catch whenever I'm close?"

"You're imagining things," I mutter, unable to stop my eyes from drifting to his parted lips. The same lips I fantasize about tasting again.

"Really?"

I glare up at him, cheeks flushed. "Really," I repeat.

Lincoln cups my face, his fingers pressing gently against my cheek. His lips hover just inches from mine.

"Tell me to disappear," he whispers, "and I will."

But I don't.

I can't. I tried it earlier, and barely succeeded, no matter how much I want to fight it. So, I give in, leaning into him, letting my lips find his.

"No more pretending," Lincoln breathes.

I echo the same words against his lips, "No more pretending."

Saying it feels like deciding to live after trying to survive for so long. I circle my arms around Lincoln's neck, anchoring myself in the moment.

A sudden clearing of a throat shatters it, though.

We pull apart reluctantly, the sudden space between us feeling too wide.

"I'd hate to interrupt..." a steward in ivory robes says, standing stiffly by the throne room doors. "But the king is ready. It's time for your meeting."

I lift my chin, silencing the heat in my face behind a cold facade. "Perfect timing," I state dryly. "I wouldn't want to keep him waiting. He seems like the punctual type."

The steward gives me a tight smile, offering no comment. He pulls open the throne room doors instead.

Lincoln's hand brushes mine, and I flick my gaze toward him. The air between us still hums with the weight of our promise, but the moment has slipped away. There are more pressing matters waiting beyond those doors, things we need to face, whether we're ready or not.

I hook my arm through his. "I don't have time to explain," I whisper. "But the Beldara bloodline are direct descendants of Althara. I don't think we should kill the heir."

Lincoln's brows tighten into a scowl as we step into the throne room.

Walls of glass surround us, flooding the space with the shifting light of the water outside. Soft ripples flow through channels carved into the floor, casting dancing reflections across the room.

At the far end, King Nerion sits on his throne, the crown of Thalassara gleaming in the light. His keen eyes watch us closely.

We stop before him and bow; the murmur of water the only sound in the room.

"Secrets don't seem to faze you, it appears. Maybe you have some of your own?" King Nerion presses, a hint of challenge in his voice.

I purse my lips, unamused. "I care for Lincoln's life more than anything. But it seems you don't share the same sentiment."

The king places a hand over his heart. "Forgive me," he purrs. "The years have grown redundant as of late. I only wished to make things more interesting."

I grip the hilt of my sword, anger pulsing through me. "A looming war and King Malvok planning to conquer the land isn't interesting enough for you?"

King Nerion reclines back in his throne, a hint of amusement dancing across his features. "I take it you went to my library. What else did you find?"

I disclose every detail of my findings—the soulfire, King Malvok's plan, and Althara's existence.

Lincoln tenses beside me. "How do we stop him?"

King Nerion bursts into laughter, his head resting against his throne as the mocking sound echoes through the room. "I think you know the answer to that question already."

"There has to be another way," Lincoln snarls.

Evie warned me back in Junia, and though I didn't fully grasp it then, her words have haunted me since. She confessed that the heir was our only hope and that, when they were ready, everyone would be waiting.

I understood now. I understood everything.

The king shakes his head, gaze lingering on Lincoln's gloves. "There is so much you don't know, boy. Do you even fully understand your curse?"

Lincoln is quiet for a long moment. "It's obvious at this point, don't you think? Unless you want me to demonstrate."

"Your father came to me once," the king says slowly. "He asked for a favor—a bargain, if you will. Because you were deadly, cursed by the Queen of Noctharn herself. But your touch does not bring death to everyone."

My heart stutters as disbelief and hope clash fiercely within my chest.

"There's one person you can never kill," the king continues, "and it's the very person you vowed to destroy."

No. My legs all but give out. That can't be.

"Liar!" Lincoln barks. "Do you truly believe we'd trust a single word that comes from your mouth?"

I rest my hand on Lincoln's arm, my touch instantly smothering his rage.

"Stop with this nonsense," I hiss at the king. "Why are you not doing anything about what is happening? Why don't you fight back?"

King Nerion studies me, unmoving. "Do you think we haven't tried? For what good is it if we can't control the soul-fire? The heir is the key to the survival of this continent, yet they hide like a coward."

"I have an inkling of where this 'coward' might be," I say, flinching at the word. I pull the worn map from my bag, unfolding it before me.

My finger hovers over the blank space beside Thalassara. "Why is this area voided off? What lies here that King Malvok refuses to mark?"

The king's eyebrows pinch together, observing me with both suspicion and curiosity.

"Old magic," he explains. "Some can see it, others cannot. I'm certain King Malvok isn't even aware that section of the map is blurred. Stare at it and tell me when it vanishes."

I fix my gaze on the faded territory. And after a few seconds, the land before me ripples and fades, morphing into neverending water.

An edged gasp escapes me. "How?" I demand, unable to comprehend what I just saw.

"This charade is boring me." King Nerion rises from his seat, and the guards converge around him. "Darian Ashfield found the Queen of Noctharn not far from there, which I assumed you knew."

Lincoln's eyes flare with fury, his fists clenching at his sides. "You've known where the heir has been all this time?" His voice breaks with restrained anger—the question laced with accusation.

"Go and see for yourself." The king waves a hand in dismissal. "I have a meeting with the prince of the very kingdom you plan to visit. Your time here is up, so be gone."

I take a step toward him, my heart pounding in my chest. "But—" the guards shift in front of me, blocking my path. I freeze, frustration welling up. "You would deny us an audience with this prince before we set foot in his land?"

"I have no desire to play more games of tales and secrets with you," King Nerion says, his tone sharpening.

Lincoln's lips curl into a sneer, his voice low but filled with venom. "You never told me what my father came here to bargain for."

King Nerion all but laughs at him. "The rest of your answers lie where you're headed next. Unfortunately for you, my patience and hospitality have run dry."

I come to Lincoln's side, placing my hand in his— grounding us both. Our eyes meet for a fleeting moment, and just at the edge of my vision, I catch the king examining us, his expression filled with intrigue.

I squeeze Lincoln's fingers, urging him to follow me. "Let's go," I order him.

We turn our backs on the king and leave the throne room.

Deep down, I know we're marching straight toward our downfall, but the clarity Lincoln sought all along is close; even if reaching it will be our undoing.

Yet as we leave the kingdom of Thalassara hand in hand, one question gnaws at me, more urgent than the rest: Am I willing to sacrifice the only real thing I have?

CHAPTER 52

MEANT TO BE

ARI

The wind bites sharper than I expected, laced with salt and filled with the muted roar of restless waves. Strands of hair slip free from my barrette, whipped wild by the breeze. The shoreline stretches just past the line of trees, like a silver thread in the distance. I keep to the shadows of the hills, moving like a ghost, every nerve taut with the fear of being seen by those who dwell in the unknown kingdom ahead.

Above, Lincoln circles the terrain, his wings slicing through the wind with ease. The fading sunlight clings to the edges of his feathers, igniting them with fleeting bursts of gold and amber as the sky bruises into deep shades of rose and violet.

The sand turns to rock ahead, and I stop, not wishing for an uncomfortable night's rest.

"We'll make camp here!" I shout toward the sky.

Lincoln spirals down from above, landing soundlessly at my side.

He whistles, long and low. "You know, sunshine, you have a gift for picking the perfect places to stop for the night. Waves, wind, and the smell of rotting seaweed in the air. It's quite romantic."

I give him a sideways glance. "Oh, I'm sorry. Next time I'll reserve us a room at a beachside inn."

He grins, expression sparkling with mischief. "As long as you sleep next to me, I guess it'll do."

I roll my eyes, but despite myself, a smile tugs at the corners of my lips. "You're insufferable."

Lincoln laughs, running a hand through his windblown hair.

"Does your hair always get this messy after flying?" I ask, noting how the wild strands fall over his forehead.

"Yes." He shrugs. "It's the only downside of flying."

I step toward him, reaching out to tuck the errant strands behind his ear. "There," I mumble. "All better now."

Our eyes meet, and heat rushes to my cheeks, igniting like fire beneath my skin. I quickly look away, searching for a spot for us to settle.

I sink to the ground when I find one, reaching into my bag to pull out a small pouch. I chew on the dried fruits, offering some to Lincoln.

I fidget with my barrette, replaying every word we traded with King Nerion in my mind, trying to push away the tightness that constricts my throat. "Just worried, that's all."

Lincoln nudges me with his shoulder. "Care to elaborate, sunshine?"

I focus on the dark stretch of water in the distance, squinting in hopes of seeing the witch kingdom. "If you can't kill the heir, then what is the point of us coming this far? We failed. We could stop now and accept our defeat." I clear my throat. "And maybe, we could live out here... together."

"No," Lincoln growls. "We will be together, but not like

that. Not yet. The heir will see death first. I refuse to believe the King of Thalassara and his lies."

I bite my cheek until the taste of iron fills my mouth. "I suppose you have a point. But—"

"Let's not dwell on the what ifs until we know for certain. What tomorrow brings is never guaranteed, and I don't feel like pondering the idea that my whole life could be a lie. I prefer to live in the moment with you."

I laugh, the sound getting lost in my throat. "Oh, what sweet words you say, Lincoln. Tell me. Are you trying to charm me?"

His mouth tilts upward as he leans back on his hands, dimple on full display. "I think I already have. Wouldn't you agree?"

My laughter fades, and a beat of silence passes between us. "I don't know how to do this," I mutter. "Any of this. Whatever this is." I stare at Lincoln, heart thudding. "How do I know I can believe your words as well?"

Lincoln doesn't hesitate to answer. "You don't. But I can promise you one thing: whatever happens tomorrow, you'll always have me, even if we can never return to Noctharn. You will have me."

His words hit me like a stone dropped in still water, rattling me to my core. I blink hard, struggling to process what he's just said—the future he sees, the one he dares to imagine for *us*. A life I hadn't let myself hope for, not fully. Not until now.

"Lincoln—" His name slips past my lips, but I can't say more. Inside me, fear and longing intertwine, none of it ready to be spoken.

Lincoln takes my hand, bringing me to my feet.

"You will always have me," he repeats, circling his arm around my waist. "I never realized anything was missing in my life until I met you. And now that I know what it is, I'm never letting it go. I'll prove to you that I'm worthy of your trust."

I can't name the feeling that rises in me, too overwhelming and fast to contain. All I know is that I believe him. Without thinking, I reach up, my fingers slipping around the nape of his neck, pulling him closer.

The voice in my head screams at me to stop, reminding me that this will never work out, that he and I aren't meant to be. My body ignores the warning, drawn in by the undeniable pull of something fleeting and beautiful.

My heart is his, even if *his* won't stay mine for long.

CHAPTER 53

SNAKE BARRETTE
LINCOLN

Ari lies beside me, her head tilted toward the sky, dark hair spilling on the ground.

"I think that one is a dragon," she murmurs, pointing up at a crooked trail of stars in the sky.

"That looks more like a rodent if you ask me," I say—half serious, half teasing.

She snorts, and the sound vibrates through me. "It does not."

"It does too. I doubt a dragon would be that small."

"And how would you know? It's a mythical creature, surely it could be any size."

"Yes, but—"

"You're impossible," she huffs out, exasperated.

I incline my head just enough to catch her expression, watching her fight a smile. "You're the one trying to convince me that a rodent and a dragon are the same size."

She stifles her laugh with her hand. I want to stay like this forever, right here beside her. But doubt creeps into every corner of my mind, filling me with unease.

I saw Ari's face when the king pointed to the voided land

on the map. She showed no surprise, only a recognition as if she'd already known and only needed confirmation. That doesn't disturb me nearly as much as King Nerion's words about my father's bargain. I refuse to accept it. My father spent his life hunting the heir. The king is wrong. I am not their savior. I am the opposite because if I cannot kill them, our fates are connected in a way I will not accept. It would mean I am cursed to stand at their side, to protect rather than destroy, and Ari is the only person in this world worth keeping safe.

I intertwine my gloved fingers with hers, our arms brushing against each other.

"What else do you see when you look at the stars?" she asks.

I swallow hard, the words weighing heavily in my chest before they even form. "I see possibilities. Futures tangled with choices I haven't made and places I haven't dared to go." I shift my focus from the sky to her. "But right now? I only see you."

Ari blinks, eyes landing on mine. "That's not an answer."

"It's the only one I have," I reply, meaning it more than I've ever meant anything. "You're the only thing I'm sure of."

She smiles subtly, but there's something unreadable behind it. I reach out, brushing a strand of windblown hair from her face.

"Ari, I lo—"

She cuts me off with a quick jerk of her head. "Don't say it. Not yet."

I search her face. "Why?"

"You can say it after tomorrow," she whispers. "After we survive tomorrow."

"Tomorrow." The word floats between us like a promise in the wind.

I slip my arm around her waist and draw her close. Her head finds its place against my chest, and I press my lips to her forehead.

She shifts, squirming against me. "Your shirt's all bunched up," she muffles against my neck. "It's uncomfortable."

I laugh under my breath. "Hang on, I'll fix it."

I tug at the corner of my shirt to smooth it down, but it catches on something.

My shirt hangs half-caught in Ari's barrette, the other half riding up awkwardly, leaving my stomach bare to the cold night air.

Ari glares up at me. "Real smooth," she jests.

I grin sheepishly. "Sorry, sunshine." I lift onto one elbow and guide her to sit up with me. "Here, let me."

I try to untangle the fabric, but it snags further, tearing a small hole near the hem.

"Owww," she howls, wincing.

"Almost there," I reassure her, spotting the barrette in the tangled mess. I pinch it between my gloved fingers and carefully work to unclasp it.

With a sudden *crack*, it gives way. I pull my shirt loose and hold the hairpiece in my hand. An unexpected vibration hums from it, and within the snake's mouth, a tiny hinge has sprung open.

I show Ari the barrette, and she freezes, her demeanor changing in an instant. Her eyes lock onto the object in my hand, like a viper ready to strike.

I tilt the barrette and give it a shake. A folded scrap of worn, yellowed paper slips into my palm.

"What is this?"

Ari's hand lashes out before I can react. She snatches the barrette from my hand, fumbling to shove the paper back into its secret compartment. Her fingers tremble as she does, face paling with each passing second.

"Ari," I growl. "Look at me."

She doesn't.

I reach forward, seizing her wrists firmly in one hand, and with my other, I steal the paper from her fingers.

"No!" she gasps, her eyes finally locking with mine. Her voice cracks like a branch splitting in a storm. "Please don't."

Tears stream down her face, and her lips part as if to speak, but only a sob breaks free, followed by another.

"What is this?" I ask again, louder now.

She doesn't answer.

Of course, she doesn't *fucking* answer.

She's hiding something, and I've known it all along.

I release her wrists and unfold the fragile paper, anger pulsing through me.

The handwriting stares back at me, familiar and unmistakable. I've seen it countless times before, etched in letters passed down from my father's old contacts, remnants of his days as the king's assassin when the queen used to help organize everything. As Noctharn's oracle, she alone told the king who must die, and he trusted her completely, using her guidance to maintain his power.

My fingers tighten around the paper as I read, each word cutting deeper than the last, branding itself onto my soul.

"Aurelia, my dear daughter, when the time is right, you will know where to go. Trust yourself and your path will become clear."

An undeniable fury radiates through me, the force of it striking me like a blow to the gut.

The life I had dreamed of with the woman before me unravels in an instant, and everything I thought I knew begins to crumble.

"Who gave you this?" I demand, my voice tight with rage, though the answer is already clear.

Ari's tears stop instantly as if they were only for show, her eyes hardening into a steely, unyielding mask.

"I don't know." Her voice is firm but clipped, like she's fighting to keep control.

Her lie tastes bitter on my tongue. I spit on the ground beside her.

"Liar!" I roar, unable to hide the wrath in my tone.

She flinches at the word but doesn't back down. Instead, she rises slowly, and I mimic her movement.

I cautiously observe her, only seeing a stranger now. "Why do you want to go to the void?"

"Link..." she pleads, but I cut her off without mercy.

"Don't call me that," I snap. "Answer the fucking question."

Her eyes flicker with despair. "I wanted to tell you. I swear I did. I wanted to tell you everything."

She steps closer, but I take a step back.

"And to think I trusted you," I say bitterly, "when you were lying to me this whole time, Aurelia." Her name feels foreign in my mouth.

"Please hear me out." She raises her hands. "I'm not the enemy here."

"YOU ARE!" I bellow, voice raw with anger. "You're everything I loathe and more."

The sudden realization dawns on me, like a dam cracking, and I see her—really see her—for the first time.

Aurelia, I repeat her name in my head. Her name is Aurelia, not even Ari. She always refused to share her last name, which could only mean...

I whip my head to the side, a prickle running down my spine. Someone is near and fast approaching. I crouch quickly, fingers tightening around my bow, nocking an arrow.

A branch snaps in the distance, and I spin on my heels toward the sound.

Ari stiffens beside me, her sword already drawn.

We press our backs together, forming a tight circle against the invisible threat.

I catch movement deep in the woods. The vines that once hung from the trees now snake over rocks and roots, racing toward us in serpentine waves.

I release an arrow, uncertain of my target. It strikes the heart of the writhing mass, only slowing its advance for a moment. But the vines lash out again, snaking around me with blinding speed, trapping me in their grip.

Ari pulls away from me, tiptoeing over the tangled growth, moving untouched.

I stare at her, stunned, watching her sheath her sword.

A wildfire of darkness spreads through me at the sight, fueling a rising heat that blurs my vision red, and from its depths, something darker takes hold.

Hatred.

Hatred for the woman I thought I loved.

I curl my lips into a sneer. "What have you done?"

CHAPTER 54

PRETEND
NOAH

The day Ari left Lumin to join the king's quest

The floorboards creak beneath my bare feet, the same sound every morning as I take the two steps from my bed to the window. I draw back the curtains to reveal the chilled glass and lean against the frame, scanning the narrow street until my gaze settles on the crooked house next door. It's quiet over there, no sign of anyone stirring, which is good because it means Ari still rests.

I let the curtain fall back and give my room a once-over. It's small and cramped, barely enough space for my bed, desk, and chair. I can't wait to leave this dump I've called home for most of my life.

I grab a purple tunic from my closet, pulling it over my head before sliding into a fresh pair of pants. I tug on my boots and catch my reflection in the old wooden mirror above my desk. I smooth my sleep-tousled hair until it's perfect. I swing open my bedroom door and stride down the

357

hall. The door to my caretakers' room is still closed, and I thank Althara that they never wake up when I leave for work. I make my way downstairs and twist the doorknob. I linger a moment, listening for any sign of movement before slipping out into the crisp morning air. The door clicks shut behind me.

The streets are cloaked in shadow, dawn threatening to break across the dark sky. I walk into town, heading toward the bookstore.

I rip a flyer off the front door when I arrive. "What part of no solicitation do people not understand?" I crumble the paper in my hand and reach into my pocket, pulling out a key. I push it into the hole, and a bell chimes as it opens.

I flip the lights on, dust motes dancing in their dim glow, and begin setting up for the day.

Every morning, I open the store. It gives my caretakers a chance to rest and keeps me away from the meaningless conversations I can't stand.

My birth mother placed an enchantment on the two strangers I live with, rendering them docile and pliable. It's a ruthless kind of control, but I don't dwell on it much because it's necessary. Necessary to protect our future and to keep Ari safe.

The bell over the door chimes at exactly 8:01 a.m., like clockwork.

"Good morning," a voice coos softly from the front of the shop. I force a polite smile onto my face and spin toward the sound, masking my annoyance. It's Octavia, wrapped in her usual dingy clothing and cheap vanilla perfume.

"Octavia," I say smoothly, stepping behind the counter. "A pleasure to see you as always."

She makes her way into the bookstore, settling into a relaxed lean opposite me. Her voice fills the space with an unrelenting flow of corny jokes and a running commentary on her daily struggles. I laugh when she laughs. I compliment her when she compliments me. I play the role perfectly, always being polite and charming when necessary.

I even pretend to be startled by a muted whistle that drifts through the store, even though I sensed Ari's arrival long before I heard it.

I straighten and scan between the shelves. Ari whistles again, and I spot her.

"Excuse me." I step away from Octavia and toward the row of shelves.

"Of course," she mumbles. Her tone is suddenly cooler than it was before, but I couldn't care less.

I round the corner, and my eyes widen in shock at the sight before me. Ari looks worn down, every line on her face telling a story of a sleepless night.

"God, Ari...you look like shit."

"Thanks," she murmurs, her voice thick with sarcasm.

I extend my hand, cupping her cheek, running the soft pad of my thumb around her already swelling eye. "Silas?"

"Yes," she whispers.

I told my mother that we needed to change her host family, but my concern went unheard.

I let my hand slide from her face and drop to my side. "Why didn't you come over last night? Where did you go?"

Ari steps back, like she always does when I question her too much. She is not one to be coddled.

"I didn't want to be told that I did something wrong. You berated me last night for the valorguards speaking to me, and I just...I just needed to be alone."

I grip her shoulder sternly, pulling her close as I lean in. "You know that's not what I meant. You're always welcome in my room." My lips brush her ear. "Where did you go last night?" I ask again.

She laughs, her body shaking uncontrollably.

I cover her mouth with my hand. "Shhhhh!"

I can feel her smirk under my palm.

"My, my, Noah, do I detect a hint of jealousy?"

"I don't care what you do and who you do it with. You know that. It is almost time for us to make our leave, and I can't have anything happen to you in the meantime."

She bats her eyelashes at me. "You wound me."

My eyes narrow, unamused. "Ari! I care about you. Is that what you want to hear me say?" I rake a hand through my hair. "I can't have anything happen to you."

She wraps her fingers around mine. "I slept on the tavern floor in the dressing room. Olen kicked me out first thing in the morning, but I'm fine."

I draw in a deep breath, as if it's the first full one I've taken all morning. Ari is both my greatest challenge and my biggest weakness.

She pulls out a crumpled piece of paper from her pocket and hands it to me. "I have something I need to tell you."

My eyes dart back and forth across it. "Shit," I mutter. I grip the paper tightly between my hands. I should have read the flyer on the door this morning. "Why do you have this?"

"Why do you think?"

"You can't do this," I snarl. "You hate King Malvok. Why would you willingly be in your father's presence when you have flown under the radar this whole time?"

"I want to see the man who wants to end my life."

"There are other ways," I shout. I pause to take a deep breath, composing myself before continuing. "You can meet Malvok the day you end his life, not like this. Please, think this through."

She rips the paper from my hands and shoves it in her bag. "You would say that. You and your perfect life, and perfect family. You never had to fight in the pits or work in the mines. You get to work here." She waves her hand, motioning to the clean, orderly bookshelves. "You have a normal life, while I've never had a normal day in my life. You have a mother who claims you as her own, a kingdom to go home to. Don't you understand?"

I seize her wrists firmly between my hands. "Why do you always have to go to the extreme? Going on a quest that will likely lead to your death isn't worth it."

She glares up at me. "Get your hands off me," she commands, her power spilling through her words. I hate it when she uses it on me, even when it's unintentional. My hands drop to my side without my consent. "I'm going. It's final. You can support me or not, but I need to do this for myself."

Ari backs away slowly, putting space between us.

I shake my head in disbelief at her pure recklessness. It's infuriating to a level I can't even put into words.

"Just don't die," I growl.

She scoffs, turning away from me. "Have a little faith in me for once."

My gaze sears into her retreating form as the ground begins to shudder beneath my feet. I can feel the roots moving, responding to the anger pulsing through me.

"Fuck," I grumble under my breath.

I drag a hand down my face and make my way back to the counter.

I guess I'll be leaving this pathetic town earlier than expected.

CHAPTER 55

LYING IS ALL I KNOW
ARI

I recognize the look in Lincoln's eyes. It's not anger, at least, not the kind I expected. It's something heavier, more profound.

Lincoln hates me. That much is clear in the cold edge of his gaze.

In his look, I see the final fracture; whatever trust we had is broken, and I know, without a doubt, it's gone forever.

There's no turning back from what I've done.

And the worst part isn't even the pain in his gaze; it's that he doesn't even try to break free. He just stands there, trapped and silent, staring at me as if I'm already dead to him. As if I never mattered at all.

I take one hesitant step toward Lincoln, my hands half-raised, not in surrender, but in plea. The truth burns in my chest, begging to be heard. I just need him to listen, to see past the wreckage and understand why I did what I did.

A voice cuts through the stillness, low and silken, curling out from the darkness like smoke.

"I've been waiting for this moment since I met him."

I pivot, arching an eyebrow, already knowing who's

behind me. "Was this really necessary?" I ask, my tone balancing on the edge of annoyance and warning.

Noah appears from out of the shadows, arms crossed, his ocean-blue eyes sweeping over the scene, admiring his work.

"Necessary?" he echoes, head tilting. "No. Satisfying?" he asks mockingly. "Absolutely."

I draw in a breath, anger flaring beneath my ribs. "You never let me do things my way," I bite out, the words filled more with hurt than rage.

Noah smirks. "I did, sweetheart. I let you run around pretending for the past few weeks, playing your little game, chasing your little fake dream. But I'd say the fun is over." His tone sharpens, smooth but cutting. "You may trust him, but I do not."

My throat constricts at his words, the air seeming too thin around me. I look at Lincoln, catching the twitch of his jaw, the barely contained fury in his silence.

He trusted me. I felt it in his touch, his smile, his honest confessions. Every part of him was open and vulnerable. Now that trust lies broken between us, scattered in the wind and impossible to piece back together. He doesn't need to speak. I already know what he's thinking. The damage is done.

"He would have come willingly," I snap. "You didn't give me time to explain."

Noah's brows lift, an amused smile playing at the corners of his mouth. "Tell me, when did you plan on doing that? You'd have been in Drahal's territory by morning. Were you planning on telling him after you fucked him again?"

I let out a clipped laugh. "Still overbearing and overprotective, I see."

Noah exhales through his nose, pinching the bridge of it. "Why must you always fight me on everything?"

I step toward him. "Why can't we ever do things my way?"

Noah's nostrils flare. "If I let you do it *your* way, nothing would ever get done." He glares at Lincoln. "But I will say, I'm impressed. You brought a worthy enough sacrifice."

"He's not—" I start, but my voice falters, the weight of it all pressing down.

For a moment, Noah's expression softens. "You know I love you," he says quietly, the words somehow worse than anger. "But you also know my mother will only accept so many things. And I doubt whatever else you brought would suffice."

Lincoln's voice cuts through the tension, and I clench my hands into fists.

"Who is your mother?" he demands.

Noah clicks his tongue. "It seems you kept him in the dark about a lot of things."

"Like I said," I interject. "You didn't give me time to explain." I fold my arms across my chest. "Why were you in Thalassara anyway? I heard you in the library."

"And if I recall correctly, you blatantly ignored me, but don't flatter yourself, sweetheart. I came for the entertainment." Noah's eyes lock on Lincoln, shining with a dark, twisted delight. "And to confirm our alliance. Things are changing and changing fast."

Lincoln spits phlegm on the ground in raw disgust—a bitter gesture only fueling the tension. The vines around him tighten, gripping him firmer as if responding to his rage.

A cold chuckle slips from Noah's lips, dripping with amusement. "You should have killed me when you had the chance." Noah marches around Lincoln's trapped form. "Did you tell her how you saw me after The Riftlands? Probably not," he huffs. "I bet you prayed she'd forget about me. But it looks like my Ari turned out to be your weakness. She tends to have that effect on people."

I roll my eyes. "I care for him. Why do you have to ruin this for me?"

Noah looks at me, his eyes narrowing as he studies me. "It was ruined from the start. Did you really think you and he would live happily ever after?"

My heart shatters. I so desperately wish that it could have been real.

"I didn't think so," he says flatly, making his way to my side. "Now, the fun is over; you and your mother have kept everyone waiting long enough."

Lincoln stiffens. "Care to tell me who your mother is, too? Since that seems to be another secret you didn't trust me enough to know."

Guilt rises like a tide inside me. There's so much I need to tell him.

Noah dips his head, casually sliding his hands into his pockets as a sly grin forms on his lips. "I've always known you were cunning, but this? This is your best scheme yet, I'll give you that."

"Shut up!" I bark, my voice cracking at the edges.

Noah lets out a lazy sigh. "Ah, how I've missed your sweet little mouth."

My eyes stay fixed on Lincoln, the ache in my chest deepening until it feels like it might split me in two. I wish I could rewind, just a few minutes, back to when he still looked at me like I was something worth believing in. Back before the truth revealed itself, before the space between us became a chasm carved by lies.

I let him be my weakness. The one thing I let myself want, even when I knew better. But weakness gets people killed, and mine ends now.

"I told you to let me go," I tell Lincoln. "You didn't listen. You insisted we stop pretending. My mother is the reason you're cursed. I've known it all along, and still, I kept you close. You've killed hundreds chasing vengeance, murdered for no reason. At least I'm working toward something greater. You just wanted to make something of your sorry life."

Lincoln stares at me as if I've driven a blade through his chest. I watch as the truth tears apart everything that once existed between us.

I don't look away. Not yet. Not until I see the last trace of warmth fade from his eyes.

Only then do I turn my back, letting the silence stretch between us, sealing what's done. Lincoln may never forgive me, but he'll never hurt me either. I am the one person he cannot kill.

Noah steps in close, his arms sliding around my waist and pulling me close. "You cold-hearted woman," he murmurs against my hair.

I lean into him, not for comfort, but for control. He's always been there, my constant, my equal in all the wrong ways.

I didn't realize how much I missed him until now.

But the moment doesn't last.

A deep, rhythmic beating rises in the distance, coaxing my gaze upward. I pull back from Noah, eyes fixed on the growing shadows above just as darkness sweeps across the sky, blotting out the moon.

Massive winged creatures plunge toward us with unstoppable force, each powerful beat of their wings shaking the air around us. They land, their clawed feet smashing into the earth, cracking it upon impact.

I stand frozen, breath stolen away. My eyes strain to take in every detail—the gleam of their scales, the smoke curling from their nostrils, the fierce intelligence burning in their eyes.

I laugh, utterly amazed. Dragons are even more magnificent than the stories ever dared to tell and bigger than any constellation in the stars.

"I'd like you to meet someone," Noah states, voice light but eyes unreadable.

Masked and armored guards slide off the beasts' backs, moving with lethal grace. One steps forward to assist a woman draped in black. Her silver hair flows down her back like liquid starlight, her blue eyes as piercing and unnatural as Noah's. Twisted silver snakes coil across her chest, the emblem unmistakable.

"Well," the woman chimes, her voice smooth and melodic, almost too perfect. "This is better than I expected."

"My mother," Noah announces, glancing my way. "Queen of Drahal and the great enchanter of the witch kingdom."

I bow low, controlled. "Your Majesty, it's an honor to finally meet you."

She offers me a ghost of a smile. "Please, call me Morsanna. Your mother and I were once dear friends." There's a sadness in her eyes, quickly buried.

I nod, keeping my expression guarded. Beside me, Noah approaches his mother, reaching for her hand.

He presses a kiss to her knuckles. "Mother."

"My son," she replies, her voice warmer now.

I avert my gaze, jaw tight.

"You brought the Beldara heir to me at last," Morsanna continues, catching my attention.

She studies me with a glint of delight in her gaze, the corner of her mouth lifting. "I'm quite proud of my son for keeping you alive this long. Truly, I'm not sure what you would've done without him."

My eyes land on Noah's smug face. "Indeed, how privileged I am to have him."

Morsanna moves with the poise of a serpent in my direction. She stops just in front of me, and before I can react, her fingers brush along my cheek.

"You look just like her," she murmurs fondly. "But also, like him."

Morsanna presses her hand flat against my chest, and my knees buckle. I double over, gasping as something buried uncoils beneath my skin.

The pressure fades, and I stagger upright, light-headed.

"There," she drones, voice satisfied. "No more hiding."

I glance down to where her hand had touched, and a seven-pointed star now glows. I brush my fingers over it, amazed at its beauty, seeing it for the first time after being hidden by an enchantment for so long.

Morsanna sighs, the sound light. "It's a shame your mother didn't stay by my side," she says, not fully grieving, just disappointed. "She would've made a formidable ally. But she always insisted it had to happen this way. That she had to die so *you* could live." Her eyes meet mine. "She believed in her visions to the very end."

I smile, unsure of what to say about a woman I have never met. My mother is now only a figment of my imagination.

Morsanna makes her way back to her dragon, the guards lifting her into the saddle once more. "Your sacrifice will serve our cause well. You'll become greater than your father ever was."

Her words feel like a promise etched in fire.

I will be greater than my father.

I know I will.

I will take everything from him because I am destined for greatness.

My gaze lands on Lincoln unintentionally, his eyes full of questions I can't answer. I never meant for him to be my sacrifice.

Noah strides toward me, the air shifting with his presence. He stops just a few feet away, staring at Lincoln, then back at me. "You love him, don't you?"

I don't answer.

"I thought so." Noah turns to face Lincoln. "Do you know what her power is?"

"Be quiet!" I order, anger coursing through my veins.

A savage smile spreads across Noah's face. He begins to move his lips, but no sound comes.

"You're already so powerful without the ritual," Morsanna says, tone curious. "I knew carrying the soulfire would strengthen it."

My heart pounds in my chest.

Lincoln needs to understand. *He will understand.*

"Lincoln," I demand his attention with my voice. "Let me explain everything. It will all make sense when I do."

Lincoln flinches, staring at me like he is seeing me for the first time, and I realize my mistake too late. "I *felt* it," he whispers. "That pull...like I'd do anything you said. I never understood it." His voice darkens. "Have you been commanding me to do what you say this entire time?"

The question guts me. I've been experimenting with ways to show my powers without the binding ritual. Sometimes it worked, and other times it didn't. Only when I was determined did it ever slip without my knowledge. It was only then that I was able to make anyone fold to the sound of my voice.

"FUCKING ANSWER ME!" Lincoln roars, the sound shattering whatever composure I had left.

"Maybe," I manage, barely loud enough to hear. "I'm not sure."

Heartbreak radiates from Lincoln through his painfilled stare. "Did you ever care for me? Or was that a lie, too?" he asks, but doesn't wait for my response. "Never mind. I don't need an explanation from you."

"I—"

"Save it."

His voice is ice, and it slices through me cleanly, leaving nothing behind but silence.

"Lincoln, please," I breathe. "Let me explain."

He laughs, bitter and broken. "You keep saying that, but explain what? That you tricked me into loving you? That every word out of your mouth was a *lie*? How would I even know what was real? I don't need an explanation from you. I don't want anything from you."

I flail my arms in defeat. "My whole life has been a lie. It's all I've ever known, but I would never use my powers to make you love me."

Lincoln looks everywhere but at me, his decision already made. "I don't love you. I never did."

"You can't deny your love for me when I know how you truly feel! I've felt it."

The veins in Lincoln's neck strain as he fights the urge to speak the truth. He exhales a sound of pure anguish. "I could never love someone like you."

A lump forms painfully in my throat, the hollowness in my chest rapidly consuming me at his declaration.

Noah claps his hands together suddenly, and I jump.

Fuck. I forgot about him.

"Speak," I command.

"Well," Noah coughs, clearing his throat. "This has been awfully entertaining, sweetheart, but we have much more important things to do." He turns to face his mother, his tone shifting to something formal, almost reverent. "We are cutting it close to our deadline."

The queen bobs her head in agreement. "Ivette," she huffs, picking at her fingernails in boredom. "Fetch your brother. Put him in the dungeons until Ari can make him loyal after her binding ritual."

A guard breaks from the line, unfastening their helmet. A tumble of dark curls spills free, and when she lifts her gaze, the world stills. Her golden eyes, alive and filled with sorrow, mirror Lincoln's exactly.

"Lincoln." Her voice trembles. "You're fighting on the wrong side. You don't know the whole story. Ari will save us. She'll save the continent. This has been the plan all along. You are here to protect her."

Lincoln's body goes rigid, his breath catching. "I killed you," he grieves. "That day in Lunaria. I saw you die."

"No." Ivette shakes her head, her expression pained. "Father cast an illusion to save me from you. Why do you think he fled here? There is so much you still don't understand." She reaches out a hand, pleading. "Join me, brother. I'll show you the truth."

A dark shadow fills Lincoln's gaze. "Join you?" he spits, "and be captive and the protector of the one person I hate most? She's no better than her father." He thrashes against the vines.

"You're all the same, using her to do exactly what he started!" His eyes find mine, burning with disgust. "I'll be the one to end you," he snarls. "My touch might not, but my arrow will."

"Do not speak another word!" I command him.

Lincoln freezes mid-breath, every muscle locked in defiance, but he obeys.

The silence that follows is deafening, and in that silence, the truth finally surfaces.

Lincoln made me want to be better. And now, he'll stand at my side whether he wants to or not.

I lift my chin.

"Ivette," I demand. "Shackle him."

She hesitates only for a breath before advancing, clasping metal bands around Lincoln's wrists. The metal hums faintly, pulsing as it seals his power away. His eyes meet mine, rage and heartbreak twisted together, before the light drains from them entirely.

I turn my back on Lincoln, making my way to Noah's side. He extends his hand, and I take it willingly.

I am the lost heir of the Noctharn Kingdom, and I plan to hunt my father like he's hunted me.

And I won't allow anyone to stand in my way.

ACKNOWLEDGMENTS

Wow...I honestly didn't expect to be writing this, and I'm not really sure I can put into words what I feel. So let me keep this short and simple.

I decided to write this book one night when I was having a mental breakdown. I wanted to leave something behind in this world, but I didn't know how. I've always loved books and how reading made me feel, but I never thought much beyond that.

I remember asking my fiancé if he thought I could write a book. All he said was yes. It was such a simple answer. Why couldn't I? Nothing was holding me back besides just starting. So I began that night.

And welp, you know how the rest of that story goes because here you are.

To Zach: Thank you for supporting me through this whole process, all the late nights and plans I had to cancel to write this book. In the end, it's all been worth it, and I'm so happy I get to live this life with you!

To Cailin: Thank you for believing in my crazy idea to write a book and listening to me talk about it 24/7. I appreciate you so much, and I can't wait for you to be the first person to read book two!

And to everyone else who's supported me along the way and everyone who continues to follow my journey on social media, I want to thank you. I wouldn't have made it this far without you.

Remember never to stop chasing the feeling that comes from believing in magic and fairy tales.

GLOSSARY OF TERMS

Animal Assignment: During the binding ritual, powerful eldarim are assigned an animal that most closely resembles them.

Belknot Root: The root that is consumed to initiate the binding ritual. When boiled, it yields a deadly form; weapons are usually coated in the oil it produces, allowing the wielder to kill any being, immortal or not.

Binding Ritual: The ritual that is performed when an eldarim turns twenty-five; the ability to claim immortality and power from Althara.

The Broken Fang: Tavern in Lumin, where fight nights occur.

The Continent: The land that all the kingdoms reside on.

Drahal: The witch kingdom, also known as The Void.

Ebonkiss: Poison that coats the sandlurkers weapons, said to be able to kill any being.

Eidolon Forest: The forest that Noah and Ari played in when they were young, on the border of the Noctharn Kingdom.

Eldarim: Term coined by King Malvok to separate the weak from the powerful, considered to be the most elite in the Noctharn Kingdom.

Giants: Beings of The Riftlands.

Gilds: Currency in the Noctharn Kingdom.

Half-breeds: Eldarim that failed to claim full power during the binding ritual who are now stuck in half-human, half-animal forms.

Junia: The kingdom of the fairies.

Lumin: A small mining town on the southernmost border of Noctharn in a lower mortal section where the soulfire mine is located.

Lunaria: The capital of Noctharn, where eldarim reside.

Noctharn: The kingdom that is trying to take over the continent, home of the eldarim and mortals.

Paradise: Home of the velka.

The Riftlands: The kingdom of the giants.

Sections: The hierarchical structure of the Kingdom of Noctharn, broken up by power and rank.

Sandlurkers: Sand beings of the Kingdom of Zalquar.

Selkith: Half-land, half-water creatures that reside in Thalassara.

Solhaven: A mortal section known for goldsmiths at the northwest border of Noctharn.

Soulfire: A crystal that is mined for in Lumin, said to expand Noctharn's wards, can only be controlled by the Beldara bloodline.

Soulfire Collection Week: One week per year when the valorguards come into Lumin to collect the King of Noctharn's soulfire.

Thalassara: The kingdom of the selkith.

Valorguard: The King of Noctharns' trusted guard, seen as the most powerful, and always has an animal assignment.

Velka: Half-human, half-animal being that resides in Paradise.

The Void: An area on the map that is hidden from the eye.

Zalquar: The kingdom of the sandlurkers.

CHARACTER GUIDE

Althara: The continent's one true god.

Ari: A miner and pit fighter who joins the king's quest.

Aurelia Beldara: Noctharn's lost heir.

Darian Ashfield: Lincoln's father, who failed to locate the lost heir.

Ella: Goldsmith from Solhaven who befriends Ari during the king's quest.

Elliot: Half-goat velka from Paradise.

Evie: Fairy healer in Junia who saved Lincoln's life.

Finley: Hot-tempered valorguard who joins the king's quest.

Gus: King of The Riftlands.

Ivette: Lincoln's sister.

Jenny: Ari's fighting mentee in Lumin.

Lilia: A mute servant in Zalquar who helps Ari and Lincoln escape.

Lincoln Ashfield: Eldarim and valorguard; son of Noctharn's most notorious assassin.

Malvok: King of Noctharn.

Morsanna: Queen of Drahal.

Myke: Ella's boyfriend.

Nerion: King of Thalassara.

The Runebrooks: The second assassin family in Noctharn that took over after Darian Ashfield's failure.

Noah: Ari's best friend since childhood.

Octavia: Bartender at The Broken Fang.

Olen: Owner of The Broken Fang.

Rami: Sandlurker and messenger for the King of Zalquar.

Rufus: The Kingdom of Thalassara's High Archivist and librarian.

Selvan: Lion velka in Paradise.

Sera: Queen of Thalassara.

Silas: Ari's drunk caretaker, who forced her to join the soulfire mines and the fighting pits.

Tharion: King of Zalquar.

PLAYLIST

Sunlight — Hozier

Rival — Ruelle

Man or a Monster — Sam Tinnesz, Zayde Wolf

Dangerous Hands — Austin Giorgio

Arsonist's Lullabye — Hozier

Gallows — Katie Garfield

How Villains Are Made — Madalen Duke

I Wanna Be Yours — Arctic Monkeys

Love and War — Fleurie

Again — Noah Cyrus ft. XXXTENTACION

Secrets And Lies — Ruelle

Fallout — UNSECRET, Neoni

ABOUT THE AUTHOR

Taylor is originally from Massachusetts, but now lives in Austin, Texas. She can usually be found with a beer, book, or coffee in hand. Her love for books started when she read Percy Jackson in fifth grade, and the rest is history.

Instagram: @taylorugrinow.writes

TikTok: @taylorugrinow.writes

www.ingramcontent.com/pod-product-compliance
Lightning Source LLC
Chambersburg PA
CBHW031111160726

47991CB00004B/1337